UPSTAIRS
AT THE PARTY

ALSO BY LINDA GRANT

Fiction
The Cast Iron Shore
When I Lived in Modern Times
Still Here
The Clothes on Their Backs
We Had It So Good

Non-fiction
Sexing the Millennium: A Political History
of the Sexual Revolution
Remind Me Who I Am, Again
The People on the Street: A Writer's View of Israel
The Thoughtful Dresser

UPSTAIRS
AT THE PARTY

LINDA GRANT

virago

VIRAGO

First published in Great Britain in 2014 by Virago Press

Copyright © Linda Grant 2014

The moral right of the author has been asserted.

A CIP catalogue record for this book
is available from the British Library.

Hardback ISBN 978-1-84408-749-5
C format ISBN 978-1-84408-750-1

Typeset in Goudy by M Rules
Printed and bound in Great Britain by
Clays Ltd, St Ives plc

Papers used by Virago are from well-managed forests
and other responsible sources.

MIX
Paper from
responsible sources
FSC
www.fsc.org   FSC® C104740

Virago Press
An imprint of
Little, Brown Book Group
100 Victoria Embankment
London EC4Y 0DY

An Hachette UK Company
www.hachette.co.uk

www.virago.co.uk

To Derek Johns, my agent of twenty-one years

Author's Note

This novel is inspired by a particular time in my own life, but the characters and the events are the product of my imagination.

I see the play so lies
That I must bear a part

William Shakespeare, *The Winter's Tale*

November 2013

Let all sweet ladies break their flattering glasses, and dress themselves in her.

I have chewed over the bones of her life like a ravenous dog. Sometimes she seems like a doll we once roughly played with when we were children. Her head is gone, her clothes are stained and torn, but he is right, we have dressed ourselves in her.

PART ONE

I

If you go back and look at your life there are certain scenes, acts, or maybe just incidents, on which everything that follows seems to depend. If only you could narrate them, then you might be understood. I mean the part of yourself that you don't know how to explain.

It is to do with growing out of strange ground, as if you came from a country almost no one has visited, and no one knows its language and customs or terrain. If I was from Timbuktu I could not be more exotic. Juan once said, 'You're from Atlantis. You're a refugee from a continent that has fallen into the sea.'

These are the reflections of my maturity. Like everyone, I lived life with most intensity when I was young, and I was one of the careless people for whom time was not a dimension.

Most of time is history, but my era was myth. Nobody recorded it because it was so marginal and childish, almost nothing we started came to anything. In our isolated Yorkshire stronghold my friends and I knew with the green force of teenage certainty, the driving fuse of insufferable self-confidence, that human weaknesses like jealousy and personal ambition were going to wither away. Men and women would play their roles in complete equality. War would be ended by the collective rule of wise female elders, the impulse to fight being some atavistic primitive urge of our fore-fathers, and our parents were coelacanths, an interim phase in the evolution of the species. There would be an end to vanity, mirrors would fall into disuse, clothes would be no more than individual costumes, fashion would cease as time came to a standstill. The present would become the eternal now. When we died our bodies would be reincarnated as trees.

Eddie says, 'Interesting. The dope must have been very different back then.'

The sense of the past bricked up is more than us not having computers, mobile phones, YouTube, Wikipedia, gaming joysticks, iPads. *Obviously* our youth was like the primitive tribes of the Amazon when it came to gadgets, but it was what was in our heads that the next generation just can't comprehend, and how we tor-mented each other with our moral certainties. How our values were made up of *ought* and *should*, and how we hammered each other to death with them.

Of course all this is hippie gobbledygook. It's Evie that I don't know how to explain and about whom I have still not worked out a way of speaking. Evie, a more primal question. More intimate and more painful. I rarely come across any Evies; Eves, yes, of course, but 'Evie' still has the capacity to give me an electric shock, attached as it permanently is to one individual. As for her brother, I have had to get used to her face embedded in his. Nineteen-year-old Evie reveals herself in his pale blue eyes, occluded now by cataracts, the bags of flesh below them, the cantankerous mouth. But there she is. There she is.

2

How to tell it? To start with, I was born in Liverpool, sea city. Liners, docks, salt wind, Beatles, African seamen, Nigerian Friendship Society, the American Bar. I'm the product of people with tricky back-stories that take a lot of time to explain and anything you have to explain is always open to suspicion. But the story, in my view, is everything.

I remember how my father lifted me on his shoulders, I remember being a giant walking through the streets of the city, my fists raised up, past Lewis's, past the naked statue, down through town to the pierhead where the ships came and my father carrying me all that way. His chest was strong and I was safe and stable, exulting in the light rain.

We went down on to a ship and the ship sailed across the water and we reached the other side, where there was a beach, tin buckets and spades, paper flags, a funfair, ice cream, candy floss, toffee apples, and I was sick.

In all his extravagance we took a taxi home through the Mersey Tunnel. Strips of amber light lining the blackness, head in Daddy's lap. Talking to the taxi driver. 'The kid's eyes are bigger than her stomach. She emptied it on the floor of a dodgem car.'

'She won't make that mistake twice.'

'Until the next time, eh, bubbsy?' He stroked my black hair. I was in a kind of heaven for which it was worth feeling nauseous.

My father's best friend from childhood was Yankel Fishoff, whom he stuck with through thick and thin because 'the Fishoffs were the poorest of the poor, no shoes when they went to school, a rind of thick yellow skin on their feet and in the winter the skin was blue and a rind of ice'.

Dad was not an aesthete – take him to the racetrack, not a gallery or concert hall – but he had a hell of a lot of respect for artists. It was not the art they made that impressed him, but the life they had to lead to make it. They were crazy and reckless and that was something he knew. Yankel was homosexual and a painter, which was a major something when you came out of the immigrant communities of Brownlow Hill and Toxteth. Daddy was in awe of Yankel's skills with a paintbrush, his struggle for recognition, his love of the Impressionists. His work was exuberant, poetic, had a vitality that came from being a serious student of Rembrandt and Velázquez, freed from academicism by loose brushwork. His subjects were couples dancing, boys playing, Moroccan markets and Brighton beaches. All human life was there, he had a flair for depicting people living, not thinking. Ringo Starr was a collector.

Yankel told me to go and look at pictures. For my birthday he gave me a book about Michelangelo called *The Agony and the Ecstasy*. That book made a huge impression on me. I dreamed of popes and painters and the ceiling of the Sistine Chapel. As soon as I'd finished it I went crying to Yankel for another book. Next he gave me *Lust for Life* by the same author. This one was about Van Gogh and now the sky became molten and a simple chair was the world.

I wanted desperately to be a painter but I had no hand–eye coordination. Only messes came from my brush. I had tantrums and threw paints across the room when they wouldn't do what I wanted, sienna yellow spattering the skirting boards.

'Never mind, minxy,' said Yankel. 'You grow up into somebody. That's for definite.'

My father said of Yankel and also of Yankel's friend, Brian Epstein, that it took guts to be gay in Liverpool in the forties and fifties, to some extent too you had to be a tough character, or you needed some *shtarker* friends to protect you, men with fists. My father was Yankel's personal *shtarker*. Dad was out nights carousing with his buddies, down to Yankel's underground speakeasy, or to the casino or to any destination with neon lights. On these evenings my mother, relieved at the rest from my father's overbearing personality, served for dinner a bowl of soup and a slice of packaged white bread and butter.

'Is that all?' My little voice breaking into tears.

My father was life, vitality, central heating turned on, platters of grilled chops and Waldorf salad and fancy chocolates in boxes tied with a ribbon. He never came home without something in his pocket. On their wedding anniversary, my mother got florists' bouquets of roses and at the bottom a bunch of sweet peas for me. *To my darling Adele.* I was in love with him, the great passion of the life of a five-year-old.

From my father I learned that when men were around there was more of everything, more luxury and abundance, and that women had to learn forbearance in the face of their big appetites, and manage the domestic economy.

'Don't you dare throw that soup on the floor,' said my mother.

'I will, *I will!* I want Daddy!'

She snatched it from me.

'You'll eat it, if I have to ram it down your throat.'

'I won't eat it.'

'Good, then starve.'

She didn't mean it, she was sick to death of my love affair with Daddy.

Late that night when I was sleeping I was woken by the sound of the doorbell. Daddy had forgotten his keys again. Through the banisters, under the Toby jugs, Daddy had his arm round Yankel and Yankel's face was all blood.

'Get a wet cloth, Edna, and some bandages. He's hurt.'

'What happened this time?' my mother said.

'Don't ask,' said my father. 'It's not women's business. And a cup of tea would be nice. Have we got any crackers and cheese?'

'In the soup again,' said Yankel through a thick tongue. 'Will I never learn?'

'You shouldn't go down the dock road, it's just asking for trouble,' my mother said. 'Can't you find someone nice?'

'From your mouth to God's ears.'

The time on my Alice in Wonderland clock read twenty to one. I went to the window and looked out on to the dark yew trees. The moon was above the rooftops of number 67. With only the luminous hands of the clock and Alice's luminous eyes to light my bedroom, for the first time in my life I experienced the sensation of *déjà vu*. I had it a lot in my childhood, not now, not for many, many years. Strange pictures came and went in my mind, elves and goblins playing on the eiderdown, fairies bouncing together, holding hands, using my bed as a trampoline. A red-eyed miniature zebra trotted over the ottoman. I began to scream.

Mummy came up. 'What's the matter, bubbsy baby? Did you fall out of bed again?'

'Is Uncle Yankel better?'

'What do you mean?'

'Did you make him better with Elastoplast?'

'What is the child talking about?' she said as if I wasn't there.

'His face was hurt.'

'Don't be silly. When did you see his face hurt?'

'Just *now*. He's downstairs.'

'There's no one here, just us, Daddy isn't even home yet. It's early. Look at the clock.'

And the clock's hands showed ten past nine.

'Daddy will come in and give you a kiss when he gets home. I'll make sure of it.'

As an adult I have tried and failed to make sense of this memory. I keep it by me. The little girl who created it is special. I refuse to allow her to be undone by encrusting time. She once twirled around the kitchen in dizzying circles until she was sick, she wanted me never to forget when I was grown-up what it was to be a child, to be smaller than everyone, to be made to do what you don't want to do, to see with such clarity how life is *not fair*. How eggs made her retch, and Struwwelpeter frightened her, and that according to *The Woodentops* clothes pegs could come to life, and that weird men lived in flowerpots, weeds could squeak a bit and Daddy's knee was heaven on earth.

I now suspect my mother's finger was on Alice's arms.

3

The fate of the only child in the time before daytime television was to have hobbies or read. I had no craft skills at all, so reading is what I did. I read a lot and I read it all very fast. I went way beyond my years. I read Hemingway under the desk at school instead of the set texts, *Black Beauty* and *Lorna Doone*. I got the school prize for an essay on *A Moveable Feast*.

I grew up to be the leader of a circle of schoolgirls, bolshy, sophisticated, ambitious, supercilious, a little bit cynical already, who smoked and wore plum-coloured lipstick and very short skirts.

We were fairly clever, though none of us ostentatiously so. We sneered at swots and nose grinders. We handed in our work carelessly and still got good marks. We didn't care what the teachers thought. We read everything that was new and particularly everything that was forbidden. Bought every Stones and Beatles record from NEMS on the day of release, quoted Dylan lyrics at each other, queued to buy mini-dresses at Chelsea Girl, sent away for a ten-shilling feather boa from *Honey* magazine, could recite by heart 'The Love Song of J. Alfred Prufrock'. Ran through Sefton Park to the Palm House and kissed boys on the swings. Drank half-pints of Double Diamond at the Phil and O'Connors Tavern, wrote poetry, stayed up on school nights to watch *Late Night Line-up*. Could tell the difference between Peter Brook and Peter Hall. Went on the Pill to prepare ourselves for the future amazements of living.

Daddy got caught in some kind of very basic Ponzi scheme involving the sale of chamois leathers and hanged himself with his best silk tie while on bail. He did it in the spare room, knocking off a silk lampshade with his dangling feet.

I imagine that this is what an earthquake or a tsunami is like. One minute you're lying on the beach drinking a piña colada under a sun umbrella, the next the whole bed of the ocean is covering your face. Or you're standing in a door frame watching everything shaking and rooms going down like card-houses. When it stops, you wander around in a biblical way, in the ruins, rending your garments.

Out has gone the sun, the land is in darkness. *No Daddy!*

My father ate an apple like this. He munched around the circumference and then pecked at the remaining rim. He cut an orange in fours and mouthed the flesh from the skin. He did not believe in peeling. 'All the goodness is on the outside, that's where the vitamins are.' How is it even *possible* that a personality as large as his could just be turned off like a light switch?

And everything that we had – Mummy's diamond earrings, the suits in Daddy's wardrobe, the silk ties, the books in my bookcase, the china horse's-head bookends, the lipsticks, the mini-skirts, the rose wallpaper on the landing, the swinging seat in the garden, the Timex watch on my wrist – all paid for by gambling and deception and crime. 'Why not?' Daddy said when the police arrived. 'Why not take from those who hate us? I know you, Inspector Ferris, I know you from Hackins Hey. You're a bastard and an anti-Semite. I'll swing for you.'

'Shut up, Harry!' cried my mother. 'You want to bring more trouble down on our heads?'

She ran down the road after the police car in her velvet

Mallorcan mules. When she came back, she said, 'Adele, things are going to be very different from now on, but look round you at everything your father gave us. He did everything for you, he worshipped you, you were all he lived for. Never forget it. It was always for his family.'

Yankel Fishoff at the funeral dressed in a black Crombie overcoat with velvet collar, black brocade waistcoat, white shirt and polished Chelsea boots.

'Look at the poof,' said one of her friends. 'Who does he think he is, Count Dracula?'

But my mother, turning on her from beneath her black hat, the black hat she borrowed from Lily Eisen who had buried two husbands and a son-in-law, the sorrows of the world weighing down the brim of that hat, said, 'Look at *your* husband, what a *shloch*, did you not dress him this morning? What's a wife for but to dress her husband? He's like something out of Paddy's market. In my opinion it's very nice to see a man who makes an effort. Old men lose interest, if they ever had any, in how they look, but Yankel is always beautifully turned out.'

'How can you think of clothes at a time like this?'

'You wait, you'll see what life has in store for you.' And the brim came down over her eyes.

I saw my father go into the ground. His brother Irving, estranged since the arrest, cried histrionically. He shook his fist at heaven. 'I remember him when he was a little boy, a little boy, I tell you! My brother, my brother. I was with him in Reece's tea room when a car backfired on the street and my heart turned over in my chest, I thought it was guns, I thought I was in the army again and I broke down in tears. Harry put his arms round me, two grown men over a pot of tea and buttered teacakes, sobbing. That was the kind of brother he was to me.'

Everyone was claiming him for their own, all the rancour at his crimes was gone, my mother was looking at the box in the earth: 'Harry, Harry.'

'Adele,' said Yankel, 'you haven't shed a tear.'

'What's going to happen to us? How are we going to live?'

'You'll live, don't worry.'

'But I don't understand.'

'What's to understand, minxy? What's to know?'

'Where is he? Where's he gone?'

'Beats me.'

'Who is going to look after us, me and Mummy? The lights have all gone out. I can't see.'

'I know what you mean, he was a big personality.'

The stone broke in my chest. The rabbi wailed, my mother and her friends stood as his weeping chorus in their hats and high-heeled shoes. Oh, Daddy, you were the light of my life and I was supposed to be the light of *yours*. Why did you do this to me?

Early the next morning, when the dawn was over the street and the lamps out there burned then fizzled, Yankel walked along the pavement, his Cuban heels clicking up the crazy-paving path to the front door, and my mother was dressed in her peony housecoat and bare legs, slippers on her bare feet. I heard the doorbell ring, I heard them go out into the garden through the kitchen door and there they were, figures in the flowerbeds burying the ormolu clock and her jewels and, deep in the ground, wrapped in a plastic bag, her fur coat. I never saw such a slightly built woman dig with such strength and frenzy or an artist take to the spade with such per-spiration and shout, 'What else needs going in, Edna?'

Our family was now under the rose bushes.

Yankel lifted a hammer and smashed a side window. Next door, Mr Hallows, the dentist, looked out of his window and saw the broken glass.

'She's been robbed!' cried Yankel.

Mr Hallows chased down the street in his pyjamas looking for the thugs, the hooligans, all the way down to the park, looking behind dustbins in case they were hiding and when he returned Yankel said, 'Poor Edna, she has the worst luck in the world. I'll call the police.'

We got a lot of money on the insurance. When you don't have

time to think, you have to think, you keep your emotions in check. You do what you must do.

Me, I was walking through fog. Monsters jumped out at me, there was something new every day. I used to go and look at myself in the full-length mirror in my parents' bedroom to make sure that I was still there because Adele was disappearing. Adele was a punctured balloon. Was anything left of Adele? The books were still in the bookcase. The Biba plum lipstick was still in the drawer of the dressing table. My copy of *The Female Eunuch* – bought in hardback, mind you, with a birthday book token – was still by the bed, half finished, full of underlinings. My dresses still hung in the wardrobe. And I'm pfffttt inside. Tiny ball of hurt, anger, longing, resentment, fear, expanding to fill the dark void left by Daddy's leaving me.

'Don't you dare crack up on me, Adele,' said my mother. 'I haven't got time to look after you. I've got too much on my plate. We're going to have to face this together, do you understand? Don't let me down. Stop crying. Don't pull that face. From now on things are going to be different, very different. Do you understand?'

My mother's friends rallied round her, all those big 'aunties' with their dyed hair and tight satin clothes who rang the doorbell bearing food and prescription medicines they poured out from their pill bottles. 'Take this, it'll pick you up in no time.' All their heads together round the morning-room table, a confederation of women who had come up together from the terraced houses of the city centre, the warmth of the old iron stoves, remembering with laughter their rayon dresses and hair piled on their heads beneath wartime turbans.

This was their world, the world of women and their no-good men, the bastards and the *schlemiels*, and their hysterectomies and pawned diamond rings, and cancers growing in their breasts and wombs. Their red-painted nails. They were hawks and eagles with talons, proud, dignified. Hair dye and lipstick were their war paint and armour.

'Life is hard, Adele. Now you've learned that, dolly. You've had the best that money can buy, but you're going to have to put your books away and start earning money.'

'I was out to work at fourteen, I was in the wages office of the munitions factory where they made the bombs.'

'I was behind the counter weighing an ounce of cheese.'

'I was engaged to a wonderful GI and we were going to go to California but he never came back from the war.'

'I had to look after my mother when my brother was killed in Italy, he was in the tanks, he was a lovely brother to me. I miss him terribly.'

And I sat there, listening to these middle-aged women in whose solidarity I could see nothing to admire, full of rage at my father for what he had done to me. I didn't want to belong where he had left me, down here amongst the women.

After the insurance paid out, my mother dug up the valuables and we moved to a flat off Linnet Lane; such sweet birdsong names these roads had, Lark, near Linnet.

'Now you,' said my mother, 'are going to have to start earning your keep.'

'What do you mean?'

'Why do you need to stay on at school? Who needs qualifications? You'll be married, I hope, in a couple of years. There are some very nice boys out there, boys with money. The Rosenblatts are loaded, one of the Rosenblatt boys would be perfect, we could be back on top of the world in no time.'

'Are you mad? I'm never getting married.'

'What do you mean? Of course you're getting married, everyone gets married, apart from the poor souls no one wants. You just need to put your mind to it.'

'You don't understand. Daddy did, and Uncle Yankel.'

'What's to understand? A girl gets married, like her mother and her grandmother before her. Even if he turns out no good, you still need a ring on your finger.'

'Oh, *Mother*.'

'Don't use that word with me. Who do you think I am?'

'My mother!'

'You little know-it-all. You could get a Saturday job, for a start. Bring in a wage, every little helps. That's right, flounce off in a huff! You'll see, believe me, you'll see.'

I was spoiled, I was insufferable, I was grieving and didn't know how because all the rituals of grief I had rejected as hopeless bourgeois relics of another generation. Teenagers aren't supposed to need to grieve, we're designed to be obnoxious. And crying in my room, my little box room overlooking a brick wall. A brick fucking wall.

But before I knew it one of the 'girls', my mother's army of girls, got me a Saturday job in Lee's on the perfume counter. Rose, iris, jasmine, geranium, the chemical explosion of Chanel No. 5 hung around my clothes like blood in an abattoir or the dust of coalmines. All the other saleswomen were older ladies. 'You've got a beautiful speaking voice, did you do elocution? You know you could get on the training scheme, you could go into management.'

I hated my life. I hated Yardley and Blue Grass. They were turning me into a ghost, a remnant. I was something you could spray into the air.

Out of the window people passed up and down the street on their various business and I was imprisoned by a till and a pile of paper bags with a punch card and a packet of Luncheon Vouchers.

'So now you know,' said my mother, 'how the old world works. Have you met any Rosenblatts yet?'

After the threat of the Rosenblatt boys, my only ambition was to make myself unattractive to as many of them as possible. To be sullen, to be damaged goods, to be seen walking down Bold Street with a boy with red hair down his back, wearing a see-through Perspex coat in the pockets of which you could see his cigarette-rolling machine, his leaky pens, snotty Kleenex. Vince from Maghull had the catarrhal voice of this dirty, windy sea city where the weather was always fresh, meaning cold winds blowing across the Atlantic.

No one knew what to do with me, it was out of control. I took days off school to ride the ferry across the river and spend a day on the dirty beach eating ice creams and sitting on the swings. I went to Yankel to ask him for a job in his nightclub. 'You go back to school, minxy. It's what your father would have wanted.'

'If he'd cared about what I wanted he'd never have done this to me.'

'I know, but your father only wanted the world for his family. If he couldn't earn it honestly, then he just went ahead and did the best he could another way. That was Harry, he was what he was.'

'I hate him.'

'No you don't. Go back to school, learn your lessons. I'd have loved to have had an education, I never even went to art school.'

But whatever anyone else wanted for me, I refused to do it. And then was surprised when I got two Cs and a D in my A levels.

'You cut off your nose to spite your face,' said my mother. 'You'll have to marry a rich boy now, won't you?'

4

Of the many Adeles I have been in my life, and I feel that I have been something of a pack of cards, the one I miss the most is the one I was when I was fifteen. I turned that age and out she came, my grandmother who died before I was born. My mother said her spirit was inside me, it had waited a few years for me to assemble my soul and make its way to me. I had, they said, her vitality and zest.

My grandfather pointed at me with a nicotined forefinger and said, 'This one is my cleverest grandchild. God grant that she not have the evil of her father inside her.'

Possessed by my grandmother's spirit, I had entered a poetry competition for schoolchildren, and won it. I won out of *thousands* of entries. All across the poetry-mad city, girls and boys sat down and wrote; mainly rhyming doggerel about pets, or jokes or limericks. One Saturday morning I produced fifteen lines. It took around half an hour and the poem had more or less written itself in my head, as if I was taking down dictation from the poetry overlords. The poem was somewhat novelistic, in that it was a portrait of an old lady –

Elsie's room is clean
and although the dust comes in unseen . . .

– a type I would never have met, only read about in books, for books were where you found life, without the effort of being in the real world.

My photograph was in the local paper. In the picture I am holding up a cheque for eight pounds. I look as Moses might have done when he was presented with the two slabs of the Ten Commandments and the deeds to the Promised Land.

The cutting is headlined, ADELE HITS AT CITY HOUSEWIVES. "'They are so insular," she declared. "Their lives are so narrow. They sit in cafés and read their women's magazines. It's all so empty and sad.'"

These remarks were an insult and a provocation. That is how they were intended. I was already making sure I would no longer be welcome.

That summer, the year I won the poetry competition, my grandfather came to stay with us for the last time before he died in the winter of old age and with the desire to be with his wife again in the grainy hereafter, sheltered under the deep bliss of God's wing.

Since her death – the floating Grandma who now inhabited me – my grandfather, who was still robust in his nineties, had led a peripatetic existence. He travelled around his children's homes like an ambassador, in a twenty-year journey across the north of England, dipping down as far south as Birmingham before pointing himself upwards again to Sheffield, then across to Manchester and to us in Liverpool. He arrived at the station with his leather suitcase which contained two shirts, some underwear, religious paraphernalia and his books. His white moustache was stained yellow with his cigarettes and he kissed the mezuzah on the door as he entered each room.

I remember him in these last years before his death, a gentle creature who stood in the garden and held out his hands with crumbs for the birds and they came and pecked the bread from his body. He walked in clouds of sparrows and blackbirds, maybe they smelled something on him that attracted them. He ate the simplest food – only rye bread, tea without milk or sugar, herring, *kasha*, boiled chicken, sour cream and cottage cheese – but he smoked the most lethal cigarettes, Capstan Full Strength, unfiltered. My aunt would buy him Benson & Hedges in a gold packet, but he threw them away: 'I don't like a fancy cigarette. Strong tobacco opens the lungs.'

For safety, his certificate for bravery didn't travel with him but was kept in the house of one of my uncles, protected behind glass and a gilt frame. 'Well, it happened this way. The year, I believe – the certificate has the date written on it – was 1913, a few months since I came to this country from Russia and even now I ask myself, Why did you leave it so long, Moishe, Morris, whatever they like to call you? The streets were very interesting in the new world, *everything* was. So I am walking along minding my own business, with my papers in my pocket because you lose your papers when a policeman wants them and they take against you. Along this road in Everton I walk, the place where they have the football now, the fellows your father goes mad for in the blue shorts, and I hear a terrible shouting in a language I don't understand, English is still almost nothing to me, but a woman who is in fear of her life can make herself understood.

'So to see if I could help, I go into the house, and she grabs my arms and takes me into the front parlour with the sofa and the cross on the wall above the fireplace and the little knick-knacks women like. Thin woman, not old, not young, not pretty, not ugly. No charms. Right in the middle of that room what do I see but a coffin and inside a dead person, but the person is on fire and the sofa is on fire and the curtains are on fire and everything has caught in flame because the candles she has round the corpse have lit the suit he is dressed in.

'The woman is talking and crying and the room is catching light and I don't understand a word she is saying because the only words I know in this language are the ones you tell a policeman, your name and your address. So I size up the situation and I think, The coffin and the corpse is burning, take it out of the house. So I ran and opened the window and I picked up the coffin and I threw it out on to the street.

'Only now do I turn round and see that as well as the woman there are two little children. They are standing at the door to the kitchen, they are hiding from me, the strange foreigner. So I pick up one under each arm and I carry them out of the house and put them down on the pavement. Now the woman is covering me with kisses, but I begin to hear the whistle of a policeman so my inclination is to run in the opposite direction, away and away and away. No good. She catches hold of my arm and she will not let me disconnect it. The policeman comes, she talks and jabbers in her language, the one I can now speak like a native, as you hear, after all the years in this wonderful country, and the policeman writes everything down in his book and I tell him my name and address and there are no further consequences, I believe.

'But not too long later, a letter arrives at my house. I must present myself at an office and I will be given an award by the Shipwreck Society for bravery! I am dressed by your grandmother in a beautiful suit she has found for me, from a recently deceased person who had no time to wear it into his own shape at the shoulders and the elbows and the knees, and I go to the Exchange Building which is more wonderful and fine and modern than anything I ever saw in Kiev. Men in suits and moustaches and beards and watch chains shake my hands and I don't understand a word they are saying, they give me my certificate and I say my four English words, "Thank you very much," and we go home and I am for a few days a hero.'

This was the only practical thing my grandfather ever did. He was really a mystic and a scholar and his soul flew like the birds into other realms.

'What a story!' I said.

'I notice you don't ask if it is true.'

'It never entered my head.'

'That is the power of stories, never forget: they make like truth.'

We had in our garden one of those swinging seats, a lavish, floral upholstered sofa which rocked gently back and forth amongst the rose bushes and antirrhinums. His accent was very pronounced, he wheezed out his words but I sat there enraptured by him, in my little mini-dress with the Peter Pan collar, sleeveless; round-toed patent shoes with Cuban heels.

'I'll remember.'

I have done all my life.

'Now bring me a glass of whisky. If your father has the Haig & Haig, that I would like.'

I went into the house and opened the cocktail cabinet. It lit up as soon as the scroll key was turned in the lock and in its mirrored interior reflected back to infinity a universe of cut-glass tumblers and goblets winking hysterically at each other, and a jar of Maraschino cherries in case by any chance anyone ever wanted to make a cocktail and had the recipe for one. I poured a glass of Haig & Haig. No ice: my grandfather abhorred chilled drinks, an abomination from America.

I carried the glass on a tray back out to the garden with a glass of Coca-Cola from the fridge for me, and saw him sitting in stillness, the birds gathering around him, pecking down at worms beneath the glassy blades of grass, and I thought he had died there in the mild sunshine.

But he opened his eyes, took the glass, sipped as though he was drinking the elixir of life, and I said, 'Tell me, Zayde. About the dybbuks.'

'Yes, any learned man knows about these in a way that the common people don't. They don't belong to the Books, not to the Torah nor to the Talmud, they are from literature, a play. A man with an imagination made them up to frighten fools. The dybbuk enters a man's body and takes possession of it. What does he do to deserve this? There are many causes, but in my opinion, and here I am in agreement with Teitelbaum, the Satmar Rebbe, the best cure is psychiatry.'

'You mean it's just madness?'

'Maybe, maybe not. I am not an expert in modern thinking.'

'Now tell me about the *ibbur*.'

'You are my cleverest grandchild. Only you know about the *ibbur* and what's more knows how to ask.'

'You told me before!'

'But you want to learn, you want to go deeper into this territory of the mystical. Now this is a very complicated condition, and one which is not helped by psychiatry. Yes, an *ibbur* is a kind of possession, but a very good, very welcome kind, when a righteous soul decides to occupy a living person's body. You may not even know that you have been possessed, you won't go round making *mitzvahs* wherever you walk, it's not like that. Your soul has been impregnated temporarily because the *ibbur* is itself the soul of a departed person who wishes to complete an important task or carry out a promise, or perform a duty that can only be accomplished in the flesh.'

'Do you think you were possessed by an *ibbur* when you saved those children?'

'Me? The person who is possessed doesn't know so how should I know? But the person whose soul is owned by a *dybbuk*, that's a different matter. Everyone knows the biggest *dybbuk* possession of all.'

'Who is that?'

'Hitler! May his name be wiped out.' He turned and spat on the grass, knocked the ash from his cigarette on to the spot and rubbed it in with the sole of his shoe. 'In hell he will feel that.'

'Do we believe in hell?'

'Whether or not there is an afterlife is a big question, but for certain people, a hell is created just for their sins alone. And Eichmann is there with him, still dangling at the end of the rope we hanged him from in Jerusalem. But you, my Adele, you have large soul and it shines a light in front of it, like a coalminer underground has a torch on his head so he can see in the darkness. Hashem has placed this light inside you for his own reasons, if you want something, tell a story. Everyone likes a story, you transfix them and make them forget what they wanted to say to you. How do you think we are here and not there?'

'Where?'

'In the old land. My wife, *alava shalom*, made up all the stories because that was her kind of head. You turn up at the border and you tell them a story, but it's the story you have guessed that they want to hear. You change your name, so what?'

'But at school they teach us to be honest and sincere.'

'That's not for us, that's for people who don't need to make any sudden moves. I tell you again, you are my cleverest grandchild because you see beyond the film of this world and the next.'

'I do?'

'Yes, I see it in your eyes.'

He kissed my cheek and I felt the bristles of his unshaven chin. Nothing could be more English and suburban than this swinging seat, the mowed lawn smelling of sweet grass, the fence on which birds perched momentarily, the neighbours' houses that overlooked ours.

My mother came out in her summer sandals and laid a card table with delicacies for my grandfather to consider, a glass of strong tea with a slice of lemon next to it and a sugar cube, a plate of biscuits she had made, a slice of sponge cake.

'In all these things,' he said, 'there is sugar, and sugar is poison. Take it away.'

'What do you think tobacco is?' said my mother.

'I'm living, aren't I?'

5

Brooding over the blue-and-silver canisters of Rive Gauche (one of the great florals and the perfume I adopted later in life, my old standby), I got an idea. I thought, This is a really ingenious plan but it depends for its execution on believing with all your heart and soul that it is true, forgetting completely that you have made it up out of your own head. But if you believe, it *is* true. No one ever say I am not my father's and my grandfather's child.

Here is what I did. My mother had bought twenty-five copies of the paper where my poem had appeared, cut it out and sent it far and wide to every relation. Of the last three, folded in an envelope, I removed one and sent it with a covering letter to America, to Allen Ginsberg, care of his publisher.

The reason for choosing him was that we had the same surname. In the letter I said that I supposed that we were related, and that like him I was a poet and that I was only fifteen when I wrote it but already I was published.

A month later a postcard arrived. It was a postcard of a picture of squiggles, black and white. Like spaghetti. In the writing space he had written:

Dear Cousin,
To write worth a damn is a fine thing, and you write more than
a damn.

The first thing to notice about this brief message is that he had
swallowed without question my assertion that we were related,
which we couldn't be, because when they got to the border to
leave, my grandmother gave them some false papers. My grandfather was on the run from the Tsar's army, he was a deserter.
Ginsberg was just a name that came into my grandma's head
because she knew exactly how to become new people in a new
land. This ability has descended unto me and I too know how to
use it to my own advantage.

I sat down one evening and wrote a hell of a letter to the vice-
chancellor of a university that I chose specifically because it was
brand-new and I had the idea that they would be less picky, more
open to suggestion. The place had no patina of age or fame. It
was built of concrete, not Cotswold stone, so it should be able to
afford to take a risk on someone like me.

I wrote that letter, addressed to the vice-chancellor personally,
in which facts skirted round the edge of the paper, unheard in the
clamour of the grandiose claims I was making for myself, and the
witness statement of my 'cousin' Allen Ginsberg. This remains my
greatest work of fiction, my plea to be admitted to the English
Department with my C and two D grades. I demanded to be
released from the perfume counter.

The letter was passed on to the head of the department, a
Professor Emmanuel Fine. He invited me to come for a personal
interview.

Now, I was very well read beyond the school syllabus, in an
autodidactic way. Early on I read *The Bell Jar* and one thing I was
certain of was that I would not let myself go mad. Strait is the gate,
narrow is the path. My sanity was very precious to me, I had no
business being careless with it. I was making my own way in life
with no fall-back position.

Emmanuel Fine was bald with a fringe of grey hair surrounding his head, like a dissident Soviet physicist. He had an accent and an office lined with first editions of Henry James and had arrived at this provincial concrete campus via Prague, Paris and New York.

'Interesting story,' he said, looking at me hard, as if I myself was a forged manuscript. 'How did you forge the postcard?'

'I didn't, he wrote it to me.'

'Maybe he did, but are you actually related to him? How do you know? Who told you? Any evidence?' The boredom lapsed from his mouth, he was slightly enjoying himself.

'That's what my grandfather told me.'

'Our grandfathers are all liars, mine was, yours was. Still, it's quite a good attempt. I'll hand you that, you have something, I'm not sure what. What do you think of D. H. Lawrence?'

'I like Gudrun and her coloured stockings.'

'Do you now? That will annoy a few people.' He asked a few more questions about what I had read and where my inclinations lay in literature. We chatted on about Keats' 'Lamia' and then he stopped me in mid-sentence and said, 'OK, I've heard enough, I'll think about it. I'll be in touch.'

This is how I came to be at university, I came at it as if I'd shot myself from a cannon aimed across a river at a fortified target. I passed through the glittering gate to knowledge, to the concrete campus and its plastic-bottomed lake, its ducks and drakes and population of girls and boys with immaculate examination records and me the impostor, trying to learn how to speak and dress and not be dragged back to the cut-glass bottles and the Rosenblatt trap.

I always knew that I was an exception and it was best to tell as few people as possible. My story was too histrionic, it had none of the bland, beige certainties of our lives in those times, not even in Technicolor while they were actually happening.

And for a long time, I forgot all about the women. The women who knocked on our front door with platters of fried fish and cakes wrapped in tinfoil when my father hanged himself, who told their secret sorrows to each other. I did not understand that they were the real thing and I should not underestimate the power of women's friendship, even when the lipstick bled into the lines around their mouths and their face powder stood in dusty crevices around their noses.

6

Picture me, dressed on my first day at university in a yellow midi-skirt, emerald-green tights and black patent shoes. I look like a daffodil in a plastic pot. My sallow complexion, thin waist, narrow shoulders, prominent collarbones and freckled arms. A musky fragrance on the skin, not unpleasant, quite sexy. The demanding eyes. Smoking incessantly, my hair falling from a central parting in two curtains, straightened by laying it on an ironing board and pushing the hot iron over the strands till the split ends singed. Tiny burn marks on my dresses from falling strands of tobacco. Only eighteen. Scared, intimidated, bold, short-sighted, too vain to wear glasses.

The train crossed from west to east, towards the rising sun. I saw a bald landscape of hills. There were fields, there were woollen sheep, the landscape had once reared up in folds while sleeping and sunk back into an eternal bored dream.

I was still reading *The Female Eunuch* and thinking about the whole tasting-your-own-menstrual-blood thing and whether people said this kind of thing because they meant it or was it just for effect. I could imagine girls I knew being very literal about doing this, but surely it was a metaphor for something, if only I could work out what. If it was a manifesto I wasn't sure what its intellectual message was, but I thought she meant that our ownership of sex was also the ownership of our souls.

I ate a cheese sandwich my mother had packed for me and read on. Women were afraid, women were hungry, women were muted. Yes. Because men were life and passions. (To me.)

After I finished the sandwich I moved on to the packet of salt-and-vinegar crisps. I looked out of the window again and counted sheep on the hills. I made myself put up my front. A front is a very important aspect of yourself in Liverpool. You cannot show vulnerability, they will be on you like a pack of dogs.

At the station we were met by students representing our colleges who ushered us into mini-vans and drove us to the campus. The town was a wash-out when viewed from the route away from the station. Its secrets were well hidden down medieval streets the width of a cycle lane. In the van we were all packed, seated on our suitcases, with no idea whether the person you were jammed next to would ever be seen again. One or two had already pre-ordered scarves in the university colours, black and orange stripes, and were wearing them. It was a cool October morning but in the van they were sweating, throttled by hot wool the colour of wasps.

I queued for my room key and carried my case up the stairs along a breezeblock corridor to a breezeblock study-bedroom with a single bed, a desk, chair, Anglepoise lamp, bookshelf. It looked bare and full of possibilities. I quite liked it. I felt I could make an impression here, with no ormolu clocks or cut-glass whisky tumblers. It could be quite Elizabeth David: austere, Protestant, unadorned and contemporary with just a white bowl with a few green apples in it, as depicted in the colour supps. It was all very exciting and different. I started to feel very *keen*.

Across the hall was the same room, but doubled, with two of everything and one girl in it, standing by the window looking out at the traffic on the road which led away from the campus back into town, as if she was going to leap out and run after the car in which her parents were speeding away back home.

Gillian Braithwaite. A plumpish type girl hidden behind enormous ointment-pink-rimmed glasses, with sandy, curly hair corkscrewing itself around in coils, wearing a maxi-dress with leg-of-mutton sleeves. Her head stuck out of the sagging neckline as if she was Alice in the process of shrinking, and the dress was about to swallow her up.

Standing in the door, I said, 'Oh, hello.' She turned round and greeted me with a frightened smile, as if a lion had walked in which she must do her best to appease.

'Hello! I'm Gillian, you must be Dora.'

'No, I'm Adele.'

'It says Dora here in my induction pack.'

'I'm not with you, I'm in there.'

'You've got the single room. What luxury. I'm from Leeds. I haven't come far, have I?'

More girls tramped along the hallway carrying suitcases, all of us eighteen or nineteen, a mass of raw material being pumped into the system of the university, waiting to be moulded into new shapes. Girls of all sizes and, on the floors below and above us, boys, male and female layered like a cake. Boys with their own inadequacies, trying to leap the ditch of unfamiliarity with even more bluster than us.

'Would you like a cup of coffee?' she said eagerly. 'There's a kitchen along the hall. Mummy bought me a set of mugs, I'm dying to use them.'

'OK.'

She trotted off in her ankle-length dress.

I could hear someone say, 'I'm Caroline but everyone calls me Caro. I'm from Fulham, what about you?'

A low voice: 'Burnley. Lancashire.'

What genius had paired all of us together? Or decided that I was not to be a pair, was to be the third wheel, the one always observing the awkward attempts to say, as I could hear through the breezeblock walls, 'Good-night, sleep tight!' to a complete stranger?

Along one of the covered walkways, I saw some parents holding a girl by each arm. I noticed the mother's hair, a blond plait wound round her head, a style you rarely saw any more, only in photographs of an older time. A stout body, blocky from the shoulders down, and the father in a grey windcheater and trouser legs flapping. As I looked at this triptych there was something about the girl, and the way she seemed to be being *dragged* along by her father, that reminded me of a sick dog which somehow understands that the visit to the vet is a journey to a lethal needle.

I could not see her face, only a matching plait of fair hair which, unlike her mother's, reached down her back and was tied at the end in a tartan ribbon, a very childish hairstyle.

She turned to her mother and said something. The older woman nodded, and they stopped and she bent down to examine a moorhen. In profile, had it not been for the plait and the tartan ribbon, I might have mistaken her for a young man. She was angular, features sharp as in a line drawing, practically a stick person in which the only circle is the head. This gauntness did not have any associations for me. When she stood again, she seemed more relaxed but looking up I think she must have seen me standing at the window watching her, because she stared straight back at me. I saw a helplessness in her, a terror.

I thought, She should not have come, she's not up to it. It's not for everyone.

I opened the window to eavesdrop. 'Lorraine!' I heard her father say. 'This won't do. We must crack on.'

She nodded, said something I could not hear, and, with her held by the arms, the three of them proceeded on until they reached the doors of the next college and I watched them, very curious at what it might be that Lorraine was so afraid of.

We were all nervous in very different ways, even the most excited, including Gillian and, I found out a few weeks later, the cosmopolitan Caro along the hall who had never been to the North and had no idea what to expect and if she would be served primitive foods she didn't recognise. But to be practically *dragged* along by your parents, to be frog-marched to university! I thought, Don't make her do it! Let her go home if she wants to. And for months I watched out for her, for her long plait with the tartan ribbon swinging against her back, but I never saw it again. I knew she had not survived the first month and had rung her parents and they had come for her, defeated. Some people fail the very first test of freedom.

Gillian came back holding two cups of coffee in mugs decorated with Union Jacks. 'Sorry, sorry,' she said. 'It was such a wait for the kettle. But look! Mummy packed me some biscuits as a surprise.'

'So what's your subject?' I said.

'Music.' She pointed across the hall to her double room and the case of a musical instrument on her bed.

'Is that a violin?'

'Oh no, it's a viola.'

'What's the difference?'

'Well, to start with it's slightly bigger and the sound is more satisfying, it's quite mellow. It's such a lucky dip which instrument you end up with, isn't it? I *wanted* to play the oboe but I'm asthmatic so that ruled that out. Then I started on the violin but my hands were too big but actually I'm glad I ended up with the viola because although there aren't many solo parts, violinists are ten a penny and it's hard to get into a youth orchestra. So it's all worked out very well for me. Would you like to touch it? I can take it out of its case if you like. It's not terribly, terribly old but it's from the French town of Mirecourt. In the seventeenth century the Dukes of Lorraine installed violin makers they had brought over from Cremona. They found the pine wood from the nearby Vosges Mountains. Of course, the viola is a lesser instrument than the violin and we're the butt of the jokes of the orchestra, it's considered a very unpretentious instrument. Would you like to hear a viola joke?'

'OK.'

'Here's one. How do you get a viola section to play *spiccato*?'

'I don't know.'

'Write a whole note with *solo* above it.'

I had no idea what she was talking about. My failure to laugh or even smile saddened her for a moment but soon she brightened up again.

'But I still do love it, my viola. Do you know Haydn's Sixth Symphony? You can hear the beginning of the day, that moment of coming out of sleep, it's *all* violins, then as the light becomes stronger the oboes and the flute and the bassoon and horns come in. You can hear birds and cock-crows, it's lovely and there's nothing much for us violists to do at all. But then there's Debussy's *Afternoon of a Faun*, which is also about morning, but not a rational daybreak like the Enlightenment. It's drowsy, it's coming out of the unconscious slowly, you can still hear the dream state and there we are! Us violas! We have a part to play. I'm rabbiting, aren't I? Well, that's me summed up, music, music, music, that's all I am about.'

She fetched the viola and held it out to me, her eyes like toffee apples behind her huge glasses, so I took it from her and tentatively plucked at one of its strings with my fingernail. It made a low thrum. 'That's C!' she said. 'I could teach you how to play if you like. You've already made a start.'

Seeing her smiling, blushing, as if she had anticipated rejection as soon as she spoke but could not help herself, as if she knew that there was something too foolish and too enthusiastic about her, I looked at her more carefully. I saw that her fingers were always moving, she was hearing music in her head, she talked and talked to hear herself over it.

And I expected Professor Fine to walk in and say to me, 'What, *you*? Did we send you the wrong letter? Why would we accept such a schemer? I know your type, I know it very well, and you bore me. Your father, by the way, he robbed me of every penny.' Rrrobbed. The rolled r of the wily émigré.

I gave the viola back to Gillian and she put it back in its case. We drank our coffee.

'Are you expecting someone? You keep looking up at the door.'

'No.'

She examined the poster of Marty Feldman I had put up on the wall. She said, 'How funny, what a sense of humour you have. Can I see your record collection, by the way? Have you got any Simon

and Garfunkel? I like them. I don't like *much* pop music but I make
an exception for "Scarborough Fair", it's so sweet.'

Another girl appeared. It was early afternoon and she was wearing a dressing gown, a thick brown woollen garment which made
her look like a giant teddy bear. She was one of the prettiest girls
I have ever seen, with that peaches-and-cream complexion that
lasts only a few years, light brown shining hair cut in a page-boy
style and hazel eyes.

'Hello,' she said, 'I'm Dora, Dora Dickie. Isn't it an awful name?'

'When did you arrive?' said Gillian. 'I'm your room-mate, how
could I have missed you? Did you come while I was making
coffee?'

'No, I've been in the bath.'

'But where are your things? Haven't you unpacked?'

'I will soon. The water doesn't run terribly hot.'

'Maybe they'll raise the temperature when the term starts properly,' I said.

'I hope so.'

'It's rather funny to have a bath in the middle of the afternoon,'
said Gillian.

Dora ignored her. She smiled at me. I introduced myself. 'Are
you any relation to *Allen* Ginsberg?'

'Oh! I never thought of that,' said Gillian.

'Yes, of course. He's a cousin. In fact we all met up the last time
he was in London, he bought me an ice-cream soda and he told me
what rubbish D. H. Lawrence writes.'

'I've only seen the film,' Gillian said. 'Alan Bates is rather gorgeous.'

'Lawrence's view of class relations is distorted, I think,' said
Dora. 'And he has no idea about the Woman Question.'

'No, he doesn't,' I replied. 'Don't you love Gudrun and her
coloured stockings?'

'You don't look well,' Gillian said to Dora. 'Why don't you lie
down and I'll bring you a nice cup of tea? I'll just finish my coffee
and I can wash out the mug. I've got biscuits.'

Dora looked bad, she was clammy and her eyes had gone strange, like frosted glass in a bathroom window.

'Yes, you really should go to bed.'

I went in an hour later to see how she was. I still see her face rising from that awful dressing gown, and the teddy bears arranged on her pillow, childishly.

'Are you all right?'

'Come and sit next to me. I need a cuddle.'

But I stood, rigid by the door, unable or unwilling to offer any comfort. She laughed.

'How appalled you look. Don't you cuddle your pets?'

'I don't like animals.'

'No! How could you not? I miss my dog so much.'

Two days later Dora disappeared overnight. Gillian said, 'I'm really worried. Where could she be?'

'Don't be so innocent. She's in some boy's bed, fast worker.'

'But she took her toothbrush.'

'That's just good planning.'

On her return Dora slept for twelve hours. In the evening, still in the hairy dressing gown, she went to the shared kitchen and made a pan of potato soup. She offered me a spoonful held up to my lips. It was white and tasteless, apart from a slight hint of pepper. 'Don't you like it? Mummy makes it, it's so comforting when you have the sniffles.'

This invalid food seemed to revive her, because she regained her colour, got dressed and clumped along the corridors in a pair of wooden clogs with yellow leather uppers attached by brass nails. She unpacked her books, which had arrived by trunk. They all had difficult titles involving words like *empiricism* and *hegemony*. Above her bed she had attached the definitive poster of Che Guevara, who gazed out across the room at the middle-aged figure of J. S. Bach on the opposite wall, a complacent visage examining a piece of paper as if he was a merchant looking for discrepancies in the VAT.

7

When I applied to the university I didn't know anything about it. I wasn't completely sure where it was. In fact, it had its own story, unknown to me. It turned out that I had unwittingly applied to be a lab rat in a giant social experiment; a benign one, but architecturally the whole place had been designed to embed a certain principle that was to mould our education and our future lives.

The campus, when I visited it last month for the first time in nearly forty years, looked like a fossil uncovered from the Palaeolithic era: low, beige, concrete, confidently and futuristically Modernist, consisting of a series of prefabricated buildings interlinked by covered walkways, open on both sides to the lashing winds from across the Pennines, and set around an artificial plastic-bottomed lake stocked with ducks, Canada geese and other wildfowl, the names of which I no longer remember. Someone remarked that it looked like a spaceship that had docked to collect an experimental cargo of passengers. That was us.

Over the years, the university has sprawled out into the surrounding fields and when you leave the original site, if it were not for the grey roof of the sky you could be in the azure uplands of Silicon Valley. The old buildings, modest in scale, are dwarfed by the brasher, more recent structures and have stained quite badly. No patina of antiquity has made the concrete boxes look distinguished. Eventually they will have to be demolished.

The land on which the university was built was acquired from the estate of a seventeenth-century manor house, russet-bricked in the mellow autumn sunshine which was when we all saw it for the first time. The house itself was now the headquarters of the university's administration. Topiary was planted in the garden where I once played croquet with Bobby and understood for the first time the essential viciousness of the game. Now, forty years later, the shaped trees are enormous, as if giants had dragged their rooted feet on to the lawn.

A few weeks after I arrived it sank in with queasy despair that there was nowhere to go but where we already were. We students had walled ourselves in, robed our bodies in that concrete cladding. The university was so new that the ancient city with its hulking cathedral had no student bars or student quarter, it turned its backs on us, we were not wanted. Many pubs would not serve male customers with long hair, so we were limited, socially, to the campus. Musically it was a dire period, the time of glam rock, which we despised: knitted tank tops, kipper ties and huge lapels. Gary Glitter, Alvin Stardust. Everything that had been our recent youth was both exhausted and exaggerated. It was the age, though we didn't know it at the time, of celebrity paedophiles. We were becoming ridiculous when we were barely twenty.

One evening I sat on the floor of a dining room watching the New York Dolls. The Dolls had an urban stink to them, they smelled of hot-dog stands, drains, the rasp of the subway train. And they seemed to us malevolent, they would do us damage. We sensed a change coming that we still thought had nothing to do with us.

Both we students and the university itself had been conceived in the early years of the New Elizabethan Age. Spaceships, the conquest of Everest, the four-minute mile, whiz for atoms. Our parents grunted and moaned and cried in ecstasy in their beds, sweatily shooting sperm out into ova. The young Queen arrived back from Kenya to sit, dressed in a Norman Hartnell gown, on a gold throne at Westminster Abbey and have a heavy crown placed on her crisply permed head (that frightened submissive face slightly haunts me now, in this the diamond-jubilee year of her coronation). At this time our founders were mapping ideas for the post-war era. They had watched the human soul become subjugated to the all-encompassing idea, which is invariably shod in steel-capped boots. Their plan was to defeat ideology with a quiet, humane liberalism of human rights, equality and a spirit of public service.

Our founders wanted us to celebrate all the human weaknesses, our frailties, foibles, idiosyncrasies, the many small ways in which we are ourselves, not robots. People had proved to be fragile, they could easily be smashed. The founders encouraged us to be robust in our scepticism.

The freedom of the university was the plate on which our lives had been handed to us. *Real* freedoms, for the administration had decided it would not act *in loco parentis*. There were no rules. No gating and, apart from attending tutorials and handing in some essays, we were left alone to do much as we liked, which of course we did, and some followed their own self-destructive impulses to hell and others survived. Lectures were an optional extra.

We were encouraged to question, doubt, answer back, retort, rebel. If we wished to dress in outlandish clothes, that was our right. If we wanted to follow daft Eastern mystical practices like transcendental meditation, om-ing away at the crying sky, then we were free to do so. If we wished to blow our minds with hallu-cinogenic drugs on a path to enlightenment, then no one would interfere.

In those days the government paid us to spend three years being students, which meant, in those days, a way of life suited to Renaissance philosopher-kings, until we were turfed out blinking and unprotected like baby koalas ejected from the womb on to the alien, leafless world of an Antarctic ice floe.

We were a tiny oasis of unreality in a world that itself is semi-forgotten, a time when the university computer took up a whole building and was tended by maths students in white lab coats. On the other hand, we were, I suppose, pioneers of environmentalism, chewing indigestible substances – brown rice, brown bread, brown sugar – while our parents still ate processed cheese and instant mashed potato and thought it was Progress. A few of us really did hug trees.

On our first real day as undergraduates, once we had settled into our accommodation, we gathered in the concrete rotunda on tiers of seats, nine hundred of us. We were only a few years out of childhood, the boys boasting faint lines of hair on their upper lips. Our founder addressed us. He spoke of 'revolting students'. Better revolt, he told us with smiling paternal middle-aged benevolence, than be 'contented cows'.

I thought, This is amazing! If only the perfume-counter ladies could see me now. And then I knew I had to forget that the perfume counter had ever existed or that I had ever been behind it. No one is going to understand you, Adele. The past is in hiding. That girl wasn't you. She was a succubus. A succubus is a devil who inhabits a woman's body and consorts with men in her sleep.

8

'But who *is* this dishevelled person? Is he a janitor? Is he a porter of some description? Where is his broom and where is his dustpan? Oh, look, he's going behind the lectern. Could it be? Surely not! And yet it is!'

F. R. Leavis in an open-necked shirt revealing far too much of a brown, wrinkled chest was delivering a lecture. 'I was going to talk to you today about *Antony and Cleopatra* or *All for Love*. But I won't.'

There were two empty seats on either side of the boy. No one, looking at him, would submit to his vertical and horizontal inspection. It was his aloneness in the lecture theatre that drew me to him, I thought his singularity might make him easier to deal with than the lines of recent A-level students, uniform collections of clever swotty pupils, good at all subjects and with no back-stories to speak of, let alone complicated ones inciting suspicion and an examination of discrepancies and continuity errors.

He tapped my arm with his finger without turning round. Two silver bangles shook on his right wrist below the sleeve of a navy wool blazer fastened with brass buttons. In profile he looked like the portrait on a coin, of an emperor or a Mediterranean king, bronze and implacable, gazing forward into the edge of the known world, across the serrated rim of the currency.

'What?'

'You will sit on my scarf if you continue your descent.'

'This?'

'Exactly.'

'Is the seat free or not?'

'Oh dear. Oh, really. Well, never mind, we must proceed as we mean to go on and accept whatever is presented. Sit.'

He slipped a bangle from his arm and placed it on mine. 'Now we are married for the duration. Of the lecture, of course.'

Once the talk commenced he fell silent. At first his hand took conscientious notes, the remaining silver bangle rotating round his wrist and occasionally clattering against the gold sleeve-button of the blazer, then the hand lolled on the exercise book, played with its own buffed fingernails. When eventually the lecture suddenly dried up, mid-thought, and the speaker disappeared from the plat-form and walked out of the room, leaving us gaping, the boy said, 'He's too squalid for me, I shan't come again. What about you?'

'I thought he was awful. What a rambler. Is he senile, do you think?'

'That is one theory.'

'Who's Tom? He kept talking about his friend Tom.'

'Tom Eliot, I suppose. Shall we have coffee? Have you found any that is drinkable? Not in my college, what about yours?'

'No, all the coffee is swill.'

'At home we have Turkish coffee, grounds you can stand your spoon in and plenty of sugar.'

I gave him back his bracelet.

'No,' he said, 'I think you should keep it. At least for the time being, at least until we have had coffee. You must be aware that I like to be known as Bobby but my real name is Jahandar, posses-sor of the *world*.' I was in the process of introducing myself when he began to pull from the pocket of his blazer a piece of paper. 'Have you seen this?'

He handed me a flyer for the Gay Liberation Front. The G had an arrow growing out of its side, like the male symbol.

'Is this *your* line of enquiry?' he said, slightly winking, looking at me with a complicit smile on his fawn lips which had a trace of a sheen, as if he'd applied Vaseline to them.

'What do you mean?'

'Are you a Sapphist?'

'*No*, not at all.'

'Really? I'm quite surprised. You do give out that impression. There is something rather masculine and *hard* in your face compared with all these schoolgirls, so I thought you must ... Anyway, what one wishes to know is whether one would actually want to be liberated. I'm really not sure. One does feel that the types who are likely to attend will be very energetic and enthusiastic and talky. One can't help feeling that there will be a lot of discussion. Discussing is the coming thing, it's why we are all here, and in my opinion that's a mistake.'

He made the eighteenth-century gesture of a yawn, patting his hand over his mouth. All this *one* instead of *me* was very stylish and affected and I started to imitate it because nobody I knew, not even the exotic yet familiar Yankel, had ever referred to themselves as *one*.

Bobby's nickname was acquired after he had been caught going down on a prefect when he was fourteen and he took it as a badge of pride and honour. 'But not Bob, that's a game-show-host name.'

I hate nicknames, they are bestowed by bullies and belittlers, and I tried to call him Jahandar but he raised his hand, 'No, no, no, it's *Bobby*. Please. I must insist.'

He had taken a wrong turn and found himself on the concrete campus of this sixties university designed by Fabian socialists to turn him into a useful member of society, when he did not believe in things that had a function attached to them. Give him a cup and he would deplore its handle. I was enchanted and terribly proud that he had chosen me to be his fag-hag and wrote Yankel a letter all about him, to which I received the reply *Send us a picture*. Dearest Yankel. I miss him.

A note in my pigeonhole a few days later invited me to tea in his room, where he made a great ceremony of brewing a jasmine infusion in a small metal pot, and pouring it into small leaf-green china bowls. He offered me a plate of stale Ladyfingers. I picked one up, it was extremely dry in my mouth. 'Darling, you dip them. See, watch me.'

'Do you mind homosexuals?' he asked me. 'Are you prejudiced at all?'

'Me? Absolutely not. My father had a great friend who was gay. He came to the house all the time.'

'The older generation were so persecuted, poor chums. I remember watching TV with my parents in our sitting room in Muswell Hill among the velvet pelmets and there it came on, on the news, that we would be able to do what we wished with no horrid police-man leading us on and entrapping us. I think I let out the smallest sip of breath, a feeling of such release because I was only fifteen and the world ahead was being fashioned to suit me down to the ground. Of course, no one noticed and my father just began ranting in Farsi about the *koonis*.

'When I was a teenager, I used to think that God had made me this way by mistake, that there were a few of us who didn't turn out as intended, perhaps a faulty mould was the explanation and I would brood and brood on it in my bedroom and wonder why we had been allowed to live if we were not quite right. Things went wrong in the kitchen and Mummy threw the failures in the bin, a jelly didn't set or her cream sauce curdled. Then I thought that we were an experiment, some plan of God's to work out what would happen if ... but the "if" was beyond me and I stopped trying to solve the secret of my life and just live the gorgeous thing I had. And that's all I'm doing now, that's all. And of course you must do exactly the same, whatever gorgeousness is in store for you.'

'Do your parents know now?'

'Good heavens, not in a thousand years. My mother thinks I

dress precisely to attract the ladies, poor dear. She's not Iranian, by
the way. She's Irish. She was once a tightrope walker in a circus.'

'You're not serious?'

'I never know the answer to that question. Perhaps university
will teach it to me, we'll see.' He leaned back on his single bed,
serene, smiling, his great brown kingly nose tilted towards the
ceiling.

Like me, he had been allocated a single room. 'I suppose,' he
said, 'they didn't trust me to share with anyone. Of course, I do
prefer it but it was awkward at the dreadful first-night party when
I didn't know a soul. That's why I think I might very well go to this
liberation group. To find some *simpáticos*. I wish you were my tutorial partner. Mine is some girl who simply never speaks. It's quite
tiring for me, I have to prattle to fill the silences.'

'Don't you sometimes just want to be left alone?'

'Oh, please, darling. That is the worst fate of all, to be left alone.
I could not *bear* it. Have you read *Brideshead Revisited*?'

'No, it's Evelyn Waugh, isn't it? I've read all the early ones,
Decline and Fall, *Vile Bodies*, *Handful of Dust*. I love his absolutely
pared-back style. What's it about?'

'I'll lend it to you, it's marvellous. I've read it six times. I can see
you as the lovely Julia, in a way.' He screwed up his face and laid
his head on one shoulder.

'But we have so much reading to do already.'

'And are you planning to, actually?'

'Well yes, don't you have to?'

'It's not school, we can do anything we like.'

The next time we met, when I invited him to my room, he looked
up at the poster of Marty Feldman. 'Ah, the Hebrew gentleman.
I thought you were too.'

'Not only that, I'm related to Allen Ginsberg.'

'Poor you, what a dreadful fright that man is with his appalling
beard, with food and God knows what else stuck in it. Can you
imagine kissing him? Yuk. Though I have had my moments with

Hebrew gentlemen. Do you ever go to Bournemouth and stay in one of the Hebrew hotels? I spent a weekend there last year loitering amongst the pines in the evening shade while those Hebrew families walked ponderously up and down the promenade. What eyes the gentlemen in their suede shoes made at me.'

I laughed. I choked on the little cake he had brought. Let him say what he liked, at least it was interesting and fantastical and strange. His reflex was to tell lies so big that they seemed like truth. To make you doubt what you thought you understood, carelessly or with intent, not with malice or unkindness but because he knew how. I was a liar too, but not like this, not lies with imagination; I lied without art, only for my own advantage and on nothing like his scale, baroque lies, lies with ceilings decorated by Michelangelo and Tiepolo, instead of little sneaky ones such as who ate the last biscuit.

When I got to know him better he would occasionally lower the mask of antique campness and you saw what lay beneath. But for now he was all tinkling bracelets and dark eyes beneath girlish lashes. I adored him.

'But I don't like the way you dress at all,' he said. 'I'm going to find *gowns* that would suit you. I see you as a Venus in furs, I see you in jewels. A Cleopatra of the Yorkshire moors. Yes. We'll go shopping. I'll pay.'

9

The cold I had always known came westerly from across the Atlantic, heavy with rain and the smell of other continents, my home, my sea city, or it blew east over the Pennines and had exhausted its rain on Manchester by the time it reached us. On the campus surrounded by the concrete blanket of its buildings, the artificial lake trapped the damp in our hair, our ears, our bones.

Bobby did take me shopping and his most generous gift was a second-hand fur coat; it was made of rabbit, I think, and shed its hairs like a cloud as I walked. I turned its collar up against the wind. My long hair spread in lank locks over the furry shoulders. My lips were darkened with purple lipstick. I went along with him because I had no dress sense of my own to speak of. A number of garments were brought back from London during his weekend visits home. He got them in the old-clothes stalls in Portobello Road Market. He had an incredible eye. 'I want you to be *flamboyant*, I think that's your style. You are very thin, quite frail and waif-like really but with this rather hard, closed face above your reedy body. We need to take that into account. I see you as an orchid – yes, you are definitely hothouse.'

Occasionally I went into town. It was usually a fruitless journey, the place had so little to offer us: a cathedral with a rose window, medieval streets, the river, an Indian restaurant. We ate all our meals in college or prepared baked beans on toast in shared kitchens. A new shop in town opened by former students sold strange things: brown rice, soya beans, loaves of brown bread so dense you could brain someone with them, brown sugar, brown lentils and blackish joss sticks with the face of some bearded Eastern guru looking out from the packaging.

The owners lived out on a farm in the country, which they called a commune. They all looked the same, the boys and the girls, their long hair, their trailing loon pants, their velvet smocks twinkling with mirrors, their smell of patchouli and their kohl-rimmed eyes. The girls were all called Sarah and they seldom spoke and so were judged to have a wisdom denied to the talkative. Curtains of blond hair falling from their foreheads framed large blue expressionless eyes which were lowered to the cover of an album on which they rolled rather beautiful, tight joints.

I bought a bottle of patchouli oil and dabbed my neck with it. The smell knocked me for six, it was so different from the perfume counter, musky and old and brown. I began to walk back to the campus but a horizontal band of rain blew into my rabbit coat and it gave off an animal odour that mingled with the patchouli and I decided to take the bus.

A familiar figure was waiting at the stop, the damp hem of her maxi-dress stained with rainwater and the heavy case of her viola slumping her left shoulder.

'Have you just been to that terrible shop? There's nothing nice to eat there at all. Ooh, you do pong.'

I asked her how she was getting on with Dora.

'Quite well. She says the most interesting things. But I like you better, obviously. I'm so proud that you are my friend, I've never known anyone like you before. I think you're wonderful, so unusual, and I'm just boring Gillian who will go back home to Leeds in three years and be a music teacher and then I'll marry

Robin because he is going to be a lawyer and Dad will die of happiness.'

'I didn't know you had a boyfriend.'

'He is in the sense that we go to see concerts together and we've kissed a little. We haven't done . . . that. I suppose you have.'

'Of course.'

'I knew it. Was it nice?'

'I liked it.'

'I hope I do. I don't know very much about it, to be honest. I'm awfully worried that I'll do it all wrong and break something.' She laughed. 'I do like boys, you know. I like their forearms best of all, hairy forearms, they're lovely. There's a boy I see in the library who rolls his shirt sleeves up to the elbow when he's writing and I keep sneaking peeks at him and going bright red. Obviously he doesn't notice, because he doesn't notice *me*. Why would he?'

And we were so cold at the bus stop, me blowing on my hands to warm them, that Gillian felt inside her pocket. 'Oh, look what I found.' She drew out a pair of Fair Isle gloves. 'Let's have one each.' I took the glove and put it on. She reached out and put her bare hand in my bare hand and we stood chained together by flesh, her viola in her spare hand, my multi-grain wholemeal loaf and jar of tahini in the other, until the bus finally arrived and I withdrew it.

A couple of days later she knocked on my door. 'I've got a present for you.' She handed me a small packet. 'Can't you guess what it is?'

'Biscuits?' The whole student accommodation was consumed with greed for Bourbon creams and chocolate digestives, it was all they seemed to talk about.

'Don't be silly. Open it.'

I saw her excitement, I knew that whatever lay inside the wrapping paper meant a lot to her, possibly too much, more than it might mean to me.

It was a pair of Fair Isle gloves. 'Just like mine! Well, not identical because all Fair Isle gloves are different, it's the way they're made, they have no more than two or three stitches in any given colour so they're like a piece of music, an atonal work, for example. And don't you think it's amazing that if you look at the other side of a piece of embroidery it seems so random that it would be harder to create than the proper side?'

I put the gloves on and held up my hands. 'Perfect fit,' I said.

'Now you will be warm.'

'Look, you must borrow my fur coat some time. Borrow it now for a few days.'

'Oh no, I couldn't do that. It wouldn't be me at all.'

'Why not? You'd look lovely.'

She blushed. 'When I have my first fur coat, I would want it to be a mink like Mummy's.'

'How bourgeois.'

'I know! It's terrible, isn't it, but you see that's what I'm like. If I had your ... maverick style, I could be someone different, but I don't even want to be.'

'I think that's sad.'

'Yes, I understand. But it's OK. I'll be a mother and wife and what will you be? A free spirit, roaming round the world!'

'I very much hope so.'

'Then my gloves will keep you warm.'

Within two weeks I had lost the gloves and was very sorry about it. Not just because they kept out the damp of the Vale but because Gillian was too sweet a girl to be careless about.

Towards the end of term I saw a couple coming towards me on the covered walkway. They had appeared as conjoined twins, out of nowhere. Separately, they seemed not to have previously existed; no one ever claimed to have seen them before alone. Already they had acquired a reputation, and were known as Evie/Stevie. The boy had the white, possibly even powdered, face of a Pierrot from *Commedia dell'Arte*, and a dry red mouth. He wore spotless white dungarees and black baseball boots. Evie was dressed identically and, extremely unusually (I had never seen this before), they both had very short hair, sheared and standing upright like a hedge, hers almost white, snowy, his hair dyed black and red like a railing that had partly gone to rust. But the most extraordinary thing about him was that he had a small gold earring in each ear. Now I had seen men wearing one earring, but two? There was something about this statement so provocative that I didn't know where to look so I lowered my gaze from his face and noticed that he was wearing my gloves.

'Where did you get those gloves?'

'My mum knitted them for me.'

'I think they're mine. I had a pair that were identical and I lost them.'

'No, you're wrong, I know they're mine because of the hole in the finger. Did yours have a hole?'

'Not when I lost them.'

'Well, there you are.'

And I just stood there, numb and furious, while Evie looked at the gloves as if she was trying to remember where she first saw them, possibly thinking that they were mine, but what did it matter because he looked so good in these girls' gloves and theft was not theft but the appropriation of things to their rightful owner, who might not have been the original one. There being some kind of natural karma at work in the universe which operated like a school prize day, handing out its gifts to the most deserving recipients. She would be thinking these thoughts because they were the ones that Stevie would have already taught her to think.

Bobby said the same kind of thing but it derived from supreme selfishness and was almost touching in its neediness for lovely items. Stevie's philosophy was ruled by the laws of disinterested cosmic justice.

10

Dora was setting herself up as the hostess of a political salon. It was there that I met for the second time, after the incident with the gloves, Evie, temporarily uncoupled from Stevie.

How to describe her? The pale cropped hair, the eyes widened. A condition in which the lid did not reach down to cover the upper whites and irises so she looked permanently surprised, amazed, occasionally even frightened of something that was just behind you, glimpsed over your shoulder and that you could not see when you looked round.

What else? Her height. Much taller than me. Five feet nine or ten. I was always looking up at her, towards that strong dimpled chin, the one point of certainty in an ambiguous face.

You saw her and Stevie walking together through the covered walkways beside the lake and they were completely unapproachable but Dora, who had absolutely no imagination, was immune to the toxic togetherness, had barged up to Evie and said, 'Look, I have a discussion group in my room on Tuesday afternoons, and you should come this week. We're examining the Woman Question.'

Evie, Dora said, claimed to have no idea what she was talking about but turned to Stevie and gave him that incredulous look, as if she was asking him to take this *person* away from her, remove her from their presence, but may also have been an asking for permission, because he said, 'Oh, but yes, you must.'

Evie turned back to Dora and said, 'Well, then, yes, I'd like to find out more.'

'But what about me?' Stevie said. 'Aren't I invited?' He gave Dora such a cutting smile, and the clown mouth turned down like a dramatic mask of caricatured self-pity.

'No, you can't come,' Dora said. I have noticed that very pretty women can get away with the most appalling rudeness. 'You're not wanted. It's women only this week.'

'So what about men, what's to become of us in your feminist world?'

'You'll just have to learn to make the necessary adjustments.'

The place was full of salons and soirées. Bobby's was literary. He read aloud passages from Proust and the literary sensation of the season whom I had not made a run at, Lawrence Durrell, while we drank sherry and smoked small black cheroots that he handed round in a silver cigarette case with the initials FTD engraved on the lid, stolen from the table of the lounge bar in a pub in Chelsea. 'Now is there a true reality?' he asked. 'Is it not all just *point of view*? There is this tiresome sociological habit of *authenticity*. Well really, what could that possibly mean? What is the authentic self after all? What is a man and what is a woman? Are we, I mean those of us here who feel these things, not just a third sex? Or are we the floating world?'

He turned to me. 'Do you know that very silvery couple?'

'Evie/Stevie?'

'Is that what they're called? Yes, them.'

'I know her, but only slightly.'

'I think we should try to bring them along to our little group. Make sure he comes. I can't decide if he's delicious or foul with his ring-pulls at the ears, but he reminds me of the young Jean Cocteau, he has the same impermeable sheen of charisma.'

Everyone knew them and wanted them and courted them. They were desirable people, even before they had opened their mouths. Stevie had read and knew about everything, or he wanted to know and would get round to it soon: the *Whole Earth Catalog*, *The Tibetan Book of the Dead* and a load of other ideas that were current for half a day. He could talk about Gramsci and Marcuse and orgone boxes and only fell silent when Bobby began to speak about Peter Brook's production of the *Dream* at the RSC, with the fairies all played by grown men, muscular, swinging in on trapeze bars. 'But did you *not* see it?' said Bobby. 'I thought everyone had.'

I sat down on the floor with my back leaning against the door of Dora's room. Dora herself occupied the chair by her desk. Evie was on Gillian's bed. It was the first time since the business of the gloves that I had seen her close up. If you took a photograph of everyone in that room, a group portrait, you might survey, as you looked through the lens, a number of attractive girls, Dora in particular, but when the photo came back, the only person you would have eyes for was Evie. She was something else, an ethereal light.

She mesmerised me. I wanted to look and dress like her but this was not possible. I was dark, sallow, chain-smoking; a 'soiled angel' was how Bobby had described me.

Dora told us to go round the room and introduce ourselves. We gave our names, our colleges, the subject we studied. Evie said she was studying philosophy main, English subsidiary.

Another girl who drew my attention was a sociologist named Rose Wright, with long romantic fronds of untidy chestnut hair she pushed constantly from her eyes and an emphatic and forceful way of speaking, as if she did not consider it possible that anyone would disagree with her. She seemed to think that her opinions were as unarguable as pointing to the sky and saying, 'That is the sun.' And yet she said everything with the friendliest of smiles, there was nothing aggressive about her. It was as if she was generously sharing a bag of sweets.

She said, in an entirely non-belligerent manner, that she was here because she believed the Woman Question needed to be considered in the context of revolutionary struggle not bourgeois individualism.

Dora said, no, we want to be free.

Rose said, there is nothing but conflict and society.

Dora said, well, that is true, but why can't we make radical gestures? Why can't we redefine interpersonal relationships on new terms?

Rose said, what do you mean? That just sounds like a stylistic mannerism. You're abandoning the base for the superstructure.

A girl called Ruth said, I think the problem for our generation is that we have nothing to rebel against, so our revolt consists of no more than petulant gestures. We've been cosseted by the welfare state, blanketed by free higher education, cocooned in free medicine, so we tell them they're fascists and they laugh at us. I mean really, what exactly *are* we all rebelling against?

Dora said, how middle-aged, how trite. The important thing is that we're all performers on the social stage, actors who—

Rose said, no, no no! There is nothing but conflict, it is that which drives everything forward. If the Woman Question means anything it's not *postures* or *gestures*, it's the workers who—

Dora said, look, is this a group or an encounter?

Rose said, what difference does it make?

Dora said, well, we've all read Goffman.

I said, I haven't.

Dora said, but you must have done.

I said, I don't know who he is, what has he written? Gillian, have you read Goffman?

Gillian said no.

I said, there you are.

Rose said, oh, bloody hell, we really are starting at the beginning, aren't we?

I said, but I've read Germaine Greer, what about her? Do you think the tasting-your-own-menstrual-blood thing is to be taken literally or is it a metaphor? Has anyone actually done it?

Nobody had.

Dora said, anyway, enough of this I've got something to show you. She removed a magazine from her desk. What do we think of this, it's new.

Rose said, ah, *Spare Rib*, I know about that already, it's a bourgeois trick. It will *never* be read by the workers. She had a shoulder bag made from two pieces of velvet, its strap an old curtain rope from which the tassel had been cut off. I've got something much better than that in here.

Dora said, are you a Trotskyite?

Rose said, ist, not ite. Yes, I am. Are you a Stalinist?

Dora said, of course not, I'm a free thinker.

Rose said, that just sounds like liberal mess and muddle to me. Like the English Department. Do you know, some of them study without any kind of methodology or underlying theory?

I said, I'm in English and I don't even want a theory, I just like to read novels and poetry.

Dora said, oh, there must be a methodology or you're in limbo.

Rose said, on that we agree.

I said, but I'd like to see that magazine.

Rose said, which one?

I said, the *magazine*, not the paper, the bourgeois individualist one. Where did it go? Who's got it?

Rose said, OK, but give mine to the girl next to you.

I handed the paper to Gillian, who examined it as if it were hieroglyphics.

Evie said, my boyfriend says the only conflict is between authenticity and the pose, he thinks—

Dora said, we're not interested in what men think, we're here to make ourselves heard.

Rose said, no we're here to work against.

Gillian said, against what?

Dora said, everything, of course.

Rose said, no, only class and imperialism and racism.

Evie held her hand up to her white throat and fiddled with a silver chain.

I caught her eye and smiled. She smiled back. We were complicit in something, weren't sure what. She was the one I wanted to get to know, not sure why.

Gillian knocked on my door.

'I've had coffee with Rose,' she said. 'She's from Leeds too!'

'Wasn't she a nightmare? Did you understand a word she said?'

'Not really, but I still thought she was nice. She grew up near me. It's a friendly feeling to be with someone who has the same memories as you do, and has been to the same cinemas and the same shops. We got quite nostalgic. It will be lovely to have someone to see during the holidays. I mean, I've lots of friends, and of course there's always Robin, but someone who bridges the two worlds is fab.'

'Good for you.'

'Well, I'm glad you approve. I wouldn't want to have a new friend you didn't like.'

'For heaven's sake, do grow up. I'm not your mother. You can be friends with anyone you like.'

She looked at me as if detecting for the first time qualities I had not tried to suppress but which she had up to now ignored.

'But I worship you.'

'Oh, for God's sake, please don't.'

'OK,' she said, hurt, her shoulders hunched up. 'I thought you liked me but perhaps you don't. You lost the gloves I gave you. That means something, doesn't it?'

'I'm genuinely sorry I lost your gloves, and I think they were stolen by that Evie girl's boyfriend.'

'Do you think so? He seems horrid to me.'

'And me.'

'And she's ... weird. It's hard when you look at her to know if she's a girl or a boy.'

'Yes. It's all a bit unsettling isn't it?'

After that, I would come across Rose deep in conversation in the pit by the dining hall where primary-coloured sponge cube-shaped chairs were arranged around the silent TV. I only once saw it turned on, later that year, when the kitchen and dining-hall staff received permission to serve lunch late, so they could watch Princess Anne marry Captain Mark Phillips. It was the first royal wedding of our lifetimes; we had no idea how significant these occasions would later become because we laughed and heckled at the screen, at the tiaras and all the antiquated pomp of a dying age, and I still hear the voice of Rose behind me saying, 'Will you all just shut up and have more respect for the workers who have given up their paid break to be here? It was the women of the working class who have only just won the right to equal pay.'

And more quietly, to Gillian, 'This, in a nutshell, is what we call false consciousness.'

11

They were burning off the old town gas. New gas, hydrocarbons from beneath the sediment of the North Sea, was being pumped into the city. Primitive organic matter in a deep coma for a hundred million years woke, combusted, turned into flame, drove the energy that powered the university computer. The cancelled coal gas burned in braziers along the roads. Workmen in donkey jackets, rough trousers and heavy boots watched the pyres waste themselves in the cold air. We were living in transitional times and hardly knew it. Whatever was happening, it was not happening to us. We remained in the playpen of student ideas.

I lay in bed and smoked. I stared at the ceiling. I thought, You know, you're going to get away with this.

Professor Fine had stopped me one morning as I was hanging round the English Department noticeboards. 'So, you got here. Liking it all right?'

'Yes, very much so.'

'Excellent. How's your cousin, heard from him lately? Any more postcards to show me?'

'Er, no, nothing recent.'

'Ha ha. Well, be sure to share anything that does come. I'll see him I'm sure when I'm next in New York.' He raised his shoulders in an attempt at a laugh, heaving them up and down as if he was carrying coal.

Each term, Bobby reappeared with some new show of magnificence. After the first Christmas it was a car Daddy bought him, a Hillman Imp the colour of acid-green pear drops. In the spring he sauntered into the college bar, ordered a double gin and tonic, spirits kept in for the lecturers and visiting parents, and said, 'Darling, guess what? I've inherited a *house*.'

'Who has left you a house?'

'A friend, a dear friend.'

'I don't really understand. How old was he?'

'Quite old, sixty-two, and he died rather slowly of cancer and I would go and see him in hospital in Hampstead, which is where I will live one day, by the way. Do you know it? No, of course you don't but you will, we shall all live there and go for walks on the Heath and look at the pictures at Kenwood and meet for coffee and cakes at Louis'. I have had to cross London from east to west, a direction which is highly complicated and involves monotonous waiting at bus stops, so he appreciated the frequency of my visits and he has left me this little house, but that's not the best of it! No! The really exciting thing is that it is on an *island*. A Greek island, in the Cyclades, the far-flung Cyclades. Do you know them at all? I haven't seen it yet myself, just pictures, but it looks like it will suit me down to the ground. There are two bedrooms and I'm going to spend the whole summer there and I wonder if you would like to come with me for a month, just so I can tell Daddy that I'm with a girl. And there will be photographs of us sitting together hand in hand as love's young dream and he will be satisfied.'

'Does he really have no idea? Are you sure?'

'We are all performing ourselves, I'm sure even Daddy understands that a performance is required. I perform for him, I juggle, I ride a unicycle, whatever he wishes.'

'We're the great pretenders.'

'I know. You and I are the ones who understand what a silly confection authenticity is, the supposed spirit of our age. Have you ever sat at your mother's three-sided dressing table and seen yourself reflected to infinity? That is what we are, reflections of reflections. We think all the time about what we sound like and how we appear. We are discarding outdated versions of ourselves. That's why I like you. You have the big secret I'm not remotely interested in, I just enjoy that you're putting on an act like me. Will you come? It would be such a help, and we would have a marvellous time. I can cook, you know. I can do many things.'

'Yes, yes, what did you think I'd say? But will it cost a lot of money?'

'Something can always be done, these things are managed. So we are settled. How glorious.'

12

Gillian said, 'I've had the most lovely holidays going for coffee with Rose and meeting her parents. They are so unusual. Her father is a journalist, just for the local paper, he doesn't approve of Rose's politics of course, he's a member of the *Labour* Party, yuk.'

He was a veteran of the Spanish Civil War. He had some kind of wound on his leg inflicted by the nationalists and walked with a limp. He could recite Lorca in Spanish from memory and wore a leather cap on his head above a blue cotton jacket. Small, intense, like a Yorkshire terrier he yapped at injustice. I had never heard of him then, but I skimmed with interest his obituary in the *Guardian* in 1996, where he was described as the Orwell of the provinces.

'I saw such *things*,' Gillian said.

'Like what?'

'How people really live.' She outlined slum housing, condensation on the walls, toddlers dying of bronchitis. 'Girls the same age as us, and they are so oppressed and beaten down by injustice and poverty and ill-health. Our fridge is always *full* of food, there's so much waste, we buy too much, and we all have too much, far more than we need. I've been in a liberal fantasy all my life.'

We were walking round the lake, woken by spring, the birdlife warming its feathers in the sun, drakes chasing ducks among the reeds. The squawking females were held down by male beaks on their necks and forcibly inseminated. 'What an atrocious act of violence,' I said. 'I don't suppose they have a clitoris so there can be no pleasure in it for the poor females.'

The sky was shot with strands of blue and daisies appeared on the grass, small white childish faces.

'Please, Adele, don't change the subject, this is important. I looked at Mummy in her pearl necklaces and mink stole. And a mile away people are so unhappy and ill and impoverished.'

'That's just bourgeois. Middle-aged taste. Don't read too much into it.'

'You can't reduce everything to a matter of style, Adele, it's shallow. Rose says that in the Soviet Union everyone adores classical music and the workers read Tolstoy on the underground. It's possible, she says, to have a working class that is educated and cultured, not watching moronic television. Imagine free concerts, imagine going to the Bolshoi any time you liked.'

In the distance, on the other side of the lake near the medieval manor house, close to the topiary garden, I saw Bobby seated on a shooting stick, reading.

'I used to think, Why can't we just let things happen?' she said. 'But now I believe that might be too passive. Rose says we must put our shoulders to the engine.'

'People like us have never seen an engine in our lives, unless it's our father's Humber Hawks.'

'Daddy has a Rover.'

'That's a doctor's car.'

'I know. He is a doctor. He's a consultant, actually. In hearts. My brother is going to go to medical school too. We have everything, don't we? What about you? Do you have siblings? What does your father do?'

'It's just me and my mum now. My father's dead. I had an older sister but she died before I was born, she was only a few days old and there aren't even any photographs. No one ever talks about her. I didn't find out until I was about ten when I overheard one of my mother's friends whispering about it in our kitchen. She said, "Edna, you must never have got over the loss," and Mum said, "I know," and burst into tears. I don't understand why they're so secretive. There's nothing to be ashamed of.'

I offered this as a diversion from queries about my father. It was true but I had half forgotten about it. I could psychoanalyse myself for years on end wondering about this little ghost in our house who had been brought home to what would become in future my room and had died of something no one would mention. My mother shrugged when I asked her and again her eyes welled with unusual tears for she was not usually a crier. But I was not that kind of person, not the type in those days to be haunted, or looking for some missing part of myself. The little girl. She had a name but it was not spoken.

'Oh, what a sad story. You must come and stay with us in the holidays. You could both come. I mean you and your mum.'

At the thought of the unification of these two families I said quickly and clumsily, 'No, I'm spending the whole summer with Bobby.'

'Well, that will be nice too.'

We turned into the library and walked up to the top floor and laid our belongings out on the chocolate-brown corduroy armchairs overlooking the greening perimeter of small but genetically ambitious trees.

A few minutes later Evie arrived and set herself up at a desk with her books. I saw her reflection in the glass that overlooked the lake and turned to wave to her. She came over and said, 'Can I talk to you? Have you time for a coffee?'

We had only just got there, but it was never too soon to break off and walk down the stairs to the café to drink cups of Nescafé and eat cheap, subsidised biscuits. It was the first time I had seen her since the start of term. She did a strange thing as we walked down the steps – she took my arm. An old-fashioned gesture. You saw older women walking this way in town, pleasant, intimate, asexual. Nobody walks this way any more, it has died out; in the past men would walk arm in arm, but we no longer attach ourselves to each other, we prize our own gait too much to lean. We are all individuals now, and walk alone.

Amongst the tea slops she said, 'Oh, Adele, I need some advice. Have you heard about Peter Ellory?'

'No. Who is he?'

'He was my supervisor. He killed himself on Good Friday. He drowned himself in the lake.'

'But I thought it was too shallow to drown yourself.'

'You're such a heuristic thinker, did you know that?'

'I don't even know what it means.'

'You operate by common sense.'

'Is that a bad thing, intellectually?' It sounded as if it must be. We were all here to rise above common sense, even empiricism was sneered at. Derrida and Foucault moved like early shadows across the water, creeping up on the English Department with knives in their chilly fingers.

'Well, it doesn't really matter, the point is, he did drown and he left a note so it wasn't an accident.'

'But why? Why did he kill himself?'

'I don't know, they haven't told us.'

We looked out at the reed-rimmed waters.

'It seems such a strange, soothing death,' she went on. 'The water lapping over your face and the ducks nibbling your hair. I can't stop picturing it. I keep thinking of him all alone over Easter before they found him.' Her glassy blue eyes filled with tears for a moment.

There was a wall of strangeness around her. I could not understand her hesitancy, the sense that she had no idea at all of her own charisma. She was always staring at something over your shoulder, as if a ghost was dancing holding a feather, and when she turned her face back to you it was full of doubt. Only when she repeated Stevie's mantras did she come to life, speak with firmness and conviction.

'You mustn't think I'm telling you this to gossip,' she said. 'We've all been assigned new supervisors and philosophy is such a small department there aren't enough to go round so they've given me someone in English. His name is Tony Blount. I saw from his list you're with him. What's he like?'

Professor Fine had put me in with Tony Blount to irritate him. Blount was the greatest authenticist of all, the ur-Leavisite, in his denim suit, denim cap and pointed beard. He said he thought Virginia Woolf was almost certainly a technical virgin, she was unsexed. He had not read *The Bell Jar*, and he thought Sylvia Plath's poetry was 'schoolgirl scribblings'. He spoke Welsh fluently and was officially a bard. I think he had a certificate to prove it. He recited at eisteddfods and was completely ridiculous.

'Oh, he has the most preposterous ideas of women that he's got from his god, D. H. Lawrence. One has to put one's foot down, that's a must.'

'I don't think I have ever put my foot down with anyone.'

Bobby walked in through the glass doors. 'Oh, there you are,' he said, 'I've been looking for you. I'm so *sick* of this dreary lake and this dreary concrete. Shall we go into town and have a cake?'

'I'm up for it,' I said.

'And will you join us?' he said to Evie. 'And where is your delightful alter ego?'

'He's at his tutorial.'

'What a shame, will he be long? We can easily wait.'

'But he has a lecture after that.'

'What a *good* boy to go to lectures.'

'I know. He's very assiduous, he always believes there's something new to learn, even from our lecturers. But a lot of the time he knows they're wrong.'

'Well on this occasion I really must have a cake so we will have to go without him. Next time, next time. Come on.'

I said, 'Evie has just told me she has never stood up to anyone, she can practise on you. Don't go if you don't want to.'

'Don't confuse her, poor thing, you can be so charmless, Adele.'

'But I would like to come,' she said.

'There you are, she has stood up to *you*.'

She was wearing a white ankle-length dress and her black base-ball boots. A knitted cap with a knitted peak covered her short hair. We went to the car park and got into the Hillman Imp.

'Do you know,' he said, when we had barely left the car park, 'I've changed my mind. I thought we might drive to the coast. Or do you think that's too impulsive?'

The notion that one could simply get away from the confine-ment of the town had not occurred to us, one was either here on the campus, in the medieval streets, or at home in our parents' living room.

'What's on the coast?'

'Towns, and they have marvellous names, Robin Hood's Bay, for example. Shall we explore?'

'But Stevie won't know where I am.'

In those primitive times there were hardly any methods of com-munication. Telephones existed, they were attached to the wall in the porter's lodge under a metal hood, you queued with handfuls of money to ring your parents. To attract the attention of friends you could leave a note for someone in their pigeonhole or, as some students did, attach a notebook and a pencil by a piece of string to your study-bedroom door on which messages could be notated. We all wrote and received letters and embellished our handwriting with distinction, we cared a lot about whether we looped the letter t or made a Greek e, and practised dotting our i's with circles and worried about whether our lines unguided by ruled paper sloped up or down. We tried to master italic and copperplate. But the main means of talking to someone was face to face.

We did not know, as we walked past the computer building, that something in embryonic form was being grown in there, at present no more than a few cells attached to each other, primi-tive but promising, out of which would come the palm-sized telephone you kept in your pocket or your bag, so you were acces-sible anywhere at any time of the day or night. These futuristic,

Star Trek-type gadgets were so far from the imaginations of us students in the humanities that it never occurred to us that one day we would cease to be beyond the reach of anyone, that we would be back in the harnesses and reins our parents attached to toddlers. Had we this foreknowledge we might have felt uncomfortably that we were going to be less free, more childlike and accountable to an order that we would be bound to find oppressive. Odd, that we clamoured for freedom and already had it, in the form of out-of-order telephone boxes and second-class postal delivery.

I said, 'You can do what you like.'

'But we plan every day, we have an outline . . . '

'That's ridiculous.'

'No, it's a form of art. It's a kind of activism, as well.'

'You are the celestial twins,' said Bobby. 'I suppose you are both Gemini.'

'No, I'm Scorpio and so is he.'

'I am Capricorn, a young goat. But Adele is Taurus, obviously.'

'Are you?'

'Yes, I am. Look, let's just *go*.' I drummed my fingers on the dashboard. 'I'm so bored and so confined. I want to see what's there. Aren't you curious, Evie?'

I had been so desperate to get away from the perfume counter I had not checked exactly what it was I running towards and I missed my sea city, my home, my Liverpool home where people were cutting and witty and rude and men and women drank too much, smoked too much, and there had always been a ship to sail away on when life became too constricting.

But Bobby had seen what I had not noticed. 'Do you have a headache, darling?' he said kindly. 'Or is it your time of the month?'

'I do have a headache, yes. I wake up with them some mornings and they take a long time to go away.'

'I thought so, you look like someone who suffers from a bad head. Have a pill.' He took an enamel box out of his pocket and handed it over his shoulder to her. 'They are mostly aspirin, but there are other painkillers in there. Just choose one, like a lucky dip.'

'Are any of them dangerous?'

'Certainly not.'

She reached in and took an oblong tablet with an indentation along its middle. 'Oh, my mouth is so dry, I can hardly swallow it. It's always dry.'

'Then we'll stop at a shop and buy a bottle of lemonade.'

13

'It's a gloomy landscape, isn't it?' Bobby said as we reached the edge
of the moors. 'Is this where they buried the murdered children?'
The North was all the same to him, a stretch of nothing from east
to west.

'You mean Hindley and Brady?'

'Yes, that wicked pair.'

'But that's not in Yorkshire,' said Evie, 'it's Lancashire. Do you
remember it, Adele? Do you remember when the children were
going missing?'

Edward Evans, Lesley Ann Downey and John Kilbride. Then
Pauline Reade and Keith Bennett. The bones of the children
howling in the wind. And I was saying, 'Who are those children,
Mummy? Why are they on the television?' But she turned it off
and brought out plates of cakes and other sweet things and said a
curse in a foreign tongue.

Bobby drove like a widow to the shops. His foot held the accel-
erator as if it was a fragile glass lozenge. 'Are we going to stretch
our legs?' he said.

He wore petrol-blue suede loafers with gold snaffles.

'No, let's just get there.'

'Well, I need to take what the Americans call a comfort break but for the life of me I cannot see a tree for miles around.'

'Just turn your back,' I said, 'we won't peek.'

He stopped the car and gingerly stepped out on to the moor. Cars passed occasionally, and lorries headed to the ports.

I felt that we were suddenly out on the rim of the universe, cold and alone. I hated nature, especially this bleak nothingness, but Evie began to hum, then to sing.

'You have a lovely voice,' I said.

'Thank you.'

'Mine's like a crow, I won't join you.'

Bobby made a golden arc in the ancient folds of the moorlands.

A while later we arrived at Scarborough, and stopped at the high promontory where a ruined eleventh-century castle was an invitation to get out and smoke. After running around like unruly kids for a few minutes we continued down into the town and sauntered along Marine Drive, past the grandeur-in-decay that all these seaside towns were. Evie once again took my arm, and Bobby linked hers into his, so we proceeded like conjoined triplets, Evie in her long white dress, her eyes rimmed with kohl, doll-like, and Bobby in his brass-buttoned navy-blue blazer, a tight cornflower-coloured jumper through which his cold erect nipples poked, a cream silk handkerchief tucked into a breast pocket and his petrol-blue loafers. Me, looped alongside them, pale-faced, in bell-bottom jeans and cheesecloth smock burnt with small holes from my cigarettes and my fur coat shedding dead-rabbit hairs.

We passed a hotel which would one day slip down from its headland into the North Sea. 'There is something here,' Bobby said, 'that reminds me, ridiculous as it may sound, of the Venetian Lido, I mean the hotels with von Aschenbach stalking the beautiful boy. Let's have tea in the lounge.'

Evie objected.

I said, 'You should never be intimidated by those places. My father always said that nothing was too good for his family.'

She replied, 'It's not that, but I must be careful with money. I don't want to waste it on fancy sandwiches.'

'In that case,' Bobby said, 'we shall slum it and have fish and chips.' Fishcakes were cheaper than battered cod and plaice so Evie chose those and I copied her. They tasted of wallpaper paste. She left most of hers on her plate but I gobbled mine up. Bobby asked for scampi and was refused: 'None left.' He had plaice, but no chips: 'Far too fattening.' He was an early refuser of carbohydrates. We took our food down to the beach. Tremendously cold winds for May were coming in off the North Sea. Off the horizon the oil rigs rose, pumping our new gas. Beyond them, the coasts of Denmark and Germany. Jagged and unknown. Hamlet and Goethe. A tanker on the edge of the sea.

We took our shoes off and walked along the sand. The sea roared down on us. Evie looked more animated than I had seen her and she did a little dance in the surf until I said, 'Your feet are turn-ing blue, you idiot!' She was a Greek statue come to life in the white dress and her baseball boots dangling from her fingers by the laces.

'No, it's lovely.' And she ran further in, and further, lifting her hem and holding it between her teeth, so you could easily see her white underwear. The water above her ankles, rising and splashing to her knees.

'Don't drown,' I cried.

The sun was on her pale hair, her cheeks were painted rose-madder, the sea had splashed her up to her waist. She was stumbling back up the corrugated sand through the icy, splashing water, losing her footing, correcting herself, her arms outstretched with a boot held in each hand. The water was shades of gunmetal grey, shards of petrol blue, the roof of the sky lifting and lifting. We were surging with excitement like the sea. Everything was dynamic, in motion, Evie was grimacing with the cold but she was also laughing and shouting, she was calling something out that we couldn't hear and when I cried, 'What, what did you say?' she answered back that it didn't matter.

'She'll freeze,' I said.

'You will hold her till she's warm.'

She was still advancing stumblingly towards us, growing pinker and pinker in the wind; she was all you could see from shore to horizon. The seabirds dipped their wings and rotated around her.

'Tomorrow we will learn what is true and what is not,' Bobby said.

'What are you talking about?'

Evie reached us, stained almost to the waist with seawater.

'Headache all gone?' I said.

'Yes, I feel great.' She laughed. 'If only we had a camera, if only Stevie could see me now, he'd be amazed.'

But none of us had a camera. Almost nothing that took place in these times was ever recorded. I am doing my best now, from memory.

'I don't know how you're going to get warm,' Bobby said. 'Of course you can have my jacket but it won't dry you. Perhaps you can wrap up in Adele's fur coat.'

'Of course,' I said, and began to take it off, but she said she would just come in under.

'That's what I was going to suggest,' said Bobby.

Cautiously I put my arms around her. I have never felt anyone so cold. She was taller than me, but still she bent to rest her face against mine. We stood together and her icy breath was on my cheek.

'Let's go and find some cups of tea,' I said. 'That will warm you up.' I felt her arms tighten around me for a moment like those of a child who had found her mother after a long absence.

We sat in a tea room for a while, warming up, Evie refusing a cake or a scone or a biscuit even when Bobby offered to pay, and when the pubs opened Bobby said he would buy us both a drink instead. Evie seemed to have no objection. We sat at a table and he came back from the bar with three single shots of brandy. 'Look at lover-boy,' a man called out as he saw Bobby sit between us. 'Which one of your birds is going spare?'

'Both,' said the barman. 'Nancy boy.'

When we drove away from Scarborough, I thought again of the boys and girls buried on the moors, of the bodies unfound, and of the trust of children. There is always the memory that returns when you are an adult of the afternoon you dared each other to jump off the roof and you think about the self that could have been, passive in your wheelchair, a child for the rest of your life, guarded and cared for by your parents, because you exercised the right to daring, you did it, you leapt. Of the child I had been who had not believed my parents' distrust of all strangers, who talked to them and took their sweets, which turned out to be kindly meant, in that instance, and I was not deep and dark under the moor. I was so delighted I was alive, unlike my dead big sister without even a name to call her own.

'I have heard about a restaurant,' said Bobby. 'It's somewhere near here. I'm sure we could find it if we look.'

'But we must go back,' Evie said.

And I said, 'Yes, we must. It's late. There's a band on in college tonight.'

No reply came from the driver's seat. The road darkened and the landscape dimmed until there was no shape out there and signposts appeared and vanished behind us.

'Slingsby,' said Bobby, 'it's in the village, I think.'

But when we got there, there was no restaurant, just a pub. He went in to ask. A few lights were on in the houses.

'It's not *in* the village, it's actually out in the country but I have directions, we'll be there in no time.' And we were.

I still see it, the curtains drawn and the light leaking from the sides of the frames, a rouge glow. What kind of building had it once been and why had some optimist decided to open up on this deserted spot with its blackboard menu on which were chalked dishes that were probably the product of the poacher's gun? I have searched for it many times, but like all dreams it is not to be found,

and no one remembers it, even when I passed through Slingsby last
year and asked at the pub, but no one knew. Someone had been
here 'for ever', but for ever was twenty-five years, and it was forty
since we had sat in the Hillman Imp and listened to Bobby cry.

The door was locked. The three of us banged our fists on it. A
man opened up and asked us what we wanted. Bobby said, 'A table
for three.' We could see past him to a square room in which middle-
aged couples were hacking away at haunches of meat. Lamps with
saffron-coloured silk shades were on each table and the light they
shed lit the place up like a brothel, all those middle-aged women's
faces rouged and lipsticked and the red bleeding round their mouths.

'You have to have a reservation.'

'Well, we shall wait until someone has finished. Look, they're
drinking coffee.'

'We don't serve students.' The man was wearing a velvet jacket
and a maroon cravat round his neck. He was the type of English-
man there were many of in those days, with war records, and a
disinclination to expand their consciousness, having been already
far too expanded on the Normandy beaches or the Burma railway.

'It's hopeless,' Evie said. Her white dress was stained with the
salt of the seawater and a damp smell rose from her baseball boots.

'Why ever so?' asked Bobby. 'I'm sure they can accommodate us.'

The man pointed at me. 'Look at her for a start, in that stinking coney and raggedy jeans. We expect people to dress for dinner.'

All the men were wearing ties and the women in silk blouses
with bows strangling the neck or a garment called an evening
kaftan. The sight of them, loading pâté on to Melba toast and raising it to prudish lips, seemed to infuriate Bobby.

'A man like my father would order the most expensive dish on
the menu and a bottle of champagne.'

'A wog with an expense account? Ha ha.'

'How *dare* you?'

'How dare I what? I'm under no obligation to serve anyone and
anyway, we're full. On your way, poof and take those two tarts with
you.'

As we walked back to the car, Bobby said to me, 'Do you think it will always be like this? Am I fated *always* to be turned away?'

'Of course not. He's just an ignoramus. In London it must be very different.'

'I must remind you that we are Persians. We go back to the time of Darius and Xerxes. You should see Persepolis. And Adele, your people are carved there too.' Tears on his face.

Evie was in the front seat this time. In the darkness with nothing to see outside I began to look at the nape of her neck. She had shorn it hard so that a fuzz of blond hairs stood up erect like iron filings. The pale hair, the pink skin. I wondered what it might be like to kiss that neck. I shifted in the seat and looked down at my hands. When I looked up again she had taken her cap off.

'Try it on, Adele,' she said, turning round to me, smiling. 'It might suit you, you never know.'

'OK.'

In Evie's cap, I tried to feel like Evie. Bobby, looking in the rear-view mirror, said, 'Oh, you do remind me now of a boy I knew once. He got a blow job from Joe Orton on a building site off Holloway Road, that little peaked cap bobbing up and down. So he always wore one after that.'

I tried not to look at Evie's neck. I looked out of the window. Shapes and shadows beside the road. A hare ran across our path, and a fox. We reached the sodium lights of the town eventually. When we got back to the university it was ten minutes to ten. My books were still on the chocolate-brown corduroy chair in the library. I had been gone all day and the building was now left to drowsy librarians and students cramming for finals, jacked up on coffee and amphetamines. I gave Evie back her cap. 'No, you must keep it, wear it so we'll both remember this day, the good parts, I mean.' And she ran off to find Stevie, her musty dress streaming behind her. Bobby walked off curtly to his room and I was left by the dark lake until I went to the bar and found Gillian in conversation with Rose.

I went back to my room and smelled her, inside the knitted cap. How her eyes were blue.

14

'*I have seen old ships like swans asleep*
'*Beyond the village that men still call Tyre.*'

Thus spake Bobby from under a straw hat.

'James Elroy Flecker. Do you know him? Died aged only thirty in 1915, but not of the war, poor thing, of TB. Coughing blood in a hospital in Switzerland, on the magic mountain. His death was considered to be as catastrophic to poetry as that of Keats, though of course his Parnassian lyricism was completely swept away by the war. I don't think he is much remembered. The department sneers when you mention him, a consular officer, too bourgeois for their modern tastes. But the drowsy rhythms, the brown slaves and Syrian oranges ... I think it's marvellous. The wood of the deck turning back into trees.'

But Bobby declaimed these lines on the shoreline of the English Channel, for there had been a misunderstanding. His benefactor had not owned the house in Greece, that had only been rented; he was leaving him his childhood home in a Cornish china-clay port.

I set out very early one morning when the sun was barely up and with a shirt tied around my midriff and hipster flared jeans I made good progress hitchhiking from Liverpool in various vehicles, lorries and sports cars, family saloons and the back of a motorbike, until I crossed the Tamar and passed over Bodmin Moor and down past Lostwithiel. The van driver, who was delivering pasties, pointed, as we descended the hill, to the other side of the estuary where the town rose in a pale pastel triangle along the waterfront. We inched on to the clanking car ferry.

On the other side I got out of the van and made my way up the slip, past the Mission to Seamen, and the Odd Spot café, the old gasworks and the abandoned branch line. Sea town. The street was white with china clay from the boots of the men who loaded the ships and tramped in after work to go home or drown the dust in their lungs in the Lugger. The front door of Bobby's house was set with a brass knocker in the shape of a dolphin. The house was called Peneagle.

I picked up the knocker and banged it against a brass plate. The house shook from the impact. When the reverberations were over, Bobby answered.

'Oh my God, you are actually here! Wait till I show you everything.'

He was wearing a striped cricket blazer and espadrilles on his bare brown feet. We passed through a dark front parlour into a second room. Now the house was full of light, light from the sky and from the river.

'This may be a port in miniature, but it has everything a port has. You'll see.'

He led me down the stairs to a lower floor which let out to a rear courtyard planted with pots of dead marigolds. Slippery green steps to the water and a ruler-width strip of grey beach on which seagulls strutted and rose into the air, screaming. On the opposite bank a boathouse had a roof that slipped over one window like a hat on a drunk.

'Here are our sleeping rooms. Choose whichever one you like, they're both foul, but I promise we'll put them all in order. The bedding isn't too damp.'

'What is this place? Who owned it?'

'Dear Peter, of course. He was born in this bed, though not, I hope, on that actual mattress. Well, you'll have to shut your eyes and think of something else if it was. It was his father's house, he was a ship's chandler. Apparently they called him "Smiler" Varco because he was always of an '"appy disposition". He would row out to the ships and supply them with ... chandlery, whatever chandlery is. Do you know? I've no idea. Rope? Baling hooks? The shop wasn't here, it was up the road on the other side but he kept his boat moored by the wall and look, there it is, still ship-shape, apparently, if anyone would like to risk it. Not me. I have been to the pub and they have told me everything. How my dear Peter was a clever little grammar-school boy and got a scholarship to Cambridge and he came away from here and eventually bought a house in Frognal, which he left to his niece who can't stand the nasty damp of this one, and so here we are. Not in Greece, but second best. I plan to make the most of it and I hope you will too.'

The parlour was dominated by a horsehair sofa, an armchair upholstered in mustard velveteen with an ivory antimacassar decorating its back, an oily patch dead centre from a long-deceased head. A gate-leg dining table under an oilskin cloth, a Turkish rug depicting a tethered camel in an oasis, and on the wall a reproduction of a Bible scene in which Jesus is being betrayed by Judas, who holds the silver coins in his outstretched hands.

A single bookcase held damp volumes of Georgian verse, James Elroy Flecker a few inches from Edward Thomas. The books bulged from their places in the shelves, the spines swollen, splitting, an overwhelming stench of dead and forgotten writers. Who, for example, now read Lascelles Abercrombie or Fredegond Shove?

'Come on. Unpack, we'll go for a walk while we still have the light.'

The road into town occasionally widened slightly to make room to step aside when a car passed along the single lane, then it descended sharply to the left down a short slope until we came to the main street. There were many useful and useless shops. A stamp collector's paradise. Marine supplies. A betting shop. Antiques. A pipe and tobacco shop. A café which announced on a sign in the window that it closed at lunchtime.

Two sturdy women in outdated mini-skirts above fat cold knees lounged outside the Lugger.

'As I told you,' said Bobby. 'The place may be small, but it has everything a port has.'

I heard the sound of boots marching behind us and the women waved, brightened, made kissing sounds with their lips. A group of five Russian sailors was walking in convoy with a commissar at each end. They held something bulky under their jackets.

'Look at our girls, completely indifferent to morality. It's rather a Methodist town but no one seems to mind. And here come their temporary boyfriends. Peter always said you could get anything you liked here. Contraband booze and cigarettes. During the war, there was said to be a Spitfire for sale, in parts like an Airfix kit. But that's probably just a legend.'

The road kept twisting, widening, narrowing. We skirted the church, then another pub, a butcher's shop, turned the corner and walked up a steep hill, turned left until a long vista of villas and the open estuary lay ahead of us. Palm trees and pines. Slightly French. The houses looked like the homes of retired naval officers, doctors and bank managers from Truro and Bodmin. Seaside air, rather than port air.

'Look at the poor Grand Hotel, all shut up. It must have been something in its heyday, do you know Kenneth Grahame is said to have stayed there and written *The Wind in the Willows* in one of its bedrooms? Though Peter said that book has been claimed by every river in England. Come on, let's see what we can see.'

The padlock on the iron gate had been forced. We opened it easily. Up a flight of stone steps through ruined ornamental gardens where a faded sign advertised CREAM T AS, we reached the windows of the lounge bar. The empty bottles still hung over their optics, the whiskies and gins and rums and bottles of advocaat and Fernet Branca and Martini Rosso. A beermat lay on the floor as if it had been hurled at someone. The leather club armchairs were covered in shifting clouds of white dust.

'So depressing,' Bobby said. 'Peter told me this place used to be a haven for the gentry in the fifties, lots of colonels and their ladies, dressed for dinner, cocktail handbags and black tie. Nobody comes here any more. It went bankrupt and the owners did a runner.'

Yet its position overlooking the estuary and the open mouth of the sea was magnificent. My father would have battered his way into a place like this, would have been the vulgar Jew with his cigar and silk tie, standing at the bar ordering Chivas Regal and a touch of water and my mother blazing in jewels and the scent of Blue Grass perfume. All smashed up, everyone and everything.

'Of course, one day, in the future, a place like this will seem romantic and stylish,' he said. 'The run-down appearance will have its day, you wait and see. For who could have possibly predicted that *brown* and *orange* would ever prevail, and yet they do. So the dusty chandelier and torn banquette will rise too.'

'Do you think? I imagine they'll pull it down and build flats.'

'Oh, I hope not. It must slowly decay with the seasons, like the Coliseum, battered by the coming of the barbarians until it's back in vogue. Come on, darling. There's someone we're going to meet who will explain all these matters.'

We walked on until we reached a cove and a small sandy beach sheltered by high rocks.

A handful of houses faced the water. One had a sign outside advertising TV repairs and another a pile of junk, wheels and bits of boat engines piled up against a wall. A man appeared to emerge from the water, but it was just a trick of the evening light.

'And here is my new friend Rami.'

The person walking towards us along the sand wore a white woollen robe embroidered at the neck, from which his high bald head fringed by black coarse hair stuck out like a toffee apple on a stick. Over his face he raised and lowered a papier-mâché mask in the shape of a dog so you received intermittent glimpses of a

terrific beak of a nose, black eyes and long brown cheeks scored
with vertical lines, as if someone had tried to carve him. When he
reached us, standing by the municipal toilets, he stopped, smiled,
and revealed powerful white teeth of the type the wolf must have
tried to keep hidden from Little Red Riding Hood. Then he bowed
with one arm held behind his back, as in a school production of a
Shakespeare play, and laid the mask on the wall by the door, which
smelled of piss and Jeyes Fluid and blubbery seaweed which had
blown into the urinals.

'This is Rami, also known as the Rabbi,' said Bobby.

'What do we have here?' he said, looking at me.

'Why does Bobby call you the Rabbi?' I said, flustered by his gaze.

'Everyone calls me the Rabbi, because I once trained to be one.
I don't think young Bobby knows that, he thinks it is because I'm
a sage.'

'And are you still religious?'

'Of course. But I worship the old gods.'

'Which ones?'

'Anubis, Osiris, Sobek.'

'But how ridiculous. They're made up, just men with animal
heads.'

'And we are animals with the heads of men.'

He smiled warmly once again and showed his bright teeth.
Cornwall was full of such characters in those days, the West
Country was very cheap to live in. The town was a place to which
those who were down on their luck gravitated, people who hadn't
quite made it or were running away from life. A pop star who had
had a number-one record lived with his wife in a house that was
still lit with oil lamps. Upstream someone had rigged up a recording studio in an old sawmill and the recording engineers would row
down with a cargo of records and sell them in the pubs. You could
buy anything you wanted, grass, contraband cigarettes, vodka all
the way from Russia. A free and easy life and Rami had arrived
here from over a strange sea and rented the house at the beach and
was setting himself up as guru-in-residence.

'Come tomorrow,' he said. 'I am going to slaughter a sheep.'

'Why would you want to do that? Isn't there a butcher's shop in town?'

'You don't want to be smeared with the blood of the sacrificial lamb?'

'No. Why would I? Why would anyone?'

Rami laughed. 'The veneer of civilisation needs to be scraped off you with a strong knife. We'll do it.'

'No you won't.'

'We are all going to be friends,' Bobby said crossly. 'Now, Rami, aren't you going to invite us in?'

'Of course. Forgive my lack of manners.'

The house was square and white, had two gable windows and lay slightly back behind a row of terraces at the beginning of a footpath over rocks. Obviously Rami was a painter, what else could he have been?, and his pictures were a series of psychedelic mandalas. I knew we were in for an evening of the higher drivel, and walked about listening to him bore on about the ancient gods and other hippie wisdom. He poured us both glasses of cider. I said, 'Have you got anything to eat? I'm starving.'

'Of course. A girl with an appetite. I like it.'

Night finally fell; I was exhausted. We ate bread and cheese and pickled onions and a slice of fruit cake. Rami and Bobby talked about Zoroastrianism and the merits of air burial. The waves were brilliant white, smashing on the beach, and the painted mandalas smelling of wet oils made me dizzy. On and on the evening droned until I fell asleep on the chintz sofa and when I woke up Bobby was gone and Rami was trying to lift my arm to pull me up and lead me, I suppose, to his bedroom.

I had been dreaming of Evie and Stevie walking round the lake together and I looked up to see his bald head shining under the lamplight, sweating slightly, though it was cold.

'I'm not moving. Leave me alone.'

'What a lump you are, my dear. You have no mysticism. Jahandar was wrong about you. You have the most impoverished soul.'

'I don't care.' And I went back to sleep.

I woke in the middle of the night for a few minutes. My grand-father told me I had a great soul, I was the cleverest of his grandchildren, I was my grandmother reincarnated. But what did he know? He was just an immigrant who ran a baker's shop. Rami was an intellectual, he said I was soulless. Sometimes I thought I was, or my soul was in hiding. I dreamed my soul was folded up like a piece of paper and embedded in the shell of a hazelnut and buried in the forest under an unknown tree. I was looking for it. My dead sister ran ahead, through thickets of brambles impassable to me.

When I next woke it was light and the house was silent. I lit a cigarette and smoked and thought. I forgot where I was and then I heard him moving through the house, his piss in the toilet, so I got up and left. I walked off along the esplanade past all the sleep-ing houses winking their windows at the sea, through the town that was rising, the shops opening their shutters, the baker's van, the paper-boy, the ferrymen walking down to the car ferry and the china-clay workers in their boots, clanging in the morning street.

I didn't belong here, but then you could ask, did I belong any-where? So I felt as at home as I ever did.

The door was not locked. I pushed against it and went into the house. Bobby did not stir. I was terribly hungry, and could find nothing in the kitchen so I went out and walked back towards the car ferry where I had seen a café the day before. I ordered beans on toast and after half an hour I had scored a summer job working as a waitress. And that is how the summer would turn out to be, with me in a grease-spotted uniform serving a full English to sailors and dockers in the mornings and learning a new/old language, Cornish, a few words of which I still remember – *Durdatha whye*!

Rami photographed Bobby and me sitting holding hands in cafés. Bobby took the film to the chemist to be developed and put the prints carefully in an envelope. 'For Daddy.'

'Can't you just tell him?'

'No, never.'

'He must be a terrible puritan.'

'It's not that, it's that I *want* to please him.'

'But why?'

'You must understand that pleasing Daddy is something Mummy and I have devoted our lives to. It's what we live for. Because he is strong.'

'Are you frightened of him?'

'No! Never. I respect and admire him, and I love him. His strength is what we love. It would break his heart to know his son is a pansy. He thinks that in Persia all men are manly and only women cry and read poetry. He's the type of man who is a rock, immovable. You don't argue or negotiate with rocks. You look up to them.'

'I bet all Persian men aren't strong.'

'Of course not, but weakness is not part of Daddy's world. He doesn't see it and no one wants to point it out to him. It would break his heart.'

Years later I met his father, the man of the souk, in of all garments a trilby, a vile little hat with a feather sticking out from its band. He held his hands like paws, was plump where Bobby was trim and muscled, and still I saw the family resemblance, those hedonistic eyes for which all flesh was fruit.

15

There was no sheep-slaughtering the following day, or the next, and a week or two went past before Rami announced that he was ready to barbecue on the beach. He bought the animal still alive from one of the farms. He and Bobby carried it tied to a piece of wood by its feet, hung upside-down, making baaing sounds of terror. It was huge, I had no idea how large a sheep could be.

'OK,' Rami said, 'we've got it, so now we're going to kill it.'

The knife lay on the wall by the public toilets, it was sharp enough to slit the sheep's throat, the farmer had told him exactly how to do it, where to make the cut and to do it quickly and with confidence.

I did not grow up with animals, my mother thought the animal kingdom primitive and dangerous. She was frightened of dogs but hated cats. Mice were an abomination. Birds remained safely outside. Horses were terrifying merchants of death on whose backs the reckless rode and would spend their lives paralysed from the neck down after a rearing-up and a crippling fall. Animals were things you braised, grilled, roasted and fried and, when all of those uses were exhausted, turned into a nutritious soup, the scraps of their flesh floating among the carrots and dumplings.

But even I could see that the sheep knew something; the sheep

could see this situation was not going to end well for it. As if it
understood I was a girl and might have a tender heart, it kept looking at me with an appeal in its eyes. *Help me.* But Rami had paid
the farmer for the sheep, some sum reached after negotiation and
taking advice from the owner of the Odd Spot, who knew about
meat. On the beach a fire of pine branches had been prepared and
the flames rose, reminding me of biblical burnt offerings. In the
kitchen rosemary and thyme lay ready to accompany the baa-lamb
to its final destination. I've no idea where he got those herbs from,
the shops sold few fresh vegetables.

'Are you going to do this now?'

'The sheep isn't getting any younger,' said Rami. 'We want a
juicy roast.' He picked up the knife. 'I can guide your hand and you
can do it yourself if you like.'

'What a horrible idea. I can't bear it.'

'Soft heart? Don't be so squeamish. People killed human beings
with their bare hands during the war. I was there when—'

'I'm going into the house.'

Bobby's eyes were gleaming. Nothing bored him. 'Well, this is
going to be an experience,' he said.

I went indoors and sat at the back of the house among the can-
vases. They seemed awfully stupid and repetitive. Too abstract for
me. I wished there was someone here to sleep with apart from
Rami because I wasn't going to sleep with him. I wished there was
a boy my own age amongst the hippies of the town who did not
look as if he were made out of straw and dingy sacking. I thought
again of the nape of Evie's neck. It was very confusing. If Evie was
not with Stevie then what if ... But Evie was Stevie's right arm
and he was her left so they were a single person. And Stevie's looks
made me feel a little ill.

A while later, when the screaming had stopped, I went back out
and saw the sheep lying on its side, its blood draining out into the
sand.

'Now we have to skin it. I'm going to make a jacket of some
kind out of this pelt, or maybe a waistcoat.'

I went back in again and looked at the mandalas until my eyes crossed. About an hour later, the sheep was finally undressed. I saw for the first time what bodies really are, the muscle and bones and sinews. Rami had decapitated it and Bobby walked off into the trees to dig a hole to bury the head. 'Otherwise we're going to attract a whole world of ants and flies,' said Rami. 'Your little friend is not what you call a big girl's blouse, is he? He did not flinch.'

Rami barbecued the meat. Bobby made the salad. We ate the sheep and I have to admit that it tasted great but the stench of spilled blood lingered on the beach and sickened me. Out in the night air, the sky was large and marvellous. Rami pointed out the constellations.

Even then I already knew I had a story here about the house on the beach and the lamb we killed and ate, the dome of stars, the coarse cider we drank with it, the taste of salt on a muscled arm. A story was building and as with all stories, it was better in the telling than the living. My mother would say, 'You tell such tall tales, it never happened like that,' but my father said, 'Leave her alone, she has an imagination.' I just thought I could make things happen in the way they should have panned out, with the loose ends tied up and some roles reassigned. Later, I learned to keep these loose ends open. This is how a story survives, lives on, because the ending always needs supplying in the imagination of its audience. My father got it, he had dramatised his own boyhood in many directions so you no longer knew what was true, and it had occurred to me, when I was sixteen, that this didn't actually matter, because my father was a man made up of the stories he told about himself. He and Yankel Fishoff had come up from the streets together and made themselves into legends.

The next day the bones of the sheep, sheared of most of its flesh, lay beside the embers of the fire. The insect world had come out and found it, a dog was running towards the bones, barking, panting, saliva running from its black lips. When I saw it I was sick and the lamb lay on the ground in a new configuration.

16

A letter arrived at the house for me from Evie. She and Stevie were hitchhiking through Ireland and would return to England on the ferry and make their way to the West Country. They would crash on the beach or find a room somewhere. She was really looking forward to seeing me, and so was Stevie. Bobby said, 'Well, I shall have the chance to get to know *him* better. Keep her occupied for me, darling.'

At this time, the old houses on the waterfront were turning empty. Modern homes had been built above the cove, with gardens and garages and central heating, and the people of the town were ascending up top, were becoming top people. They said the old houses were damp and hard to maintain; there was nowhere for the children to play and nowhere for the cars. They were making a suburban exodus. What was happening to the waterfront houses was the town's transition between the old and the new gas. We had no idea at the time. The top people stopped walking down to the shops with their baskets. They could get a bus to St Austell which had a small supermarket. The top people worked on the port and the railway and the new old-town people were still to arrive. Bobby was the first, maybe earliest arrival of the incomers but everyone thought he was just part of the hippie crowd which came to Cornwall for a few years and left, or dissolved into the sediment of its everyday life so only a greying ponytail behind a shop counter would denote a person who had originally arrived here to renounce civilisation.

Some of the old houses were owned by the squire, whose pseudo-Gothic pile on the hill and his landholdings were one of the economies of the town, along with the port and the scallop boats. The Big House was enormous; it was hard to see because it stood immediately above our heads, only from the water could you glimpse its crenellated roof, modelled by the Victorians as an imaginary abbey dissolved by Henry VIII.

I found Evie and Stevie a little house just across the road from us. It wasn't on the water and the back window faced up the steep rock, green with algae and white with the droppings of nesting birds, which made it very cheap and so everything was arranged.

Until this visit I had hardly exchanged a word with Stevie, and I was curious about him as Bobby was. After the car trip to the coast, Evie and I had often had coffee and talked about our seminars and I had admired her clothes and she had looked down at them as if she didn't know what I meant. But when they were together it was hard to be with them because they formed an invincible unit and you felt like a third wheel. I didn't know what to make of them coming. I thought, He's going to puncture something, or rearrange it and make a mess. Bobby will make a pass at him and probably be rejected. Or he'd say OK, and make Evie join them, make me join, there were all these sexual possibilities that Rami would dream up, the various permutations, part of an external pattern that was in the grand process of readjustment, as we creaked on towards the imminent Age of Aquarius.

The thing was, we were still young enough to be quite confused about a lot of things and being ordered to be confused about our sexuality to be cool made everything even more uncertain, while all the time we professed to being right about everything and grown-ups wrong. Evie's neck.

When they arrived, and unpacked and looked around the house and Stevie pronounced it dark, and Evie said to pay no attention to him, she was delighted, we went to the pub. Rami, predictably, turned up almost at once. He adored new meat.

'Let me inspect the arrivals.'

Evie looked scared when he examined her. She reached for Stevie's hand but you could see he was fascinated by Rami.

'*Two* earrings,' Rami said. 'Very interesting.'

Soon the two of them fell into a discussion of arcana.

'I know something about that,' said Stevie, who snacked from a smorgasbord of fashionable ideas. They began to talk about Gurdjieff and Ouspensky, who were mystics then in vogue.

'A is both A and not-A but in Aristotle's formula A can be both A and not-A but not at the same time,' said Rami.

'Exactly,' said Stevie, as if he had found a soulmate.

I had been up since dawn, into my nylon uniform serving bacon and eggs and strong tea, then splashing in the shallows of the cove in the afternoon. I fell asleep for a moment, but Rami gently woke me by touching my inner elbow. I felt pierced, erotically pinned down by as if by a lepidopterist. Evie was trying to follow the conversation, Bobby interjected with a few observations about the goddess Shiva.

Stevie began to talk about Scientology. He was curious about it, wanted to know if it was possible to 'go clear'. Rami said, 'Now *they* are charlatans. A religion invented by Americans.' Stevie said, perhaps, but everything was worth investigating.

'You shouldn't make postures,' Rami replied.

I said, 'So, what's your dog mask but a posture?'

He said, 'The girl has woken up and thought of something to say.' He tickled my chin. I told him to fuck off. He laughed in a bellow. 'Oh, a good one,' he said. We were all very tired, drunk and emotional. Rami watched Evie, Bobby watched Stevie, I looked out of the window onto the street.

At one o'clock we packed it in for the night.

Bobby said, 'I enjoyed that.'

I said, 'Did you?'

I read for an hour. Poems from the benefactor's shelf. *You won't find another country, won't find another shore.*

What liars these poets were. I would.

Evie and Stevie stayed for nearly two weeks.

'When we first met I didn't look anything like I look now,' she said as we made our steep ascent up a narrow track amongst the yellow flowers with cows staring at us in a huddle. There were awkward gates to cross, stiles and other methods of closure, and below us the sea was turquoise in the sun. The sky was very high above us, we were still young enough to be burning with love of life and freedom. A farmer's wife sometimes put out a sign advertising cream teas. It was a time of our lives when we could eat anything we liked and never put on an ounce, and we were both thin and strong. We thought we could walk for ever. And we were walking in summer sandals or flimsy canvas shoes.

'In what way?' I said, surprised, for Evie seemed to have come from the womb looking original.

'Oh, I was very different, shy, nervous, actually really frightened. I wanted to go home as soon as I got to university. I met Stevie on the first day. What a stroke of luck, because if I hadn't, I know I wouldn't have even unpacked, I'd have spent the night and left the next morning. But Stevie was very kind to me and we talked for ages on the grass outside the rotunda where we got that lecture about not being contented cows, which I didn't even understand, and he convinced me that I should stay.'

'What did you look like?'

'Oh, ridiculous, I had a long blond plait tied with a tartan ribbon. I could nearly sit on my hair.'

The memory returned to me of my own first day, of standing at the window of my room and the girl by the lake being pulled along by her mother and father, the woman with the plait tied around her head. But the resemblance between that terrified girl and Evie, now in a halterneck dress, and the way she and Stevie caressed each other, was so slight that I was certain it must be a coincidence.

'I owe everything to Stevie,' she went on. 'You know *Pygmalion*? Well, that's me.'

'In what way?'

'Every way. He even gave me a new name.'

'Your name isn't Evie?'

'Oh, no. It's Lorraine. I hate it, I always have, wouldn't you?'

'And who then is Stevie? Is that not his real name too?'

'Oh yes, he is Stephen, but he wasn't Stevie till he met me. He's a miner's son from Newcastle. Can you imagine? How different everything must be for him?'

'Then how does he sound so middle-class?'

'His school sent him for elocution lessons because his teachers couldn't understand him. He's had that voice forced on him, he can't even relax back into his old accent. He feels he's stealing everything he can find, he says he's entitled but I don't think I'm entitled, do you?'

'I don't know. Is to want the same thing as being entitled?'

'I'd say to wish.'

'For me it's want.'

'Then you are more like Stevie than you think.'

We walked on until we were tired and then we lay on the hillside and watched the ships and Evie reached over and picked up a strand of my hair. 'I've forgotten what it feels like to have hair you can wind round your finger.'

'Help yourself.'

'I'll grow it again one day. I'm sure I will. It can't stay like this for ever.'

'Have you seen what it looks like at the back?'

'On my neck? No. Stevie loves it though, he's always kissing it. He says I'm like a boy.'

I wanted to kiss it. I had to stop myself. I stood up and looked along the estuary where little yachts were circling in a race. Evie stayed lying on the ground looking up at me, smiling. Happy, lazy, young.

'You know, I'm very surprised and pleased that you and me are friends. I thought you were terribly stuck-up at first, such a hard face, but that's not true is it? You're quite funny when you want to be but you do seem to be standing your ground a little too firmly, well, that's what Stevie says.'

'And what do you say?'

'I think you're nice.'

'I don't want to be nice, I hate the idea of nice. Nice is just feeble.'

'You know what it originally means etymologically?'

'Yes.'

'Then I do believe that you are apt and to the point. In your way. I don't really understand it, though. Gillian told me you had a sister who died.'

'I did, but she was only a few days old, and before I was born.'

'Like a twin you never quite see, who is always out of sight. I have a brother, he's a bit older than me, not much, but he looks out for me. I can't imagine my life without him.'

'Has he met Stevie yet?'

'No. I've told him I have a boyfriend and he's pleased on one level but he still wants to keep an eye on me. I don't think he really understands the idea of Stevie. George is terribly opinion-ated, and a little bit rough to be honest.'

'In what way? Is he violent?'

'In the sense that he has a temper, yes. But he would never hit anyone, at least I don't think so. But he's not a thinker. At all.'

'Is he not at university too?'

'Oh no. He's in a band. He plays drums and he lives on a sea-going barge on the Thames so he can practise as much as he likes, bang bang bang away all night and no one will be disturbed by him. I think you'd like him. He'll come and see me when he's not busy and I'll introduce you. He's very *robust*, not like me.'

'I don't think of you as particularly frail.'

She looked at me and said, 'Oh, you are kind, I do like you. I hope we're always friends.'

'Even though I'm a ... ?'

'What?'

'A something thinker.'

'Heuristic.'

'Oh, yes. Not like Rami or Stevie. I don't understand what they're talking about, do you?'

'I do. Rami is a danger to Stevie. I've told him so but of course he won't listen. He's a bit enchanted.'

'Why is he a danger? Because he fancies him? Bobby does, obviously.'

'No, because Stevie is looking for a cult. It started with him wanting us to be the originators of a cult, we would be the two gurus and we'd have followers. People would give us part of their income. It's stupid, who would give us money? But Rami will attach himself to us like a parasite sinking itself into the intestine. I know he will.'

'Rami is so ridiculous. How can anyone take him seriously?'

'But Adele, you don't take anything seriously, so how can you say who will and who won't?'

We came back with the early-evening sun, along the path above the sea, down into the wooded lane and on to the beach, past Rami's cottage, shut up, the doors closed, no sign of life in there. And Evie and Stevie's house was empty so we went over the road to Bobby's.

Bobby was sitting with his legs dangling over the sea wall, reading Lawrence Durrell. It was the book of the season, we were all waiting for him to finish so we could borrow it next. An evening breeze rose up across the water, carrying with it strands of my hair and sheets of newspaper, and the surface of Bobby's cup of coffee moved and rippled. Now the sun dipped down below the surface of the sea. '*Thalassa!*' he cried. 'We are in the womb of life.'

'But where's Stevie?' said Evie.

'He went to explore the rocks, ages ago.'

'I hope he comes back soon. I hope he hasn't fallen.'

'Nonsense, he will be at Rami's house, I'm sure of it.'

'I don't think so, there was no one in when we passed.'

An hour later Stevie and Rami turned up together. They had been to Truro, where Rami had had his ears pierced; he had strung a piece of long red thread between the hoop in his left ear and the one in Stevie's right, so they were tied together now, until Bobby, looking at Evie's face, advanced on the pair from behind with a pair of scissors and cut the cord.

One hot day on the town quay we fell into conversation with a strange woman. She was, I am guessing, in her late forties. Her name was something like Sylvia or maybe Sonia or Sybil, I don't remember, and she had an odd accent, sometimes it was the clipped cut-glass vowels of the middle classes before the war and sometimes she would lapse into Americanisms, like that old word *gotten* which came from England with the Pilgrim Fathers and has died out altogether here.

'I'd like to show you my clothes,' she said. 'I have a fabulous collection. 'I think you'll be interested.'

'OK.' Stevie was once again with Rami, they had rowed up river to visit the recording studio and find out what was going on in there. Bobby was writing something indoors. Evie and I were bored, the town had exhausted all its fascination for us. A few days ago an insect had stung me on the face and my upper lip was swollen and itching. A doctor told me there was nothing to worry about, it would soon pass, but I felt like a monster.

We followed her up the path beside the church, past the library and along one of the secret lanes we had not penetrated in the shadow of the walls of the ridiculous Gothic mansion.

'What happened to your face?' she said to me.

'I was bitten by something.'

'Do you have a cream for it?'

'Yes.'

'I'd stay indoors if it was me. I can't stand being ugly.'

'Thanks a lot.'

'Here we are.'

She unlocked a faded blue door and let us into a house which was decorated not in the musty styles of the half-abandoned houses of the old town but in what I could only pin down as a *London* way. Glazed ceramics. Rag rugs on a bare slate floor. An austere chair.

'This is really nice,' I said, looking around. 'Wow.'

'Wow what?'

'I don't know. It's just a bit amazing.'

'Thank you. But it's not my house, I've just borrowed it for the summer. From friends. A few of the bits are mine, of course.'

'Have you been coming here long?'

She made a vague gesture with her hands. She seemed to me like one of those china dolls that need regular dusting, distant and admired on the mantelpiece, but when she took us upstairs to the bedroom and opened the painted wooden wardrobe, she began to speak knowledgeably of the clothes in there.

'This is a St Laurent trouser suit,' she said to Evie, as though I wasn't there, because she winced when she had to look at me. 'It's from the 1969 collection and it's already a classic, of course, I bought it in the sale, but the cut and the styling are superb. I'd have thought it would be made for you. You can try it on, if you like.' The blinds were down over the window, the room was very shadowy, you could hardly make out the furniture from the marks on the floor. She turned her back. 'I won't look while you're undressing. Women's bodies don't really interest me.'

Evie looked at me, as if to beg me, as the stronger party, to tell the woman that she did not want to be dressed by her, but I was too curious to see what she would look like in the trouser suit.

She struggled into the hot wool and presented herself, looking trussed, as if she was the sheep being carried by its tied legs. A new word, one that I had seen in a dictionary but never used, came into my head. *Androgynous*. She looked like an optical illusion, the eye shifted from one sex to the other, her gender wouldn't stay still, it wavered, and Evie herself was shifting all over the place. She put one foot forward in a man's strut, and her hands on her hips in a fashion-model pose. She laughed.

'What do you think?'

The woman appraised her. 'I knew it was right for you. You can have it for fifteen pounds, which is a terrific bargain.'

Evie looked as if she had been surprised by a snake.

'I don't have fifteen pounds!'

'Well, what's your offer?'

'I don't want it, I can't afford it even if I did. We're only students.'

'But why do you want to sell it?' I said. 'Won't you want it again when you go back?'

'Oh, you exasperate me. You children have no idea. I need that fifteen pounds more than you don't need this trouser suit.'

Evie was fearing going home to Stevie in the trouser suit and having to explain how she had parted with so much money, and how he would tell her she was too easy to push around. I suspected that he would respond with extreme coldness of a kind she could not easily endure.

'Well, I'm sorry,' I said, 'but we can't help you. Anyway, the trousers are too short.'

'They can always be taken down, there's a good hem in them. Let her speak for herself.' Everyone including me was always telling her to be vocal, to stand up to our bullying.

But mutely Evie undressed and we ran out of the house as the little babes in the forest would run from the gingerbread house.

When we got back to Bobby's house, Stevie was lying on the sofa wearing nothing but his earrings, reading a Scientology book. His body was very white and his penis, semi-erect, a shade of violet. Rami and Bobby were sitting at the table looking at him. Bobby was saying, 'You know, darling, you should put on a little weight, some muscle definition is always nice, don't you think, Rami?'

'He's a study in colour, all the shades of grey and ivory and the purples and violets and blacks, and some silver. I would need to take photographs for a preparatory sketch.'

Stevie looked up. 'Hiya, babes, where have you two been? You look hot, take your clothes off, be cool.'

'Oh, yes,' said Rami, 'we should all take our clothes off.'

'We've just been trying clothes *on*,' said Evie and, addressing Stevie, told him about the strange woman we had met who had tried to force her to buy her trouser suit.

'I know her,' said Rami. 'One of the pioneers, she came here in the sixties thinking she'd escaped from the rat race. But that crowd has moved on and she's something that got left behind on the beach. The remains of beauty, like eggshells.'

We had come face to face with middle age and disappointment and we found it horrifying. We felt sad for her and fearful of her. From now on we saw her sometimes in the tea rooms, alone, with a cup of coffee, writing in a notebook, and Bobby said, 'Obviously not love letters.'

None of us took our clothes off and eventually Stevie put his back on and Rami cooked for us all, he made a paella which was the first time any of us had had this unfamiliar dish of rice and fish.

'We go to bed alone,' Bobby said, 'apart from Evie and Stevie, which is so silly when you think of the possibilities, how dull you all are. I feel quite petulant, I shall have a sulk in the mirror.'

17

Of all of us, the one who had been affected most dramatically and most unexpectedly over the summer was Gillian. The first thing I noticed, as I turned round to hear my name called out from several feet behind me on the covered walkway, was that the maxi-dresses had gone. She was wearing denim dungarees covered in badges advertising causes. She was a plump noticeboard for anti-war protest. A thin-faced Oriental man with a wispy beard looked out from her bosom.

I paused to allow her to catch up to me; she broke into a trot, she had lost a little weight and was lighter and faster on her feet. The sudden movement let up a frightened flight of birds from the lake; when she reached me, she embraced me and kissed me on both cheeks.

'How *brown* you are,' she said. 'You must have had a fantastic summer and I want to hear all about it of course, but for once I have something to tell *you*. The summer I've spent, it was amazing. I saw incredible things and I learned so much. Rose and I were inseparable, we hitchhiked to London together and went to a demonstration, I felt so alive. I've been stuck my whole life in a room with the windows shut and outside everyone is waving and shouting at me and I'm hearing them for the very first time and wondering how on earth I could have ignored them for so long.'

It seemed to me that commitment had made an unexpected improvement in her appearance. Despite her stocky figure, the dungarees suited her, she did not seem so overwhelmed by cloth as she had in her too-large dresses and you could discern a round and quite womanly shape which some boys could find attractive.

The huge surprise was that she had given up her room in college, when back in June she had expressed no intention of ever leaving for the town. She was moving everything out to a shared house on Thorpe Street with Rose, her well-known boyfriend Brian, and a couple of other comrades.

I said, 'What do you mean, comrades?'

'I've joined! I'm a member, I've been recruited. I was so happy when they said they wanted me and I had to be interviewed and I passed!'

My friend was now part of one of the many Trotskyist sects that littered the political landscape in those days, whose names included the words *socialist*, *Party*, *workers*, *revolutionary* and *international*, like Scrabble tiles in various permutations. I could never keep in my head which was which, for the rivalry between them was based on differences not visible to the outside world, as if you were supposed to tell one ant from another.

She had somehow failed the test we did not then know we were all being put through, of rejecting ideology. In the lab that was the campus, she was a rogue element. But you don't turn down happiness when you find it, and Gillian was ablaze with love of humanity and had set herself the task of recruiting *me*, though Rose had warned her that I was riddled with bourgeois deviation and a tough nut to crack.

'But what about your music?'

'Oh, music music music, my whole *life* has been music. In Leeds people used to live in houses called back-to-backs. The back wall of one house is fastened to the back wall of the one behind it so there's no ventilation. Don't you think that's appalling? We are so lucky, we have more food than we can ever eat, we're sitting on a mountain of glut. Look at the butter mountain, the wickedness of it.'

Then Rose came over to the primary-coloured sponge chairs with her boyfriend Brian who said, 'We've got hold of a van so we can move you out tonight. And have you heard the news? The Egyptians have crossed the Suez Canal? Surprise attack. This is an extremely important moment for the anti-colonial struggle.'

Everyone knew that Brian was supposed to be very clever, that he had come, a year younger than everyone else, straight from Charterhouse, that he was on track for a First and did not intend to turn up for his finals, that he believed that fairly soon universities would be abolished and replaced by free institutions of learning open to everyone, where Marx would be at the centre of the curriculum. Brian had five identical red shirts in his wardrobe and spent several minutes each morning repinning his badges on one of them for the struggle that lay ahead in the day. He was full of hope and bombast and enraged by human weakness, he despised his own reflection in the mirror for its feeble struggle to grow a Zapata moustache on his angry round face, for emphasis.

'How wonderful!' cried Gillian.

I am not sure that Gillian knew at that stage in her recruitment where the Suez Canal was, which continent even, or what Rose was talking about. I certainly didn't, for it was a time in my life when I did not read newspapers or watch TV and the great events of those times were unknown to me. I lived through my own portion of history oblivious to it. It took me many years before I understood how to read a newspaper, to follow news you have come in in the middle of, like the Biafra famine or Vietnam, not understanding the causes and origins. I had to start with a new conflict to make sense of it.

But from then on, Gillian would acquire a shell of predictable responses to any question. I noticed how, when you tried to argue her out of it, she would raise her eyes up and turn them to the side as if she was reading from an invisible book or script that she had been taught but could not entirely remember. She was auditing another language. The chain of words came out link by link, the truth had been revealed to her and it was complete. She had a system. With this system, she had been assured, everything could be understood, since, as she now learned, even buying a loaf of bread was a political act, and she could bore you to tears at your elbow in the shop while you were waiting to pay for it.

Everyone said that this condition of talking nonsense was temporary and she would snap out of it by Christmas. I thought so too because I had seen her with her viola, had heard her play Bach on it. I still think of her when I listen to Jacqueline du Pré: each of them was overwhelmed and destroyed by something that caused them to lose sensation.

They bore her off and from then on I would see her every day outside the college dining room, selling her newspaper, and occasionally I would buy one. The little fanatic became a figure of fun at the university, one of those fixtures everyone would later remember: her awkward approaches and stumbling explanations of the great causes of the day. Always her eyes raised up and to the right to the great script in the sky and you only bought a paper because you felt sorry for her.

She lost a little more weight but she was armoured now by dogma. She had a boyfriend, an appalling boy called Jim who publicly humiliated her in the coloured sponge cubes of the JCR because she had not managed to finish some boring beige-backed tome by Lenin. He would stroke her cheek and then turn his hand into a fist and lightly punch her with it; not a blow, a gesture. But she said she was learning everything from him, and that she loved him. I didn't believe her. No one like her could love a thing like him.

'But you see, Adele, the difference between you and me is that I believe in something and you, you're just unwilling to open yourself to the world. What's wrong? Why do you have to be so grudging? Humanity is there to be loved and pitied and inspired by.

Life can be beautiful or we can make it beautiful. Don't you want to be a part of that?'

'I don't want to be part of anything.'

'You're missing out, you don't *know* how much you're missing. We could read texts together, I could introduce you to such ideas.'

'Yeah. But no.'

18

Everyone was leaving the campus that autumn, only the swots were left behind, the types who sent their underwear home to be washed by Mother. Apart from Bobby, who had no intention of moving out. Evie and Stevie had taken a flat together. Dora had organised a house. I had waited for a better offer but did not get one so I had to move in with her.

Our house was on a road that followed the path of the railway line. The larger rooms had once held upright pianos and potted palms. Significant traces of the late owners lingered on. Wrought-iron bedsteads, marble-topped washstands, black Bakelite handles on the doors. As a latecomer I had the smallest room but it over-looked the garden, not the trains. It had once been part of the maids' quarters, a china ewer and basin were still in the pine wardrobe and a cracked chamberpot lay beneath the bed. I don't think anyone had gone up there for years. The room smelled to me of the menstrual blood of these unhappy girls of long ago, of their sweat and of their stale unwashed clothes. I painted the walls green, we were all in a frenzy of painting, each imposing some embryonic sense of our young selves on our environment.

I had survived a year at university and no one had come to take

me away. My pretences had gone undetected. I was metamor-
phosing into a different kind of girl, one who had never known the
perfume counter or the Rosenblatt noose or the smell of fried fish.
Who she was was currently beyond my capacity to say. I did not yet
know myself.

We rarely went into the garden, only to clear away a patch of
weeds so we could sit outside with a cup of tea and a cigarette on
a mild day. Did I say we all smoked? Everyone did. The air was
always ash grey, no one could live without their cigarettes, we were
addicted to instant coffee and nicotine. We ate bags of chips and
tried to cook soups and the recent sophistication of quiches. But
cigarettes were jammed at all times into our mouths, we only took
them out to fork food in. We walked everywhere to save money
and we were thin and pale and nervy.

From my bedroom window I saw the nests of birds in the upper
branches of the trees, and the horrible starved cats jumping on to
the fence from the paths they made tracking in the long grass. It
was a filthy old house as all student houses were then, with an
Ascot heater which unpredictably burst into flame and spat out
scalding-hot water for a couple of minutes. The rooms were fitfully
warmed with gas fires fed by ten-pence pieces in the meter, and the
old gas mantles were still visible on the walls from the era before
electricity.

Every day we had milk delivered and it was kept out on the windowsill in the kitchen: we had no other source of refrigeration.
There was a scullery to keep food. The walls had been colonised
by mottled black and grey slugs. Dora laid salt trails for them. She
went to the council to ask about methods of extermination. One
day I found the hole through which the slugs were entering and
stuffed it with a piece of newspaper. The slugs skulked outside in
the garden. Dora said my solutions were simplistic.

19

Not long after we moved in, Dora decided to form a consciousness-raising group, an idea that came from America, from the chicks who had broken away from the male domination of the anti-war movement. In fact we were no longer to call ourselves chicks, we were *women*. We must all sit round and talk about those aspects of our lives that we were too ashamed to tell anyone and out of this we would both raise our consciousness and achieve solidarity. As she understood it, we would come to realise that what we thought was unique to our individual selves was actually part of the condition of being a woman. I don't believe any of us, at that time in our lives, considered ourselves to be women. We were girls; women were creatures with lines on their faces and a beige mask of make-up concealing them.

By this stage I had read two feminist books, *The Female Eunuch* and Kate Millett's *Sexual Politics*. I thought they were both immensely interesting and confirmed what I had thought aged fifteen of housewives having morning coffee in cafés leading empty lives.

Apart from the kitchen there was no communal space. Every room in the house had been turned into a bedroom in order to cover the rent. Dora had found it, being the most resourceful of all of us, and had awarded herself the best room, on the first floor, what would have been the master bedroom when the house had had a master and, as she pointed out, the women had no vote. Not the wife nor daughters nor maids. This is where the consciousness-raising group was held, in Dora's room, on whose walls the posters of Che Guevara had been replaced by Simone de Beauvoir with her fine nose, expressive eyes and her hair in what seemed to be a French pleat.

It was an early-November afternoon in our fourth term. We felt we were all really on to something. We were absolutely on the verge. Of what, we didn't know, because we were certain it was about to be revealed to us if we wanted. What was going on, I now see, was that we were making it all up as we went along. Any revelations would come from our own mouths and hearts.

I came too late to get a seat near the fire, I kept my rabbit coat on. Dora was klutzy. She didn't have a good idea of her size, her spatial awareness was off, and she kept bumping into things because she could not internalise the outer limits of her body in relation to objects like furniture. Her beauty was in her skin, her china-doll blue eyes and the shining hair, but the body itself was big-boned, lumbering.

I thought how some people move with grace and others don't, but Dora's clumsiness was what made her powerful; you were always having to take her into account, where she was and what she might do next. She was perfectly well aware of this and laughed at it. She could be so charming, so keenly observant about some of her failings, but not others. I think this was because she was the daughter of two teachers, didacticism was in her blood.

Now, having regained her chair by the fire, she held her hand up for silence. Who does this but a natural leader? 'I'll start,' she said.

She began by telling us that she had arrived at university eight weeks pregnant, had had the test two days before she arrived. The room erupted. Everyone was gasping and crying out and shaking their head and making expressions of 'Oh, poor you, how awful, you must have felt so lonely knowing no one.' Except me. I was going back over in my mind the hot baths and the potato soup, thinking, So that was what was going on.

'I tried to get rid of it in the bath,' she said, 'which turns out to be an old wives' tale even if the water had been hot enough.'

I saw her standing in the doorway, smiling, a smile of greeting to new people she would have no means of avoiding, and keeping that secret because she did not trust us not to reject her. But neither of us would have done. Or I wouldn't, of that I was certain. Gillian might have seen things differently, I don't know. I don't really know what Gillian thought in those early weeks. People were complete mysteries, and you saw them every day.

'In the end I went to the college doctor. It was the most humiliating experience of my life. He examined me with this enormous metal willy, a speculum, and he had me lie on my side and he said, "Blunt end up."'

Everyone cried out again. I said, 'How revolting, what a pig.'

'Then he said I could have an abortion. I went to Malton for two nights, that's where they do it, that's where the abortion clinic is.'

'All on your own?'

'Yes, all by myself.'

'But what about the boy?'

'Chris – he was just a summer romance, he was starting at Kent that week and the only way I could reach him was by letter.'

'So did you write?'

'Yes, I did, but he didn't answer. Too terrified, I suppose. I saw him last Christmas, he came round on Christmas morning with a present for me, and we pecked each other on the cheek on the doorstep and that was it. He walked away and Mummy said, "Aren't you going out with him any more? Did you have a row?" and I said, "I've grown out of him."'

As Dora would have known, this story occupied most of the first half of the meeting. Evie was there. She looked stunned, tears kept coming to her eyes and she pushed them away. 'Awful, just awful,' she kept saying. 'Oh, poor you.'

We talked about abortion, she was the first girl I knew to have had one. No one had travelled on the train with her, or held her hand or given her a word of sympathy while it was happening and the brute of a doctor regarded her as a lump of inconvenient flesh. I think now that we didn't really see the point of the story, which was how alone she must have felt, and how it had altered her. How she had need to draw a group of people around herself and that the only way she knew how to do that was by organising them. But why wouldn't she have done so? It was a university, and that was its ethos. Ideas and groups.

No one wanted to go next.

Dora said, 'Adele, come on, you're not the type who holds back.'

'Nothing to tell,' I said.

A girl called Jenny suddenly put up her hand, she was bursting to speak, and she said, 'Well if she doesn't want to go, I will.'

What happened next was that Evie, who had left the room for a few minutes after Dora's revelation (to change her tampon which was becoming uncomfortably full, she told me later), returned to find an agonised silence after Jenny had said that she had never had an orgasm and thought she did not like sex with anyone. No one really knew how to respond because it was our power, as liberated women, to be sexual, and this girl sounded like the heroine of a Victorian novel. She did not lie back and think of England but lay instead composing her history essays, while the bump and grind went on on top of her.

When Evie returned she looked refreshed and relaxed. I have now forgotten how much our hormones, the monthly ravages of our periods, affected us all. No one talked about it then and they don't really now. I don't mean premenstrual tension, mood swings, the once-a-month bitch. I mean the difficulty in controlling the flow of blood that was gushing out of you and the terror of the stains it left behind. Of borrowing tampons when you had run out, of palming them in your hand so they could not be seen, of the shared flats of girls who all, according to the dictates of the moon, mysteriously found themselves in sync with each other, and of the poorer households of mothers and daughters wiped out financially by the monthly need for cotton wadding all in the same week.

Dora looked at her. For Dora, Evie remained the tantalising enigma and the challenge. Dora saw Evie as Stevie's creature. She was determined to break the two of them apart with her bare hands if she could. The abortion had turned Dora against relationships; she brought boys back to her room for one-night stands, she considered this an aspect of her growing autonomy, to leave after sex as a man might; not for her the neediness of begging him to stay the night, of two mugs of coffee by the bed and talk of how he liked his eggs for breakfast.

So the sight of this couple on campus who could not be prised from each other had become part of her agenda.

'Evie,' she said. 'Your turn.'

Evie did that thing with her eyes. She opened them so wide that you could see the whites above them. I think there is some word in Zen Buddhism or Hinduism to describe this, it means a soul which is in trouble. From then on, her eyes often appeared like that. I was the only one to notice that day, because she was looking directly at me, not Dora.

I thought all she was going to say was how she had come up to the university with a long blond plait with a tartan ribbon tied at the end and was really called Lorraine. I couldn't see the harm in her sharing it.

But she said, 'My mother was raped at a dinner dance. I don't know if my dad is really my father. My mum says she doesn't know either. Not that she's ever talked about it but my brother found out and he told me. I didn't even know what rape was at the time, because I didn't know what sex was.'

Evie kept looking round the room for a response and found nothing. We were all in shock. I knew she must feel she had been railroaded into it. If she had not come back at that precise moment into the room, that smiling expression of relief on her face after she had changed her tampon, it would have been someone else's turn, another girl would have volunteered, or Dora would have pushed me into making my revelation, and that would have been how I had cheated my way into university from the perfume counter.

I don't know how Evie had the guts to do it, but she must have seen those encouraging faces and thought that now the moment had come when she could . . . what? Why *did* she tell us? What did she think would happen? Was there a feminist point she was making? But this seemed unlikely because it was Stevie who was the political one, she was the philosopher. And maybe if even one of us had said something encouraging, or asked a question, we might have found out more, shed some light on her childhood and on her. So for the longest time I thought that this was the moment we had all missed, the path not taken, and it haunted me. Or rather, she did. Evie herself has haunted me because for most of my life she has been a ghost.

When she had finished these devastating sentences and turned round to look at me, what she had seen was my face withdrawn from her. She didn't insist on taking my hand so it stayed clenched around a cigarette.

Dora told me recently, 'I remember you sitting there with your fag smouldering, I could see the body language you were using, and that was you all over, wasn't it? *Noli me tangere*. Don't touch. You were always so tense, your shoulders and neck, you looked like you were holding yourself rigid, and everyone wondered why, because it's not like you were ever a repressed personality, so it must have been some kind of self-protection.'

20

Two days later Stevie stopped me on the steps of the library, he actually barred his hand across the door while smiling at me. Some people have a smile like a watermelon slice. He could make his mouth do something to create a favourable impression. So he was smiling and preventing me from opening the glass door at the same time. I looked at that hand that was in my way. He too seemed to have lost my Fair Isle gloves now and his fingers were bluish, his skin translucent. He was wearing a woman's coat with a fur collar which he had pulled up around his neck. The coat was green and the fur was grey and his hands were blue and his dry watermelon smile betrayed a hint of lipstick. There were lines of kohl around his eyes.

I think of his elocution years, the hows and the nows and all the brown cows till he reached a kind of flattened Received Pronunciation. And how he might have gone away at the end of each term with his home clothes in a case and changed into them in the toilet at the bus station and become once more Steve who had left and gone to college in order to make something of himself. A nice boy, out of his depth.

'I'm glad I caught you,' he said. 'Evie is quite upset. You didn't seem to react in the way she expected. You see, she wouldn't even have said it if you weren't there. She thought you were the most unshockable. So she doesn't understand. She's in pain, she needs your help and support. You have no idea how fragile she is. She thinks of you as a friend and she needs friends, lots of them.'

'I know she's vulnerable. I saw her, on the first day, through the window with her parents, they were practically dragging her round the lake. When she was still Lorraine with a plait. Before you took her over.'

'No, that's not true at all, we took each other over, I'm not Svengali. If anything, she is, not me.'

'How is that even possible?'

'Look at my face.' He pointed to his eyes. 'That's what *she* does, with her tin of kohl. If I could have changed her, believe me I would have done. I'd have made her happy and she isn't happy. She's so hard to live with, Adele, you don't know, how can you? Her mood swings, she can spend all day in bed, she zones out into another world and you can't get through to her. I do love her, you know, I'm trying, I'm trying, but I don't have any experience of how to be with someone who is suffering. Can't you just be a little bit kind?'

And then I saw that he was indeed out of his depth. That Evie had become a kind of invalid to him, and that he was not coping, that his own kindness might have already been used up. It had never occurred to me that Evie might be, for someone like Stevie, a handful, because they had seemed on the surface so well matched, so fully a mirror of each other. But I was still insisting that he had built her from scratch for his own purposes, because that was the only explanation that fitted the circumstances.

'It would go a long way if you just apologised for not under-standing.'

At that time, when we were at university, the greatest crime was not to understand. Not to understand a play, a novel, a poem, an idea. So that was a challenge to me.

I don't know why I found this revelation of Evie's so difficult. If

I psychoanalysed myself I would come up with the idea that I reacted badly to the idea of families fissured in some way by acts of violence, that I saw my own situation reflected there. But that's to over-complicate it. I think that I was frightened. That if I became emotionally involved with Evie, in trying to soothe her troubled soul or whatever it was, I would fall in love with her. Because I was drawn, I was. To the nape of her shaved neck and her beauty and strangeness. And I did not want to be the person who loves a woman. I had escaped from ghettos and I did not want to go back to one, I lacked Bobby's conviction about his sexuality, how he had always known. And I was not running from the centre of the world to its outlaw edges because that's where I felt I was already. My hanged daddy.

There are people who are the centre of attention at parties and there are those sitting in corners. And there are those who stand in the door frame between two rooms, watching, turning. Assessing the possibilities on either side.

It was in my mind to run, but Stevie wouldn't let go of the door. No one else was approaching, either from the steps to enter or from the interior of the building to exit, and I was pinned there, and he was so physically easy in his androgynous clothes, prepared to wait all day until I agreed.

'Please,' he said, 'she needs a little tenderness. Go round to the flat. She's in now. And you can meet her brother George, he's staying with us. In fact, why don't you go straight away, it would mean the world to her.'

What could I say? I walked off with the idea that I was walking towards my fate, to something that was going to happen. I went into town thinking of what I would say to Evie and was stopped twice by students making their way to the campus, and we stood and smoked cigarettes in the cold air, chatting while I delayed my arrival at the flat which was at the top of a house on a road that led to the river and the path alongside it which flowed idly right out of town. The grass verges widened away to make a flood plain. In the distance were houses and I sometimes saw people walking out of them with their children. There were people living there who had no connection to us or our lives, who would go on living by the river as successive waves of students came and went, and this made me half understand that our existence here was temporary, that we would be replaced and that our feeling of being the centre of the universe was a fallacy. It gave me the chills.

Everyone kept the front door open. The idea of locking up was alien to us. I climbed the stairs and knocked on the door of the flat which was ajar and it was opened by her brother.

I looked at him and saw again Evie in the trouser suit in that dim room in Cornwall, her hands on her hips and the leg extended forward, but where she had seemed both sexes together, in George the sex was just the one, masculinity. And yet they looked so alike, I could see her face in his and when she walked up beside him and I was confronted by the brother and sister, I felt that I had turned in that doorway and seen someone enter the room.

Evie went into the kitchen to make coffee and George followed her. I had always found the flat a claustrophobic space. There was a heavy smell of patchouli coming from a corner of the carpet and a dark brown stain on the robin's-egg blue of the wool.

I could hear their voices in the kitchen, I heard George call her Lorraine and she was pleading with him to chill out. They came back in. George was carrying a tray with three mugs and a plate of biscuits.

George picked up a biscuit and handed it to Evie. She shook her head. He still held it out. 'Eat it,' he told her. 'You're nothing but skin and bone.'

'I'm hardly ever hungry.'

'Well, that's not right, you know you should be.'

As if to change the subject, she looked at my dress. It was second-hand, what was not yet known as 'vintage'. A black dress, beaded at the sleeves and collar, empty frayed spaces where the beads had been shed. 'I bet it would look good on you,' said George, looking at me, not her.

'Try it on if you like,' I said.

'Really? Can I?' Her eyes widened and I saw again the sight of her irises ringed by the whites.

I pulled the dress over my head and when I handed it to her and I was in my pants and tights, I held my arm over my braless chest while he looked at my yellow cotton knickers which showed through the tights and that mound, growing damp. I was standing facing him while Evie was enrobed in cloth, trying to find the neckline for her head to emerge from.

When she got it on, the dress was too big. I was thin then, but she was thinner, maybe half a stone less than she had been in the summer.

She went to look in the mirror. I didn't really think the dress suited her, she had a short waist and not a great deal of curve in the hips, but I was astonished by what she said next. 'I look really fat in it, what a shame.'

'Don't be ridiculous. If you're fat what am I?'

'Oh, but you have a lovely figure, doesn't she, George?'

'Yeah. Give it back, Lorraine,' said George. 'Adele's shivering here.' He went on looking at me and I went on looking at her, at how her ribs stuck out and her pelvis was like an anvil with skin stretched over it, until our clothes were exchanged and we were right again.

Evie said, 'You might not be the only performer in our family, George. Stevie thinks I should take up acting. I'm going to audition for Hermione in *The Winter's Tale*.'

'Are you now?' said George. 'Do you think that's a good idea?'

'Why not?' I said.

'It's a lot of stress, I don't think it's in Lorraine's best interests.'

For the second time in an hour she was being spoken of as a patient or invalid. It annoyed me. I said, 'You should do what you like, don't listen to anyone else. Maybe I'll audition too for another part and we can do it together.'

'Oh, would you? That would be wonderful.'

George said, 'Are you going to see the New York Dolls tonight? That's why I'm here.'

'I've never heard of them.'

'We're all going,' said Evie, 'you can pay on the door. Do come.'

'You should come.'

'Should I?'

'Definitely.'

Back and forth I looked, between them, until my eyes came to rest on him. Evie clapped her hands.

'Oh, this is going to be great!'

21

You reached George's barge across a slippery gangplank in the dark
and he held out his hand to me as I crossed. When I was inside
that vessel then we were separate from the world. At night you
could hear the black water rippling as police boats patrolled the
river. They were looking for corpses, for the waterlogged dead, the
suicides. Bodies were brought out under a bulging yellow moon.

The tide would go out, the barge would lurch in the mud,
George had all kinds of special duties to attend to; it was like living
on a ship at sea, he told me, but without masts or rigging. He was
always up there scraping and painting when the weather was fine.

One thing I'll say about us in those days is that we were not
bored and we were not cynical. We were still in the early stages of
excitement about being adults. George kept his childhood stamp
collection on the barge and went mad when it got damp. He
showed me the little perforated squares of Madagascar and Ceylon,
they were beautiful tiny paintings of birds. The Madagascar eight-
franc was a red engraving of a long-tailed bird, a little like a
peacock, with a second bird in flight behind it. The 1938 Ceylon
stamp, with George VI in the corner, showed a woman in a sari
picking what George thought were leaves from a tea plant.

'Postal history is very interesting,' he said pompously. 'People think it's just for schoolchildren but you can learn so much about the world from a stamp album.'

I think of his collection now as a poignant early form of the internet. I fell in love with his stamps and the way his spade-like fingers picked them up delicately between tweezers and he stared down into the zones of their internationality. Then he would put them away in a metal box, kept locked, and we would head out into the city's unconquered territory.

On Friday mornings I would set out from the university, hitch-hiking down to London to see him. I learned how to use the tube and recognise the colours of the lines, heading west on the green cord that led to Gunnersbury. Along the towpath I heard his sticks beating the skins.

I remember slices of the river with the streetlights dappling it, the odour of damp, the roughness of his orange shirt, the heaviness of his donkey jacket, the thin plastic patches on the shoulder, the slime of the gangplank. It was ironic that I, the challenger to D. H. Lawrence's misogyny, had fallen into a Lawrentian passion with a man, it was all about sex.

London was downbeat, depressing. It seems to me now, look-ing back, very poor, or at least the parts we inhabited. The glamour of the sixties had passed away and we were left with the mud-flats of a retreating tide. The power went out. The lights went off. The electric fires went grey. The televisions were dark. The toast-ers were unpopped. Table lamps were dark under their fringed shades.

So that period of my life when I should have got to know the city for the first time was spent on the rocking barge. Mainly in bed, watching the sun rise in the mornings through the fog on the opposite bank, shrouding Kew Gardens in blank memory.

I didn't learn the geography of London, but the geography of George and of the lands inside his stamp album.

22

Evie and I auditioned for parts, she got Hermione, me, nothing. I was asked if I was interested in doing wardrobe but, having no skills with a sewing machine, I declined that resistible offer. And Evie was unable to learn her lines. Five times she asked me to go through them with her and each time she failed. It was possible that she might have been able to act, to become someone else as her brother did, but she couldn't get over the first hurdle of memory. I thought this was quite strange because at school in our day, memorisation was everything for exams, before coursework and continuous assessment.

> Since what I am to say must be but that
> Which contradicts my accusation, and
> The testimony on my part no other
> But what comes from myself, it shall scarce boot me
> To say, 'Not guilty.'

Boot me. It defeated her. She simply couldn't remember it, and stumbled on until she got to the firm ground of her innocence. She was absolutely hopeless. She tried and tried, but it became obvious that she would not make it to the first night. Eventually she lost the part. Another girl took it on, quite an ordinary person, nothing about her of a royal presence which is why Evie had been cast in the first place – because she had a deceptively haughty disposition which was really just nerves and shyness.

But the girl was more ordinary than anyone at first knew. She wasn't a student, she was from the town.

The way I would describe her is *lamby*. Her name was Denise and she wore a dirty lemon-yellow fake-fur coat and had colourless fawny hair and a pinkish face and was completely unmemorable until she started acting, when she could do what Evie could not. She had those lines down in a flash, and she was really talented. Not anything more than talented, nothing about her made your heart stop, but she could get away with making a little into a deceptively satisfying something which lasted until the end of the play. She said those lines as if she meant them, as if she really had been wrongly accused.

I acknowledge that she should have got the part from the beginning. She had auditioned for it but everyone was taken in by Evie's ethereal white-blond beauty. The director, one of Bobby's GLF friends, wanted her for the poster. And anyway, Denise was *from the town*. Many in the Drama Society had thought that to cast her was on some level cheating, she did not belong. She had not been lifted off to unknown planets in our concrete spaceship.

The director said he could use Evie anyway. She would appear at the end as the statue. She would stand there frozen and come back to life. There wasn't much to it and the lack of resemblance could be got over by lots of make-up. And was she not supposed to be a ghost? Who actually knew what a ghost looked like since they did not exist?

They say that everything changes during the course of a play. People cease to be who they are and cease to love who they love. During a play you are put in a box and shaken.

Denise, boring, unremarkable, overlooked until now, had some makeover in the part of Hermione. She wasn't good-looking enough for it but became so in costume and greasepaint and it wasn't fair. We had so ignored her that we hadn't understood what we had on our hands, this person from the town who illegitimately hung around the JCR and the bars, listening, trying to insert an elbow into the conversation. There was something persistent about her: once she assumed a form she seemed to be everywhere. You could not pass from one side of the campus to the other without Denise bumbling towards you and greeting you as if you were friends and we would haughtily acknowledge her with a nod or a small 'Hi.' I sometimes wonder if she might even have been in the room the afternoon of Dora's consciousness-raising group because she always managed to get herself invited and when she wasn't invited she would simply arrive, and was so unnoticeable you didn't rarely care.

After a month of rehearsals, I heard the most shocking piece of gossip from Dora, who had seen them together in the tea rooms in town, holding hands. The incredible had happened, the campus was alight with it, or those parts of the campus we considered its stylish nucleus, the ones who mattered.

Stevie was *with* Denise now, of all people. When Dora told me in the queue for Scotch eggs and potato salad at lunchtime, I went straight up to him sitting in the college bar on his own with a pint, reading, that black and red head bent over some book of arcana he had sent away for, a mystic piece of Eastern rubbish. And I actually grabbed his ears, I took him by the gold rings of his earlobes and twisted his head up from the page and said, 'What the hell is going on? What have you done to Evie?'

'Ow! Let go!'

'How could you?'

He said, 'Look, I told you, I've tried, I've tried, I've tried. But I can't help her. She's ill.'

'What do you mean?'

'She's not what I thought. She's . . .'

'You took her, you made her into something she wasn't, it's all your fault. And *Denise*, how is that possible? She's just so incredibly boring and ordinary.'

'Don't say that. Denise is a lovely girl, she's simple and affectionate. Do you think Evie ever showed me any affection? She doesn't know how, all she does is demand, she will suck a boy dry – not because of selfishness, I mean her extreme vulnerability. You have to look after her, you have to go out and bring people back to apologise to her. I had to come after you. Every little thing is a blow that strikes her. And what about me, has anyone ever thought what I need? Denise does. I'm only a boy from Newcastle, not Superman. I can see what you're looking at. No more eyeliner every morning as soon as I've had a wash. She liked me dressed in her clothes. At home she would make me put on her dresses but I wouldn't go out in them. It was a laugh at first, then it stopped being a laugh. I don't know what she wants. Oh, it's all a mess.'

I could not doubt his sincerity. He was close to crying, but I did not feel sorry for him, I was too fired up with contempt for Denise to take his side. Had I looked closer I might have noticed that he was in the early stages of dissolving, like a fizzy aspirin dropped into a glass of water. He was starting to lose a little of his definition, maybe the lack of kohl round the eyes was the start of it, and his hair was a little longer, his face not as pale but more freckled and indistinct, as if he was getting ready to leave us and go back to his normal life. If I had been a more responsible person I would have suggesting counselling, but then nothing like that was available in those days, just the loony bin next door.

From the bar, I went into a tutorial on Melville and came out and went home and when I got back to our house she was in the kitchen with Dora who had her arm round her. I burst in and said, 'How can he even touch that stupid girl? She's ridiculous.'

Evie said, 'I've tried, I've tried so hard but his standards are so high, he wants to live each day as if we're making a new future and every act has to be a moral one. Did you know, he let a beggar come and stay in the flat? He let him sleep on the sofa and the next night he said he wanted the bed and Stevie said we should give it to him. I said, but where will we sleep, and he said, you take the sofa and I'll sleep in the chair. You have had a bed every night of your life and he's lying on the pavement in Market Street. Just this once. But it wasn't one night, he stayed for nearly a week until he came into the bathroom when I was in the bath, and he sat on the edge watching me and then he started to take his clothes off and I screamed and Stevie came in and then he told him he had to go. You're too beautiful, he said, I was a temptation and you could hardly blame him for wanting me. I feel like he was hanging me high from his morals, or maybe he was punishing me.'

'Maybe at heart he hates women. So many men do really.'

'Dora, what do you mean? How could they hate us?'

'Ask your mum.'

'I have a brother. He loves me and looks out for me, he doesn't hate women. You've met him, Adele, do you think he hates women?'

'No, I'm sure he doesn't.'

'What's he like?' said Dora.

'He has a stamp collection.'

'Oh, did he tell you about that? He's normally a bit secretive, he thinks people will laugh at him. He must have liked you if he told you about his stamps.'

'What kind of stamps?'

'Pictorial,' I said. 'Ceylon and Madagascar.'

'Oh, he must have *really* liked you then, I'm so pleased. One day we'll go to London and stay with him on his barge, we'll turn up when he doesn't expect us and give him a surprise. Will you come, Adele?'

'Of course.'

What else could I have said? I was forbidden to tell her. George said it was something the two of them had to work out together, when she was less frail.

23

After Evie and Stevie split up, Evie moved in with us. Dora made
two girls share a room to free up a single for her. We tried to take
care of her. There was no counselling service at the university
because of this determination that we were free to make our own
cock-ups of our lives. Nor could we have predicted that the actions
of the people we regarded as the walk-on parts in our little drama,
the crowd scene, the science students, would hold up a mirror to
her fragile mental health.

Some boys in the Maths Department were trying to make a
primitive robot. They gathered in one of the college bars in the
evenings and sketched out their proposals. The idea was to con-
struct a Frankenstein contraption that would walk around the
campus issuing orders through a voicebox, and eventually after a
lot of failures they had a crude prototype.

I don't know what the mechanism was inside the figure but they
had bought a dressmaker's dummy and done it up in a white dress
and placed a papier-mâché head on it with a blond wig and you
knew as soon as you saw it who it was meant to be: Evie as the
statue Hermione on the poster that was plastered all over the
campus, on every college noticeboard, in the corridors of the
student accommodation and on flyers on all the dining-room

tables. Everyone would have seen it, for two weeks it was ubiqui-
tous, inviting the drawing of beards and moustaches and devil's
horns on Evie's face, and some delinquents had defaced her with
a penis peeking out from the folds of her dress.

The robot was christened Hermione and for a few days they
dragged her round the campus, trying to make her voicebox work,
they were using her to play practical jokes, to deliver challenges to
students in the Physics Department, to stuff her skirt with stink
bombs. They were getting up to all kinds of mischief with her
until, on a lovely evening of delicious sunlight when everyone was
outside drinking beer and white wine and lemonade, and girls in
Laura Ashley frocks let their long hair fall across their faces, and
boys in loon pants and cheesecloth shirts wooed them with tightly
rolled joints assembled on the back of Joni Mitchell albums, they
accidentally pushed Hermione into the shallow water. Bored now,
they waded in and dragged the sodden body across the lake to a
reed-fringed island occupied by Canada geese and ducks. They got
her to stand upright again, propped up by empty wine bottles, cer-
emoniously kissed her and left.

I don't believe there was any malice in what they did, it had
nothing to do with Evie herself; I suppose they had only seen her
as a figure passed along the walkways, one of the eccentrics of the
university whom they would have understood was part of the self-
appointed Zeitgeist to which they did not belong.

When I got to the campus for my tutorial, she was already half
rotting, green with slime from the water. Someone had thrown a
tennis ball at her and caught her in the face. I went to the porter's
lodge and told him they had to get rid of the thing. He said they
already knew about it, it would be rescued and dismantled after
lunch. We had no phones in our house. So Evie, on her way to her
own tutorial, couldn't have missed it.

Psychologically, what could it have meant to her, to see herself
so parodied? I don't know, I never got the chance to find out
because my birthday party was that night.

*

Someone had filled the bathtub with green jelly and furnished it with spoons, but the bath had a scum around it and I don't think anyone ate even a mouthful. Later that night Bobby fell in and wallowed there, looking up at me as if to say, 'If I don't, who will?'

We had a kitchen full of Blue Nun and Hirondelle and a couple of party kegs of beer. There could have been food, French bread and blocks of orange cheddar, but I don't remember any, apart from my birthday cake, which Gillian's mother made. A woman I had never met. Gillian went to Leeds and brought it back on the train. It was a chocolate cake and my name was iced on it in a curly italic script.

The house throbbed, it shook with the new Stones album, *Goats Head Soup*, almost unknown today. Stevie and Denise were not invited but they turned up anyway. He walked in, dressed in ordinary jeans and a T-shirt and a funny little hat and came towards me holding a flat square present which could only have been an LP. 'It's the Dolls. I know you wanted it. We come in peace.'

'What are you doing here?'

'I've always liked you, Adele. There's no reason for us to be enemies.'

'Go. Get out, you're not wanted.'

'Why don't you ask Evie what she thinks? It's only fair.'

Evie was dancing with Dora, both of them flailing their hands about. I went over to her and asked her if she wanted me to tell Stevie and Denise to leave. 'I don't care. I'm tired,' she said. 'I've danced too long. I'm going to lie down for a while.'

'I'll come and check up on you later.'

'Oh, will you? I'd like that.'

The house was full and hot. Many people were arriving that I did not even know, the stairs were full of my birthday presents, books of poetry and pots of eyeshadow and coloured stockings and posters and a dictionary and a novel and a fountain pen and yellow ink and Caran d'Ache crayons and a little glass bird which got trampled on and smashed. We were not pale moths in our white party dresses drifting across night-scented lawns, we were streaked with sweat and blue glitter was flying about and getting in people's eyes. Bottles of Hirondelle and Blue Nun smashed in the kitchen, crowding each other off the table, and spilled their Muscat syrup on to the lino floor.

Around ten-thirty, Emmanuel Fine and his wife turned up. It had been my idea to invite them. I made an appointment and sat in his office and he looked at me with an expression even more bored than when I had last met him, and I said, 'Do you ever come to student parties?'

He looked up from his papers at me as if I was what in fancy restaurants they call the *amuse-bouche*, a little thing you pick up and pop in your mouth before the first, serious course.

'Parties, with ten-shilling bottles of wine and a chunk of cheddar cheese and a roll of French bread? Ha ha, please, grant me some taste in entertainment.'

'It's my twentieth, I thought you might drop in.'

'I never had such an invitation before, no one was bold enough to make such a ridiculous suggestion, which would guarantee refusal, of course. I should come so I might appear fab and groovy? "The gear", is it? No thank you. Most kind, as the English say.'

'Well, I think you should. You say the sciences must talk to the arts, but the faculty won't mix with the students.'

'I have had a drink in your bars, isn't that enough for one lifetime? Do you propose to persecute the poor refugee any further?'

'Where are you from exactly?' I said, because I had grown up among people who came from somewhere else.

'A name from history. You are too young to know anything about that. You have the great privilege of stupidity and ignorance. I envy you children your innocence.'

His jowls drooped on his shirt collar, behind his dusty glasses his eyes swam slowly like small fish.

'But what would you do instead, if you don't come?' I said, ignoring these mysterious pronouncements. I couldn't believe he would have a better invitation than my party.

'Oh, my wife and I will eat a good dinner and then I will retire to my study and at nine o'clock I will join her for an hour of television. Priscilla marks out suitable programmes in the TV magazine she buys every week. You think it's boring, don't you? It *is* boring, a boring life. I don't want any more excitement. I enjoy being bored.'

'I can't offer you boredom.'

'Correctly so. At twenty you wish for drama – no, melodrama. I've had quite enough drama, and melodrama is for nitwits.'

'But if you change your mind, this is the address.'

And yet he did come. We all crowded round Professor Fine's suited figure, his wife in a long black velvet skirt and a red silk blouse, pearl earrings in her ears and a tiny gold watch on a pendant bouncing between her breasts. 'What fun,' she said, looking round.

'Now where,' he said, 'is the birthday girl?'

'I'm here,' I said, trailing glitter, it dropped on his polished black shoes. 'I didn't think you'd turn up.'

'Mrs Fine persuaded me. She says we never go anywhere.'

We showed them round the house, took them to the bathroom with its bathtub filled with jelly. 'Ha ha,' he said, 'very witty. In Prague I once took my clothes off and walked into the student dining room carrying nothing but a large wooden spoon. Can you remember why, darling?' He turned to his wife. 'She wasn't there, of course, but still she is the receptacle of my memory.'

Someone had put on the Dolls. 'Can I have the pleasure?' I said, and held out my hand to him.

'Priscilla? What do you say?'

'Dance, darling, why not? You used to adore the foxtrot.' Her iron-grey hair was frozen in a mass of curls.

'How exhausting,' he said, when the song had finally finished. 'Didn't it go on for a long time? I'm quite out of condition.'

After this, I saw him across the room talking to Bobby, who had arrived with some GLF boys in embroidered Afghan waistcoats and tentative suggestions of lipstick.

Bobby had brought me a gift, an inlaid wooden box. 'I didn't *buy* it, darling, I shoplifted it in Venice because I couldn't possibly afford anything as pretty as this and my friends should only have nice things. I don't know what you could keep in there but I'm sure you'll think of something. Foreskins, perhaps. You look beautiful, by the way, a true star, is that glitter organic with you? Are you manufacturing it in your bloodstream? The young men are *panting* to be star fuckers.' He looked around. 'It's all very lurid. Lovely.'

Bobby laid his brown hand on Fine's tweedy arm. Priscilla held the other ever more tightly. Fine's face had completely lost the heavy *ennui*, Bobby leaned forward and whispered to him. Fine swallowed, I saw the whole gullet moving. Bobby escorted them to the door. I turned back and went into the party.

After this arrival and departure I was very elated and very full of *rush*.

'Do put my present away,' Bobby said. 'I risked detection and arrest to get it, don't let it come to any harm.'

'I'll take it to my room and check up on Evie.'

The door was closed. I knocked. 'It's me, Adele.'

'Oh, come in, come in.'

She was lying askew on the bed reading a red-backed school exercise book. Every child of our generation tore through these in our schooldays; our mothers usually kept them when they were used up as evidence of our handwriting and our gold and silver stars. Printed at the back were the times tables.

In these books we wrote our little essays and handed them in and they came back with our marks in a different-coloured ink. There were paper-bound rough-books for notes and books with a stiffer board for formal compositions. It was a brand called Silvine and on the cover was a crest in the top left-hand corner surrounded by wands of what looked like laurel leaves. Two dotted lines invited you to inscribe your name and your subject. When we got to the sixth form we abandoned them for the sophistication of the ring-bind folder.

There were three more of them on the floor by the bed, bound together with an elastic band, and Evie's packet of cigarettes next to them and a box of Swan Vesta matches.

'Can I have one?'

'Help yourself.'

'Look, are you OK? Do you need anything? If you're cold I could make you a hot-water bottle. I don't mind. If we can find the kettle.'

'You're so kind,' she said. 'I feel looked after and loved.'

Then she reached out and took my hand and it lay in hers. After a moment she picked it up and kissed it.

'I like you so much. Do you remember when we went to Scarborough and we were dancing in our bare feet in the waves?'

'You were, not me, I was just standing on the beach watching you.'

'Was I? I thought you were in the water too.'

'No. I don't like getting cold.'

'Well, you warmed me, didn't you? Under your rabbit coat.'

'Yes, I did.'

'I wish you would warm me now.'

'Of course I will, I'll put the blankets over you.'

'I don't want blankets.' And she drew my hand towards her breast.

I pulled it away.

'Oh, no,' she said. 'I've got it wrong again.'

'What do you mean?'

'Did Dora not tell you?'

'Tell me what?'

'I don't know, maybe I misunderstood her, I feel so muddled up all the time. I just want to sleep so much, but I can hardly ever sleep.'

I took my hand out of hers. 'Of course I like you, Evie, who wouldn't?, but that's not my ... I've got someone, I just can't talk about it at the moment. When I can I promise you will be the first to know. Absolutely the very first.'

'I didn't realise.'

'Dora can be very stupid and wrong at times.' I stood up. 'I have to go now. I'm going to put the blankets over you and close the window. It shouldn't be open, it's the noise from the garden that's stopping you from sleeping.'

Walking down the stairs my hand recalled the cold skin of her breast, its clamminess and whiteness. I rubbed my hand against the fabric of my dress. I don't know what I would have done if she had offered me the nape of her neck, how this story could have ended very differently, but she didn't.

I found Dora outside in the garden, talking to Rose and Gillian.

'What on earth did you tell Evie? What did you say to her? She just told me she fancies me.'

Dora smiled that innocent, delightful smile. 'Oh good, she did pluck up her courage.'

'You're mad, I don't want to sleep with her.'

'Don't you? I thought you did. You're always looking at her.'

'No I'm not.'

'You are so. You eat her with your eyes.'

'Not *her* . . . Look, she's in a terrible state, someone needs to look after the poor girl, you know she can't sleep?'

'I could take care of that,' said Gillian. 'I've got my mother's Valium. I brought some back from Leeds.'

'Why?'

'Mummy gives them to me, just in case. The whole world takes Valium.'

'How many do you have?'

'A dozen, they're in my coat pocket.'

Dora said, 'Give them to me, I'll take them up to her.' I went back into the dark throng of the kitchen where the main dancing was and it was midnight and I was twenty and Gillian unveiled my cake which we went at with knives and spoons and forks, anything we could get our hands on, stuffing it into our mouths and laughing.

'Save some for Evie,' I said.

'I'll take a slice up to her,' said Gillian.

She came back down a few minutes later. 'The Valium has knocked her right out. She's sleeping. I left the cake on the bed.'

'Good.'

And on and on the party went, all night, until all that were left were boys passed out in pools of beer and a girl sitting under a tree in the garden weeping and Dora surveying the wreckage, saying, 'In the morning we'll need a rota to clear all this up.' I took all my presents in my arms and brought them to my room and fell into dreams writing a letter to my darling George, the story of the night, but with no mention of his wounded sister lying coldly in bed all alone.

24

Next morning there were early movements in the house, steps on the stairs, moans and laughter. Outside my door someone coughed as if they had been standing there waiting.

The silence went on, the sun made a watery reluctant appearance through dirty windows without curtains. Then a knock.

'Only me.'

Gillian entered carrying two mugs of tea.

'What are you doing here?'

'I came over to help clear up, but no one's awake. You think you hear noises, but there isn't anyone there, you're all still snoring.' She put a copy of her socialist newspaper on the bed. 'I know you think you don't want to read it but there's loads of interesting articles this week. You might find a minute to pick it up later.'

I had also heard sounds on the stairs and the low voices, and had thought I was dreaming. Outside a huge bird was perched on the windowsill with a twig in its mouth, stooping, flapping, rising. A train began to rumble past on its way to the coast, the low shudder on the rails out of our enclosed valley with its monotony of weather and frequent intermittent showers that rested and fell, rested and fell. I felt for my cigarettes by the bed and lit one. The smoke rose as a column to the ceiling and dissipated. Gillian's eyes followed it too.

'Thanks anyway, but I won't.'

'You can't blame me for trying!'

'I suppose not. What a party that was.'

'I *know*. How did you get the head of the English Department to come? And then he did the Twist, how funny.'

'Is that what he was doing? I thought he'd hurt his knees.'

'Drink your tea, it'll do you good, you must have a bit of a sore head this morning. Don't get up until you're ready, I'll make a start downstairs.'

'You don't need to, there's loads of us here, we can do it later.'

'Yes, I know there is, but I like to help. It will be nice for you to come down and see a little order restored.'

'Isn't order bourgeois?'

'Oh, no. We must keep ourselves neat and tidy, ready for the revolution.'

'You don't honestly believe there's going to be a revolution, do you? You can't, I don't believe you, it's just something they've taught you to say. You didn't use to be like this, you cared about your music and you used to talk about the viola, and now you just don't any more. It upsets me that you don't. Music is the real you, you must know it is.'

'I *do* believe. I feel these things very deeply, Adele. How I used to be seems terribly selfish to me now. People have so very little and they hardly have anything more to hope for because of our awful capitalist system. When you have seen the poor you burn with the disgrace of it, of living in a country with such easy abundance, and then there are girls our age who have lost their children to chest infections because their flats are so damp, condensation running down the walls. And then when you find out that it's not inevitable, that there's an *explanation*, that it all fits and makes sense, I don't see how you could not believe that it will and must change. Take joining the Common Market: everyone thinks it's great but it's just a businessmen's club. There's nothing there for the workers. I can bring you some articles about it if you like.'

'I'm honestly not interested in the Common Market. It's very kind but it's not something I ever think about.'

She looked at me with such pity, as if I, lying in bed, arrogant, smoking, twenty years old that very day, make-up halfway down my face, lying on drifting piles of blue glitter, was as sad a case as her poor dead babies.

'Well anyway, later you're getting your birthday present from me. I didn't bring it in case it got lost in all the mess. I've bought you a record. You might not like it at first, it's not pop, it's classical. Chopin. It's a bit selfish really. But it goes to show I haven't completely forgotten about music.'

'I don't mind. Put a record on now.'

'Can I? What would you like?'

'Anything, you choose.'

She took an LP from its sleeve and looked with dismay at the dust. 'Do you have a record cloth?'

'No.'

'Oh, it's so scratched, you should take better care of your records, really.' She put the record on and came and back to sit next to me. 'So, tea in bed, your birthday. Isn't this nice? Simon and Garfunkel, like the first day.'

'This seems so dated now,' I said. 'So wishy-washy and dreamy.'

'Oh, I'm wrong again. Wrong again.'

'It doesn't matter.'

We could have sat there together for another hour in this peaceful reverie of our youth, of our freshness and innocence, but the tea went right through me and I had to get up for a slash.

'You're covered in something brown,' she said as I got out of bed. I looked down at myself, encrusted in a sticky mass of crumbs and icing.

'It's bloody chocolate cake. Did you put it there?'

'Yes, I thought you might like a nibble before you went to sleep.'

'I didn't even notice it.'

'Never mind.' She sat by the bed looking at me dressing. 'You have a lovely body. Like a painting.'

'But no tits.'

'Yes, it's unexpected. Mine are a burden. They have hardly any sensation when Jim touches them, isn't that strange?'

'Do you really like Jim?'

'Not really.'

'So why do you go out with him?'

'We're not allowed to have special friends who aren't comrades, it limits the choice a bit.'

'What happened to that boy you were going out with at home?'

'Oh, poor Robin. He's so terribly unreconstructed. University hasn't made a bit of difference.'

I got dressed and we came down the stairs from my attic bedroom to the chaotic disorder of the house. Dora was sitting at the kitchen table in her teddy-bear dressing gown eating toast. 'Has anyone checked up on Evie?' she said.

I struggle to tell this story in a way that makes what happened not seem inevitable, but that wasn't the way it felt to any of us. It was inconceivable to us that we were vulnerable, that life itself was fragile. There was a sheen of permanence to everything.

'I haven't seen her since last night.'

Dora said, 'I think I'm going to make Mummy's lovely potato soup.' I made a retching motion with my finger behind her back to Gillian, who laughed with her hand over her own mouth. 'And someone needs to drain the ridiculous jelly from the bath.'

'I'll do it,' Gillian said. 'I don't mind at all.'

'Then I'll take Evie a cup of tea,' I said. If she was awake, I thought I might disobey George's injunction of secrecy and tell her about him and me and she would be happy and I would be happy and he would be, and happiness would rule the world and that would be that.

When I came back down a few minutes later I felt that I had seen something that was not permitted for us to experience; that there had been a mistake. This was not supposed to happen to me twice. Once, Daddy swinging (I did not discover his body, Mummy did, but I ran into the bedroom because I didn't believe it when she came down into the kitchen, chalky, saying, 'Adele, will you make me a cup of tea, your father's just gone and done a terrible thing. I don't think I can even lift the kettle to the sink').

I remember walking back up the stairs with the other girls past a torn poster of a Dalí painting, the melting clock, and bottles skittering down the steps as our feet collided with them, bouncing and breaking as they descended down the runners to the hallway.

'I can do first aid, we learned it in Guides,' Dora said. 'She's probably just unconscious.'

But as we entered the room we all saw it was no good. How was it possible that all that was left was her thin body, her white-blond hair, her kohl-rimmed eyes rolled back in her head and the plate of birthday cake still on the blanket beside her, its fork laid down next to it, rimed with chocolate icing? It was ridiculous, why couldn't you just stick a hand through time and correct it?

25

We had not been lied to by our founders when they said that the university would not act *in loco parentis*. It was Sunday. I rang from the phone box at the end of the road. The switchboard operator, on the other hand, accepted the urgency of the situation and gave me Emmanuel Fine's home number.

'I hope this is important. We're in the middle of Sunday lunch here. If it is to thank me for coming to your party, a note would have been sufficient.'

'A student has died. Evie Pugh. We don't know what to do.'

'Who is she? I don't recognise the name.'

'It's Lorraine Pugh on the files. She's philosophy main, English subsid, but Tony Blount is her supervisor.'

'She is, she was? Is she dead or not dead?'

'No, she's dead. She isn't moving or breathing.'

'Oh dear. I am sorry. You must call the police at once.'

'We've done that.'

'Very good, well that's it really. I'll go into campus later and get her parents' number from the files and drop it off to you.'

'But we thought you would come round and help us. You were only here last night, you know the address, it can't be far, can it?'

'As I say, we're in the middle of lunch and she didn't die on university premises. I don't have any further responsibilities. I could give you Blount's number; try him.'

I rang Tony Blount, also in the middle of Sunday lunch.

'How very unfortunate. But now she's dead, she's not actually my supervisee any more. I don't quite feel that I should take responsibility, it's not really a university matter.'

'But we don't know what to do.'

'Of course you do, you're grown-ups. You say you have already notified the police, and I will have someone inform her parents later today. I think that's it really. You'll manage, you'll see. Please don't cry. No, you *must* stop that at once. The situation will be bound to have its own momentum and you will be carried along with it, there are procedures and I've no doubt they will be followed, and our task is to approach an event like this in a way that behoves our higher principles of poetry and thought. Weeping has its place, of course, but I think of Lawrence at these moments, dying of tuberculosis at the Villa Robermond, so much yet to—'

I put the receiver down on its hook before the money ran out.

The GP turned up, the university locum, a youngish man with a tweed jacket and black leather bag. 'I haven't seen this before but I've heard about it. I deduce that what has happened here is that she's fallen back to sleep, been sick in her throat and choked on her own vomit. The regurgitated food – is it cake of some kind? – is all over her face, you can see where it's dribbled out of her mouth. There will have to be an autopsy. Did she take any pills, do you know? We'll soon find out. Don't worry. This is more common than you'd think, I'm afraid, so let it be a lesson to you. Drugs are awful things when mixed with food or alcohol, but will you listen? I expect you will now.'

Rose and Brian arrived. Brian proved to be a tower of strength. He turned into an efficient system for getting things done in the right order. 'It's just logistics,' he said. 'His father's a major in the army,' said Rose. 'We don't like to talk about it, but Brian has a rather military mind.'

Together with the doctor, Brian arranged for an ambulance to
come and take away her body. He took over all the phone calls. He
closed the door to her room until the police arrived. He became
cheerfully insulting when they got there, which they seemed to
take in a matey way. 'Looking after the girls, are you?' they said.
'Takes a man, doesn't it?'

The Pughs must have been phoned because they arrived later
that evening on a Sunday train and stood by the door with the
long-broken bell, looking up at the windows, banging on a door
that was always kept unlocked, and, when Dora answered, walking
through the hall, looking up the staircase, as if both intimidated by
the size of the house and fastidiously appalled at its decay.

Gillian wanted to make them a cup of tea. 'What a kind girl,'
said Mrs Pugh.

We all looked at her, at this middle-aged, somewhat heavy-set
woman with a blond plait pinned round her head and watery blue
eyes and a Marks and Spencer nylon navy polka-dot dress, who
had once been an object of such desire that she had been trapped
against a wall and attacked and her cotton knickers lowered down
past her suspender belt and a man had rammed her with his cock
while she cried and said, 'Oh, no. No, please.'

Dora said, 'Oh, we're all so sorry,' and hugged her. The two of
them stood together in an embrace and Evie's mother wept on
Dora's shoulder.

'And who are you?' said Mr Pugh.

'I live here as well, I found her this morning and called the university.'

'Is it always such a mess?'

'No, there was a party last night, it was my birthday.'

Mrs Pugh looked up and stared at me. 'My Lorraine will have no
more birthdays. Remember, Dennis, how she loved her jelly and
ice cream? And the doll we bought her, the big doll?'

He nodded, tears in his eyes.

'But *you* have had a birthday. And everyone here will have more
birthdays, including me. It is not right.'

I stared at her solidity, the gold locket round her neck and the cameo brooch at her neckline between the two points of the collar, the two pearl earrings in her ears and the gold watch. The same woman from the lake, only a year and a half ago, once seen through glass from a high window, now bulkily pushing against me, who had a birthday and would have more birthdays.

We took them upstairs and showed them Evie's room.

Mrs Pugh kept patting her hair with her hand as if she feared that it was not her plait that might come undone but her head itself might fall off. Mr Pugh picked up one of the records that was lying on the floor and turned, very suddenly, into the kind of father that many of us were familiar with, as if he had no idea at all how to express whatever it was he was feeling and resorted to playing a character from the television.

'It's rock and roll that is the evil in this world,' he said. 'I'd send all the long-hairs to prison on dry bread and hard labour.' He ripped the album cover in two with his hands.

'Actually, that's my record. Evie borrowed it last week.'

'Which one of you is Evie?' He looked round at the room of girls.

'It's what we called her, we never knew her by another name.'

'Why is that then?'

'Stevie called her Evie.'

'And who is Stevie when he's at home?'

'Her boyfriend. No, her ex-boyfriend.'

'Well, I never heard of a boyfriend. She never said anything to us.'

'I don't know how we're going to break it to Georgie,' said his wife. 'He thought the world of his sister.'

At the thought of George I began to cry so loudly that I leaned my forehead against the wall of Evie's room.

'What's the matter with that one?' Mr Pugh said. 'She's taking it terribly hard.'

Dora looked at me and raised her eyebrows. Gillian said, 'Oh, cry, Adele, cry, it's good for you.'

Mrs Pugh looked round the room at all of her daughter's belongings and said, 'I don't think we want this stuff at all, it's not her.
She came back that Christmas with her beautiful hair all cut off
and it was like she was a different person. I don't believe she was
any happier, do you, Dennis?'

'I don't know, these are women's conversations.'

'She *wasn't* happy,' Dora said.

'Why was that, dear?'

Dora began to advance an explanation and I left the room and
went to my own, lay down on the bed and watched the birds flying
round outside the window, looking for shelter from the falling
night.

When I came back in, I heard Mrs Pugh saying to her husband,
'Didn't she take the books, Dennis? I was sure she had them. I've
looked high and low.'

'She must have brought them back at Easter, they'll be at home
somewhere.'

26

Who is to blame?
I, said the fly. I made her die.

'It's your fault, Dora. Why on earth did you have to tell her I wanted to sleep with her? She must have gone into a black depression, humiliated like that. I'll never forgive you.'

'It was an easy mistake to make, let's be honest. You know everyone thinks you're gay, don't you?'

'No, why would I?'

'You should think about it. Anyway, rationally it has to be Gillian's fault, after all she gave her both the Valium *and* the chocolate cake. She admitted it to the police. She's lucky they didn't charge her with handing out drugs without a prescription.'

Gillian said, 'I know, I know, how can I live with myself? I've been so stupid.'

'Don't be ridiculous, you were only trying to be kind, you're a kind girl, everyone knows that. Evie died of your *oughts* and *shoulds*, Dora, of your fucking moral experiments.'

'What about you? Do you think you're so innocent in all of this? You left her alone after that massive rejection.'

'But it was my birthday and my party.'

'You could have spared an hour.'

'I didn't know! How could I have known?'

'Anyway, I don't think Evie wanted to live, I think she was suicidal. It was suicide, in a way, and could have been prevented.'

'Well why didn't you say something before? If you thought she was suicidal, you could have mentioned it.'

'We did talk about her going into hospital for a few days, just to calm her a bit, she brought it up herself. But I thought it was a terrible idea: you don't want to put yourself into their hands, they'll do awful things to you those psychiatrists.' She began to talk of something called the Anti-Psychiatry Movement. 'Perhaps the insane are really well and we are the mad ones.'

'Oh, shut the fuck up, Dora, you do talk absolute drivel at times.'

'What exactly are you doing here, Adele?' she said, looking at me with her calm, serious face. 'I mean in all honesty why are you even at a university? You have no real interest in the life of the mind, do you? You seem to operate on some primitive instincts, hunches, intuition, guesswork. I've watched you and you still haven't a clue how to *think*, I mean to be rational. There is something about you that's ... unvarnished. Do you even wash properly?'

I burst into tears.

'You don't understand. You ...'

How can I talk about Daddy hanging by the neck, the light going out in the world, wanting to be loved and being afraid to be? How can I talk about George who loves me but won't say so? What do I say about our nights together on the river and what we do? Why is everything always in hiding?

'See how you react so emotionally to criticism? That's exactly what I mean.'

Gillian said, 'What a horrid thing to say. You've really upset Adele. You should apologise.'

Stevie came round. 'It's my fault. I take all the blame.'

He sat in the kitchen like a collapsed string puppet, his arms and legs askew on the chair. We all wanted him to be the guilty party, we needed a scapegoat and now we had one, we loaded him with our sins and drove him out.

And I have to admire the way he just sat there and took it, while we subjected him to our mock-trial with its predetermined guilty verdict. 'If you hadn't turned up last night she wouldn't have needed to go up to her room, she might have stayed a while longer,' I said.

'Yes, you're right. I'm sorry. I'm so sorry.'

He dropped out that week. He went back to Newcastle and we heard no more of him. Dora-the-efficient took Evie's clothes to a charity shop. A week later I saw Denise wearing them, walking down the street in a green chiffon blouse with jeans as if the stupid bitch thought she could turn herself into something other than a nonentity by what she *wore*, of all things.

She continued to pretend to be Evie until all of us left and she remained, as if, having taken on the clothes of someone else, she was stuck in them.

27

Our final year at university was spent under the shadow of Evie's death. We were the same people we had been, but for all of us it was the first time that a person our own age had died and we had been implicated. Her death left us less sure of ourselves, less invincible, but with a spurious wisdom that we had been through tragedy together. That we were darker, more mature, wiser individuals. We wore our sadness as a new set of more sophisticated clothes.

I felt decapitated. But eventually I grew a new head, doesn't everyone?

One by one we all moved out of the house because of bad memories and the embarrassment of meeting every morning in the kitchen, making tea and eating toast by the gas fire, those same guilty faces from the Sunday morning in May. Eventually Rose and her gang took it over, it became the politicos' house, and Gillian moved into my room.

George grew too violent even to talk to on the phone. I was afraid of him and his drum kit. The last time I saw him, I hitchhiked to London and waited all day and all night on the barge for him to come, but he was up in Yorkshire in our old house, packing up Evie's things, and when he eventually arrived home he was drunk, he threw her record player into the river with all her records and her books and I was holding him from behind, round the waist, trying to kiss him. But he was raving and I knew then that our life together was sunk under Kew Bridge like her stuff.

In the autumn of our third year I started sleeping with a very nice boy called Peter Warren. He was a history student who did something immeasurably strange to us in those days, he shaved his hair into a skinhead buzz-cut. He would not talk about why he did it except to shrug and say that long hair got in the way, he preferred his face in the mirror like this; he was an assiduous shaver of his own facial hair. He just didn't like hair. It was the way of the future. I was fully absorbed by the nape of his neck.

In the middle of the term I came down with glandular fever. I slept up to seventeen hours a day and Peter looked after me. In my long dream-winter I was barely alive, excused from my tutorials, submerged in an underwater world where Evie and Stevie floated through a series of cloudy situations which were more real than the mattress on the floor, the green-striped Indian bedspread, the two-bar electric fire, the pile of our clothes in the corner, the posters on the wall, the bare floorboards, the smell of rain outside the window on a cement yard and Peter sitting next to me, reading about the English Civil War, that billiard-ball head bent over his book.

My eyes would open for a few minutes, he'd say, 'You OK, love? Want anything to eat? Cup of tea?'

'I'm cold.'

'I'll climb in and warm you up.'

We hardly ever had sex, I was too tired.

When I recovered, towards the end of term, I felt that, like animals in hibernation, I had narrowly survived the winter. I came out of the cocoon as a different Adele.

Bobby noticed. 'A certain crude, over-bright light has gone out in you. You are more muted and the hard look in your face has gone. Which I rather liked. Never mind.'

*

We graduated. As if we were running along a vast plain, we had suddenly hit an abyss where the land gave out and we were still only twenty-one.

We took it very hard. What I did was to go away. Gillian said I was running away. Gillian had become more opinionated and moralising. The balance had tipped between us, and she no longer saw me as her mentor but someone to be pitied for my immaturity.

I know that the dead are supposed to live in our hearts and as long as someone remembers us we are still alive. They say this at funerals. But we were all moving on into the future, and in the ground in Wolverhampton Evie was altering beyond all recognition. She would resemble the contents of a rotting compost heap, maggots by now had eaten her eyes, a soft pile of decomposition spread over the indigestible bones. Cold and alone. The horror of her death would not leave me. I remembered and remembered her, but the nape of the neck was bare vertebrae.

I went to America. I felt an urge for the wide-open country and far horizon that had grown up in the claustrophobia of the campus.

It was possible in those days to go and work on American fairgrounds, to be a ride operator in coastal resorts. I was down below the Mason–Dixon Line, dressed in orange shorts and orange shirt, handling the levers of a circle of toy aeroplanes which rode round and round a few feet above our heads. The little children spun in the air and screamed with joy or terror while their parents took photographs. People the size of mountain ranges carried buckets of fried chicken and drank from wells of root beer.

It was very, very interesting. This was just after Watergate and the boys were coming home from Vietnam. At the bumper cars the white moms and pops shouted, '*Turn the wheel like Daddy does!*' And the kid turned the wheel. The black moms and pops stood helpless. They all came on the bus from Baltimore, the kids never even saw the driver. The driver was white and Daddy was black and the things Daddy did were not the same things the white man did.

The amusement-park owner would not let blacks operate his

machines. They swept and carried away garbage. We summer ride operators lived in trailers and earned minimum wage. I saved all of it. I ate mustard sandwiches for lunch and got even thinner.

After two months at the fairground I set out to hitchhike one night on the beginning of a highway where Chryslers and Fords cruised like finned fish across the continent. The night air was balmy and the thinnest peel of moon rose over the shoreline of the Atlantic.

In later years, when everyone turned against America, when *America* had become a dirty word for Europeans, I would remember the cars and trucks I had travelled in on that epic journey, and the kindness of strangers who bought me meals in truck stops and told me their life stories. I saw a country's young men mutilated. I saw them without arms, in chairs and with canes, with prosthetic limbs and cocks that didn't move any more.

I did not go in a straight line but wandered up and down the states.

One night I was at a truck stop in Montana. A rancher with a shot deer strapped to the roof of his vehicle, its killed eyes glazed over, drove me from state line to state line. We spoke long into the night about what freedom meant. He was visiting his handicapped niece in a town called Angelus, or that is what I remember but I have never found it on a map.

The sky seemed like a cloak pierced with rents for the stars and the moon. He was a Dust Bowl child. The Dust Bowl was the greatest man-made disaster in the history of America. They over-farmed those prairies and when the rains never came the earth dried, could not hold any moisture. The sky turned black at noon, children died of dust TB, it happened to his little sister, she was three years of age when she was taken. He said, 'We have a responsibility to the land, to be good husbands to it. I don't mean the government, I mean each individual man.' A rack above his head held his shotgun and in the glove compartment there were two pistols. 'I only eat what I can shoot,' he said. 'If I can't find an animal for my food, then I eat vegetables I grow and store them in the winter. I make a garden every year.'

He pulled over to the side of the road and we kissed for a long time. The whole universe was shot with light and brilliance, bars of pink in the sky, irradiated vapour trails, a dawn like it was the dawn of the world and nothing from horizon to horizon, no houses or the glow from a distant city. If he had murdered me, he would have buried me out in the badlands and I would never have been discovered, but those were not his intentions. He was a lonely widower, the kindest of men, armed, dangerous, compassionate, ecological, a survivalist. I have never forgotten him. I count him among my lovers though we had no sex, we didn't even undress each other, just a slow smooch at sunrise on the plains.

I thought of Evie all the time. I told the rancher about her and how she had died and what had happened that night and my part in it. He said, 'She didn't die from no piece of cake. Your friend is right, she had a troubled mind. You know, you complicate things too much, you think too much. Is that how they go on in Europe? I've never been there.'

You have no idea about the badlands, how they pacify the brain then make hallucinations. A European eye cannot cope with such monotony without fabricating illusions.

But then I reached the Pacific coast and that was even more interesting and for a while I forgot, and I turned round and came back again, to New York, where, after Montana and Wyoming, I saw a transvestite in silver lipstick on the subway and was in the country of the Dolls. I loved New York. It was Daddy and Yankel's true city. I came alive there, back to life.

PART TWO

28

All of us eventually wound up in London, apart from Peter Warren, who got a First (as did Brian, who turned up for his finals after all) and went to Edinburgh to do an MA.

In London Dora once again organised a house for us. It was a squat in Newington Green, near a roundabout and opposite a chip shop. Everything was poor, we were poor. Under that roof we waited for something, for the change that was obviously coming. Something I had seen in New York. I had returned with a Patti Smith album.

Those early years were the ones in which we were building our future lives from almost nothing. We had lost all our student privileges, had been expelled from Utopia, and we were young women on the dole. Bobby had moved back home to his parents in Muswell Hill.

He came one day to visit us with an American boy from Long Island called Howie who wore red Converse All-Star baseball boots and jeans rolled up at the bottom.

Howie said it probably wasn't possible to stay up all night in London but he would try. He once sent Bobby out to find him heroin to see if it could be done and Bobby obligingly came back with some. They went to my room and injected it and came back looking relaxed. Bobby said, 'That was lovely but I don't think I'll do it again, it was *too* good.' At two in the morning, Howie demanded chocolate cake. Bobby exploded. 'Find chocolate cake in the middle of the night? Don't you *get it*? Drugs are one thing but all the shops are bloody *closed*.'

Howie was probably what we were all waiting for, he was a visionary. He told me to cut my hair so I cut my hair. He told me to wear drainpipe jeans and a leather jacket so I wore drainpipe jeans and a leather jacket. He said, 'You should be a singer in a band.' I said, 'I can't sing.' He said, 'You don't have to sing, just shriek.' I said, 'I can do that.' For a few months I was lead singer in an all-girl punk band playing upstairs in pubs during the heyday of the Slits and Cunning Stunts and Siouxsie and the Banshees. Howie was correct, you did not need to sing, just bawl, and I could bawl. Me at my zenith.

I was in a very androgynous phase in my life, when I wore my hair short, in a quiff like a fifties American car mechanic, and my jeans were rolled. My lips were very dry, they flaked. I was cold all the time and discontented. I heard about my George from an amplified distance through Howie. He was getting famous but not as a drummer, he'd left that line of work. He was still in the music business, but he managed a few bands.

If we had had the internet I would have spent my time obsessively looking him up, I would have stalked him in cyberspace, but he existed only as rumours and traces. Sometimes there was an item about him in the music papers and his face, Evie's face, with his arm round some act he had taken on, and when they were female I cried.

I remembered the night of the New York Dolls when he had put his hand on my leg as we sat on the floor and his breath was on my face and I tried to see, when he turned his head, the nape of his neck but his hair was still long. Now he had cut it and I wanted to rotate the head in the photographs.

*

Howie went back to New York and became the doorman at Dance-teria. There is documentary evidence on YouTube that he discovered Madonna.

The band broke up and I got an entry-level job eventually on a tedious little magazine for the Canal Boat Association, subbing articles about locks and sluices. Dora decided she would retrain to be a youth worker.

'You see, there can't be any lasting answers until we completely rethink how we see young people in society. All our institutions just want to socialise them in preparation for them going into the workforce and becoming obedient little members of society. Adults have to accept young people as social equals and not kids expected to play adult roles only in those areas that are convenient for us, like the army.'

Shut up.

Rose went into the law. She became a barrister so she could defend the workers against the crimes of the state. She had some mysterious Establishment connections she would never explain to us, access to a higher world of privilege. Dora thought her mother was an Honourable, related to an old Yorkshire landed family, who had rebelled against her class and gone off to Spain and come back with a journalist. 'But didn't you think,' she said of her old rival, 'that she always had that sheen of class confidence? Wasn't it a bit funny that they went on summer holidays to Scotland and stayed with friends? I mean, who has friends who could put up a whole family? My parents were both teachers. We had a caravan and went to Wales.'

And we became even more suspicious of Rose when she announced that she had tickets for a box at the opera. It was 1977 and the last week we lived in the house in Dalston. The council had turned off the water, they were trying to get rid of us. We had not washed for days, we smelled of damp clothes, mouldy bread, sour milk, mildewed shoes. Our hair was greasy and filthy. But everyone had an outfit suitable for the opera or could lay hands on one. We bought silk opera coats in second-hand-clothes shops, and paste diamond necklaces. Dora decided to wear a pre-war men's dinner jacket and a tight short black skirt over knee-high leather boots. I had a bias-cut satin dress in oyster. Gillian turned up in a cocktail dress borrowed from her mother. Rose was in a red, embroidered Chinese bed jacket with a feather-boa collar. Only Brian arrived in jeans and donkey jacket.

The market at Covent Garden was derelict. The fruit and vegetables had gone south of the river but the developers hadn't yet moved in, for it was that strange hinge period, between eras, when men still wore flares and wide-lapelled jackets and kipper ties and the prevailing decorative colours were brown, orange and avocado. The opera was *The Magic Flute*. Gillian brought the score with her. 'I've been before,' she said, 'but never a box, not even the stalls, just up there where you feel a lot of vertigo. I wouldn't have come, of course, if the tickets weren't from Rose, but she wouldn't see me wrong, would she?'

As we waited for the curtain to rise, stinking in our moth-eaten clothes, looking down at the middle-aged bourgeoisie with their programmes and chocolates on their laps and their eyes raised looking through opera glasses, a spotlight swept round the auditorium and came to rest on the box opposite ours.

'It'll be us next,' I said, preparing to rise and wave. 'We should have all worn tiaras.'

'Isn't that the Queen Mother?' said Gillian.

'Bloody hell, it is,' cried Brian, and rising to his feet, shook his fist at the woman in canary-coloured taffeta and the Crown Jewels on her grey perm. 'Royal parasite! Troops out! Victory to the IRA!'

'Shut up, Brian,' Rose said. 'We'll get thrown out.'

'Who cares? The bloody *Magic Flute* is away with the fairies. Masonic piffle.'

But Rose had already ordered and paid for interval drinks for us all and I wasn't losing my free gin and tonic, so I pulled Brian's donkey jacket hard and he fell back into his seat.

At the interval I glimpsed a familiar figure at the bar, drinking a glass of champagne. He wore a white polo-neck sweater, a navy smoking jacket with frogging, dusty black patent shoes and an ivory silk scarf. It was Professor Fine, his other hand lightly held over Bobby's buttocks. I turned away and did not draw it to anyone's attention. It upset me, I don't know why. I wanted Bobby to fall in love with a boy his own age and be normal. I wanted him to be happy and I did not see how he could be happy with Emmanuel Fine, his study, his glasses, his first editions, his boredom and sarcasm and his wife who wanted to go out more, away from the television set.

29

And then we were evicted from the house and went our separate ways. The old times at university finally closed up, that whole tent folded. The first person I lost touch with was Gillian, who was said to be working full-time for the Party as their office administrator. Music had turned to vapour. I saw her once in the early eighties on Tottenham Court Road, wheeling a brown baby and looking harassed and red-faced, still in her workers' dungarees, but she caught my eye across the stream of traffic and she cried out, 'Adele, Adele!'

A bus came past and I sidestepped the situation by getting on to it. It was not a nice thing to do but, turning back on the platform, I saw her standing in the street with a small hand raised from the pushchair, an infant fist emerging from the lemon-coloured blanket, its dummy hurled into the gutter in an act of frustrated rage, I suppose at being ignored while Gillian was waving at me, and she knelt down to pick it up from amongst the empty crisp packets and the other detritus of the city street. Her bent head, that untended and untendable jumble of curls, was already greying. I felt like such a heel, such a miserable low-life, that I jumped off the bus again as soon as it reached the traffic lights, but she had disappeared, maybe down a side street or just into the thronging crowd passing the electrical shops with their peculiar new goods such as computers and Sony Walkmans.

The further away we were from Evie's death, the more we wondered if we would carry her along with us or leave her behind in our shared past. We made new friends who had never known Evie, and then Evie became a legendary figure, someone who, when we three were together – me, Dora, Rose – shut out everyone else. We had no contact with her family. Still our conversation turned again and again to the night she died and we worried away at that old bone as if a dog had dug it up from a broken grave.

Bobby, our aesthete, got a job at American Express. I'm not sure what he did there. He went to work in the West End and wore a perfect dark suit and gleaming white shirt, with a silk tie my father would have killed for, in maroon with a tiny pattern of lavender seahorses. Because Bobby was born a London person he had no need, like the rest of us, to put down roots. The city lit up with the available spaces in which he could operate. He never had what I thought of as a home, he was a house sitter and dog walker and cat stroker/feeder for people with nice houses and flats.

He rang me at work in 1982 and asked me if I would come for supper because something had happened and he wanted an old friend to sit with him. Bobby had always been oblivious to the political events that were taking place, he never read a newspaper or watched TV and only listened to classical music on the radio. He had been walking past the bandstand in Regent's Park at lunchtime and he had been about to take his silk scarf from round his neck, lay it on the grass and sit down to enjoy the music, when the band struck up one of the tunes from *Oliver!*.

'And you know I can't bear show tunes. So I pressed on, and just heard the horrible blast when I was at the other end of the park. But that was enough, darling. The bodies of the police horses and the bandsmen strewn about in the trees, oh, the poor horses, the poor, poor beasts. I never learned to ride, I wanted to badly enough but Daddy would not permit it. All day when I close my eyes I see those broken hooves in the grass and now I'm afraid to go to sleep. Darling, I feel so horribly shaken, like a clock thrown against the wall. Explain it to me. *What* is going on? Who would want to blow up a bandstand? Someone who hates music? Surely not?'

We had climbed out of the window on to the balcony with cups of tea and sat out amongst the scent of the nicotiana plants. In the darkening garden below, cats passed and repassed across the lawn. A church reared up, bulky, losing definition, dissolving into the bosky air, and humidity hung in our clothes.

It was a perfect evening except there had been murder at lunchtime. The city felt febrile and anxious. Waste bins vanished. Station concourses overflowed with rubbish. There was nowhere to leave luggage. London was a series of terrorist-made inconveniences. Bombs and bombs and bombs. Our ears became attuned for potential explosive devices.

'I will not go to the Heath tonight.'

'Oh no, you mustn't. Have an early night, you must be terribly shaken up.'

'I am, and anyway the Heath in summer has certain limitations. Summer always brings out the Australians. They *flood* the market. They will only venture out of their Earl's Court bedsits in the summer, they're used to practising their buggery at opportune moments at barbecues on those deafening beaches of theirs. They don't have the talent of the British to sodomise behind a bush in the November drizzle. In fact I don't think I shall go to the Heath again. One must grow up.'

'I don't see the attraction of it, I never have.'

'Really? And you have never seemed particularly romantic. But perhaps you do want a suitor, standing at the door with a corsage and chocolates.'

'Oh, Bobby, what are you going to do with your life?'

'I don't suppose that I shall do anything with it at all. Why should I? In fact I know that I shall do precisely nothing. What I *do* do, I do terribly well already so what is the point of all that striving? Money is the thing. Having plenty of money so you can just lie on the sofa with a glass of wine and watch the patterns the shadows make on the wall. That's enough for me. Of course it has to be financed, more or less everything does. I'm not an unworldly aesthete, Daddy didn't bring me up to be one of those. I can't stay at American Express for ever, it just doesn't pay enough for me to be more idle. I have a plan.'

'What plan?'

As upset as he had been a few minutes ago, now he smiled and looked across the treetops.

'Well, you see, I have heard – that is, it has been drawn to my attention by one of my colleagues – that there is what you might call an "agency" that could suit me perfectly. You just have to take the tube to Heathrow and there they are, in their hotel rooms, waiting for you. In and out, they pay by credit card – I have to carry the machine with me – and then the agency pays me at the end of the month, once their commission is taken off. It's such a perfect arrangement. No hanging around on the busy Heath with those bloody shivering surfer boys. Apparently sometimes they even send a taxi for you. Mostly Arabs, I believe, but that's all right, I don't mind one bit – anyone, really, as long as they're clean and don't impose too much with the need for conversation about their dreary businesses or their uninteresting wives in yashmaks or whatever they're called. Oh, just *look* at your face, darling. And there I was thinking that of all people *she* would understand because she understands implicitly the concept of the means to the end. Isn't that how you got to university?'

'But it's not the same thing at all. Wouldn't it . . . I don't know, eat away at your soul or something?'

'My soul is not so fragile that it can't withstand being bummed by a businessman from Iowa. Have you never had bad sex? That's all it is. You can be such a provincial bourgeois at times, do you realise? Look how you ran away from poor Evie, didn't even try it once! Darling, I've always understood that sex is basically trans-actional. Each of you wants something from the other in exchange for whatever it is you have to give. Since I was a child that's how it's always been. For sweets and ice creams at first, and then for money. I got all kinds of things. I got a car, you remember the Hillman Imp, surely?'

'You said your father gave that to you.'

'My father? Don't be ridiculous. He wouldn't give me a rope to climb out of a building if it was on fire unless he had extracted a promise that I would tie my own hands with it when I was safe. When you were growing up, did you know in your heart that your parents loved you?'

I considered this for a moment and in the answer flooded.

'Yes, of course, I was their princess.'

'Ha! I thought so. You see, I don't think that what Daddy has ever felt for me is love, or if it is love, it is a kind so all-devouring you must protect yourself from it, you will be eaten alive. I think it's probably because of him that there is a certain coldness in me that I don't feel I'm at liberty to do anything about. I adore my friends, but giving oneself heart and soul to another? No, I can't really imagine it. Too inconvenient, too messy, too much like dealing with Daddy. I think I would become all too subservient if I ever fell in love, and fight like anything against that. My condition is a wonderful thing, it means I can sleep with anyone really. It's all going to be fine. But tell me about you: any scrummy boys you're seeing?'

'Oh, there's always someone. I don't have any trouble finding them, but they bore me so.'

So Bobby rose, through the eighties, seemingly immortal, advancing into his mid-thirties in Jermyn Street shirts and Crockett & Jones shoes. Smelling of Eau Sauvage. Often photographed in newspapers sitting at a table at La Gavroche, captioned *unknown companion*. Maturing into a better-dressed version of his father, with smoother features, some small tucks done to his eyelids, a fine line tattooed by the lashes. Carrying a kidskin man-bag, wrapped by a strap around his wrist, containing his card machine.

He had turned into the kind of person whom the papers

describe as 'always jetting off'. To islands and coasts, villas and small palaces, to vanish for a month and return, bumped into on Bond Street carrying a copy of the *International Herald Tribune* as an accessory, a fiction of his style. 'I sometimes skim it, darling, occasionally they like the pretence of intelligent conversation for a few minutes before we get on with the business at hand. I'm investing everything I make, I shall be retired by forty and rich. Then I think I really will buy that island in the far-flung Cyclades. Put three summers hence in your diary. We'll see if we can track down old Rami, too, wherever he is.'

30

When I met his father, coming out of the hospital lift in 1991, entering the corridor that smelled of boiling gravy and sterility and blood, he picked up a finger and pointed it at me.

'I recognise you. The Hebrew fiancée. Why did you desert Jahandar? It might have been different if you had been true to your word and married him.'

'I'm afraid that was just a deception. I was never his girlfriend, we never as much as kissed. He wanted to please you, that's all.'

'I don't believe it. I am Persian. Persian men are *strong*.'

He gazed at me with a lascivious stare as if he were judging a beauty contest. 'You have a little look of Ava Gardner about you. That is a woman. I sold her a carpet once. Are you sure you are not related? Or maybe Elizabeth Taylor. Yes, you have the same mouth. You have a very beautiful mouth, do you know that?'

'Jahandar has never slept with a woman.'

'Outrageous. No son of mine is a kooni. Something has brought this about, maybe an injury to the head.'

'He has been gay all his life, he says he has always known.'

'How is it possible to know such a thing? I did not know I was a lover of women at three years old. I tell you, it's brain damage.'

His ridiculous trilby hat, his plump fingers, his suede loafers. I felt mildly sorry for him. He threw his hands into the air, an expression of helplessness. I was reminded of my own father, the same slightly womanly emotions. Both of them in different ways sensualists; for Bobby's father it was sex, for mine it was guzzling and smoking.

'And what about now?' he said. 'You could still marry him for appearances, for the community.'

'Nobody is going to pander to your hypocrisy. We love Bobby as he is.'

'How? The little whore is covered in brown blotches and his body stinks.'

31

When Bobby died he left me the house in Cornwall. This did not suit his father at all and of course he contested the will, and when that didn't work he threatened me, he tried to wear me down but no one who is the daughter of Harry Ginsberg will be robbed of bricks and mortar. He made angry phone calls in the middle of the night, and he rang my employers and told them I was a thief and a tart, but I was about to be made redundant so it didn't matter what he said about me and no one would have believed him. Because to them he was exactly what Bobby had said, a funny foreigner, just a wog with an expense account.

We had left university in the middle of a recession, and struggled to start careers. In the end we had all managed to find a berth somewhere, even if our jobs were not what we had ever expected. As we approached forty, here came another recession. Rose had predicted a crisis of capitalism from which it would be impossible to recover, that the whole rotten apparatus of the bourgeois state would crumble in front of our eyes, that the workers would seize power on a wave of pan-European revolution. She had said this with such conviction that I half believed her, not understanding economics, but when there was no revolution she said these things sometimes took longer than one expected.

From the Canal Boat Association I had risen and risen to become the features editor on a magazine founded in the nineteenth century by men whose faces and true unfathomable natures were obscured by whiskers; black, blond and russet moustaches held in place by specialised wax; feet shod in highly polished Chelsea boots. Smokers of stinking cigars, devourers of steaks and chops with strong sauces, admirers of Jerome K. Jerome, whose portrait hung above the receptionist's desk (unmanned, we couldn't afford a meeter-and-greeter since no one ever came, unless it was writers delivering their copy and hoping to get in out of the cold to hang around waiting to be offered coffee and biscuits). We were the last gasp of Grub Street.

Illustrious past and present contributors included George Bernard Shaw, P. G. Wodehouse and Alan Coren. We had a small, loyal, ageing American and Canadian subscription base and I had once almost tempted Saul Bellow to write for us. When he was in London I took him out to lunch at Rules and gave him our pitch. Bellow was the kind of guy not safe in taxis or under the long white tablecloth of the first-class restaurant. I think he liked the food and he enjoyed the fustiness of our surroundings but he looked at the pages I showed him and said, 'Give it to Updike, he understands this Waspy material.'

I had a golfball electric typewriter, and we even had a fax machine through which distant contributors' copy would roll out impressively like a simple printing press, as if it was already typeset. One notorious hack was so late with his pieces, so insistent that his fax machine was broken or ours was, or we were out of paper, that he would extend his deadline until almost the moment when we were supposed to go to press and it would be too late to mark him up, let alone edit him. One day I called his bluff and told him it had arrived. 'Marvellous,' I said, 'terrific stuff, everyone has read it and we're not going to change a word.'

There was a long silence at the end of the phone. An ontological moment, said the managing editor, who was supposed to take care of budgets and expenses and issue the paltry cheques to our writers but who spent a few hours of the working day at his desk perfecting the art of the dactylic hexameter.

At the other end of the line I heard, 'Well, you know, I'm not entirely satisfied with it, just let me do a few tweaks, I'll have it over in half an hour.'

'No, no,' I said, 'believe me, it's *perfect*.'

When the magazine came out, he said, 'You didn't publish my piece. What happened?'

'It was just *too* good,' I said, 'it showed up the rest of the dross.'

He stood there in his deerstalker hat, many-pocketed mackintosh, checked suit with flared trouser, a large stubborn ginger figure from an earlier age.

'OK,' he said, finally. 'Can I have that in writing?'

But I was beyond caring and so I typed it out on the golfball typewriter, tappety-tap, it made a high-speed sound like mice at the keys. I loved that machine. I handed the sheet to him and he disappeared, into the early nineties, the decade where self-reinvention ran finally out of steam.

Had the job of editor become vacant, I might have got it after that stunt. Nobody in the building had any feel for advertising, including the advertising manager, who spent lunchtimes nipping out to the London Library to borrow a book for his doctorate on Thomas Pynchon. All the schmoozing business was left to me, I was the only one who was considered to have any talent for it. The owner got in someone to analyse our readership with a view to targeting advertising. Our regular purchasers were aged fifty-five-plus and living on fixed incomes. We went bust in the recession.

After Bobby's will finally cleared probate and the old man was defeated and went back to Muswell Hill (and the Persian-carpet shop had a perennial closing-down sale in the window without ever closing), I went down to Cornwall to take a look at the place, to find out if it was worth anything.

I had refused to reach the point in my life, common to a lot of women I knew, when I was supposed to panic about being alone. It was true that I had always dealt with relationships carelessly; if anyone was unable to commit it was me. I have been desired inopportunely, I have been propositioned on buses and tube trains, walking down the street smoking, sitting in a café with a cup of tea and a lipsticked stub in the ashtray, in airport departure lounges and of course at parties. I have had my share of drunkenly driving off with a man to a flat and a bed and a morning cup of tea and a goodbye on the doorstep. See you around, baby.

I had been that person and for a long time I thought I would always be that person, but you get older, your waist is no longer thin, you get colds more easily, you think you would rather stay at home and read than cross the city to get to a party. And these opportunities dry up without you even noticing. This freedom you wanted is an illusion, it's nothing to do with you, it's about being young. It's all about your unlined face and perky tits.

It was more tiring to sit in front of the mirror and put on my mascara and draw an accurate line above my lids and dash the blusher in the right spot on my cheeks. Brush my hair and struggle into my tights, my clothes, my shoes.

'Whatever you do,' said my mother, 'don't let yourself go. Because I can see you're letting yourself go, and you'll never find a man that way. I can see grey hairs at the back of your head. You need to take care of that. Put your war paint on, dear, then you can face the world.'

'I don't mind about not finding a man.'

'You're such a women's libber, much good it'll do you in the long run. I've been without your father for twenty years and it's not such a bed of roses, you'll see. I've looked for a boyfriend but who wants to be a nursemaid to an old man? And the young ones aren't interested, are they?'

'Oh, Mummy.' She had come more and more to my attention. Daddy seemed now like a character from a half-forgotten early-sixties film.

*

The last time I had seen the town was at the end of the seventies, when a crowd of us tried to hold a ceremony which Rami had devised to commemorate Evie. We lit a bonfire on the beach and chanted incantations, her spirit was supposed to be in the waves and the sails of the yachts but it wasn't, it was in a cemetery in Wolverhampton beneath a marble stone the colour of pink brawn and her name in gold. LORRAINE PUGH 1954–1974.

I took the train along the sea at Dawlish, across the Tamar to Par and came out to find no taxis waiting. An elderly woman was getting into a mini-cab and I knocked on the window and asked the driver how I could get away and he said there *was* no way, unless you pre-booked, or rang the office from the phone box or waited for the bus which came every two hours. But the old lady asked where I was going, and it was to the same town so she said she would let me share with her.

We came down by a different route from the one I had travelled long ago, and I saw the estuary laid out like a hand, with the ships lying at anchor in the harbour under breezy skies, and the pines framing the scene, as if to encourage you to think, fleetingly, that you had taken the train from Paddington and, without crossing any sea, had found yourself in the Mediterranean. The houses were dragee pink and powder blue and lemon yellow and straw green in the sunshine.

Always I felt the mood of exultation at this sight. It was before the internet. Only advertising executives had mobile phones. Even if I had had a phone, there was no signal. The world was swallowed up behind me and I was in a place where the only way I could be reached was by letter.

They dropped me off at the slipway to the foot ferry and I walked back up through the town along the esplanade, past the church, pub, butcher's, fishmonger's, picture gallery, knick-knack shops, fudge shop, tea rooms, and what I noticed was that four restaurants had opened since I was last there. Silver-service establishments with handwritten menus in the window advertising lobster, scallops, crab, fresh sea bass and bream, in garlic and butter sauce, or Pernod sauce, and Caesar salad to start followed by sticky toffee pudding and a cheeseboard.

I saw the yachts in the harbour and the shops I had always ignored which serviced them with marine supplies, and the voice of my father rose in my mind saying, 'I'll tell you what, there's a few bob down here now. This is a place that's coming up. Smell the money, darling.'

Bobby had not been here for some years, and the odour of damp hit me in the chest as soon as I opened the door. The walls were streaming with condensation and the furniture was half rotted. Large holes gaped in the sofa and legs of chairs had been devoured by woodworm. The books in the library were in terrible condition. Spores of mildew had found their way into the house, the spines were powdery and fell away from the bindings in your hand. Mouse droppings lay along the skirting boards. Mouse piss stank out the kitchen.

We had not seen a lot of each other in the years leading up to his illness. *He* knew what would happen, he was just waiting for the positive test as if it was inevitable and there was nothing he could do to dodge the death bullet. '*Inshallah*. The oldest known song in the world says it all, darling. Do you know it? It goes like this. *While you live, shine, have no grief at all, life exists only for a short while, and time demands its toll.*'

When he was ill he came to live with me for a few months. I had a little one-bedroom flat I had bought. First he took the sofa-bed, then I took it, then his father came to claim him and removed him back to Muswell Hill to the bosom of that Persian family to die.

When he was with me he battled with breath, with standing up, with holding a spoon to his mouth, with reading a page of poetry and listening to one side of a record. Then, when he could only lie there in his Jermyn Street pyjamas, looking rather like the elder Steptoe at only thirty-eight, I told him everything. About my father's tie and the back of Evie's neck and George, and he smiled and said, 'I always knew it, darling. And was he a handsome brute? Would I have liked him?'

'I don't know.'

'Do you think he was a *little bit* gay?'

'Possibly, I don't know.'

'Well, everyone is, aren't they? You and I both know that. And might he have liked me, do you think?'

'Of course, of course he would.'

And once, when I was blending out-of-season strawberries for him to drink through a straw, he said in his weak voice, from the sofa-bed where he was lying with a copy of *Vanity Fair*, reading a few paragraphs of an article about Donald Trump, 'You know, there is, I think, a coldness in me that I am not quite at liberty to do anything about. I think it comes from protecting myself against my father. Have I ever said this before? I don't remember. I mean against his authority and his needs and his vanity and his disappointment in me. I've never mentioned my brother, have I? He's ten years older than me and he went all the way to Australia to get away from Daddy. I haven't seen him since I was eight. His name is Karim, I believe he changed it to Ken and he is married and I have nieces and nephews in Cleveland. *Cleveland.* Have you ever heard of such a place? Clever of him for escaping his fate with Daddy but how far he had to go. And darling, really, what are *you* protecting yourself against? You must know. But you don't have to tell me if you don't wish.'

I thought, But you must protect yourself to survive. But that would have been tactless as he wasn't going to.

Bobby told me things. Some of them are well known. I heard from him about glory holes, where a man stuck his cock through a hole in a cubicle wall and another man sucked it. I thought, what woman would get dressed on a Friday night, sit in front of the mirror and paint her ageing face, spray her hair, perfume her wrists and neck, step into her tight bodycon dress and patent high heels and go out to sit in a stinking box waiting for a cock to stick its way through the plywood separation?

I was not a romantic, but *this*?

Sex, desire, love. The whole mish-mash inseparable. If I had turned into one of those women in her late thirties who begins to panic because she has not sealed the final deal I'd have thrown a rock at my reflection in the mirror. I was doing fine, my mother's wailings notwithstanding. But I had banked on Bobby always being around. There had to have been a point, when everyone knew about Aids, when he could have said, 'Stop, enough.' Maybe he was already ill, maybe he wasn't. Some men I knew were asymptomatic for a long time even though the test results were positive, but still, why not withdraw? The house in Cornwall was always available to him, he could have lived, if only in a small way, but his appetites increased. He liked the Hermès handkerchiefs and the Gucci loafers too much. I think that by the end he had almost forgotten about the Cycladean island, he had got used to lusher islands in the Caribbean. The house in Cornwall was shut up, neglected, gone to rack and ruin. Me, I would have chosen living, with all its let-downs. I am not a romantic about death. It's just a big nothing.

Oh, Bobby. Is anyone still alive who remembers him apart from me?

Has his brother forgotten him too?

Inside the house the mildewed James Elroy Flecker and the Edward Thomas and the other Georgians and post-Georgians together with the biographies of Jane Austen and Strachey's *Eminent Victorians* and Vasari's *Lives of the Artists* remained, dripping wet. I could hardly bear to spend the night there, the sheets smelled so of must and damp, but there was no choice. Next day I would make a start on clearing out this library of lives.

32

I went to the estate agent the next morning and asked her to come and have a look at the house.

'These old places,' she said, 'no one wanted them twenty years ago, everyone was moving up top. Now all the top people are complaining because they've been priced out of the old town. Bit hilarious. It's their own fault, they should have stayed where they were and waited for the yuppies to arrive. Now look, I could put this on the market for you *as is* for ninety-nine. It will need a lot of work, and of course it isn't a family house, only two bedrooms, but you have water access and mooring so that adds on quite a bit. Or you could knock it into shape yourself for the market and then, to be honest, who knows what it might go for? Up to you, but I don't think we'd have much trouble selling it. It could go like a flash with the right marketing.'

My father said: 'Bricks and mortar, Adele, people always need houses, everyone's got to have somewhere to live, never throw money away on rent, you're just enriching the landlords. Line your own pocket to keep your hands warm.' There was a certain amount that I could do to the house to make it appear more

presentable, appearances being everything. I decided on this halfway
measure.

There was no one left in the town I knew. A family was living
in Rami's house at the cove, an NHS psychiatrist, his GP wife and
their two red-haired children. A winter of sewage contractors had
just finished months of work relaying the pipes for the whole town
and leaving in their wake a number of babies to wives whose husbands were away at sea on the scallop boats. The hotel had
reopened under new management. When I passed I saw BMWs in
the car park.

I worked on the house for a few days. I hired a skip. The carpets
overlaid a slate floor, the house twizzled back in time until it
became an old plain cottage overlooking the sea, where masted
sailing ships set out for France and other romantic destinations
across the Channel. Under the wallpaper was old distemper. With
all the rubbish removed, even without a lick of paint, the house
could, to certain sophisticated eyes, seem stylish in a primitive way.
I quite liked it. I could spend a summer here if I went on having
no work. The estate agent came back. 'Oh, yes. Even without
doing up, it's more than ninety-nine, it might be one-ten.'

'One-ten?'

'Easy.'

One night I decided it was boring to eat alone at the kitchen table
so I walked through the town to one of the new restaurants. The
dark, dapper owner served me a drink in the bar and gave me the
menu and behaved in a charming, gallant way to a woman dining
by herself. He had a table by the window for me, and I had a book.
I was reading the short stories of John Cheever for the first time.
I'd come late to them because I couldn't see the interest in suburban American marriage and its discontents, I was yet to read
Updike. Saul Bellow was my guy despite his rejection of my literary offer: *Such sums as I made, made themselves. Capitalism made them
for dark comical reasons of its own. The world did it.* I was going to
make at least ninety-nine on the house for merely sitting down

next to Bobby in a lecture theatre and, in latter days, disposing of his soiled pants.

I chose pâté and Melba toast and the lobster with Pernod and he led me up the stairs to the main room, which fell silent when it saw a woman by herself as it usually does, as if you can look longer at a person alone than a couple, because there's no threat of back-up. Or that people alone are halves and halves don't compute.

The back of the head of someone you have slept with is one of the most familiar parts of their body and to me the back of the neck has been the primary erotic zone. You wake up to it in the night or in the morning. You see how far down the skin the hair grows and you know by heart the mole tickling the flesh beneath the ear, the lobe of the ear fatly thickening, the triangular trapezius muscle rising into the neck and the shoulders gripping the cargo of the head.

The waiter brought my pâté and I was sitting with my white napkin half falling from my lap to the floor with my glass of wine raised to my lips but not reaching them. Over his shoulder I saw the woman he was eating with. I recognised her as his wife, the very small, Irish, Chihuahua-like creature he had married. I had seen their photograph in the papers. The Chihuahua was a make-up artist, she specialised in horror-film prosthetics. Across the white cloth she was raising her forefinger at him to say something I did not want to catch but did, about how he must eat less red meat, how the fish was fresh from the sea and full of omega oils. 'You look pasty,' she said. 'You need to lay off the chips.'

'But I *like* chips.'

He liked chips. He *liked* chips. I knew that.

But the restaurant did not do chips, it offered boiled new potatoes as part of a selection of vegetables. He had ordered the steak, it was the only meat on the menu. She, like me, had gone for the lobster. They had a bottle of champagne in a chrome bucket by their table. I was making do with one glass of Pinot Grigio. I pierced the flesh of the lobster claw and withdrew a pink morsel. She did the same. She looked up and saw me and raised her fork.

'Good, isn't it?' she called.

I nodded, smiling, trying to make a distant, uninterested expression – don't pop my bubble, lady – and lowered my eyes to John Cheever. I was trying to return to my thought, which was Now this is how to write, look how he gets a sentence to turn on a dime, like a poet, but George was in the process of turning round, his back was starting a shadow across my table. He was moving with half a smile on his face, but as his shoulders revolved and he saw me, he seemed to want to correct the motion, to return to his previous position, which would depend on neither me nor his wife having noticed what he was doing. So he was stuck between her and me, and there were only two directions he could go, or only one without appearing (to her) rude. The owner was walking towards me with a side salad. The other tables were bent over their plates forking fish into their mouths or advanced already to the sticky toffee pudding and dessert wines.

I tried to smile. A great piece of muscular stupidity spread across my face. 'Hello, George.'

His wife said, 'Hey, do you two know each other?'

'Adele and I had a brief acquaintance long ago.' The coldness of this remark hurt me, it was a little humiliating to be honest, as if he had signed a love letter *Yours sincerely* or *Yours faithfully* (which is even worse, the sign-off when you don't even know the person addressed). Yes, yes, it had been brief and perhaps it was true that we had been no more than sexual acquaintances. But it wasn't like he'd put his cock through a hole in the wall. We had glittered together when we walked along the street, surely I couldn't have been mistaken about that.

'I don't want to disturb you, I'll let you get on with your meal in peace. Nice to see you again.' I lowered my eyes to my fissured lobster, looking like a hand that would reach up and take my throat.

'One-night stand?' said his wife.

He turned back to the table and began to saw away at his steak but she continued to look at me with raised eyebrows as if to say she was going to get to the bottom of this. And he leaned towards her, and spoke, and then she nodded and said, 'Ah, OK.'

It was down to me to resolve this situation as fast as possible by refusing pudding or another drink, but when I called for the bill and rose to leave, he stood up and said, 'Just a minute.'

We walked down the steps to the bar and he said, 'What are you doing here? Are you following me?'

'Don't be ridiculous. Why are *you* here?'

'I've bought the recording studio upriver, everyone knows that. And what are you doing here?'

'I was left a house, a house I came to in the seventies, I've just come to clear it out so I can sell it. Evie was here too, did you know that? She was here one summer.'

'I don't call her by that name so why do you have to? She's Lorraine.'

'Yes, Lorraine. Sorry.'

He touched my arm, in fact he bruised it, or so it felt. The owner called out did I not want to stay and have a drink at the bar, they usually had a bit of a lock-in, but I said no. It was still only nine o'clock when I passed the church and walked up the silent streets. The bells chimed and a rush of rooks flew upwards in fright. The street was no longer white with the dust off the boots, of the china clay under the moonlight, all that was passing away.

33

'So where was she?' He was talking as soon as I opened the door to him, he was staring at me as if I was hiding something behind my back that I was trying to keep from him. He always had that way of barging in and taking over the space and furnishing it with parts of his extended body.

'Give me a minute, for God's sake, I'll put my shoes on and show you.'

'You've not changed.'

'I have, I have.'

'You seem the same to me.'

'*You* don't, you're just flashier and bigger and wealthier. Is that a diamond in your ear? What are you *wearing*?'

'That's nothing, it's something you have to put on when you're in the business. The kids these days need intimidating.'

Her face coming and going in his.

'Has anyone ever told you that you look a bit like Patti Smith?'

'Yes, quite a few times.'

'We didn't know about her then, did we, when we last met? She was still below the radar. You could have been her, you could have been a double act. You were in a band for a while, weren't you? I heard about it. I never came to see you. It didn't seem possible, though I was very curious. Were you any good?'

'No, I wasn't. That's just a shard of my life.'

'That's all life is, anyway. Show me where Lorraine was.'

I felt a terrible self-consciousness, as if I was prone to blurting out thoughts that should remain secret, when you think you are going to say, as if you have Tourette's, 'But I've always loved you', without knowing what it means or if you mean it.

The house across the road on the landward side was raised up from the street, you couldn't see through the windows. A car approached, we smeared ourselves against the wall so it could pass.

'I know how we can look in. Follow me.' I took George along the alley that lay behind the row of three Victorian cottages from which the rock rose up to the squire's garden and a stream of algae-coated water flowed down a gulley all year round. Pansies and begonias were doing their best in the shadow of the cliff, growing out of a concrete planter. A woman was out hanging her washing at the end of the terrace and I told her we were here just to look through the windows because I had known the house once.

She said, 'I recognise you. I have a good memory for faces. You came here with that foreign boy across the road.'

'I did.'

'Well then you're welcome, m'lovely.'

'It's a long shot, but do you remember the couple who came to stay here one summer, a young boy and girl both with short hair?'

'Oh, yes, I do, like a pair of twins, brother and sister. I thought it was incest at first.'

'They were friends of mine, *this* is her brother.'

'Well then, you go and look as long as you like, there's no one in there at the minute. They come and go so fast you can't be bothered keeping up with them. Ken and Doris used to have it but he died and she moved up top. We used to be dinner ladies at the school together but I don't see her much any more, her son's got it and he makes a mint from the rent. My son will do the same when I'm gone. I said to him, Mark, hang on to this old place, it'll be your pension one day.'

She turned and went back to her washing line to hang out her tea-towels.

The house was so dark it was possible to imagine figures moving across the rooms, through the furniture. I mean passing around the tables and chairs and sideboards and then up the stairs to the bedroom where Stevie had stood at the window and said, 'Even from here there's not much of a view,' and I had said, 'That's why it's only three quid a week, what did you expect?'

'That was a disappointment,' George said. 'I don't know why I bothered.' He turned and stared at me. 'Except, I suppose, because I wanted to see you.'

I flushed and burned in the alley. The woman had gone inside. There was just us there, under the rock. 'We call this an entry, where I come from,' I said. 'And there are girls with up-the-entry eyes.'

'Are there?'

'Do you want to come over the road and have a cup of tea?'

'Yeah, we should do that.'

We sat out in my courtyard and watched the pilot boat go out to fetch a ship in. 'You'll see it come back in about twenty minutes. There's always a lot to look at out here. Sometimes the sailors are on deck and I wave to them and sometimes it's a navy ship and they're all out there in their summer whites saluting.'

The pilot boards the ship and takes control of the bridge, he guides the ship through the channels of the deep-water estuary out to sea. The pilot boat goes ahead, as if it were a toy car. When the ship is ready to depart, the pilot climbs the ship's ladder down to the boat and they return to harbour.

'And after hours, if you want to go to the other side you must apply to the night ferryman who smokes black cheroots, black as the night, with the coal glowing in the darkness and the sound of the engine starting and the water rushing. He'll bring you over, m'lovely, if you like.'

'This is nice.'

'Yes, it is. Do you want to buy this house from me? It would be a good investment, done up.'

'Are you included?'

'Yes, all in.'

'Done up?'

'Do I need it?'

'Not really. You've held your own, babe. I like that.'

34

A few days after he had come to see the house where Evie had stayed, I heard George's voice calling me but I could not tell from which direction. I went out to the street but he wasn't there and then I went out to the back and looked down over the sea wall to where he was standing below on the water in a rowing boat, the oars waggling uneasily in the oarlocks, his hands around his mouth crying, 'Adele, come on down.'

'Where are you going?'

'Upriver. Put on your shoes and get into the boat.'

'How?'

'There's a fucking ladder.'

'I'm not going down that, those steps are treacherous.'

'Don't be such an arse. Get down here. I'm taking you for an adventure.'

I started to lower my feet to the steps, but the first rung cracked under my weight. I knew I would kill myself, that I would crash into the water and be swept out to sea. I pulled back up again and said, 'It's too dangerous.'

'Oh, all right, get on at the pontoon then.'

A few feet from the house the lifeboat lay at anchor, sturdy, industrious, orange, with a prow that meant business. Yachts had temporary mooring. I walked down in my jeans and cotton shirt and flip-flops, and George was reaching me as I arrived, very strong his chest against the oars. I got in the boat.

George said, 'Here you are,' and kissed me on the nose. 'Steph's taken the kids to the museum at Charlestown. They'll be gone all day.'

'Why didn't you go?'

'I hate museums.'

'Whose is this boat?'

'Mine. I bought it yesterday. Had a couple of lessons. Got a tide-table book. Don't know what's in there. Probably doesn't matter.'

We moved on upstream. The river had a regatta feel under a sparkling summer sun. Birds whose names I did not know flew overhead and perched on buoys. Little sailboats lay at anchor and we weaved in and out of them. On the bank you could see the cars that brought the clay down to the port from the dries, on the tracks of the mineral railway.

George had a map of the estuary in his pocket. 'Have a look at this. Where should we go?'

'There's a pub that does good food. And well upstream there's a very pretty village Bobby told me about, but I never saw it myself.'

He rowed on, his chest expanding and contracting, barely out of breath.

After quite a long while, longer than I'd imagined it would take, we reached the pub, but George pointed with an oar to another pill. 'Let's try up here. Seems quiet. We can have a drink later.'

'The pub will be closed later.'

'No it won't.'

And that seemed to be that. He appeared to believe he could keep the pub open by the force of his personality, his tendency to brutishness. We rowed up, or rather he did, and I lay back in the boat against the cushions until we were shaded by overhanging trees. It was all very, very quiet. Not even birds made a sound. I thought about a conversation we had all had long ago, that summer when Evie and Stevie came here, about how everyone can be classified as a character from *The Wind in the Willows*. This was Bobby's idea. Dora and Gillian were Ratty, always busy. Evie was Mole, brooding. I was the Wayfarer Rat, who only appears for a chapter, the siren of wanderlust. Bobby was Toad. Rami was Badger. Stevie was an apprentice Badger. George I reckoned was another Toad, one of life's demanders and wreckers, people whose mess you must clean up.

A couple of real wrecks, sailing boats with broken masts, were aground on the bank. Up a shadowed inlet we could see the façade of a Georgian house facing the river, its back to the countryside. In the middle of the pill a summerhouse floated on a platform. A man was out on deck, drinking a glass of wine.

'You see, there are all kinds of places you can escape to if you look hard enough,' George said. 'There are secret places, and we've found one, haven't we?' We were drifting from side to side, the boat was barely moving. George took a hip-flask from his pocket. 'Have a gulp of this. Best Scotch.'

'Is there nothing to eat?'

'Who needs food?'

I drank and then I laid my head in his lap as he obviously was intending me to do and we drifted and drifted and I was looking up at the sky, thinking of how you could do something and there would be no consequences and yet you wanted the mess that followed, you would wallow in it. I would gladly have taken George with the Chihuahua and the two children and all the drama and the tears. He began to stroke my hair.

'I'm sorry we left it the way we did,' he said. 'But the times were the times.'

'Yes, and we were very young, just kids.'

'Just starting out. And now we have all our worries and responsibilities.'

'Unzip your jeans, will you, darling? Or should I do it?'

'No, I will.'

I was naked in the boat, he was still partly dressed. The man in the summerhouse was looking at us through binoculars.

'Don't be self-conscious,' George said. 'Let him look. Your body is more voluptuous now, I like that, you were too thin before. I always fancied Patti and now I've got her. But a better version.'

I saw the lenses flash in the sun. I lay down in the boat and George pushed himself inside me very suddenly and so we rocked and rocked.

'Just lie there for a minute,' he said. 'I want to look at you. Your face, mainly.'

I closed my eyes. I opened them again. He was looking down at me with what I thought was a kind of fondness. But who knew what his expressions meant or what he really felt? The man in the summerhouse had gone. There had been a boat tied up to the raft and it had gone too. We were alone again and the house up the inlet was all shuttered.

'I'm getting cold.'

'I know. Put your clothes on, I'll get us out of here, we'll sail away.'

But where there had been water now rose soft mounds of mud isolated by pools of river. George struck them with the oars, but we made no progress.

'Oh, fuck, the tide's going out.'

'Now what?'

George looked round. 'When does the tide come back in?

'How should I know? Look at the tide table.'

'I don't understand it, to be honest.'

'Are we going to have to stay here all night?'

'Shit.'

We spent two hours in the boat. We talked about what Evie had said the day of Dora's consciousness-raising group, that story about her mother being raped and her father maybe not her father.

35

'I saw your mother once, you know, through the window on our first day, with an old-fashioned plait round her head.'

George said, 'Oh, that terrible hairdo. But she said it uglified her, and to Mum that was important. She hated the idea of attracting men's attention. And she wanted Lorraine to have a long plait like her, with a tartan bow, a child's plait because it made her look like a child so maybe she wouldn't attract boys either. But I think maybe she was also envious of our normal lives and that was reflected in some of her behaviour. She could be spiteful. She took away her first lipstick and hid it in a drawer. People are fucked up. They tell stories to themselves in order to make sense of their contradictions. Sometimes the most psychotic behaviour is just a story. Mum was hard to grow up with. There were no rages or anything like that, just a lot of inexplicable deceptions.'

'What was Evie like as a child?'

'*Lorraine.* Why do you keep calling her that? I'll throw you overboard if you say that name again.'

He produced a series of memories. When she was a little girl in her plaits with tartan bows and white ankle socks and the same blue leather starburst Start-rite sandals I had had. Evie digging in the garden for worms and beginning to eat them until her brother looked out of the window and saw her and pulled the wriggling thing from her mouth. Evie with her bunny rabbit, Peter-Peter, holding up his lifeless head from the straw of his cage and George turning *her* head away from his limp ears and the shit he had been lying in. Evie doing her homework at the kitchen table, her mother laying down a glass of milk next to her. Evie and George riding their bikes through the suburban streets, past fences and pillar boxes and phone boxes, to the shops where they bought their comics and Black Jacks and foam shrimps and all the sweets that were four for a penny.

Evie and George making plays for the audience of their parents and her mother laughing and clapping. Evie in the bitter winter of 1963 when they found a hill in the park and slid down it on a tea tray, exactly as I had done in our park, and all the children of England that frozen season. But I had had a red duffel coat with real bone toggles and my father walked with me in his thin leather slip-on shoes, looking out at the snowy expanse that had been the grass. 'Are you sure you don't want to go back and sit by the radiator with a book?' I said, 'No, I want to sledge.' He said, 'OK,' and I did it once and fell and cried and we both came home with our feet soaked, my mother made tea and sliced cake.

Now I said to George, 'Tell me when you first found out about your mother.'

As he began to speak, he put a hand on my breast as if he owned it, and kept it there, as if it was part of his own body. I hear that when paraplegics speak of touching their leg, it's as though they are touching someone else's leg because they cannot feel any sensation, but still, they know it's theirs. The mud was not receding at the sides of the boat. The cows and sheep on the hills wandered about to some unspecified timetable.

George said, 'There was a time, but I don't really remember it, when Dad was not there and Mum was pregnant. I was about two, coming up to three. Dad went out to work one morning and apparently he never came back at night for his sherry and his dinner.

Mum said I was the little man of the house, she stood me on the kitchen table and looked me in the eye and said, "You're my lord and master now, in sickness and in health, eh, Georgie Porgie?" I was named after the old king. Do you remember his head on the back of the pennies?

'Then after a while Mum went away. I went to my Gran's. Mum came back with a kid in a carry-cot and then sometime after that Dad reappeared. Time isn't measurable when you're three but it was a few months after. And that I know because of the diary. Mum had a secret place. It was in the bottom drawer of the chest in the bedroom, under her knickers. There was a tin box in it with roses painted in enamel. It might have had chocolates in it once. The way I found it was that I bought a knife from a boy at school. Mum didn't approve of knives and this wasn't a pen-knife, it was a knife with an engraved ivory hilt and on the hilt there was an eagle. It was *fantastic*, I saved my pocket money for a month to buy that knife off him and when I brought it home Mum took one look at it and she let out a shriek, which wasn't like her at all.'

Now George had started to act the part of his mother and of himself as a boy. He raised the imaginary knife in his hand above his head, he made his other arm reach for it but not be able to reach. He was a muscular man, a bit fat, sitting in a rowing boat becalmed on a Cornish creek with his pants still undone and his cock limply dangling and now he was a comic blonde lady with a plait wound round her head. Not bad.

'The blade had a leather case, she took it at that end, and then she ran out of the room. When she came back her arms were crossed and she made her lips seal and put a finger over them. All she would do was shake her head when I asked her where the knife was so I had to go and look for it. I spent a week turning the house over and it never occurred to me to look in the drawer where she kept her pants, because the idea of a knife in with Mum's droopy grey cotton knickers was a bit much, that was the last place I would have looked. Their bedroom was the place where they had this private life you just didn't want to know about. When they stop being

Mum and Dad and turn into strangers who fuck. Lorraine never believed they fucked, she was absolutely certain Mum wouldn't have wanted to, and she kept on saying we were adopted and she wouldn't believe me when I told her that Mum went into hospital with a big bump below her chest and came back out with her. But Lorraine was a very, very naïve kid. I used to worry what would happen to her the first time she saw a boy's todger so I showed her mine. For education.'

'What?'

'For crying out loud, don't look at me like that. I didn't *touch* her, I just said, here's the way it is, Lorraine, all boys have one of these, so you'll have to get used to it. And she said, well what do you do with it, so I explained, because it was too much for Mum to tell her the facts of life, the bad memories, though we didn't know that at the time, I just assumed she was a prude or squeamish, and Dad certainly wasn't going to, not just because fathers didn't talk to their daughters that way, but because he never talked about anything, he didn't believe in conversation.

'It was left up to me and a bit about the birds and the bees she got at school. I can picture it now, Adele, the two of us in the shed where Peter-Peter used to live and the hutch still there, half broken, Dad's bulbs over-wintering, my packet of ciggies hidden behind a broken flowerpot and me and Lorraine sitting on the floor and me unzipping my short trousers and showing her. She said, what's that behind, I said, that's balls, and she said, what are they for?'

'Jesus, George, no wonder she was fucked up, you fucked her up yourself. The poor kid.'

'Don't be ridiculous. It was just a flash in my shorts, that's all. Let me get back to my knife. Mum kept everything in this tin box in the bedroom and when I'd run out of everywhere else to look I went in there one Good Friday, when she was downstairs baking a simnel cake which is some Easter thing Dad liked because our gran used to make it for him when he was a kid before the war. So she was busy and I went in and I looked in the bedside table and her dressing-table drawer, and then I knew it was all or nothing, I'd have to go for the chest where her underwear was, so I opened them one by one and let my hand feel inside past the knickers, with my head turned away in case I saw gussets, then I pulled out this box. And I could hear the knife sliding around in there, the hilt banging against the sides.

'I grabbed the whole thing and took it down to the shed. Dad was digging outside, the spade hitting stones. He was always digging fucking holes, and no one ever knew what he put in them, except I suppose plants he started to grow, and every year, on their anniversary, he would pick Mum a bunch of flowers, big bronze chrysanthemums and the stalks would all be hacked down to the ground. He was banging the spade against the rockery to dislodge the dirt and I was in the darkness of the shed with the door closed and the light coming from the dirty window which looked out, stupidly, onto the neighbour's fence.

'My knife was there in the box, I got it out and held it, and looked at the fantastic eagle someone had carved. What I wanted to do with the knife was threaten bigger boys at school. That was the idea. There were letters in the box, and birthday cards and Valentine's cards, and a dried flower wrapped up in tissue paper and this big round rubber thing in a pink plastic box which had a white dust on it when I picked it up. And then there were these red-backed school exercise books with lined pages. Remember them? Four, strapped together with a rubber band. And writing inside them. A *lot* of writing.

'I took the knife from the box and returned it back to the house and to the drawer. I suppose Mum knew, but there was this bigger thing, the exercise books, and what she was more worried about than the knife was whether I knew what was in them.

'She just went on hiding the notebooks, they travelled all over the house. They spent a year inside the grandfather clock before I found them again. Next they were shoved behind the bookshelf where Dad kept his A. J. Cronin novels and Mum's Barbara Cartlands. I turned myself into a boy detective, like in my comics.

The fourth time I found them I was fourteen, but it still took me years to piece it all together and in the end I got bored and just went and asked Mum when I had the gist of the story and she realised the game was up and she said, "Fine, so read, and then you will understand." So this bloke raped my mother and then she was pregnant with Lorraine. She couldn't get rid of her. She didn't know anyone who could tell her how it was done or who you saw and anyway, she never had any money of her own, Dad took care of all that, she only had the housekeeping and he'd have known if she'd spent that all in one go and asked for more. She couldn't make up a story.

'Dad moved out, then he came back. That's what happened. And eventually Lorraine found out too because I showed her the books where Mum had written it all down, her diaries. But Dad, when he did return, to his credit he was as much of a father to her as he ever was to me. He accepted her even though he had to change his bank account, which wasn't an easy thing to do in those days. Mum wrote about all that, having to go in and close his account and look this man who had raped his wife in the eye and say, I've come to make a withdrawal, Lassiter. Not Mr Lassiter. Or Captain Lassiter, they were still using their officer titles after the war, jumped-up little fascists. He took everything out of the Midland and went to the Trustees Savings Bank, and he had to get references. That wasn't easy. The Masons closed ranks around Lassiter because that's how it was, he was a worshipful master, and Dad was just a tyler which meant he kept the robes amongst other things, which they gave him because he had a draper's shop.'

'God, that's bleak.'

'Isn't it just?'

'Are your parents still alive?'

'No, Mum died eight years ago, from cancer, she was only sixty-six. Dad carried on for a bit, then he tripped in the street and a car ran over him. Bust his leg, he never recovered, had a heart attack in the ambulance on the way to hospital. Died a couple of days

later. Probably for the best, he was useless on his own, that generation can't even boil water. Anyway, it's over, the two of them are
gone and my sister is long gone, I'm an orphan and it's just me and
my kids.'

'What about your wife?'

'Yes, me and Steph, but I mean blood relations.'

He put an oar down in the water but still it reached the bottom.
The descendants of the sheep we had burned on the beach long
ago were still grazing in woolly clusters. A line of cows were being
marched along an invisible lane. I thought, Could we just get out
and clamber along the bank and make it to that house? But the
bank looked completely inaccessible, covered with wild black-
berries and tree roots.

'When all's said and done,' George was saying, looking at me,
not putting his arm round me though I was shivering, 'what do you
make of Mum's story?'

'I think it's an important one. About what happens to women.'

'Just women? What about Dad? He was wronged and persecuted
too. His shop never recovered, really. We always struggled to keep
our heads above water, to be respectable and keep up with the
mortgage.'

'Can I read them?'

'What?'

'The notebooks.'

'Even if I wanted to, I couldn't. I wish I knew where those exercise books went. I haven't seen them for years, not since Lorraine
died.'

'What happened to them?'

'I don't know. They disappeared.'

'I think I saw her with some school exercise books the night she
died, the last time I saw her.'

'Did you now? They were in her room?'

'Yes, by the bed.'

'They weren't there when Mum and Dad came and they weren't
there when I came to fetch her stuff. Believe me, I looked.'

'How strange. But then I wasn't the last person to see her alive, Gillian was.'

'Who's Gillian?'

'Just one of the girls, you wouldn't know her, a little fanatic in her way, sad case.'

His body was a haven but he was sitting stiffly, denying it to me.

I said, 'Look, is this the beginning of something, or what?'

'Let's see what happens if we ever get out of this place. This is a ridiculous situation we're in, two landlubbers on the water. Can you swim?'

'I can.'

'Well I can't.'

'It's a stupid question anyway, there's nothing to swim *in*.'

The hill was silent, the sheep had gone. No birds sang and the wrecks began to look nightmarish, like pirate galleons in the shadows. The river was beginning to creep up the side of the boat but still George dragged his oars against the bottom.

Finally, when we were freezing cold, we heard the sound of an engine coming from the mouth of the pill. The shadow of a motor boat was moving through the water. It got closer and we saw two young men standing, their hands on the tiller. They were short, squat, their heads bristled like blond pigs. One of them was smoking a pipe, a short corn-cob thing.

'Ahoy!' George cried.

'You stuck?'

'Yes we are, we're fucking mired.'

They started laughing. 'Too right. Stuck. Want a hand?'

'Can you help us out of here?'

'Think we can.' They looked at each other and doubled up with the pain of their laughter.

One of them took off his shoes and lowered himself into the water. His feet were like a hobbit's, furred and with prehensile toes. He waded over to us and attached a rope to our stern. Then, pulling us behind him, he walked us through the channels into deeper waters. 'We know this riverbed like our wives' faces, don't we, Bert?'

'Better.'

'Now, how you getting back? Rowing? You'll be against the tide.'

'Oh God,' said George.

'Or do you want a tow?'

'Yeah, please.'

'It'll cost you.'

'Anything you like.'

'Ten pound.'

'Done.'

We moved swiftly on the rising tide to the mouth of the pill and then headed towards the estuary, like a king and queen in our pomp and majesty, tired, cold, embarrassed. It took only a few minutes to reach the pontoon, but we had been gone for hours.

I got out of the rowing boat with a sense of relief at our rescue and panic that I would not see him again. He winked, that old gesture of complicity.

'Don't forget about Mum's notebooks.'

'How am I supposed to get hold of you?'

'I'll be in touch all right, no need to worry about that. Give me your number.' I wrote it down on a bit of paper. 'I've gotta go.'

He rowed off down the river back to his wife and kids.

Across the river the boathouse with the roof slipping sideways was dissolving into darkness. A light came on. Everything was mysterious, everything was profound and I was in the process of being kicked somewhere.

36

The smell of 1974 when we first slept together was of patchouli oil and Old Holborn tobacco and long hair singed on the bars of an electric fire, bent towards the red-hot filaments to light a cigarette, the stink of the dirty Thames rolling below Kew Bridge.

And the smell of 1991 was the plastic of taxi seats on which we sat together watching London blinking and twitching under late-afternoon winter streetlights, ink on newsprint, George's Lucky Strikes, and Opium – that heavy vermilion Oriental scent: sandalwood, cedarwood, myrrh, opopanax, labdanum, benzoin and castoreum. It was everywhere you went, you walked into a restaurant and the perfume from the bare shoulders of the women rose, waving the sex banner. The autumn and winter of 1991 smells of sex.

It smells of the sweat of George's neck, of the ginger shower gel in the bathroom and the laundered cleanness of the sheets when we got into bed and the sloughed-off cells and semen stains and sometimes the menstrual blood that came from me. Sex is dirty work.

Sometimes he hurt me by twisting my breasts too hard, sometimes he asked me to slap him on the face for his own pleasure.

One time I was bending over to pick up my clothes from the floor when he lunged at me and came in from behind. It was agony. I said, 'How could you do that to me, after what happened to your mother? Don't you get it?'

'That wasn't rape, that was affection. Affection for your pretty little arse.'

'I'll kill you, I'll get my revenge.'

'You won't, you don't know how. You can't hurt me, Adele. I'm beyond that. I shed all my tears when Lorraine died.'

Once I was sitting by the window with a white towel wrapped round me and he just stared and stared and I was looking down at the street, at the taxis and all the rumble, and he said, 'Don't move,' in almost a whisper. And I had to stay there while he looked and this was our most tender moment. After all the devouring and hitting and raping, he just let me be. I was an unfamiliar version of myself, quite happy, at peace by a windowledge in Soho.

And had I gone on sitting there for longer, I think he would have left his wife and we would have been together, twisted the whole situation round so that the past was severed, finally, and we were just Adele and George. But I turned round, like Mrs Lot. Was turned later to salt, salt tears.

Like every mistress who has ever lived since the invention of the telephone, I was waiting; and once, enraged by the passivity, I said that I hated my powerlessness.

'Look,' he said, 'you know my situation, this is how I have to operate.'

'But what about me, what about the way I operate?'

'In this situation, you don't operate. I'm lying for you. And I have more to lose than you, I have kids, you don't.'

'You have money, I don't even have a job.'

'I can get you a job, if you want.'

'What kind of job?'

'Something in the business, let me think about it.'

The following week I got a call from a music magazine who had heard from George's assistant that I was available and would I come in and interview for features editor. The office was in Soho, and this made it very easy for us to conduct our affair at his convenience, over lunchtime at the room he took at the Groucho Club.

Every time we met, he said, 'Did you find those books yet?'

'No, but I'm on to it.'

'Good.'

'Is that the only reason you're sleeping with me?'

'Don't be ridiculous. I adore you. But the books are important. I'd like them back.'

'How much do you adore me?'

'I love your skinny legs and your little pot belly, I like the way the skin puckers on your arse. I appreciate that you always wear lipstick, that your gob is always the first thing I see when you walk into a room. I'm enamoured of the colour and the gold tube it's in. Your pussy is nice and tight and the skin inside there is like satin. I could drink your bleeds.'

'Oh, oh! What? You go too far.'

'No, I'm mad about you. Are you mad about me?'

'Yes, what do you think? I've always carried a flame for you.'

'I know you have. I saw it in your face when I turned round that time in the restaurant. I saw your eyes, your beautiful dark brown eyes. We're moving towards something here, it's happening, isn't it? Don't you feel it? Don't you?'

Obviously, I assumed that what he meant by this was that he was going to leave his wife.

If only I could find those red Silvine exercise books and get them back to him. I was sick, I was mentally ill with love for him. I would have done anything. You can be completely axed to the ground by love, that's the only explanation. You're down to your roots. This *was* love. What a monster.

37

Of all the people I had known at university, the only one left in my address book was Rose. That she was married and had a child was somewhat unexpected, the conventionality of her circumstances were not in what I had thought of as her own specifications for the future. She told me she lived in Brixton, but if she did, it was quite a walk from the tube station and the high windows of her house overlooked the park. The map might have argued that she lived in Dulwich and that leafiness and a nearby delicatessen were the constituent aspects of her new life.

She came to the door dressed in jeans and a silk shirt, the casual day-off uniform of working women that season. I was wearing it myself. Her shirt was emerald, mine was chartreuse. We snapped our fingers at each other. A bag with a gold chain for a handle was draped over a post on the hall stairs.

'Isn't that Chanel?'

'Oh, yes, well spotted. I succumbed to it one day. You have to make an impression.'

'I love this house.'

'It's good, isn't it? Floor-to-ceiling windows in the sitting room. We were lucky. We bought just after the crash when the prices slumped. But let's get out of here, there's a door to the park at the end of the garden. Let the nanny look after Sophie. That's what I'm paying her for. The kid runs about so.'

We walked down the long garden and emerged through the fence into a circle of grass.

'Another person who has a kid is Gillian,' I said, as a means of opening the exercise-book door, 'I saw her in the street with it a few years ago, though you would know better than me about that.'

'Oh, poor Gillian. I haven't seen her in an age.'

'Why not? Do you not both go to meetings, or whatever it is you do?'

'Ha bloody ha. I haven't been in the Party for years, I completely grew out of those people. They all started to seem utterly ridiculous, juvenile. Our heads were full of the most extraordinary rubbish and I was as bad as anyone, if not the worst for a bit, I was such a bully and a beast. There was nothing real about it, it was all just play-acting, because we had been given the time and the space to play. That's what the freedom was for us, so we could work through this childishness. And then, as if the scales dropped from my eyes, I saw that bloody Dora, that know-it-all, was right, particularly about all those senior male comrades grooming fatuous little students to become part of their harem.'

We had reached a gate and entered a small walled botanical garden of plants which caught Rose's attention again and again. 'Oh, look at those wonderful Chinese lanterns!' We navigated the flowerbeds until we came to a pond surrounded by a rockery and sat down on a bench. It was very pleasant to be surrounded by green and colour with fat, oily-looking orange fish moving sluggishly around in the water below us.

'Cigarette?' she said. We lit up. We were the last people we knew who still smoked.

'The thing about you, Adele, was that you managed to escape all the nonsense because you were so extraordinarily primitive. Too primitive to have a higher consciousness. Poor Gillian struggled with that assertion because she idolised you. I suppose you must have changed, but as I remember you, you were always just sitting there, smoking, narrowing your eyes, one leg crossed over the other, picking at the rips in your jeans. Looking at us as though you barely understood what we were on about, yet with this nasty force of survival. I don't mean that unpleasantly. I was intimidated by you, everyone was. Your case was interesting because you seemed to be immune to the comrades, however much they lusted after you, and they all did.'

'You're kidding. I never even noticed them.' I tried to remember who she meant, the boys in their donkey jackets hawking newspapers with straggling hair and Adam's apples like eggs in their necks, rising and falling. I was completely oblivious, I was in a dream.

'They were always nagging me to recruit you and I said, it's a waste of time, she's unreconstructed. You have to understand the boys mostly joined the Party because it was the only way they could get any sex. Then there were the older ones, the organisers, who we started to meet when we got to London, appalling people, dandruffy men who spat at you when they talked and wore any old clothes they didn't even bother washing. You had to deliver those young girls to them like sides of meat and they were *slavering*. God, it made me sick. And if they were ghastly then the ideas were even more preposterous.'

For some minutes she went at the slogans of our youth with a hammer. She had always been good at that.

'What happened to Jim, Gillian's appalling boyfriend?'

'No idea, so many of them passed through the organisation, really forgettable people. I barely even remember him.'

I looked round at the vegetation. The plants had names as me and Rose and Dora and Gillian had names, and the names were on little sticks or labels. Rose was the type who knew what they were, in English and Latin.

'As I said, I saw her on the street a few years ago, wheeling a pushchair.'

'Ah. That *was* particularly awful, I don't think I even want to *talk* about it. You will have to ask her. The thing is, Adele, I always feel rather responsible for Gillian, she was far too frail and gentle to be a Bolshevik, lacking that deep, homicidal nastiness that kept the rest of us going. And I'm sorry to say that it was the propaganda of people like me that led her to that way of life, and then in her eyes I went off and betrayed the cause I got her to join. She rang me, you know. She was in tears: "Why are you leaving? What's wrong? Don't you understand we're making a turn to industry and we *need* you?" I still feel guilty about her. She was such a sweetheart and she adored my father. He was very protective of her and said, "Rose, you should leave this girl alone, let her play her viola in peace."

'But I wouldn't listen because I thought our politics were newer than his, and he and his generation hadn't really *tried* to change the world, and we would, it would be terribly easy. Because of course, yes, they had fought and defeated fascism, but that's not actually building anything, is it? It's a defeat of an enemy and they had cleared the way for us to create on the empty ground they had given us. Dad fought in Spain, but he seemed to me quite conservative in so many other ways, as if all the vision left him, the fight itself knocked out the stuffing. And what was left was this dull piecemeal alteration. Welfare state, council housing, NHS, expansion of education. Yawn. I actually put my hand over my mouth and made that cynical gesture. To my own father.'

'We were goldfish, weren't we? Who didn't know that our water was a bowl.'

'Yes, that's an interesting way of putting it. More than you know, actually.'

People poured into the walled garden. They eyed us on the benches as if they thought there ought to be some time limit for sitting there, like a parking meter. Small children ran and screamed and one fell into the pond and was fished out with a mighty wailing. I laughed.

'Have you got her phone number?'

'Whose?'

'Gillian's.'

'Why on earth do you of all people want to talk to Gillian?'

'Do you remember Evie, and the night she died?'

'Oh yes, Evie. An unusually fragile type, much more so than Gillian. Almost certainly some mental-health problems. Which the university did nothing about, complete dereliction of duty, in my view. Her parents probably would have had a case to sue.'

'Sue who?'

'The *university*. Yes, I'd have done that, had I been them.'

'But that's not the kind of case you take, is it?'

'No. But I'd have advised them to.'

'I thought the law was a bourgeois instrument of something.'

'The state. It is. But unfortunately without the law which has grown up since the Middle Ages, without *habeas corpus*, for example, all you have is anarchy. You're worse off without the law. Then they really can mow you down.'

'Is there anyone you wouldn't defend? A rapist, for example?'

'With my reputation I doubt if I'd be instructed, but yes, I would if I was. Under English law everyone is entitled to a defence.'

'A child murderer?'

'Why not? The child's mother is there in the court, but so is the defendant's mother. Everyone has a mother and you never know what life has in store for you, Adele. You just never know.'

I noticed that Rose had acquired a habit, a visual tic, of agreeing with the points she had just made by screwing up her eyes and nodding. She seemed quite emphatic about life's unpredictability.

She looked round at the strolling couples and said, 'They really, really want this bench, don't they? Shall we get back? I'll give you Gillian's number.' She reached into her shoulder bag and produced a strange gadget, an early electronic organiser. I took out my little gold-backed leather address book and wrote it down. The walled garden was lush, beautiful and claustrophobic and we went out into the wide park and back to her house, where we sat in the kitchen for a while as she began to prepare food for a dinner party, talking while the ash from her cigarette fell into the mayonnaise.

She was still very attractive, I thought, and she wore early middle age lightly. Her hair was bobbed and polished. Her nails were manicured. She seemed more adult than the rest of us, but then, despite the childishness of her ideas, she always had. Her kitchen was full of unusual gadgets, her husband was upstairs working on a home computer. He was a management consultant, this was not as bad as it sounded, Rose insisted, he advised charities on how to organise themselves for the future, how to obtain funding and when to merge or change their name to something more palatable for the modern era. They were modern people.

The mayonnaise glossed and thickened in the blender. Rose looked round the kitchen. 'I have so many fucking gadgets. I have a melon baller and cherry pitter. I buy them in an addictive way, these stupid accessories no one needs. I don't know why, they'd need a shrink to get it out of me. I'll be a kleptomaniac next, I'll start stealing piping nozzles from John Lewis.'

'We might once have said that what you're doing now is being chained to the kitchen sink.'

'I have a dishwasher. And the nanny deals with most of the chores of motherhood. I don't clean up my own messes. It's not the same thing at all. Absolutely not.'

38

I went to see Gillian in early September. The messages on her machine had gone unanswered for two weeks and then she finally returned my call in a breathless way, as if she had run to answer a long-ringing phone.

'I'm sorry, I'm so sorry, I've been away, I just put my suitcase down and saw the messages you left and I wanted to get back to you at once in case you thought I was ignoring you and you know I'd never do that.'

'Can I come and see you? There's something I need to talk to you about. It concerns Evie, do you remember her?'

'Oh, Adele, how could you say such a hurtful thing, after everything we went through that night? Of course I remember her, I remember everything. Yes, come and have tea with us. I'll bake a cake, it would be so lovely to see you and catch up on all your news. And I have news, too! Very exciting things are happening in my life. You'll be quite surprised, I think.'

'Everything you do surprises me, in a way, Gillian, and I can't say that about many people.'

'I'm blushing. And you were always the interesting one. I expect you have much more exciting things to report than me.'

She lived near Russell Square. It was enviable to live in Bloomsbury – I was nowhere near town – and the building had been designed by the same school of municipal dreamers who had imagined our university campus, with Utopia in mind, and I thought how poor Gillian had been the one for whom their worthy plans had reached accomplishment. The flats rose in widening tiers, like an amphitheatre with balconies across which washing was stretched, and a few plants burned in the summer heat. The shops below were poor and terrible.

'I know it's only council, I was rehoused when I had Ruby, but I love it here, I'm so grateful to live near everything and you can walk into town, I hardly ever take the bus or the tube, it's so easy. I never want to move and the neighbours are lovely. Mummy and Daddy hate it, but they hate almost everything about my life so that doesn't matter. Now come in, the kettle's waiting to be boiled and the cake is on the table.'

It was then that I observed that Gillian, who was dressed in a denim skirt, an oatmeal-coloured T-shirt with stains, and Birkenstocks on brown, hairy legs, had round her neck a gold crucifix with the figure of Christ writhing on it, bouncing up and down on her breasts as if Jesus was trampolining.

'What's that?'

'What?'

'Round your neck.'

She giggled. 'You're so funny. Most of my old friends notice straight away, but you, you're still the same vain old thing, aren't you? Why don't you wear glasses like me? Anyway, I thought you'd be surprised.'

I looked around the flat. Half of the bookshelf consisted of revolutionary literature, those beige-backed volumes of Marx and Lenin's complete works, produced in Moscow and imported to the West in their millions, and Isaac Deutscher's biography of Trotsky. *The Prophet Armed; The Prophet Unarmed; The Prophet Outcast. Russia – A Marxist Analysis. The Employer's Offensive. The Struggle for Socialism. The Meaning of Marxism. Revolutionary Silhouettes. Antonio*

Gramsci: An introduction to His Thought, Parliamentary Socialism by Ralph Miliband.

Like the mummified corpse of Lenin laid out to be viewed by visitors in Red Square, or the ceremonial objects found in the tombs of the pharaohs after millennia in the silence and darkness, they had about them the odour of death and ancient history. In some other world, the Soviet Union was choking the life out of itself and here, propped up in front of the books, as if they were a row of china ornaments, was a series of small, highly coloured, palm-sized pamphlets pronouncing the Good News (*Christ is Risen, Christ Died for Your Sins, Rejoice! You Are Saved*).

A cake, a Royal Doulton teapot with matching plates, cups and saucers for two, a milk jug and sugar bowl were laid out on the table by the window. On the walls were framed family photographs of Gillian and a frightening little girl, growing older, bigger, more belligerent with each pose, the kind of kid who runs around making a noise and says the unspeakable thing that everyone else is thinking.

'That's my lovely daughter Ruby. She's at school at the moment, you should catch her later. The tea service came from Mummy, she has so many, you know. She's determined that the flat should be nice, it's all she *can* do really. We've just got back from South Africa. We went to see Ruby's father but of course he's terribly busy.'

'Who is Ruby's father?'

'Oh, he was a comrade from the ANC when I met him, just visiting, of course. We had a few happy days together.' She smiled and her glasses, no longer huge and ointment pink, but smaller and rounder, magnified an expression in her eyes of wistful memory. 'I know what you're thinking. But it was meant to be. I don't know what I'd do without Ruby. She's the world to me. And my neighbours. I'm terribly lucky. You learn so much from the most unlikely people. Kindness, for one thing.'

'But you were always kind.'

'I didn't know how to be kind to myself, I thought I was so

feeble and useless. Now sit. I'll put the kettle on and we can make a start on this cake, it's Mummy's recipe.'

After we had drunk tea and eaten cake, and Gillian had told me the good news about how Christ was risen and I had nodded politely and she had suddenly held her hand to her mouth and cried out, 'Oh, but I forgot you're Jewish,' Felix arrived. He was about sixty and wore the kind of trilby hat Bobby's father had had clamped on his head. I could see him standing on doorsteps, insistently ringing bells, not giving up until someone answered, inserting his brown slip-on shoe on the mat by the doorframe and speaking in a heavy monotone about Jesus this and Jesus that. He looked like a man with a doctorate in moral disapproval: of fare evaders and adulterers.

'He came here on the *Windrush*, you know,' said Gillian. 'Isn't that marvellous? And all the doors were closed to him but still he managed to get on. He's a ticket inspector on the buses.'

Felix went to the kitchen, moving across the lino with flat feet as he would do when traversing the swaying upper deck of a bus, and got out an enamel mug from the cupboard, the kind whose handles heat up to intolerable degrees unless you have asbestos hands. He had asbestos hands. 'He doesn't like fancy china, do you?'

Felix had not yet said anything. He was a practised glarer. He sat down next to us and poured himself some tea from the pot. Gillian cut him a large slice of cake, which he took on his plate, inspected and smiled.

'You always make a beautiful cake, girl.'

Looking round, what there was no sign of in the room was a musical instrument. A record player and a line of old LPs, some cassette tapes, that was all.

'Do you not have your viola?'

'Oh, no. You see it was worth a lot of money and the Party made me sell it, for the funds.'

'What a wicked thing to do. Those people were always evil, do you not think? Rose told me some terrible things about them.'

'No, it wasn't very nice, was it? And I don't know how I will ever be able to afford another. I work part-time, clerical jobs. It's enough to get by, with Felix's wages, but not enough for a viola. And Ruby is quite musical, but we can't afford an instrument. And here we are in another of Thatcher's slumps. But tell me all about you. I've hardly heard a word for so long.'

I explained about Bobby's death and my inheritance of the house, and my new job on the magazine. Her eyes filled up at the bad news of Bobby. 'How horribly sad. He was always such a lovely boy. And did he have a special friend who loved him?'

'No, I don't think so, that wasn't really the way he was made. He was a loner.'

'I couldn't live like that, what about you? You were always the most glamorous of all of us, the boldest. I used to look at the bourgeois press and expect to be reading about you. Are you married or anything?'

'No.'

In the absence of Felix I suppose I might have told her about George because she would have understood the personae in this heightened drama and it might have even been possible to explain what was going on with me, and how I had arranged to get so stuck in this volatile, obsessive relationship, of which I had some hopes. She would have held her hand to her face and told me to stop, but then so would anyone. I had confided in a couple of friends and they had screamed slightly at my recklessness, but then they could not be made to understand about Evie. And I had not actually said anything about Evie to them.

We rambled on, Jesus bouncing, Felix sitting next to us saying nothing, and eventually the girl came home, very large, her school blouse straining across her chest, her skirt already too small, and she said hello to me, nothing to Felix, kissed her mother with a banging motion on her face and cut herself a piece of cake. They were all looking at me as if I was a visitor from another world, who had come possibly to bring *them* good news of some kind. Maybe that they could move to a bigger, even more centrally located flat.

Finally Gillian said, 'You mentioned poor Evie on the phone.'

'Who's Evie?' said the child.

'A girl we knew at university. Sadly, she died.'

'What did she die of?'

'Drugs,' said Felix.

'There are already drugs at Ruby's school, and she's only just turned twelve. It's heartbreaking.'

I was having difficulty trying to pierce the membrane of the past to go back to that Sunday morning in the house, seventeen years ago, when Gillian had sat by my bed and we had listened to Simon and Garfunkel and heard noises on the stairs.

Ruby said, 'I like your earrings.'

'Thanks.'

'Did they cost a lot?'

'Not much at all.'

'Mum, I want some earrings like that, with sparkles in them.'

She leaned across Felix, took hold of my earlobes and tugged at them sharply.

'Here, have them. Are your ears pierced?'

'No, but I can get them done tomorrow. Mum, will you take me after school?'

'Adele, you shouldn't have done. Ruby, give them back straight away.' But Ruby had run into her bedroom with the earrings and I had got rid of one of the superfluous members of the party.

Felix said, 'You have something on your mind, girl. Spit it out. We can't wait all day. I need a wash.'

He made me uneasy sitting there with his trilby still on his head, slurping his tea, but George's need for the exercise books had to be appeased.

'OK. Gillian, the night Evie died, you were the last person to see her. Is that right?'

'I suppose I must have been. I've gone over and over that night in my mind and I've prayed to God for forgiveness, haven't I, Felix?'

'She has.'

'When you saw her, what state was she in? Was she asleep or awake?'

'She was awake, no question of that. We talked for a minute or two, she was feeling a bit groggy and there were things all over the floor by the bed, so I tidied up a bit, just to make it a bit nicer for her.'

'What did you tidy up?'

'Oh, coffee mugs, two or three I think – I know it was more than one, because I would have washed them if I'd been able to get near the sink but the party was so crowded. And her lovely dress, I put that over a chair, and there must have been other things, but really it was a terrible mess with so many knickers strewn about every-where. I know there were some old school exercise books, but I don't think they were Evie's, because I had a quick peep and they were diaries, from years before. I can't imagine whose they were, so I just put them in a pile by the wall.'

'But what happened to them?

'Didn't her parents take them away when they came?'

'No, they couldn't find them. What exactly did you do with them?'

'Adele, don't be so sharp. I'm telling you everything I can remember. I just piled them on the floor, there was no bedside table or anything. And I gave her the chocolate cake and she said she was feeling very sleepy and then she asked me if Stevie and that awful girl had gone, and I said I thought they had, so that all seemed to be all right, and I gave her a kiss and turned out the light and she smiled at me. And then I closed the door. But whatever I did or said, I think it must have been the reason she died.'

Until then I did not think anyone as harmless as Gillian could do any wrong. Doing wrong is the province of stronger types, like me and Dora and Rose. People with faulty opinions, an air of self-righteousness or in my case my supposedly primitive instincts. Now, looking round at the flat and at the closed door of the intim-idating girl, I thought it might be possible to blunder through life accidentally knocking people over when all you wanted to do was give them a helping hand.

After I had washed up her afternoon-tea dishes, and accepted a couple of pamphlets ('I know you'll just leave them on the tube, but that doesn't matter, someone else will pick them up'), she walked me down the concrete steps of the building to the station.

'Now you know where I am,' she said. 'I'm always here. I'm very happy, you know. I don't think I've ever really not been.'

'That's a form of genius, I suppose.'

'And you so discontented.'

'But discontent is to want something better, not to be a placid cow in the field, munching.'

'Didn't they say that on our first day? Not to be contented cows.'

'I'd forgotten.'

I kissed her on the cheek. I can do that now, I am loosening up.

'How funny, you've never done that before. God does work in mysterious ways, doesn't he?'

39

In the winter, George was after a new stamp. His collection had grown since the single album he tried to keep from rotting in the dampness of the barge. In his house in Chiswick his stamps were kept in their own temperature-controlled room. He was, he said, 'one of the leading collectors of postal history in Britain'. I started laughing. He looked at me with the hurt expression of those whose fate it is to always find themselves misunderstood in some matter close to their heart. 'Can you even spell philately?' he asked me.

'Probably not, I've never had any cause to write it down.'

'Well, I can.'

I knew George was a little dyslexic. He wasn't particularly good with pens and paper and his spelling, when he had written me letters, made me cringe. I'm so glad now that our affair took place in the age of phone calls and not in the age of texts and emails, where I would have had to see his struggle with *thought* and *liaison*, words that slipped from his fingers like a bar of wet soap. And so I, who never referred to his difficulties with the letters of the alphabet, thought it was odd that he was so obsessed with stamps which are the means by which letters, the composition of our thoughts to another person, were sent on their way. The Mercury of the postal era before we all fell into the digital sea. But I understood and sympathised with him for loving the pictures, the postal paintings by unknown artists of another century, tiny windows into other lands. He only collected pictorial stamps of the Far East and had no interest in modern covers.

The stamp he was after was issued in Madagascar in 1895. The postage printed on the stamp was a shilling which must have been fairly expensive at the time, he said. Its colour was slate blue and it showed a pair of robed individuals walking along a jungle path past two postboxes and beneath them, in large letters, was printed KIROBO. Or so George told me, because when I eventually saw it I could barely make out the image. By that time my astigmatism had worsened, there were no contact lenses available for my prescription and I was too vain to wear glasses with George. So what happened was a slight blur, the stamp was a blurry, undifferentiated haze of blue.

George said he would go and see the dealer in person to take a look at it and have a chat with him about other stamps he was trying to track down. I was ancillary to this visit. A winter trip by train to the south coast. The New Forest. Little ponies. A walk together along the beach past the pine trees behind which Bobby had once hidden, making eyes at the Hebrew gentlemen in their suede shoes who made eyes back. Or so he said. He could tell a great story if it burnished his image and to him the whole world was gay, it was a huge party in which the heterosexuals were unlucky onlookers who sooner or later would loosen their inhibitions and join in.

George had never been to Bournemouth, but I had. My family had worked its way through all the Jewish hotels on the seafront for our summer holidays where I, a teenager, played ping-pong and was organised into social activities suitable for Jewish adolescents to prepare us for early married life. Fashion shows and flower-arranging lessons and bridge classes where inquisitive boys, who at night taught you how to smoke cigarettes and laid their trembling hand on your thigh, were inducted into the mysteries of the baize card-table.

In the card rooms our parents played kalooki, a game known exclusively to Jews, like some family secret we are too ashamed and uncertain of the reception to be able to own up to. Those summers in the fifties and sixties I remembered as always being fine, without any rain, me in shorts, my hair in bunches, and my father dressed in his flashiest, wolfiest manner with my mother on his arm, got up in turquoise satin like a tightly upholstered sofa. In Bournemouth Harry and Edna *sauntered*, they walked up and down the promenades like crown princes and princesses from Monaco. My mother brushed her eyelids with pale blue shadow and frosted her lips in fuchsia pink. We travelled down the cliff on the funicular railway, my father in a hounds-tooth checked sports jacket and open-necked shirt, and on the sand we rented deckchairs. Neither of them undressed or took off their shoes. No one went in the dangerous water. If there were any rock pools with crabs and starfish on that long even strand I never found one. The air smelled of Ambre Solaire and Blue Grass and kosher sandwiches wrapped in tinfoil, prepared by the hotel, with odorous salamis inside. My parents lay in their deckchairs looking out at the horizon of the English Channel with suspicion, as if they expected to see a U-boat surfacing any minute.

I booked a room in the inaptly named Tudor, an art deco Jewish hotel in which I had once kissed short, hairy boys named Malcolm and Norman from Cheadle and Finchley. The room was under the name Mrs Ginsberg and they must have expected a retired couple who wanted the set menu soup-and-sandwich lunch followed by an early-afternoon tea in the lounge while the light was still available.

The hotel's hard, chalky whiteness pierced the murk of December. Like all art deco buildings, it reminded me of a cruise ship. I thought it was rather beautiful. I hoped that George might even like it and enter into the spirit of the semi-joke once we were away from the afternoon-tea tables and antimacassars on the backs of the velvet tub chairs. We took separate trains. At the desk I said my husband would be joining me with the luggage. When he arrived he told them he thought I had the luggage. He signed the register as Mr Ginsberg and said he would pay cash up front.

'Your wife is waiting for you,' the receptionist said to him, poker-faced.

George had an old-fashioned taste in lingerie and perfume. On the bed, I was doused heavily in Opium and wearing a set composed of black plunge bra and crotchless knickers. George had found them for me at a shop in Soho and posted them to the office, where I opened the package and saw scarlet tissue paper and laid out the items over press releases for the new Nirvana album.

I didn't want to wear this stuff, but what could I do? I had produced no exercise books to keep him happy. The bra was padded but it was slightly too tight around the back; when I took it off, it left welt marks. I spotted a grey pubic hair sticking out over the black lace. I plucked it out with my fingertips and it hurt. The afternoon had the aspect of a coming disaster, I had nothing to read but I wasn't supposed to read, I was supposed to just lie so he'd open the door and see me like that fucking painting, Manet's *Olympia*, with a black bow round my neck. He'd have belled me like a kitten if he'd dared but George was not that confident. He was *very* confident, but there was something about me he remained unsure of. There was a place beyond which he lost control. He knew it and so did I.

So I lay on the bed in these tart's knickers, looking round at the brocade honeycomb pattern of the bedspread and the stiff satin of the matching pelmet, and the tea- and coffee-making facilities with packets of shortbread biscuits and a trouser press in the corner over which I had draped my dress. I thought I could smell fried fish rising from the lift shaft.

Let's get it over with, I said to the ceiling, as one so often does.

Then George turned up jubilant with his Madagascan stamp.

'You look ... nice.'

He understood he had made an error. I was in all the wrong clothes, they can alter your personality, you know, if only momentarily.

The constant sound of the lift mechanism creakily rising and falling and the heavy footsteps on the fawn nylon carpet in the hall, the imagined smells of chiropody and out-of-date medicines induced a sense of being dosed with laughing gas. I could hear them padding along, my mother's girlhood pals, now old ladies with their dyed hair back-combed into bouffant shapes, and their powdered faces. Kind, suffering, Revlon smiles. 'Adele? What are you *wearing?*'

The afternoon proceeded to various failures. After I had arrived at a miserable semi-climax, enough for George to feel he could raise his numb tongue and give it a rest, he asked if I minded if he turned on the TV.

'There's a BBC2 documentary on about Charlie Chaplin. He's my idol.'

We were both now passing time until our trains home.

'Of course, go ahead.'

We lay under the blankets and sheets in each other's arms like a pair of department-store mannequins arranged into the simulacrum of a couple in love. There had to be a spot on earth where we could be, easily, together. It was just a matter of finding a place. But it was not the Tudor. 'What is so great about Chaplin?' I said. I was prepared to salvage the day with education. Chaplin had always struck me as infantile, a babyish taste of early film-goers who had nothing more sophisticated to entertain them.

'Watch this bit. You'll see.'

The Tramp is running from something, he rushes through the door of a trailer to hide. Inside there is a lion, sleeping. He tries to noiselessly reverse out again by reaching his arm through the slat to open the door from the outside, but only manages to lower the latch and lock himself in. His task is not to disturb the lion and wake it up. Various noisy distractions like a barking dog and a screaming girl threaten to rouse it. The girl faints then after a few minutes the Tramp brings her back to life, splashing her with water from the lion's dish, and she wakes up and unlatches the cage. But once he is free to escape, the Tramp has a change of heart. Now he wants to impress the girl; he behaves as if he is a lion tamer, affects nonchalance and bravado until the roaring lion suddenly frightens the life out of him and he runs full pelt until he reaches a telegraph pole which he races up like a cartoon character. Once safe, he starts to do acrobatic tricks with the same sudden sense of liberation from life's dangers. I cried with laughter.

George took my hand. This is a very intimate gesture when you are in bed with someone. It is greater than sex, it signals togetherness. We were one for a few more minutes.

'Do you see, babe, that in his films men are always bigger than him. He's at the bottom of life's heap, the most fragile, even dogs and car doors are his enemies.'

He talked as he held my hand, with the other jabbing repeatedly at the screen. 'Only with a girl can he be a man, because only chicks are more vulnerable and smaller than he is. Women make him feel big, they make him feel like a tough guy, he's always showing off to them but at the same time he has this terrific dignity, and that's what makes him Everyman, human in his essence. Not even Shakespeare can write the universal little guy: his heroes are kings and princes, his ordinary characters never have the full set of emotions. Chaplin has *every* emotion, including nobility. His films are maybe the most sophisticated of the twentieth century, he's doing something far beyond himself. His sincerity is unbelievable.'

We went on watching the programme together from the bed and we stopped being celluloid people ourselves and dissolved into Adele and George and were tender with each other. This was the only good part of our day together and I knew it at the time. Though not how much worse it would get in a few minutes.

'Here's *City Lights*, maybe one of the greatest movies ever made, where what you think you love and what you love aren't the same thing. He loves her because she can't see his rags, she loves him because she thinks he's rich. What do you love me for, Adele?'

'That's always an unanswerable question, unless you're just inviting flattery.'

He smiled. He did not do this often, he was one of nature's scowlers, but when he smiled the sun came out.

'I think I know. The other amazing thing about Chaplin, which is why I believe he was the greatest actor who ever lived, was that while he is always the little tramp in his bowler hat and cut-away coat, half the time he is acting a woman, he just falls into it, can you see? Watch him. He understands women from the inside because he's always a little less than the ordinary man, less mas-culine. So he can dance like a ballerina, he can express emotion like a screen siren just with his face. It's incredible.'

'But what's that got to do with us?'

'I'll show you.' He got out of bed and sat in front of the dressing-table mirror. His reflection was blocked from me by his back. His muscular neck expanded and contracted, his head raised and lowered as if he was attempting to mould himself into another form. And then he turned around and began to speak in a kind of simper.

'Oh, Stevie, let me put your make-up on. Just a little liner round the eyes.'

He looked grotesque, with his head, the dark hair starting up from it in waves, coquettishly on one side.

'What are you *doing*?'

'Don't you see her?'

'Who?'

'You must do. I'm Lorraine!'

But I just saw a lumpy, fattish man wearing invisible drag and I started laughing again. Nobody had ever laughed at George. He looked at me like a wounded bear, a circus performer with arrows in its side. He got dressed, patted his chest to make sure the stamp was still in the inside pocket of his jacket, and set off along the piny promenade of the Eastcliff and I never saw him again apart from in the newspapers and occasionally TV where he loomed out of the screen, and Evie's face was indeed buried in his features. I saw that quite clearly then.

40

One day, when Eddie was maybe two and a half years old, I turned the key in the door on a winter's afternoon when the lights in the streets had already come on. The sun had set, leaving a grey blurred line above the rooftops, flecked with other shades of grey and black and pinpricks of white. My mother, trying to busy herself with grandmotherly duties, was staying with us and in her generation's belief that electricity was a resource like diamonds, she had not turned the light on in the hall. She thought electricity could run out if you used too much of it. I tried to explain it was infinite. I told her about the oil rigs in the North Sea, along the horizon from the Yorkshire coast, the days when the town gas was replaced by the new clean gas from the bed of the ocean. I had watched Evie dance in the shallows of the water.

The overcast sky from the garden in the rear sitting room of my ground-floor flat was enough for her, and her grandson sitting on her heavy lap, being entertained by old tales from a vanished world, songs she sang in Yiddish, which she had sung to me.

'Shlof meyn kindele, shlof.' Sleep, my little one, sleep.

She told him stories of forests and bears and men on horseback and magic rabbis. These narratives flowed from her memory, sleeping for many years since my own childhood, and rushed out into the room with the Heal's dining table, the poster of Patti Smith from the cover of *Horses*.

My mother was holding out for my return, when in her calculations it would finally become economical to flick a switch on a side lamp and wake up the light.

The flat had a small front garden, very small. I passed along the short path and put my key in the lock and opened the front door and I heard, from the blackness of the tiled hall, a voice say, 'Hello, Mummy.'

How did he know it was me? What was it in my movements, the sound of my heels on the hard floor that he recognised? And why was this the very first time he had ever greeted me as if we were equals, a pair of adults, formal, welcoming, and I was not simply the nourishing body that grew him inside me and fed him and came to him in the night when he cried because he was hungry or a tooth was jaggedly pushing through the soft throne room of gums, or he had a cold and his small nostrils could not cope with the congestion of snot?

In the blind blankness of the hall I reached for the light and saw him standing, holding his yellow bear with blue trousers and green bow tie in his left hand, the other hand with its thumb clamped in his mouth and the mouth smiling, and the thumb dropping from it, not needed to comfort him because *Mummy* was home. I put down my briefcase and lifted him to me and felt his heart beating and hugged him until he began to choke against my chest and was unable to breathe, and my mother came in and said, 'Cup of tea, dear?'

She went into the kitchen to put the kettle on. 'I've baked some biscuits, we can have them with our cuppa. The little one had a tantrum this afternoon, I couldn't do anything with him. His trousers were drying on the radiator and he wanted to put them on and I said he'd have to wear something else, he was lying on the floor kicking his legs up and down, I had to laugh and when you laugh at him it makes him furious. His little pecker was flailing around and his bottom was smacking the carpet. Such a sight. I wish I'd taken a picture. He'll laugh himself when he's older.'

Why did I have him? Everyone asked me the same question and to this day I do not know. Because he was George's child or Evie's nephew? I can't say. I just assert that everyone was right about me, that I was primitive, and some atavistic instinct took hold and I couldn't have an abortion. I had no idea what I was doing. I did not know what life had in store for me, the stink of baby shit – which does not smell sweet, whatever the propaganda – the cease-less wailing, the terror that they have died without you noticing. I would check him in the night to make sure he was still breath-ing.

My mother was asleep on the sofa-bed. Every time she came to stay she took over the flat, her rollers, her hair lacquer, her tubes of Revlon lipstick, her old slippers, her half-slip drying on the clothes horse in the bathroom, her medicines in the kitchen, her tub of bran in the cupboard, her gold jewellery by the sink, her Harold Robbins paperbacks and the *Radio Times* with her pro-grammes ticked off.

'Men,' she said, when I told her I was pregnant, 'are the same the whole world over. And you are my daughter and I am proud of you, whatever they say, I will always stand up for you. Men break your heart, you can only trust another woman.'

There we were, the three of us. I had fallen back down among the women and children, where meals were meagre and laughs were short and dreams were small. Exactly where I had tried to escape from in my Daddy days.

In the first years of Eddie's life I sometimes forgot that I had him and that I was a mother. I would make arrangements to see friends and fail to remember that I had not booked a babysitter and would have to offer my apologies and cancel. Once, I was woken in the morning by his screaming and could not, at first, work out what the noise was. And then I thought, with surprise followed by fleeting despair, He's still here!

But nothing could save me from my son. Having a child pushed me sheer away from the centre of my own life into a corner of it and I resented it. I was outraged. Especially if you are still a child yourself, muttering the universal 'I want, I want, I want' under your breath as you hear him for the twenty-sixth time (you have been counting) get down out of his new big boy's bed which has arrived this morning to replace the barred cage of his cot. Getting out because he can and he wants to. *He wants*. He wants, you want? Who wins? He does. You can give up on this duty, of course it is possible, but so morally wrong that you want to send people to prison for doing that. Your thoughts against them are murderous. You would bring back the death penalty for child cruelty until you have to slap yourself and say, it's love that's talking, and hormones.

For years I smothered my son in kisses until he wriggled out of my arms and it broke my heart that they reach an age when you can't pick them up any more. Once I took him to the doctor to have his inoculations. 'Go and sit on the nice lady's lap,' I said, and off he went as good as gold and climbed on to the knee of the nurse and smiled at her. She stuck the needle in his arm and for a long moment incredulity at this outrage gave way to an expression of such betrayal, as if he knew that he had learned the very worst lesson: that no one can be trusted. You sat on the nice lady's lap and she hurt you. And then he began to scream. I was helpless, tears in my eyes. All I could do was try to hold him but he did not want to be held and that I night I cried as I lay in bed, thinking what I had done to him and how I had to. It was the start of me trying to touch people to make things better, to learn how to relax my stiff neck, being of a notoriously stiff-necked people. (Now my neck is partly locked with bulging discs.)

And I remember standing outside the toilets in John Lewis, a store where men seldom came and only to assist in offering an ignored opinion on the choosing of carpets and beds and washing machines and kettles, or to have their clothes selected for them:

'Hold still, Jim, let me see if this jacket is the right size.' It was the only place in London where you saw a queue for the gents', a line that extended back to the double doors, bladders filled with tea and intestines still digesting scones from the Place to Eat. And my little boy, aged eight, was in there all by himself, being too old to go to the ladies' with his mummy, now standing at a ceramic urinal with his little willy aiming a fine golden arc of piss at the white wall, being looked at, devoured visually, possibly sidled up to and touched in all the wrong places by these purchasers of blenders and cotton tea-towels and beige leather blouson jackets and three-packs of socks. Every one of them looked like a paedophile.

I wanted to elbow them out of the way, walk in and rescue my little boy who was taking too long, far too long. Until eventually he came out again, with his red and yellow backpack weighing down the shoulders of his T-shirt, containing his Game Boy and his crayons and his cardboard box of juice and our phone number and address written on a laminated piece of paper. I had to restrain myself from throwing my arms round him and smothering him with wet, terrible kisses. Now he is twenty-two I must force myself not to hold his hand when he crosses the road.

My boy is called Eddie Fishoff. At the moment he still does not know who his real father is, though obviously that it's not Uncle Yankel who bought the house in Cornwall from me and with whom we spent our summer holidays, later with his stepdad, my very bald husband Juan, the software designer from Buenos Aires, who enjoys high living of various types and whom I met on a plane and followed him to the back. I did this as an act of, as Stevie would have called it, working against. Against the nappy pail. Not many marriages start that way, with a vertical fuck in a plane toilet passing over Sardinia, but ours did and that's all there is to it. Eddie was at home with Grandma at the time, being sung to. So it worked out in that respect. Eddie has a father whom he calls Padrone. 'What's for din-dins, Padrone?'

41

The early years of Eddie's life, before I met Juan, were assisted by an unlikely helper, and I don't mean my mother. For some years I had been living in an off-beat area of London, a dip or former bog at the foot of one of the city's highest hills from which the television and radio transmitter darted out its signals sparkily. The valley below was a black spot for FM radio, a crackle zone. Nor did it have a tube station, on the London map we were *terra incognita*.

The magazine job George had got me was a success. I moved on and up quite quickly to a newspaper colour supplement, editing features. It was another world, working for a paper, one floor away from the newshounds and the football and cricket correspondents. I thrived on the atmosphere and the quick jokes and the general sharpness, the sense of waking up each morning relishing a crisis. My editor was of a withering disposition.

'Oh, don't commission him, he's the type who sits down in a restaurant and says he fancies something *salady*.'

I was a little older than everyone else. This was a new experience for me, coming from that generation born young, and to stay young for ever. I took every precaution to stop my grey roots from showing and began to dress expensively. I thought I could get away with cutting a soignée figure at morning conference and not saying too much.

But I went home to Eddie and my mother, a situation I didn't say too much about. A lot of people didn't even know I had a kid, they wouldn't have believed it of me. I didn't look the type.

The park had a café, a summer paddling pool and a playground with slides, swings, static ladybird cars that jiggled, and knotted ropes for bigger, more robust kids to pretend they were Tarzan. One afternoon, while Eddie splashed in the shallow water in his Noddy shorts my mother had bought him and I tried to read, looking up every paragraph to make sure he had not fallen and was lying on his face, drowned in a few inches of water, I heard an indistinct shout, then another. The cries of angry mothers.

'Fuck off, what you doing here?' 'Aren't you ashamed to show your face?' 'Leave our kids alone.' And other mothers sat silently, as if ashamed at the abuse but unwilling to stop it.

Like a bear assaulted, with spears sticking out of its sides, the woman came blundering towards me on my bench, a grey, hollowed-out version of herself like someone in the bad stages of cancer. The mothers watched her as though they were expelling a demon.

'Dora, is it really you? What's wrong, why are they shouting at you?'

It was a few years since we had been in touch. I had last seen her at Bobby's funeral in Highgate cemetery, where we had been ignored and insulted by his father and walked off to the village for a cup of tea and inevitably our conversation had turned once more, as it always did, to the night Evie died.

She told me then that she had abandoned youth work and gone in for family-support social work. 'The kids are fine, really; I mean they'd all get on OK eventually if we just left them alone to get their heads sorted out but families need incredible help, particularly black families when, you know, they bring with them such sophisticated structures of child-raising that aren't always a good fit with the society they are trying to establish themselves in. They still maintain extended families while here, since the Industrial Revolution, we've gradually abolished that in favour of the nuclear family which is an instrument of reproducing the workforce. It's ironic that we actually *suppress* family self-sufficiency and yet as social workers we have to act as mediators between the state and the community.'

When I moved, after Yankel bought the house in Cornwall from me and I could afford a place with a garden for me and Eddie, I didn't add her to the list of people whom I informed of my change of address and phone number.

'But did you not read about my situation?' Dora said now, standing by my bench, not sitting down, her back to the angry, taunting crowd. 'It was in the papers, it was on TV.'

'Look,' I said, pointing to Eddie in the water, his blond head dewed with water, his pale chest with its plump fold of flesh over the fragile bones. 'I've had my own situation.'

'What? He's yours? You have a kid?'

'Yes.'

'Whose is he? Are you married?'

'No.'

But I could not concentrate on whatever story she had to tell me while Eddie was in the paddling pool so I went over to persuade him to come out with me, by wrapping the wet body in a towel. 'I don't *want* to,' he cried, reminding me of the years of my own 'I wants'. For what he did not want and I wanted for him were the warfare they never tell you about, not in the antenatal classes, not in the children's clothes departments, not in the toy shops where the wanting rises to its highest pitch, and still you can't hear it until the hot hand is in your own and your eardrum is being pierced.

I picked him up; my back twinged. He was getting heavy. He had his father's iron bones.

'Do you *know* her, is she a friend?' said a mother I had often spoken to, about our sleepless nights and our anxieties about the various stages of child development ('Is he late, and what does that mean?').

'Yes, we were at university together.'

'So was she always so bloody callous, your mate?'

I turned back to Dora, who had drawn a force-field of hatred around her. Eddie wriggled in my arms and screamed shrilly, I stuffed him into his trousers and T-shirt and sandals. He did not want to go. I gave him a square of chocolate, his face turned beatified, as if he had seen the beams of heaven's glory.

Dora stood and watched us, did nothing in her greyness, seemed too inhibited to help, as if touching Eddie might be regarded as a form of contamination of his velvet skin.

'Do you want to come back for a cup of tea, I'm just round the corner?'

We walked together out of the park and along the street to my flat. Eddie was hungry, I fed him a soft-boiled egg and toast soldiers. I allowed him to watch a children's programme seated on the sofa with his mouth in a round shape, his fists half clutched, another square of chocolate smeared on his fingers.

Dora and I sat in the kitchen. 'You don't know,' she said, 'about the little girl who died?'

When she reminded me, yes, of course I remembered all about the little girl who had died. Her body was covered with sores, welts, half-healed scars, whip marks and the impression in several places of human teeth. The torture had ended when a dog had been set on her, a hungry dog. She had been half eaten when her body was found. Her mother and grandmother ran away and hid in Epping Forest, leaving the body to be found by neighbours, driven mad by the howling and barks of the abandoned dog through the walls of the flat.

'Billie DeCosta.'

'Yes.'

'And what has she got to do with you?'

'I was the social worker. The head of social services was the one whose picture was in the paper, but it was me, I was the one who had all the contact, she never even met the family, it was all me.'

Dora sat on the kitchen chair looking like this ghost of herself, of the exceptionally pretty eighteen-year-old with her radiant, shining certainties who laid down the foundations of everything that had happened to us, with her soirées and consciousness-raising group and the houses she found. Dora, I think now, was the source of everything, good and bad. It was impossible to dismiss her influence.

'And then when the little girl died I thought, Just get through this, you only need to endure, get through it, because I've never been afraid of a challenge and actually, I should have just said sorry and resigned. But I thought I was right and I didn't.'

'But what were you doing in my park?'

'It's near where I used to work, didn't you know? I live on the other side of the hill. You can't see it from here – it's like the dark side of the moon to you, I suppose. I was sacked this morning. I'm so sorry, I'm so terribly sorry, and sorry is nothing, isn't it? It's meaningless. What does being sorry do? It's a rock I keep stumbling over, that being sorry doesn't bring the child back, or do anything. It's just a stupid ridiculous word, it's Christian, isn't it? If you say you are sorry, then you can be forgiven. Turn the other cheek, or something. That family was Christian, tub-thumpingly Christian, not in a humane way, either. It was terribly Old Testament and vengeful, not gentle-Jesus-meek-and-mild like we were taught in Sunday school.

'I keep going over it all in my mind. It's like a never-ending tape, the pictures and the words of the visits and how when I see it now it's all so *obvious*, how could I have *not* seen what was happening? It's so stark. I was walking into a hellish place and I was smiling, stupid smiles, thinking everything was roses and I was helping and that that household, however chaotic, was better than ours because it was authentic. And isn't that important, really? Don't you think our world is so plastic, and our relationships plastic?

They used to feel sorry for me because I had no children. I didn't tell them I had a girlfriend, partly because we're not supposed to discuss our private lives, but because I thought they wouldn't understand. I didn't want kids; Bev would have liked them but I thought that being gay meant that you lived by a different set of rules. She always said she thought that family was weird.'

'Is she looking after you?'

'No, we split up a while ago. It turned out me and Bev lived our lives by completely different sets of principles.'

'Maybe you live too much by principles.'

'How can you say that? Without principles what do you have exactly?'

'You never change, Dora. Where are you staying?'

'The police have put me in a hotel. The press are swarming over our lives. My mother is in a nursing home, she's got Alzheimer's, and they're camped outside in case I come and visit her. I hadn't left my room for six days until I couldn't stand it any more and walked down to the park, just to get away from the fucking tea- and coffee-making facilities and the view of a brick wall.'

My mother said, 'You must stand by your friend. A woman who is in trouble always turns to another woman, they're the only ones who will not desert you. Look what happened when your father died. If it wasn't for them, I'd have killed myself. What she did was terrible, but take my situation, married to a criminal who robbed everyone, even his own flesh and blood. Remember how we buried the valuables in the garden and Yankel came and helped me? Well, you don't know the half of what the girls did for me, and they got you that wonderful job you turned your nose up at. You must be a true friend to her, whatever she's done. Believe me, they're all you've got apart from a mother's love and who knows, one day you will need the favour.'

And because of my mother's unexpected intervention, Dora came to live with me for several months. She slept in the living room on the sofa-bed and looked after Eddie while I was out at work. She did not go to the park but found another place for their afternoon walks, a secret passage between the distant tube station and the hill, a disused railway line, little known in those days, undiscovered, and Eddie ran along it in the company of dogs and felt free.

Dora had been semi-destroyed more than any of us. She really had been beaten down to her hands and knees, and it turned out to be me and my family that showed her how the whole hard-hearted trick of survival worked.

'What do you people *believe* in?' she cried. 'What do you stand for exactly? How do you live, if not by principles? Isn't that the whole of everything?'

My mother looked at me and gave the Jewish shrug. I winked back. It was our greatest moment together.

PART THREE

42

So we were going back. Forty-one years after we arrived, we were returning, a party of grey-hairs and those who went to the hair-dresser every four weeks so as not to be grey-hairs. A party of people in their late fifties, me, Dora, Gillian and Brian, Rose's university boyfriend, who had accomplished all we were going to accomplish but had not yet understood this. Rose was a life peer in the House of Lords. She had been tapped to receive an honorary doctorate from our old university.

She had hired a Rolls-Royce and a chauffeur to drive us to Yorkshire. She hoped we would find this gesture amusing and take it in the spirit in which it was intended, an ironic finger up to our former teenage selves. Even Dora, who had no discernible sense of humour, could sense the outline of a kind of a joke in this proposal.

Rose was not accompanying us in the Roller. She was travelling alone, in a mundane Lexus, in order to catch up on her paperwork and emails. We received an itinerary of our three-day stay with the details of the restaurant meals that had been booked for us and the Vice-chancellor's lunchtime reception and the Chancellor's drinks party and the smart dinners. There was a dress code for each of these occasions. The baroness's secretary asked us to contact her

directly if we had any queries. The baroness herself would be joining us for dinner; she had taken a private dining room in the hotel
and our dietary preferences had been noted. The secretary asked
me, for a second time, if I was sure that I did not want a kosher
meal and what types of seafood were acceptable. Brief biographies
of us all had been attached to the email, as if we were strangers at
a conference. Gillian had printed everything out and brought it
with her in a file folder.

Our driver said he thought he could make it in four hours with
a stop for lunch. He wore a uniform and chauffeur's cap and his
name was Stefan. 'Nice day for it, should have a lovely run. Sit
back and enjoy the scenery.'

'And where are you from?' Dora asked him, for the chauffeur's
cap was causing her discomfort.

'Romania.'

'That was Ceauşescu, wasn't it? I remember the night of the
people's revolution, it was Christmas, we were sitting down to have
our lunch and we kept jumping up to turn on the TV, to see if
there was any news. It was my Dad's last Christmas before he
died and he kept telling us all to get back to the table, but we
were fascinated.'

'I know. We marched to the palace and killed him. But I was just
a kid, I don't remember.'

'After that, we thought we'd have real socialism in Eastern
Europe.'

'But instead you are riding in a top car driven by one of the
ungrateful masses who didn't want any kind of socialism. I hope
you are not too disappointed.'

Dora was lean with a proud bearing ('a lot of Alexander
Technique'), she carried her chin really well. Most of us jut our
chin out from too much time in front of a computer, making a big
problem for our necks. I have terrible arthritis in mine. Her pret-
tiness had gone long ago and been replaced by the hawkish,
handsome profile of a Red Indian.

'I don't know if anyone told you,' she said to us, when we had all settled back into our seats upholstered in mushroom-coloured leather and played with the gadgets, the seat-rests, the folding-down tables, the screen that dropped from the roof in case we wanted to watch a movie, 'I had breast cancer five years ago. I'm absolutely fine now. I had a double mastectomy, to be on the safe side. I don't miss those heavy bags of fat hanging from my chest one bit. I never could stand the bra's harness. You look absolutely great by the way, Adele, you must have terrific genes. Your mother was a very well-preserved woman right to the end.'

'Brian,' said Gillian, 'do you remember when we were marching for something or other and I tripped on my shoelace going round Piccadilly Circus and there was blood all over my knee and you were so kind and helped me up when other people were laughing?'

'We all did a lot of marching in those days, and much good it did us. I can't remember half the things I marched for. We marched in baseball boots with thin rubber soles and sometimes even in flip-flops. And then we went to the Wimpy bar and ate processed meat end-products in a bun and drank instant coffee. The last demonstration I went on was against Thatcher in Brighton. I was punched by a policeman. He broke my nose. I could have regarded this as a terrific souvenir of the class struggle, but it hurt like hell. I had to go into work on Monday and explain myself. What about you, Gillian, do you still demonstrate or have you given all that up? Did you all march against Iraq, by the way? I didn't bother, what was the point?'

'There's always a point,' said Dora.

'The war had already been decided, anything we did was just a gesture.'

'And what's wrong with that? Doesn't it build solidarity?'

'It left us with bitterness and cynicism. Better to stay at home and read P. G. Wodehouse. That's what I did. Never a wasted day when you read good old Plum.'

'And what about the class relations?' I said. 'Weren't those people parasites?'

'Oh, absolutely. No question of that, and a class that no longer exists, or not in that form. No, there are no more fearsome aunts of that ilk. But you see, I teach. And the longer I teach, the more I despise the younger generation. I know it's awful but it's almost impossible not to. One enjoys their vitality of course, but they're from the moon, the moon, I tell you.'

You could see what had happened to Brian if you had a time-lapse photograph of his life, like the speeded-up life cycles of plants, but otherwise, it was incomprehensible to me. How had any of us been that then and this now? But the 'that' was just children with moustaches and lipsticks.

I turned to Gillian. 'Are you still involved with the Church?'

'Well, hmm. Oh yes. I mean no. Of course, obviously I still think the Church is absolutely marvellous, it does so many impor-tant things, particularly in Africa, but I wish God wasn't involved, just the nice people doing what they do out of the goodness of their hearts. I've rather fallen out with God, or he has fallen out with me. When my husband died somehow God wasn't really there for me in the way I expected.'

'So what do you do with yourself now?'

'Oh, I've got a wonderful job! I work for the International Esperanto Society. Do you speak Esperanto, Brian?'

'Of course not.'

'Why do you say that? It's a lovely idea. And it will be hard work, of course, before it catches on, but the reward is so great.'

'I suppose all the best causes are lost causes.' Brian looked at his watch.

'It isn't a lost cause at all, its day will come.'

After further discussion of *lingua francas* – Latin, French, English – and languages that were dying or dead, we fell into silence. Brian put his head back on the mushroom-coloured uphol-stery and dozed for a few minutes. Dora smiled to herself and looked out of the window. Gillian took out an Esperanto diction-ary and ticked off words in it. I thought how dull passing nature was, always monotonous shades of green with occasional legs moving across it. I began to read the news on my iPad. I was made redundant a few months ago. Skills like mine, editing a magazine, which is the art of moving the reader on from one thing to next, making them read something they don't know they are interested in, were becoming obsolete. No one reads that way any more. Everything is separate from everything else.

I was not sorry to have been let go. I was by far the oldest person in the office. I was the old crone, I was a little bit ridiculous. This hurt. We were moving forward into new phases of our lives, ones in which everything to do with hope and promise had no meanings for us. We could have as much hope as we liked but any promises had already been fulfilled.

'*Et in Arcadia ego*, and to Arcadia we are returning, to see how it has changed,' I said, waking everyone up.

'You English-lit types have read too much Evelyn Waugh,' said Brian. 'You lack the advantages of a hard public-school Classical education. Arcadia is life, ego is death.'

'What?'

'In this tag, arcadia means life and ego means death. Even the dead once shared the pleasures of being alive.'

'I see.' Then back to the white lines of the motorway.

Stefan intruded himself into our little pockets of individuality to announce that it was twelve-thirty. 'The lady has made a lunch for you. She has given me directions to a very nice spot where you can have a picnic if it is fine. It seems fine. Do you agree?'

I could not deny that it was fine though I had no wish to move out of the electric comfort of the interior of the Rolls. The English sky was dramatic with scarcely moving cumulus clouds, as if they had been painted by a child's brush. Stefan had turned the air-conditioning on when we skirted Coventry but the car had begun to smell slightly, of clashing perfumes, and an ointment on Gillian's sandalled foot.

We pulled off the motorway and drove along narrower and narrower roads, canopied with summer trees, past hedgerows blooming with pretty little wildflowers, until we came to a stream, a bridge, woods.

'This is lovely,' said Gillian. 'Oooh, isn't it nice, Adele?'

'We could even go for a stroll after we've eaten,' Dora said.

'Not me, not in these heels,' I said.

She looked down at my fuchsia suede shoes. 'I don't understand why you would travel like that.'

'Well, I just do.'

'I don't think I could manage the grass, not with my arthritis,' said Brian. 'I'll have mine in the car.'

'I don't much fancy it either,' I said, picturing a blanket and hard ground.

But Stefan said, 'Don't worry, no one has to sit on the grass, I have a picnic table and chairs for you. You'll be happy, I promise, when you see what the lady arranged.'

He took out a folding table and camp stools, and a chiller box. He laid a white tablecloth, knives, forks and china plates, produced bottles of wine, white and red, and glasses. Out came a roast chicken, potato salad, a green salad, two types of bread, olives, strawberries, cream, shortbread biscuits, a box of chocolates.

'This is ridiculous,' said Dora. 'I brought my own packed lunch, I'll have to throw it away now.'

'Or save it for later,' Gillian said, 'you might still be hungry before you get there. You never know. Waste not, want not.'

We ate lunch. A swan swam past us. We all followed it with our eyes as if we had never seen a swan before, but swans, I always think, force you to look.

We were all shifting our uneasy hips in the uncomfortable folding chairs, thinking how idyllic and special this moment out of time was and how much we would prefer to be in a restaurant. We were too old for picnics, our joints did not work in the way they had once used to, the doctor had explained to me about the wearing away of cartilage under the everyday, ordinary experience of the vertical. The beauty spot was putting on a tremendous show for us, it was pulling out all the stops to impress. A kingfisher flew for a moment over the stream into the trees. Dora saw it flashing and cried out, 'Look at that!' but we had turned our heads too late. The failure of the kingfisher to fly slowly enough to enchant us enhanced a sense of discontent, that we were the wrong people in the right location. After we had eaten, Dora took out a flat plastic box with cavities in which lay a host of multi-coloured pills.

'Down the hatch,' she said.

'That reminds me to take my vitamin D,' I said.

'What's that good for?' asked Brian.

'It's sorted out a lot of mysterious aches and pains. But you have to take it for a few months until you really feel the effect.'

'What about glucosamine? Do you take that?' Dora said.

'Sadly, the studies have more or less discredited it,' said Brian. 'But there's no harm at all in half an aspirin. My blood pressure is on the high side.'

'Mine is very low,' I said. 'The last time it was tested the nurse said I had the blood pressure of a "young lady".'

'Well, good for you.'

'I never go to the doctor and I'm always well,' Gillian said.

'There's something to be said for that. What about bowel-cancer screening? Have they sent you the test kit yet?'

'No.'

'You wait. You have to poo into your own hand then smear it on a card.'

'I don't believe it.'

'Then put in the post.'

'But the poor postman,' Dora said.

'It's all sealed up. Still, fancy carrying a bag of poo samples over your shoulder.'

'And we used to say that everything was shit, meaning the world.'

The sun dappled and dappled our faces so we looked alternately young and very old. 'What has happened to us?' cried Dora. 'We're medicating and testing ourselves to the grave. I tried homoeopathy, but it doesn't work, it doesn't work at all.'

'I'm all for pharmaceuticals,' I said. 'People with HIV survive for years and years now. If only Bobby had been able to hold on for another decade; but he was right in the eye of the storm.'

'I don't know Bobby,' Brian said.

'He wasn't in your set. He was an aesthete.'

'Then I wouldn't have done, no.'

He reached into the inside pocket of his jacket and said, 'Look, I don't know if anyone's interested, but it seems to me like this is the right moment for a toke, if anyone still does.'

He held up a slim little joint. We stared at it with a sense of sudden familiarity for a long-lost object we had never expected to find again, and the unease that we had forgotten what its purpose was.

'Just me then?'

'I'm in,' I said.

'Oh, you don't still do that, do you?' said Dora.

'Why not?'

He lit the joint and passed it to me. I took a sip of smoke, then another. A few minutes earlier we had been in a rush to leave, to get away from the folding chairs and back to the leather comfort of the Rolls, but this honeyed spot in the sunlight, with the driver sitting behind the wheel, eating his own lunch and reading a Romanian newspaper, was suddenly hard to get out of. The chairs themselves were not easy to stand up from. They tipped sideways as you bent your knees to rise. Gillian took some knitting from her shoulder bag and began to softly clack her needles. Dora, erect in her seat, flat-chested under her linen shirt, looked around for more signs of unusual wildlife and Brian began to smile fatuously.

And then after a while of lazing and dreaming, of stopping being the recently-made-redundant Adele who once managed budgets and staff, she came back, walking along the path in her white dress and black baseball boots. *Let all sweet ladies break their flattering glasses and dress themselves in her.*

'And are we,' said Dora from a far distance, 'all thinking about Evie?'

'No. Who is Evie?' said Brian. 'Another one I didn't know.'

'The girl who died.'

'I don't remember anyone dying. Who was she?'

'But you were there, that night. And the next morning. You came round at lunchtime with Rose, you were a tower of strength actually. I remember thinking we needed someone who wasn't weeping and it was you.'

A long fringe of grey hair hung below Brian's straw hat, which he had not taken off in the car. There was a suspicion of a monk's pate of baldness. He was wearing polka-dot socks and leather sandals. I recalled him in beige suede desert boots and his tomato-coloured shirt sagging under badges, pushing the paper at you outside college dining rooms, chanting his slogans in a sing-song voice. I have always pictured the brain as a smooth interior with a surface veneer scored with tiny slits, into which some situations get trapped by the corner and can't escape and form there into memories until they are absorbed into the brain's capacious chambers of recollection.

'I used to have such an excellent memory,' he said, 'I was like the internet, I couldn't erase a thing. Now I ... Well, you know what happens. These domestic forgetfulnesses with keys, and cups of tea made and left to go cold, and people's bloody names. The sight of a new class at the beginning of each year is beginning to terrorise me, all those round smooth faces like the children in *South Park*, and the list in front of me waiting to match up with those identical moons.'

'But Evie was memorable.'

'Really? In what way, exactly?'

I tried to help but my tongue had acquired a new unnecessary weight, making it hard to lift.

'This is quite strong stuff,' I said eventually. 'Where did you get it?'

'It's skunk, didn't really exist in our day, a lot stronger than what we're used to. My younger son is my supplier, though he's annoyingly reluctant. Evie Evie Evie, let me try to connect. Was she was she was she that rather silvery mad girl? Bipolar?'

'Was she bipolar?'

'Probably. It wasn't called that then, but I remember a girl who had all the significant symptoms. She shouldn't have been there, she needed treatment. So she died, wow. And I've wiped the memory, or maybe it's the first sign of Alzheimer's. Which statistically is bound to come to one of us. I wonder who?'

'We all thought we were responsible for Evie's death,' Dora said.

'Was it drugs and booze?'

'Yes, and cake.'

'I love cake,' said Gillian. 'The word for cake in Esperanto is *kuko*.'

'Hmm,' said Brian. 'Time for lunch. I'm starving.'

'We just had lunch.'

'Oh, yes. Now is that the stoned munchies talking or dementia? I'll never know.'

Everything was strange. We had been in the Rolls-Royce, we had talked about Rose, I had even spoken of Eddie. Now I remembered the big girl in Gillian's flat grabbing at my earrings, tugging at me.

'What happened to your daughter, Gillian?'

'She lives in Johannesburg. I miss her terribly. You have a baby and you think you're attached for life and you aren't. But she's doing terribly well.'

'Do you speak to each other in Esperanto?'

'Oh, no. Ruby is learning to speak Xhosa. We do have a society there, but unfortunately Ruby isn't really involved. It's funny what you said about lost causes, Brian. I must tell her that, she might find it interesting. I can't ever really explain myself very well to Ruby. And she gets a bit exasperated with me. But why not, she's young and fancy-free, she must have lots of other things on her mind.'

But the real world was becoming more vaporous and implausible and the memories strengthened and soon we were speaking of Stevie, lost at twenty. No one knew what had happened to him, or that girl Denise. When I looked down at my own hands, I did not recognise them. The rings seemed unfamiliar.

Evie on the riverbank.

'I'm not smoking this stuff again,' I said. 'It's ridiculously strong.'

'I know.'

I thought I saw a tear form in his right eye, and felt a sense of sudden doom, which he later explained was just the usual side-effects of this stuff.

'I'm sorry I rolled it now, but I find it helps.'

'Helps what?'

'Oh, you know.'

I thought, No I don't. I had sat with my grandfather in the garden and he had told me about the *dybbuks* and the *ibburs* and I was still telling Eddie these old stories, I still believed in stories and how they are told and I still wondered what had happened to Mrs Pugh's notebooks which I had never been able to produce for George. Maybe they would be just lying there when we arrived, waiting to be picked up from the floor. Anything seems possible when you're stoned, aged fifty-eight, for the first time in thirty-five years. Possible, but threateningly so.

43

The campus had spread out far beyond the perimeter of the plastic-bottomed lake, running into the surrounding fields where new departments rose glassily into the grey skies. Double our own teenage years had passed since we had come there at the beginning of a now-discredited decade. The ethos of arts speaking to humanities had passed away. The colleges had no purpose other than to house bedrooms, dining halls and bars where no one drank, preferring the new student union building. As far as I knew there were no totalitarianisms left to defeat, and no sets of seductive all-encompassing ideas remained for students to fall into. The biscuit-coloured one-storey computer building was now a store room. Off-site, a multi-storey tower of glass and steel was badged with the name of its corporate sponsor.

The layout of the JCR of our college had been completely reconfigured; the porter's lodge was not in the same place, the telephone booths were gone altogether. The conversation pit and the primary-coloured sponge cubes had been sent to a landfill site decades ago. On the lake, many generations of water life had been born, grown up, hectically reproduced in squawks and flurries of wings, laid their eggs, the chicks had hatched and the old birds gone to die in the reeds.

No one was left who remembered us. All who had taught us were dead or retired. We were ghosts standing on the concrete bridge looking down at the island which had once held the ruins of the robotic Evie. The librarian said, 'No, I can assure you there was never a café on the ground floor. Though I've never looked at the original plans.'

Structurally, some of the old buildings were in trouble. One college was sliding down the slope it stood on.

Brian held forth. The construction had been based on the old CLASP system of prefabricated modular steel frames covered in cladding, invented in the fifties to throw up schools quickly for an expanding population of post-war children. CLASP stood for Consortium of Local Authorities Special Programme; cynics, Brian said, had renamed it Collection of Loosely Assembled Steel Parts. CLASP expanded out to railway stations and office buildings. It was a system simple, industrial, modern and hated. Form followed function with little decoration.

Lately the campus had become overrun with rabbits. Students went out with traps and even guns to hunt them.

Our past was fossilised inside the historic centre. It was mentioned that the old buildings would have to be pulled down one day, they were coming up to their fiftieth birthday, having been designed to last only twenty-five years. Over their walls climbing plants had been trained to soften the unrepentant utilitarianism. Brian said, 'But I think they've mellowed a little, don't you? I wonder if those brash glass palaces will do as well.'

I had the vertiginous sense of time-travelling, but there was something lost and cold and alone about our party in late middle age walking in our own footsteps. Something was a dream, now or then. The memory of our young selves burned with an intensity we had not felt for many decades. We were compromised people in so many ways and were the accretion of our compromises. The founding spirits had not warned us that this was who we would become.

The walkways were full of students about to graduate tomorrow, with parents in tow, showing these scenes of a final glory before they would be cast out, as we had been cast out, to become the people they were supposed to be. They all looked preposterously young. I fervently wished them well. I had been to Eddie's graduation last year and seen him in his mortarboard amble up to receive his degree and shake hands with the Chancellor. I did not go to my own degree ceremony, none of my friends did. But here he was in a semblance of a suit borrowed from Juan, lining up with the history boys and the history girls who wobbled on unaccustomed heels, car-to-bar stilettos which have become the footwear of choice for the graduand. The immense smiling. When I was them, I was hitchhiking across America, I was commanding the machinery of the dodgem cars below the Mason–Dixon Line.

We were thick with nostalgia.

Dinner had been arranged in a private dining room at the hotel, Rose presiding over us, laying her palm over the bill. We got drunk and stayed up until one in the morning. The next day we were hungover, with poisonous headaches, blunted by paracetamol and a cooked breakfast.

At eleven, we took our seats in the rotunda. The Chancellor and his party processed in, with Rose behind him in a grey gown with a maroon hood. The head of the Law Faculty read an encomium to her achievements, 'beginning, if I am correct, with running for president of the Student Union against a stuffed parrot named Monty and arguing with a stubborn electorate that jokes should be kept out of politics. And winning, resoundingly.'

I had no recollection of that.

Rose was presented with a maroon tube, embossed with the university's crest, two keys crossed above a crenellated castle resting on a bed of oak leaves. *In limine sapientiae* was inscribed in a scroll at the base. So we hack on, I thought, still trying to cross the threshold of wisdom.

Rose put on her reading glasses and began to speak to the assembled undergraduates and their parents as if she was addressing a party conference. She spoke of the resentment of the young against earlier generations who had gone to university on full grants, who had not worked during termtime because the administration expressly forbade it; we were to be dreamers and thinkers, not part-time shop assistants and bar girls. But we had, she reminded them, left in the middle of a recession so deep that it had led to radical and frightening social and economic change, the tearing-up of the contract written in 1948. A glancing reference to Margaret Thatcher, some titters from the parents. The children looked up at her. 'Before they were born,' Dora whispered. 'She was kicked out before they were born, they have no memory of her.'

Rose said that student radicalism, gestures however flamboyant and seemingly decisive, had given way to the quieter demand for justice. She quoted Sir Thomas More in Robert Bolt's play *A Man for All Seasons*. 'And this is something on which I rest every case.'

I thought she caught my eye, and winked at me from the podium.

And when the last law was down, and the Devil turned round on you – where would you hide, Roper, the laws all being flat? This country's planted thick with laws from coast to coast – man's laws, not God's – and if you cut them down – and you're just the man to do it – d'you really think you could stand upright in the winds that would blow then?

Applause. 'I saw that film,' said Gillian. 'It was Paul Scofield, wasn't it?'

'I have only one more of these shockers to sit through before I retire,' said Brian. 'Now where are the drinks we were promised?'

We were led out of the rotunda through the thickets of under-graduates being photographed by their parents, grey caps twirled on fingers and jettisoned into the lake, along a path through the topiary garden, past the manor house to a single-storey building hidden behind high yew trees.

It had been here all along, the vice-chancellor's residence. A Modernist concrete slab with picture windows and original fittings from the sixties. All the time we had been inserting pellets of newspaper into holes where the slugs slimed through into the bath, the VC had been sitting on G Plan furniture drinking cocktails.

The current VC was younger than we were. He was eager for our memories of the 'old times'.

And Rose, now without her gown and sugar-sack hat, in a crisp black suit and high patent shoes, her ears flashing with pearl and diamond studs, was laughingly discrediting everything we had all once stood for.

'For even Adele, who was not one iota political, came here with the understanding that we were creating a brand-new world, didn't you? Isn't that why you chose this place?'

'Actually, no. I wrote a letter to your predecessor,' I said to the VC, and related the story of the postcard, my father's death, my desperation, the perfume counter, the interview with Professor Fine who did not, I realised in retrospect, believe me, but was either amused by me or was demonstrating some kind of complicity. We were an alliance of liars.

Gillian, dependably, said, 'Oh, you are so clever and brave.'

'I wonder if we still have that on file,' said the VC. 'That would be one for the archives, wouldn't it? Not possible now, though. Three As for English, I'm afraid. We really don't have that kind of discretion any more.'

'Yes, it was completely different, the spirit was different.'

'That's probably true. It was a set of very utopian principles on which the place was set up, but we realised by the nineties that it couldn't function like that any more. We were dropping down the league tables, we had absolutely no international reputation because we were simply too small. It was expansion or die. We had to raise a fortune.'

And then he began to tell us about our long-forgotten founder, and his plan to defeat totalitarianism though the humanities talking to the sciences. 'Of course you of all people know all about that, Rose. And all the architecture was to follow through on the same principle. What a lovely idea. How nice for you all to have been the beneficiaries. Do you consider yourselves lucky? I've always wondered. Most of all, we gave you all the freedom you wanted. Today, we see ourselves as having a duty of care to our students, we don't abandon them if we perceive they're going under, we have a first-rate counselling programme, and we don't throw them out into the cruel world when they're finished. This is where the Alumni Association comes in, to match up our former students who have done well with those who are making their start. Are you all members of the Alumni Association? If not, I have the forms here.'

The joke was greater than I had first understood. We had been brought here by Rolls-Royce in order to be tapped for our wealth and contacts. But Rose had delivered to the university not her colleagues at the Bar or in the Lords, but an unemployed magazine editor, a yoga teacher, a professor of economics about to retire and a secretary. Gillian, not seeing this, blundered in with a description of the Esperanto Society, offering to set up an organisation on campus if there wasn't one already.

'I think I'll have another drink,' I said. 'Is there any champagne?'

'We'll be serving that at lunch. It's a buffet.'

'Good-oh.'

We went to another glassy building for lunch. The windows gave a panoramic view of the whole campus, you could see how tiny the old site was, surrounded by the mini-Chicago depleting the surrounding fields.

We took our plates and passed along the line to receive salmon *en croûte* and balanced our champagne glasses in little plastic contraptions jutting out from the side of the plate. There were place-settings on the table. I was seated next to the head of the English Department, a woman in her late forties. She asked me who had held her position in my day.

'Professor Fine.'

'Oh, yes. A memorable figure, probably one of the last of the generation of Central European émigrés driven out by the Nazis. Our department in those days was a tiny bit parochial and insular, very much enslaved to the English canon, and he brought to us that extraordinary polyglot mind, at home in several languages. And a . . . subtle sense of humour, I've been told.'

'I've always wondered why he let me in.'

'I overheard you earlier talking about that extraordinary letter. In those days we did take a risk on people, we were able to. I'm not even sure if the DofE would let us get away with it now. And the parents of applicants with the three As might even sue. It's a shame. Or a sham. I don't know which. Professor Fine passed away in the nineties.'

'I know, I read his obituary. Was it Aids?'

'That is what I've heard.'

'When I was here it was starting to be the time that people no longer needed to lead double lives. He came to my birthday party, with his wife. Would you go to a student birthday party?'

'I don't know. I've never been asked. I'm not sure whether or not it would be appropriate. There are much more formal barriers now between staff and students.'

'I wonder what happened to Tony Blount.'

'Who was he?'

'My supervisor.'

'Before my time, I'm afraid. But was it a nice party?'

'No.'

'I'm sorry to hear that; why not?'

'There was a girl who died.'

I told her about the party, about calling Professor Fine at home, then calling Tony Blount from the phone box and how they would not help me because of our freedom.

'Outrageous. Whatever happened to the boy?'

'He dropped out that very week. We were talking about him yesterday, no one's heard a thing about him since he came to the house the next day. He vanished. And now I hear from Brian that Evie was probably bipolar, when we thought her madness was a kind of style.'

'R. D. Laing came to the university to deliver a lecture around the time you were here, did you see him?'

'Of course.'

'And what did you think?'

'I didn't believe that the mad were sane and the sane were mad. I thought he was another charlatan. He disgusted me. Little rat-like man.'

'I wonder if we still have their files, these people you're talking about. You tell such a good story about them. I'd love to know what the administration wrote, the kind of language they used in those days.'

'And could you look them up?' We had got to the meringue shells with fruit and cream and chocolate. Rose was rising to her feet to make another speech, it was her habitual mode of verbal delivery.

And again. '*Could* you look them up?'

'I don't see why not.'

In the afternoon, we were taken on a guided tour of the town. A medievalist showed us round the cathedral, but Dora and I broke off. We took a pleasure cruise down the river. We travelled part of the way along the banks of the flood plain towards the palace of the archbishop. The wharves had been turned into restaurants. 'Do you remember that pub?' said Dora, pointing at the quayside. 'That's where Rose and Brian and Gillian used to go, to plot the revolution.' A sign outside announced that it was now a gas-tropub.

'There was a revolution,' I said, 'just not the one they had in mind.'

'Nothing was what we had in mind. That is what's so amazing.'

'You seem to be thriving.'

'Yes, I am. My yoga practice is doing very well. And I'm study-ing to be a life coach.'

'What is that?'

'Helping people achieve personal goals.'

'It sounds very useful.'

'It is. I really learned about it from your mother.'

'My mother knew about life coaching?'

'Not in the formal sense, but she was very ... I'm not sure how to describe Edna. I'd say she understood how to pass on through all life's difficulties.'

'That's true.'

'I liked her. She wouldn't let me sit around crying when I stayed with you, she gave me a good talking-to one day. It was very helpful.'

'The older I get, the more I appreciate my mother's influence. I was bored by her when I was a child, I was all Daddy Daddy Daddy, who came home showering us with coins from his pockets. My mother kept the whole thing going with her posse of friends nattering round the teapot. They were a robust generation, those women, they never went under.'

'My mother faded away in the home, she was so sweet and gentle. How did your mother die?'

'Of a heart attack on the way to a holiday in Mallorca. They covered her in the blanket, it was a very full plane. Her friend Ida had to sit next to her for the rest of the journey and held her hand the whole way until the ambulance came and took her off and then we had a hell of a problem shipping her back again.'

'Oh, Adele, the things that happen to you. Where is she now?'

'In the cemetery in Liverpool, next to my dad. I sometimes feel I've left them all alone. Where are your parents?'

'Cremated. We scattered them in the Brecon Beacons; they were great ramblers.'

'How strange this day is.'

'Is it? Why?'

'I keep wondering what Evie would have looked like had she lived, and what she would have done with her life, if she would have mutated into a completely different person, calmed down, become ordinary, even. It's hard to imagine but people do, you know, they have their little rebellion and then they return to how their nature and nurture has formed them. Look at Brian.'

'I don't think so. I don't believe Evie and life were meant for each other. She didn't really want to live. Some people don't. When I got my cancer diagnosis, the oncologist told me that there are people who refuse chemo, they can't stand the idea of the side-effects, they don't want to experience it and they choose a shorter but happier life. But the odd thing is how very few of them: most will take the nausea and the tiredness for a chance of a few more months in the world. There are exceptions and they see things differently and we'll never understand them. You see, for me, the chemo was absolutely dreadful, it was everything you hear about, but look at us now, walking around after a champagne lunch, and, as trivial as it is, I wouldn't exchange it. And I had a loving partner to see me through. But Evie, I'm just not sure. I don't see her as ever having had the potential to make old bones. She was the kind of girl born to die young.'

'No, I can't accept that. It was an accident, she died by mistake. It could have turned out completely differently.'

'You think that because of the kind of people you grew up amongst, you don't have a depressive bone in your body. You're exactly like your mother with this will to live, to make the best out of bad opportunities. It's remarkable really, but I don't think you understand people who don't have it.'

And then she took my arm, as Evie had once done on the stairs leading down from the top floor of the library.

We returned to the hotel and had a nap before the next round of formal eating. For this we must dress ourselves in cocktail attire, according to the secretary to the baroness's notes. We all assembled in the hotel bar, Brian in a suit, Dora in a tuxedo trouser suit, Gillian in a floral dress and me in a black one. Rose came down last, attired in gold.

'I'm exhausted,' said Brian. 'The pleasure is relentless.'

'Oh come on,' Rose said, 'we're just getting going. This is absolutely nothing compared to politics.'

At the reception, the head of the English Department walked over to me in low heels, smiling. 'It was rather dusty work but I've found their files. I found her first-year room-mate's file as well. Then I cross-checked and she's a member of the Alumni Association.'

It had never occurred to me that Evie had a room-mate. I had assumed that she was in a single, like me, for, from the first time I had seen her after her reluctant walk round the lake with her parents, she had always been with Stevie. Someone had known her before that transformation, had watched it take place. How Lorraine had become Evie, how her hair had been cut short, how her clothes had been acquired. Evie's metamorphosis in one memory.

'Of the boy – Stephen Graham Platt is his full name – as you say, there's absolutely nothing. Not even a note on his file to say why he left. But there's an oddity you might be interested in. The room-mate had a home address on the same street as Stephen, the numbers are only a few houses apart, so they must have known each other in childhood. Perhaps she can tell you what happened to him.'

44

I chose the old way to contact Alison, I wrote her a letter. I thought that she might find it more respectful. It was not hand-written, that's beyond me now, I haven't written anything more than a shopping list for years, my fingers ache when they hold a pen. I typed the letter and topped and tailed it in ink. I printed it out on some nice heavy Smythson stationery we'd received in the office as a PR sample. The letter looked good and I got Juan to do the address on the envelope in the calligraphy hand his grand-father taught him.

I watched the post like an old-time teenager waiting for love let-ters. This thing, this long-term situation, was only a hand away, a writing hand. Then I would know. Know what? Juan asked. The things I don't know I don't know.

We sat down one night and I told him the story.

'Were you attracted to her?'

'For a while, until I met George.'

I sometimes think that Evie was a path I didn't take but might have done. Other lives spread out like the unfurling of the folds of a fan. When you've opened it and seen all the ones you might have been, then you start to get the whole picture.

'You're not a dyke, I guarantee it,' he said. 'You remember what Freud said about polymorphous perversity, surely? In infancy we derive pleasure from any part of the body. I get off on having my toes sucked. I don't tell you because you would not like to do it. These impulses evaporate by the time we are five years old, and we settle for what is the conventional object of desire. You kids were in a playpen until your twenties, no wonder you were still experimenting with what turned you on. And who cares now but you, about these past things? It doesn't matter, darling. Leave it alone, the past is nothing.'

'Faulkner says the past isn't even the past.'

'Of course he would say this. He was crazy.'

Since I was made redundant, I have spent a lot of time in the kitchen. Not cooking, I've never been much good at that, but because the kitchen leads to the garden and in my dotage I have come to be interested in how things grow. I don't touch anything out there, I still have no idea what anything is called, Latin or otherwise, we have a young gardener for all that, but I like to watch it all changing. Eddie spends most of the time upstairs in his room, slothful, unmotivated, pulled out from life like a plug from the mains. He has developed a nice line in sarcasm, can be quick-witted, but he is subject to moods and sulks. His visual environment can be like sandpaper to his eyeballs. Since he was a baby and his eyes were first able to focus, if the style of something displeased him, he would try to block it out of his sight by resting his fingers on his forehead to make a mask. Last week he objected to the Roman blinds in the living room, which had been there for six years. The colour is ivory. He denounced it as a form of sin. His neuroses, Juan said, were just a phase. He needed something to do. He should go for a run or get a job. But Eddie could not imagine a situation where his imperative bubble of privacy was penetrated. He must do things in his own order, along his own hierarchies.

I have, in recent months, been worried sick about him. He went away to university and came back like this. Something happened. He said, 'No, it didn't. Nothing happened. Everything is *fine*.'

Eddie walking down the stairs, clumping in his big white skate shoes. Comes into the kitchen and turns on the radio.

'Am I invisible?'

'Oh yeah, sorry, Mum, no I didn't see you there.'

Am I that unremarkable now that I have no presence in a room, or is it just his self-absorption? He turned it off and walked out again. He went into the sitting room. I heard his feet stop but not the scraping of the legs of a chair. Sometimes he does this, grinds to a halt mid-movement, a toy whose batteries have run down.

Two days later I found him sitting in there with the curtains undrawn. It was evening. He had turned on no lights. The remains of a sandwich lay on a side table. Lately he has put on weight. Everything he does has started to disturb me.

'Can I have the telly on now?'

'Of course you can, were you waiting for me to switch it on?'

'No, I just didn't want to disturb you.'

'But I was *out*, how could you have disturbed me?'

'I don't know.'

One of us is mad, me or him.

'What did you want to watch?'

'I don't mind.'

'How can you *not* mind? How can you be so passive and consuming?'

'You don't get it, Mum, my generation doesn't even want to change the world. It's all shit. Shit-brown shitty shit.'

'You're depressed, that's the problem. Talk to me!'

'Not at all, I'm happy. It's the world that's having a seizure. I'm fine. One of my mates has had his mum's initials tattooed on his ankle. Is that what you want?'

He knows me too well.

45

Malmköping, Sweden

Hi Adele

Alison tells me you've been in touch with her about 'Evie'. That's a name I haven't heard out loud for many years. Did she even exist? Of course, the person who would have understood that question was 'Evie' herself. We used to discuss phenomenology which was very fashionable in the seventies, it dealt with exactly those ideas which I was quite interested in at the time, but only as a means of working out a radical strategy for change. This was the difference between the two of us, she was interested in ideas for their own sake, but I had an agenda.

Did you know she thought you were a heuristic thinker? She admired it as a quality. Because she said her head was always crowded with too many thoughts.

She didn't really understand you and she wanted to, and I told her there wasn't anything to understand, you were shallow. Obviously I meant that pejoratively at the time, but despite what I said, I always admired you, Adele. I thought you were very fine, clomping round the lake in those turquoise platform boots you used to wear and your eyes never quite focused on *anything. Do you wear contacts now? You must do, no one could go through life so myopic, with such an off-centre vision. The lens is wrongly shaped, isn't it? Like a rugby ball not a football. I hope they managed to correct that. Sweden, where I live now, is very good for eyewear. I have two fashionable pairs myself.*

Looking back, I always thought you seemed a little sad beneath that veneer of confidence and boisterousness and belligerence, not an intellectual strength, but tough. You seemed tough to me. Like overcooked meat. You were hard-balled. But that sadness, did something happen to you before you arrived?

Maybe this is a game of 'I'll show you mine if you show me yours'. You want to know why she died, how she died, who was to blame. Important questions. I also have questions, but since you're asking, I agree that I'll go first.

When I was at university, brief as it was, there was something I didn't get about Freud – that he was very pessimistic and the longer he lived, the more pessimistic he became. But I was completely focused on the idea that he had liberated us, he'd named the unconscious and in doing so he allowed us to understand that these dreams and needs and wants were not implanted in us by the Devil but were part of our innate selves, the architecture of the psyche. So in psychoanalysis, if you could access the unconscious, you could liberate yourself.

What I didn't realise was that while he might have believed that <u>at first</u>, as time went on he became very sceptical about the possibility of <u>any</u> really radical liberation. In the sixties and seventies people thought that Freud was the key to unlocking some kind of Californian self-expression, which is why so many cults sprang up. But I don't think he thought it was even desirable. He didn't consider it possible to do away with repression or neurosis. What he actually wrote, which a lot of people forget, is: 'Much will be gained if we succeed in transforming hysterical misery into common unhappiness.'

Yes, yes, the old effulgent web of student ideas is being spun. I know what you're thinking, that we will never get to the bottom of anything.

What I'm saying, Adele, is that I knew she was in trouble, and I tried to help her by getting her to liberate herself from her repression, to turn it on its head into freedom, endless possibility. I didn't think she <u>needed</u> treatment, I thought she should let it all hang out. It was me who got her to come off those anti-depressants. I threw them down the toilet. And later learned from Alison that was wrong too.

I'm sure you don't remember Alison. She wasn't the type who would have penetrated your visual field, a working-class girl from the North studying biology. Your lot regarded them as the chorus to your self-centred lives, if they had any role at all. But she and I were friends together from childhood, played together in the streets, sat down in the library together with all the prospectuses and chose which university we would go to together. She would have liked to stay at home in Newcastle but I really forced her hand, I told her I didn't want to go home every night to Mam and Dad, I wanted to find a place that was new and forward-thinking where the kids of the working class who wanted to break things open with their bare hands would be welcome. And I said this new concrete palace round the lake would be just the ticket. Both of us were of that first emancipated working-class generation to get our education on full grants instead of sweating it out at evening classes, burning the midnight oil after your job in the factory. There'll never be a time like that again, will there?

So we went together, me and Alison, not brought in cars by our mummies and daddies but on the coach with a sandwich and a packet of crisps each. Excited as toddlers. As soon as I settled into my room I went to find her, to see if she was getting on OK and that's when I saw Lorraine for the first time, standing there with her long plait and the tartan ribbon looking like she'd been led to the gas chamber, but I saw the books that

were on her shelves and we started talking and for the first time
in my life I knew I had a soulmate.

Or I thought I did.

We both went to the barber's in town and got our hair cut
together. Mine was mouse, I dyed it black. I said to her she
could forget Lorraine, the frightened girl, she was Evie now.
And that's who she became. She wasn't a virgin, by the way.
That surprised me. I asked her who her first was but she
wouldn't say. A long time later I wondered if her old man had
interfered with her, but it was already too late to find out. You
wouldn't want to ask her brother, would you?

It drove a rift between Alison and me, my taking up with her
and changing her name. Later on, when she graduated and
went into nursing, she told me that in her opinion Evie was
already not well by the time she came to university. She knew
that because the first thing Evie did, before she unpacked a
thing, was to take out a bottle of pills and put them on her
bedside table. They were called Tryptizol, a very commonly
prescribed anti-depressant in those days before Prozac. They
were of the amyltriptyline family which today is mainly used at
much lower doses to treat arthritis as a serotonin blocker, but
then it was a crude, blunt instrument and its side-effects could
be horrendous. The most common one was a dry mouth, but
there was also weight gain.

Now I was _very_ intolerant of fat girls. Alison called my
girlfriends my 'skinny birds' and it was true, I liked them lean
and androgynous. I think we all know why. If Evie put on a
pound, I noticed. So she almost stopped eating, to counteract
the effect of the pills, and that must have been the trigger for the
anorexia. Because they were making her fat, and because she
ate almost nothing, I wanted her to come off them, I nagged
away at her to stop taking them and sometimes she would be
disciplined and sometimes she would forget and take them
absent-mindedly until I threw them away. What I didn't realise
was that the side-effects of sudden withdrawal can be quite

unpleasant. You have to do it gradually, under medical supervision, and Evie didn't. Alison took a very long time to forgive me for doing that.

So you see if anyone was responsible for Lorraine's death, I was. I have always accepted that. Not because I dressed her up and she dressed me up and we played these games with each other that we shouldn't have played, but because I didn't believe there was anything the matter with her, or if there was, it would be cured by some kind of radical intervention, a political and philosophical one. And that was what killed her. It took years for me to understand how wrong I had been, and the awareness of my responsibility grew with the years, rather than lessened, because of events that happened in my own life.

I suppose we have all been punished for what we did to her. I wonder how Denise was punished, who after all was the last one to see her alive.

You ask about those red exercise books, volumes in the Devil's library I think of them as. I thought her brother must have come and fetched them. I see him occasionally, interviewed on some old documentary about eighties music, dubbed into Swedish. I see Evie, I see her ageing, I see her getting heavier, like me, the jowls at the chin like him. Years ago, I wrote to him. I never heard anything back. I wonder if I'll hear anything back from you?

That place was awful, I don't see how it could have done anyone any good. Alison had a rough time, more or less abandoned by me until she found a circle of mates eventually. I'll tell you who she became friends with: the younger girls who worked in the college canteen, the ones who served us our egg and chips and shepherd's pie. That really put her beyond the pale, didn't it, hanging out with the hired help? And then she ran for her life when she graduated and went into nursing. I went home to Newcastle empty-handed, the golden boy with no degree. And yet for me, who ought to look back on it with hatred, the time when I was at university was when I felt most alive; not even when I was very active as a Scientologist did I have that feeling of everything moving really fast. I was a lightning rod for new ideas, I was electrified by them and then they left me burned out and breathless. No one can sustain that level of excitement, who has the stamina?

Remember Rami? That summer in Cornwall in the early seventies was a life changer for me. I went back there a few years later. We had a fling. It was nice. I travelled with him for a couple of years, we had a winter in Greece when I thought I was really in love with him, but he was arrested. The police came and took him away. Someone in the village caught him fingering a little boy. I didn't see him again. He was taken to the mainland and I had no money – he'd been paying for everything and I was skint – so I hitchhiked home. And met my lady and we had a couple of kids. And so on. Then it all burned out of me. Now all I'm interested in is a peaceful life.

You realise that everything we talked about was nothing compared to what was really going on on campus, which had nothing to do with us? Do you remember the computer building? I'd look in at all those dials and switches and wonder what you could do with such an instrument. Whether it would make changes in our lives so fabulous that we wouldn't recognise the landscape if we came back from the future. It turned out you would identify the hills and the fields and the sky, it's us we wouldn't know from Adam. We're not the same people, and not just because of our beards and our fat stomachs and our Botoxed faces, but because we don't know any more how to be alone and silent. The whole world is in our hands, in our phones and our other gadgets. The internet enslaved us. We're all-knowing and fidgety.

Rami would have hated it. Except maybe the porn. I guess he would have found a way to be an artist around that.

Maybe one day I'll see you, Adele. I come to London every couple of years on business – you've just missed me, in fact. Sometime in the future, then. I stay in one of the three-star palaces off the Euston Road which promise so much in the chandelier lobby and lead to rectangular boxes overlooking an annexe, with a TV mounted on a wall bracket and a toilet you sit on with your knees under the sink. So no rush to leave this small town and the peaceful contemplation of the snow, the sky, the white screen of the computer in the moments when it's firing up, drawing me back in to the illusion of life.

Yours

Steve Platt

46

Forty years ago, one summer morning very early for snore-a-bed students, I woke, lit a cigarette, upended it on its filter on the windowsill, got up, peed in the brownish toilet, dressed in flared jeans and rubber flip-flops, and set out to walk as far as I could until I was ready for another cigarette.

I crossed the bridge over the river and walked upstream as the sun was rising pale lemon yellow and birds spoke to each other about matters concerning chicks and territory.

A woman came down to the edge of the water carrying a tea tray, a bottle of gassy dandelion-and-burdock and a plate of home-made cake. She wore a navy Breton artist's smock, jeans turned up at the cuffs at her ankles, leather sandals on bare feet with scarlet-painted toenails, and her copper hair was piled up on her head, held in place by a pencil. It looked to me as much a costume as an everyday outfit, but we all wore outlandish clothes and it was only that she was middle-aged that it seemed to me she should not be allowed to dress this way. Not if she was coming from the row of houses in the distance at the edge of the long meadow of the flood plain with back gardens of hydrangeas and hollyhocks, crazy-paved paths and bird feeders.

She stepped over a mound of whitish dog shit, an incident I don't see happen any more because the whiteness was a by-product of the make-up of older brands of canine foods with a lot of bonemeal in them. The chalkiness is the calcium left behind after the dog's body has absorbed the nutrients. A spiral of shit on the grass fixes the memory.

After this manoeuvre, she lowered herself very nimbly on to the ground and sat cross-legged. I was a few feet away from her. She called out, 'Watch your step! Dog poo!' I looked down and skirted round it and then she said, 'Well done. You're out and about early. Isn't it a lovely spring day? Come and have a glass of pop. You look a bit hot, you never know, it could be a scorcher.'

The grass was already warm from the sun, warmer than it should have been for this time of year. I took out my packet of cigarettes, my Players No. 6, from which my face was rarely separated in those days. I offered her one and she took it. We smoked, and drank dandelion-and-burdock pop and the cake lay untouched, with a dainty knife beside it with a ceramic handle painted in rosebuds. Her name was Muriel Cooper. She was part of the tiny bohemian fringe of the town.

'I'm from here originally. I studied at RADA, dear, but then I married a Yorkshireman I met at the milk bar on Southampton Row, as you do, and came right back where I started from and had children and now I just direct the am-dram society. Have a slice of cake – it's not mine, I'm no baker, it's just a Women's Institute Victoria sponge. You get given an awful lot of cake, as a thank-you. I've sponges coming out of my ears. Or do you think it's too early for cake? Have you had breakfast?'

'No, I haven't had anything. I never get hungry till lunchtime.'

'Not eating breakfast makes you fat, you'll see in later life. And I don't mean a bowl of cereal, a proper breakfast. I had mine at five, I'm the type who's up with the lark. Time for cake soon. It must be nine-thirty. I don't have a watch. I can tell the time by the sun.'

I thought she was very interesting. Her bare toes wriggled inside her sandals. The toenails were jagged as if she bit them. 'You're looking at my toes, yes, I can bite them, I'm as flexible as an acrobat,' and she picked up a foot and put the big toe in her mouth for a moment, like a giant gnawing the limb of a child.

I stayed for a few minutes, talking about plays and whether I had seen Ken Campbell's road show, which I had, how we had left the arts centre, led out by the actors, and Ken was dressed as a copper and began to direct traffic and was arrested for impersonating a police officer. 'Wasn't that the funniest thing?' she said. 'I nearly died laughing. So clever.' I swigged some more dandelion-and-burdock from the bottle, smoked another fag, then I stood up, thanked her for the cold drink and went on, upriver to the archbishop's palace on the opposite bank, turned back and she was gone. It was eleven o'clock when I arrived on campus and I had a tutorial to present my essay on Mark Twain. I was very keen that year on the nineteenth-century American novel. Over the summer I would cross the border into the twentieth and begin reading Richard Brautigan and John Barth. Aged twenty, cigarettes and printed paper were the constituent elements of my world.

When I walked up the path to the house past the tedious privet hedge (the ugliest of evergreens, even when it weakly blooms), I thought it *could* be the same woman when she answered the door because behind her on the walls in the hall were framed theatrical posters advertising long-ago productions of Terence Rattigan and Alan Ayckbourn. A console table held the sculpted head of a young girl who looked familiar, as if I had once seen the piece in an exhibition and would, any moment, be told it was by Degas or Rodin or some other artist known to everyone.

'Denise went to the shops, she'll be back in a minute, dear. We're expecting you. Shall we go to the river? It seems like a lovely day. I'm blind. Just take my arm, will you? She'll see us from the window and follow.'

She was smaller than I recalled, more sunken round the mouth, as if she'd had too many teeth extracted, and her hair was a grey frizz around her face, a fallen raincloud.

'I think I met you once before, a long time ago, when I was a student. I was walking along the riverbank and you were drinking dandelion-and-burdock and eating sponge cake. In a Breton smock.'

'Yes, I think I remember a Breton smock, it was a fashion I wore for a time. I don't recognise your voice, dear, but I saw you all come and go, you students, you waves of young girls, walking upriver in your long dresses and long hair and the boys in suede shoes and flapping jeans.'

We stood for a few minutes on the bank as she raised her face to the sun. It was a much cooler day than when we had last met, late September and the leaves beginning to curl and yellow slightly on the trees.

'Denise was very surprised when she got your letter. Those old times she thought were all over now. She doesn't have anything to do with the university. Apart from a few weeks when she was in a play. I remember when it was being built and my sister and I used to go for walks along to the village and watch the buildings going up, the lake being dug. It was all fields, you know, and still mainly is on the outskirts of town. I took Denise in the school holidays once, it must have been around 1965 and the university had just opened. There still wasn't much there, but I said, "Look, Denise, there's going to be so much excitement happening here one day, not long now, not long." There was a big hole in the middle of everything and the water birds hadn't arrived yet and the roofs over the walkways hadn't gone up either.'

'Didn't Denise want to go to the university herself?'

'Oh yes, she would have loved to. But it was all acting with her, she got that from me, and she had her heart set on RADA like me but you know what happens when ... Oh, here she is.'

Much later than Muriel, I detected footsteps on the grass and looked round and Denise was walking towards us, a figure from another age. I have tried my best not to turn into my mother, though sometimes, when I am applying my lipstick in the magnifying mirror, and the shade I've chosen has not yet been muted by a softer artificial light, I see her reflection. I see her and all her friends, those chatterboxes in their powdered glory, the spores of face powder falling from their chins on to wattled necks. And I paint it on, more and thicker, to imitate the red badge of their courage.

But Denise had let herself go as my mother and her friends had never done. She had surrendered to a dowdy late middle age, grey hair styled in a useful pudding-bowl cut and her face free from make-up to weather slowly under the sun. I would never have recognised her. Absolutely nothing was left of the lamby girl in the fake fur apart from the pale blue eyes and an amateur actress's lightness on her feet.

'So you've had a chance to catch up,' she said. 'Auntie Muriel loves the river. I've bought a cake, shall we go back in the house, it looks like rain. Or do you want to stay out for a bit?'

'Whatever you like, dear. I've had a lovely chat with your friend. She said she met me once, on this very spot when she was a student. I gave her a glass of pop.'

'You were always doing that. You were friendly.'

'I was. I liked to talk to the young people, they had a freshness of mind it was hard to come across here. Lots of ideas.'

'Too many ideas,' Denise said.

'Yes, far too many,' I said. 'And most of them were drivel.'

'I never understood a word.'

'Neither did I.'

'See, Denise? I told you there was never any need to be so intimidated by those students, they were just boys and girls like yourself, but with more exams behind them.'

Denise took Muriel's arm. We turned back to the house and I opened the gate that led through the garden to the kitchen where, sightlessly, Muriel managed to make a pot of tea with little difficulty and laid out a plate of biscuits.

'Don't forget the cake,' Denise said. 'It's in a box on the work surface.'

Muriel moved her hands smoothly along the counter until she reached the cake box, opened it and took out a carrot cake decorated with a marzipan carrot.

'You have your refreshments in the lounge. I'm going to listen to the *Archers* repeat in the kitchen. Take as long as you like though, I've got a talking book for after.'

We went into the very cluttered room of a person who requires everything to be at hand, and decorated with many photographs of family weddings and other occasions.

'I don't live here, you know,' Denise said. 'I'm Auntie Muriel's carer but I've got my own house, up the road. I come in every day to get her shopping and see how she is. She's very independent considering her age and her disability.'

'Where are her children?'

'All scattered. Susan is in New Zealand, Paul is in Manchester, Felicity and Mike are in Kent, their son was killed in Iraq. You can't expect a lot from them, now. They're just about holding themselves together with string.'

'I'm glad I remember your aunt in her prime. She made a strong impression.'

'Do you think that was her prime? I always imagine the fifties were her era, when she was in London. I've never lived there myself. I've been lots of times, of course, I'm a priority member of the National Theatre, we go a couple of times a year. Do you go a lot?'

'Not really. No one in London goes to the theatre.'

'No one?'

'I mean no one I know.'

'There you are then. Another click I'm not part of.'

She had been very hard to track down. It was a matter of consulting old university Drama Society playbills to find her last name and then, of course, she had changed it when she married and it was Dora who said that if once she had acted in university plays, maybe she had gone on acting and that was how I found her, through ringing the am-dram society, and she rang me back. She thought I had, after all the long years, a message from Stevie.

'You know, I haven't seen or heard a word from him since that week in 1974. It was the last time anyone let me take part in the Drama Society at the university, as if I was somehow responsible, when I'm the *last* person who should be blamed. I hardly knew her. I only took over when she couldn't learn her lines, *and* she was a rotten actress, she couldn't act for toffee, but she had the looks. I never had those. No one will give you a chance when you're not pretty.'

'Stevie must have thought you were pretty.'

'I don't know. He never said so. I was just a relaxation for him, a bit of rest after all that thunder and lightning he had with that girl. He was lovely in bed, I've never forgotten him, very gentle and sympathetic. It was quite ordinary sex, you know. No perversity. No dressing-up and make-up. What happened to all the gay boys from the drama society? Did they die?'

'A lot of them, yes.'

'I used to think about them during the Aids time. I did wonder. It's the only time I've ever spent with students. My son went to uni but he liked it no more than Stevie did and he dropped out. My daughter didn't bother. You don't have children, do you?'

'Yes, I do. I have a son.'

'You surprise me, I thought you might be one of them.'

'One of who?'

'Them, you know. Because of the way you were always staring at Evie, like you fancied her. And don't look at me as if I'm a naughty doll you want to shake. What do you want, exactly? Have you seen him?'

'I had an email, that's all.'

'Where does he live now?'

'Sweden.'

'Oh, how disappointing. There was always a part of me that thought he couldn't have gone far, and that one day I'd bump into him in the street, and all the time he was in Sweden of all places. I've been to Newcastle a couple of times, I couldn't believe I'd not just turn a corner and there he would be, but I don't even know

what he might have looked like when he was grown up into a man.
It's inconceivable, isn't it? You look in the mirror and what you see
is yourself at twenty-two, but that's not what anyone else sees.'

The gas fire and its artificial coals burned too warmly, she was
sweating and so was I. She cut me a piece of carrot cake and laid
it on its side on a plate. I put it down on the floor because there
were no empty surfaces in the room.

'So why are you here? What are we supposed to be talking
about?'

'I'm trying to find out what happened the night Evie died. And
Stevie told me you were the last person to see her alive. Which
surprised me. Because if that's true than everything we knew about
that night was wrong.'

'Well that's a laugh, because everything you thought you knew
always *was* wrong. I mean that rubbish you talked. So it's not surprising you would be wrong about that too.'

'I know. We were such idiots. Girls like you could have taught
us about life.'

'Oh, don't soft-soap me. I'm not a child.'

Muriel knocked on the door. 'Everything all right in there? *The
Archers* has finished and I'm starting on my talking book now. Let
me know if you want more tea.'

Denise looked at her aunt and smiled. 'You're so kind, Auntie
Muriel. We've got everything we need, we won't be long.'

'Take as long as you like. It's no trouble.'

'She hears the smile in the voice, you know. I think her drama
training gave her quite an acute gift of listening to tone. Are there
any blind actors? I don't know, but you can't really have a deaf one,
can you?'

And then she pulled her grey hair from behind her right ear,
turned her head towards me and I saw the small plastic lip of a
hearing aid.

'Me and Auntie Muriel, the deaf leading the blind, eh? I didn't
get into drama school because the other actors always sounded like
they were mumbling. I was too proud to get a hearing aid. Then I

had to. You see, people like you have no idea, you actually have *no idea*, do you, how other people live, what we have to put up with and how nothing turns out all right because it was never going to. We didn't have a chance. Poor Stevie, that he fell amongst you. He'd have been all right otherwise. That's my opinion, anyway.'

As she spoke, I began to wonder if she might have actually killed Evie, smothered her with a pillow or stuck her fingers down her throat. To her, we were self-advertised god-like creatures, drifting round the campus being paid for by her taxes from her clerical job at the chocolate factory to talk on and on about working against, to make experimental robots and abandon them on a bird-fouled island, to feel ourselves to be always becoming, never being. She must have wanted to smite us.

'And what was it you wanted, again?' she said. 'Why are you here? Remind me.'

She was tenacious in her temporary advantage. It had to be temporary, I hadn't come back here for nothing. I have been a journalist, albeit one who gets other people to do the writing and interviewing. I have determined, commissioned, shaped their stories. I understand the structure of stories, even though they are just bits of paper that will be thrown out the next day. I have told my writers to go back and ask more questions, I have ticked them off for asking the wrong ones. But what they have told me is that the best answers are the ones to which you did not even know the question. Stay schtum, let the tape roll, allow them to fill the silences between you. In the end they will spill.

So I picked up my slice of cake from the floor by the chair and took a mouthful.

'Nice cake.'

She reached up and fiddled with her hearing aid. I thought she was going to turn it off and block me.

'That party of yours. It was awful. I still remember it. I didn't have the right clothes, I told Stevie that. He said he didn't care what I wore. We were going to go on a picnic the next day, out of town somewhere, I'd looked up the times of the buses at the station, we were leaving before lunch, so he said jeans would be better because I wouldn't be able to go home and get changed if I stopped the night with him. And all those buses left without us. I'd already bought the ham and tomatoes for the sandwiches, it was a Sunday, wasn't it? Nothing was open, remember that? "Sunday closing". But we never went on the picnic because of a silly thing I did, a stupid careless thing. And you've come a long way to find out what it was and gone to all the trouble to find me. I spoke to my husband about it, and he said it was the least I could do to tell you.

'You're right, I went back to the house. I didn't know then I was the last person to see her alive, I had no idea. It never entered my head. I thought people were up. When you threw us out of the party we went back to Stevie's flat and in the morning when I reached for my pills I realised I'd left my bag at yours. Somewhere on the stairs. I panicked. My pills were everything to me. If I'd fallen pregnant my mother would have killed me, I had to go back straight away – you mustn't miss a day, you know, and we were going on the picnic. That's all behind us now, but I still remember the panic when you were late with your pills.'

'So you came *back* to the house, I had no idea. Gillian thought she heard someone on the stairs that morning.'

'Yes, I went back and everything was silent; you'd left the front door unlocked; everyone did in those days, didn't they? No crime then, nothing worth stealing. Not like now. I walked up the stairs and found my bag on the landing, nothing was gone from it, but as I bent down to pick it up Evie was coming out of her room to go to the toilet. She looked bloody awful. She was completely grey and her eyes were rolling around. To be honest, I was mesmerised by the sight of her, she was in a white cotton nightie and she looked a bit Miss Havisham, if you know the story. I was frightened for her, I thought she might fall down the stairs, so I hung on until she flushed the chain, I could hear everything, the plopping of her poo in the bowl and then she came out and saw me. I mean she saw me for the first time, I wasn't hiding or anything, but before she was too out of it to notice a thing. That's how bad she was already. And she invited me in, you know. I didn't force entry.

'I said, "Are you all right? Can I help you?" And she looked at me and said, "Oh, Denise what are you doing here?" Very dry-eyed. She wasn't crying or anything. I said I'd forgotten my bag and come back for it, and she said, "Well, come and sit with me for a minute." I followed her in, looked around, all very studenty. A few things on the walls that Stevie had given her, posters and so on. A lot of books lying on the floor against the walls, too many books for the bookcase by the window. All her clothes spread around in a mess. Her pots of eye-black and tubes of lipstick. Her knickers in a mound by the door, maybe she wanted to launder them. There was a wash-stand in the room, an old thing from when the house was first built, but whoever lived here before the students hadn't got rid of them. It was green marble with a ewer and basin on top of it. Full of dead flies and spiders. That room was so neglected. Did she never tidy up? Was it too middle-class or whatever you called it to use a duster now and again?'

'And what did you say to Evie that would have caused her to be dead an hour later?' My voice was harsh, it was thick with tears and anger.

'You sound like a policeman. My father was a policeman, that's why I never said anything. I knew what trouble there could be for me. Innocent people go to prison for crimes they didn't commit because they didn't know how to tell their story right.

'She got back into bed and I said I was sorry that I stole Stevie from her, but that was how it was. And I said something which I suppose made the big difference. I wouldn't have said it if I'd known what would happen after I left. I said she was too thin. I wonder now if she was anorexic. I didn't even know the word then, did you? I told her she was much too skinny and that Stevie liked a bit of flesh he could grab hold of, which wasn't really true, but I wanted to taunt her. She should build herself up a bit, I said. So I took the piece of cake that was lying on a plate by the bed and I gave it to her. "Eat this," I said. "It'll do you good."'

'And did she eat it?'

'No, I swear to God. She didn't eat it straight away while I was there, but she nodded and I suppose she must have eaten it after I left. She died with cake in her sick, didn't she? It was in the paper. But there was not a mouthful touched when I was there. She just went back to sleep. And that's the end of the story.'

She arrived at this conclusion so abruptly, and with a small smile that reminded me briefly in a flickering way of the lamby girl she had once been, that I was tempted to grab her wrist and force the rest out of her, but I said, 'That's not all, is it?'

'I hardly knew you at the time, Adele, you thought you were so superior to me. And now you're still behaving as if you're my lord and master. It won't work. I spent my life working as a children's librarian. I've always loved books. You lot never loved books the way I did. You *studied* them. That's not what books are for, tearing them to pieces in your head, they're to walk into and get lost in. You can't have detachment when you read a book, it's not right. Children know how to read, until it's knocked out of them. I loved the Enid Blyton books when I was little, out of fashion now, but I particularly liked the Magic Faraway Tree ones, with the lands that change at the top and the toffee that gets bigger in your mouth and the Saucepan Man. They were lovely. Evie had so many books on her shelf, and all of them looked *hard*.'

'But they weren't the only books in the room, were they?'

'What do you mean?'

'Weren't there some school exercise books? You know the kind I mean, we all had them when we were kids.'

'Oh,' she said after a while. 'Those.'

And then we were into the next phase of this encounter, where I could see that she suddenly understood why I had come and that there was nothing to be gained from me but to try to preserve whatever advantage she had.

'Before we get on to that,' she said, 'now I know why you're here, I just want to explain something to you. I was *encouraged* to go after Stevie. I would never have thought of it myself, he was completely out of my league and I wasn't even all that sure I fancied him at first. It was his friend Alison from school, who came to one of the rehearsals, who put us together. Everyone thought I was ordinary compared to Evie, and I was, but you see Alison said that ordinary was what Stevie needed. She thought Evie was doing him no good, that she could pull him under, and she said that if I went after him, she was sure I could get him because she would make sure he knew what was in his best interests. And that's what happened. He wasn't hard to get at all. I didn't need any feminine wiles, I just talked to him like a normal person and I think that's what he wanted, it was a relaxation after all the stress of being with her and worrying about her and him realising that she may not even get better.'

This Alison, this unknown girl who had unseen executed so many aspects of this situation. We had analysed and analysed and analysed how Evie came to die, and all the time there was a person with her own interests and observations and agenda.

'I see. And what about the exercise books? Did you take them?'

'I saw them when I went in. They were on the floor by the bed, piled by the wall. I thought, This must be what they do their student work in, their essays or whatever they are, so I picked one of them up while I was talking to her and I saw it wasn't that, but it was all about sex. And I was really curious, because for the minute I thought they were sex diaries, about her and Stevie, what they had got up to, and then when I looked up she'd gone back to sleep and I thought, I'll just go to the toilet where no one can see me, and have a read, but then I heard someone coming and I put them in my bag along with the pills. I ran out of the house without really thinking, or wondering how I'd get the books back.

'After she died, I still didn't know what to do with them so I kept them. You've no idea what's in those books. She had a secret, that girl, that nobody knew about. My husband says I should have sent them back. I could have sent them to her brother, but as time went on that became less possible. He's a powerful man, and not a nice one from what I read in the paper, he could have me arrested for stealing.'

The dybbuk enters a man's body and takes possession of it. Does the *dybbuk*, once the evil deed is carried out, leave the body of the possessed and fly away to enter another host? Or does it stay there, burrowing its way into the bloody supply, for ever? My *zayde* said there was no such thing, it was mental illness, but Denise did not seem mad, she was just indignant and envious of our advantages.

'A long time ago I promised her brother I would find the books. I'd like to fulfil that promise.'

'I don't think you'll like what you see. You'll be sick when you read them.'

'I'm used to stronger meat than that, I'm sure.'

'Perhaps you are. Perhaps in London there's all kinds of perversions and horribleness. But it's not really the same when it's somebody you know, is it? There again, maybe it's for the best and then you'll understand. You'll see how right I have been about everything. I'm relieved to be shut of them, to be honest. As long as I don't get into trouble. I keep them under lock and key, you know. I wouldn't want my kids to see them.'

Still she hesitated, and I saw that she felt that she was being robbed of something. 'What will you do with them?'

'I don't know, I'd have to read them first.'

'Will you send them to Stevie? So he can see that Alison was right all along about me and him. That's what I'd like.'

'I'm not making any promises.'

'No, your type never do, do you?'

There was an old-fashioned desk against the wall, built of a highly varnished oak, the type with a lid that comes down and inside all kinds of obsolete pigeonholes for writing-paper and envelopes and stamps, and a groove to lay down your pen. Some of the compartments were stuffed with recipes cut out from magazines.

She invited me to sit at the matching chair, and handed me a sheet of pale blue Basildon Bond from a block with the paper band still round it, and a biro. 'Write your address down here,' she said. "I'll make my mind up in my own good time. If I decide, you'll get them. If not, then you'll know I'm still thinking.'

I said goodbye to Muriel, who seemed unaware of the nature of the visit, because she smiled and held my hand inside both of hers for a moment and said, 'I hope you've had a lovely catch-up. Come again the next time you're up this way. Do you know where to get the bus or do you need a taxi?'

'I think I'll walk back along the river.'

'Yes, it's always nice, isn't it?'

Denise stood and watched me from the back door. The child I once was saw the *dybbuk* try to emerge from her chest, beat its way out of there, leaving a bloody cavity. The *dybbuk* wanted to leave her, it was looking for a new host in the world. Obviously not. But I have always had an imagination.

47

A couple of months later the diaries arrived, the four Silvine exercise books in a jiffy bag. Smelling of old. Smelling of damp, mildew, extinct ink, the hiding spots that they had lived in. Drawers, clocks, sheds, wardrobes, locked desks.

The sight of them made me feel a little nauseous. I thought, This is a big mistake. This does not belong to you, it is none of your business.

But the ferocity of curiosity is the primitive instinct that overrides moral scruples. I had to know.

The first page in neat sloping handwriting, composed with a fountain pen using blue ink.

31st September 1954
My name is Veronica Pugh. I was born Helga Eichel in
Kidderminster in 1924 but that name is dissolved in the sea
now. My father was a prisoner of war from the German Army.
He married a local girl and stayed here. He died when I was
thirteen years of age. I don't know what would have happened
to him when the next war started, I suppose he would have been
sent away. My mother started to call me Veronica after the film

star because Helga was a German name. I am English, how
else am I supposed to think of myself? I never set foot in that
other country. Why should he have done this to me because I
was once called Helga? A little word and it has ruined my life.
Five letters and I have lost everything.

Here's the story, as I'm going to tell it. Her version differs from
mine in that it is a little more boring and repetitive. I have left out
her recipes for lamb hotpot and complaints about service in
Woolworths, the phone calls from her mother in Kidderminster
ringing in the mustard-coloured hall of the pebble-dashed semi-
detached house on the road called, poshly, Belvedere Avenue. (I've
found it on Google Street View. Privet England. This is where Evie
was brought up. You can only see the front of the house; the rear
windows, where Evie and George's bedrooms must have been, are
inaccessible. But Evie walked down that path on to the street in
her long blond plait with tartan ribbon and George pushed his
bike round the side of the house. And masturbated, overlooking
the chrysanthemums.

Before the war Evie's mother was an apprentice milliner. Happy-
go-lucky, she says of herself. Always a smile, a nice disposition.
Plenty of boyfriends, nothing serious, did not want to be tied down
too soon. She was a dab hand with hats. In those days everyone,
man, woman and even child, wore a hat. It was a thriving industry, maybe they didn't wash their hair so often. I don't know if hats
will ever come back into fashion. Now, when you try to wear them,
they just look arch.

Veronica did war work sewing parachutes. Rumours of para-
chute sabotage were common urban legends. The pilot jumps from
his burning plane, the cords of his chute are cut. Like everyone else
in the factory she was watched like a hawk but doubly so because
she had a foreign name. She had a boyfriend in the tanks who was
killed in the liberation of southern Italy. She liked fashionable
clothes and could make her own, easily. When Reg died, she sewed
a black armband round the sleeve of her best navy suit.

After the war she met Dennis Pugh in a Kardomah tea room in Birmingham. What she was doing in Birmingham she does not say. You could drive yourself mad wondering. This was a very genteel way to commence a romance. He had a draper's shop in Wolverhampton. Clothes were coming off the ration. He foresaw a demand for romantic nightwear. Before the war he and his father had specialised in ladies' nightgowns: women came from miles around, seagulls squawking over the choice, the satisfaction of good flannel next to the skin on a frosty night or the slippery seductions of his luxury satin selection, small in number but carefully picked from the commercial traveller's suitcase of samples.

I'd forgotten about commercial travellers, those free and easy men of the roads and the railways.

George. Born in the last year of the old King's reign. Dark out of the womb with a black thatch on his head, purple in the face, heavy, nine pounds ten ounces and born by Caesarean section. A bawling child, exploratory from an early age, climbing over the bars of his cot, an alpine expedition down on to the rag-rug made from scraps of worn-out jackets, blouses, skirts. Fat feet crossing the lino to the ungated stairs, crashing down to the bottom, tumbling, gasping at the bottom, screaming and Mum running in from the lounge where she and Dad listened to dance-band tunes, Joe Loss and His Orchestra.

In 1953 she developed a dermoid cyst on her ovary, a confused egg which unilaterally decides, like a foetal feminist, to go it alone without fertilisation, develops bone, hair, skin and teeth, but without the capacity to become what we understand to be human. A freak development. Surgically removed. Two weeks in hospital and rest from roaring George. She enjoyed it and knitted a black and silver skirt and jumper set that unravelled when she sat down on a nail on the garden bench.

She got the bus on Thursdays to the Boots library to change her book. She enjoyed Georgette Heyer. She and her friends often went to a matinée at the pictures. Twice a year, she and Dennis went to Birmingham Rep. He always bought her a box of Black

Magic chocolates which she ate off her lap, and underlined the names of the actors in the programme whom she liked. She saw Eric Porter long before *The Forsyte Saga* and found him slightly sinister. I did not recognise most of the names she mentioned, I have obsessively looked them up on Wikipedia.

She sometimes treated herself to scented bath cubes on her weekly trip to Boots. She had a tiny vial of scent Dennis gave her. They went to Denbighshire on their holidays. Dennis told her about the traveller in negligées, a Maltese. She pictured him with dark hair, black flashing eyes: 'I'll bet he's another Dirk Bogarde. *What* a dreamboat, even though he took the part of a terrible hoodlum last week in that police picture.'

In October 1953, when our founders were beginning to talk of a new university in Yorkshire which would defeat totalitarianism through the arts talking to the sciences and the freedom to do as one chose without the university acting *in loco parentis*, Evie's mother got ready for a dinner dance. She had a sea-green satin cocktail dress with shoes dyed to match and a little black moiré handbag which attached to her wrist. Under this outfit she wore fifteen-denier nylons held up by a white suspender belt spotted with artificial lace daisies. Her brassiere was silk. Her glacé-leather high-heeled shoes were from Dolcis and her hair had been permed that morning. She applied a Rimmel lipstick to her mouth and brushed her eyelids with blue shadow. She spat into the palette of mascara, mixed it around with the tip of her finger and scratched the miniature brush across the surface until she had a good dose on the bristles, and applied it to her lashes. Finally, she dabbed cream rouge onto her cheeks, those apple-shaped cheekbones so many women of the forties and fifties seem to have, and the same prominent chin as Evie.

It was difficult to square this young fifties matron, aged only twenty-nine, with the stocky plain figure of the mother with the plait wound round her head whom I had seen walking round the plastic-bottomed lake. I didn't understand how this metamorphosis had taken place, or how long it had taken. Veronica in a

cocktail dress to Veronica in mouse-coloured suede Hush
Puppies.

The dinner dance was at the big hotel on Lichfield Street. Mrs
Pugh said that it was just an excuse for mutual back-slapping
amongst the city's traders and small businessmen. She seems cynical about the speeches and calls for proposals and seconders for
various half-jokey motions. But she was excited about getting
dressed up. She was looking forward to rising to her feet, holding
a glass of orangeade (she didn't drink) and toasting the Queen.

She was awfully proud of Dennis in his dinner jacket and dicky
bow. He was beautifully turned out. His clothes were always spotless, he knew how to take care of them, vigorously brushing his
jacket before he hung it up, polishing his own shoes.

After the meal, before the speeches, her bladder full of orangeade, Mrs Pugh rose, made her excuses to her husband and the others
at their table, and went to the ladies' room to powder her nose. She
walked along corridors decorated with a wallpaper embossed with
Scottish thistles. The carpet was a series of overlapping squares
embellished at each corner with rosebuds. The smell of the contents of soup tureens and gravy permeated the air. A light bulb had
blown out halfway along. She passed a watercolour of Balmoral and
thought that the hotel had a decidedly Scottish feel, as if it were
trying to emulate a hunting lodge, though she had no idea what the
interior of a hunting lodge might look like – she had imagined a
kind of log cabin with throne-like gold furniture.

The sign to the toilets was lettered in flaking gold on an oak
plaque. The heads of the arrows pointing left and right had
partially rubbed away. Although completely sober, she became
confused. She blundered on, turning to the right, past a series of
reproductions of Stubbs horses, and finally turned again just
beyond a watercolour of Birmingham Town Hall. There she
bumped into Figgy Lassiter in a plum-coloured cummerbund and
his Masons pin in his lapel, the worshipful master of her husband's
lodge, referred to by Dennis in an awestruck way not only because
he was in such an exalted position in the ancient order but because

he was a bank manager and had served in the RAF. 'He took the *lid* off Monte Cassino.'

And Figgy bore down on her, recognised her, said, 'Ah, Frau Pugh, or should I say Fräulein Helga Eichel? I've had my eye on *you*.'

Mrs Pugh became flustered. Her evening bag drooped on her wrist. Dennis knew about her father but she had told no one else when she moved to Wolverhampton. They were married in church, she wore a petrol-blue dress with a white Peter Pan collar and a confection of a hat with a dyed feather, a hat she had made herself. Only perfunctory questions were asked by the vicar regarding her unusual surname. She had almost forgotten about it.

But someone had snitched on her. She must, she thought, be on some kind of little list at the police station, the traitor's alphabet.

So she said, 'Oh, but that's not my real name, you might as well say I'm Vivien Leigh! I mean it's just *names*, isn't it?'

Figgy's upper lip was ill-defined by a soft, colourless moustache. His hair was parted on the right-hand side and the nape of his neck was still shaved in a military show of hairlessness, almost Erich von Stroheim, she thought. If anyone looked a bit German, to be honest, it was him. He stood in her way, and she was dying for a wee.

'I think Helga is the *real* you.'

'Don't be silly, Mr Lassiter. I was born here, I have never even met any of my German relations.'

'Write to them, do you?'

'No! Of course not.'

'Then they write to you.'

'Well, I don't know, I never heard a word from them and I wouldn't have understood that foreign writing even if they had.'

'How do you know they weren't intercepted before you even got them, taken away to have the code cracked?'

'Oh, don't be ridiculous. This is like something off the pictures.'

'Am I ridiculous? Me? You think *I* am ridiculous?'

'No, I didn't mean ...'

'All right, I was only teasing, give us a kiss.'

'I can't do that, I'm a married woman.'

But Figgy had taken her by the wrist and dragged her along the hall to a door, behind which were dusters and brooms and half-empty bottles of disinfectant and other cleaning products. He pulled down her silk knickers and rammed her.

'You fucking Kraut cunt, here's one for the boys. Shut your face, Helga, and take what's coming.'

Her account was formulaic and euphemistic: 'He stole my honour.' She glosses over the details, the sexual humiliation, the pain of penetration and what I assume was a further, anal entry, when he turned her around against the wall for a second shafting while he was still erect, then back for the final few thrusts and what may have been Evie's conception.

Instead she talks about the experience of floating, of being only partially there. There seems to be a squeamishness about describing the sex act, and perhaps the need to hide from her children what sex was; she might have felt that she was leaving smut lying around the house. More than smut, pornography. But the note-books were exercises in how *not* to write porn, how to evade, as if she were under the control of the censor.

She talks instead about the objects in the broom cupboard coming to life, as if they were animated creatures from a cartoon film. She wonders if she is ill, that she feels so odd and suspended above her body. Her great anxiety is about becoming aroused. That would be treachery, to herself, and to Dennis. She prefers to feel deadened and alienated, a wooden doll with a rag of a blond wig and a hole between the legs.

She thought how, up to now, she had done everything right, she had always been attractive and well turned out, even when you had to stain your lips with cochineal during rationing. She was a good mother. She made everything in the house, her skills with her hands had not left her. She made George's clothes; she arranged flowers and was thinking of taking up weaving. All crafts interested her.

That afternoon in the consciousness-raising group, when Evie told us this story, it was just the broadest outline. We were so green, so shocked, we did not get what it was that Evie was struggling to express, because for us sex was sex, a thing we were still trying to master. ('What exactly is a blow job? Does anyone know? Has anyone actually done it? Is it nice?') What her mother had attempted to explain in the notebooks was that rape to her was an act of violence and revenge.

I wondered what my mother would have said if she was still alive to read the diaries. I cannot imagine giving them to her. About her own sex life I know absolutely nothing. Wild horses would not have persuaded me to ask. I think she would have stood by the ironing board and told me, 'Men are same the whole world over, the dirty dogs.'

'Was this my war?' Mrs Pugh asks. 'Are these our war stories? Women have no tales of bravery and heroism and honour like the men do. We fight on our backs, a heavy man on top of us, unable even to struggle.'

When Figgy let go of her, and before turning spat on her breasts, she eventually found the ladies' room and sat on the toilet and wept. How would she tell Dennis was the main question on her mind.

My mother wouldn't have told Dennis. My mother would have said, 'Whatever you do, *don't tell your husband*, because he won't understand, that's just the way men are made. He won't like it. Pull yourself together and put on a smile and go back and pretend nothing happened. This is a secret to take to your grave. Are you kidding? There's nothing to gain from being honest. Or if you have to, make up a story. And make it a good one.'

In my mother's hands, this would have become one of the secrets that made the silences in the rooms I entered, when she and her friends were sitting round the coal fire with cups of tea, their heads bent together. And you thought it was all cysts and hysterectomies, but it was also abortions and rape.

But Mrs Pugh, the idiot, told Dennis as soon as she got home and the next morning he packed a suitcase and went to stay with his sister. Her next period was late. It was not possible to tell whose it was, Dennis's kid or Figgy's, of this she was quite certain because she kept scrupulous notes of both her periods and the days she had sexual intercourse with her husband.

She and George alone.

At one point she says, 'We are living without a clock.' I supposed that in her despair she meant that day and night were indistinguishable. Then I realised she meant that the clock on the mantelpiece of their lounge was broken. It had stopped ticking and refused to be wound up again.

Mr Pugh sent her money and paid the mortgage. One day she saw him from the bedroom window hesitating with his hand on the latch of the gate but when she came downstairs to open the front door he was gone. She wrote him letters. She enclosed pictures of George. 'He misses his daddy terribly.'

But after she finished the housework she went into the cold parlour every afternoon in that umber hour before winter twilight, when the fire does not yet need to be laid for your family's homecoming. Instead of reading her library book in the warm fug of the kitchen, she was writing something down, she was making a kind of record, a formal account. A manuscript which George found when he was fourteen and told the contents to his little sister, explaining, as he went along, what sex was, what a penis, what a vagina. This seems astonishing now, that a twelve-year-old would not know these things – Eddie first saw porn on the computer when he was ten – but I, aged twelve in the sixties, tugged the arm of my mother, washing up in the kitchen, and said, 'Mummy, what does *fuck* mean? I can't find it in my dictionary.'

And then Dennis must have come back eventually because the entries stop. Evie was born. Dad was home, life reverted to normal, except Mrs Pugh waged war against her appearance. She never again went to the hairdresser's to have her hair permed. The mascara dried out in the dressing-table drawer, the lipstick broke in its gold tube. The cocktail dress became dusters. The long plait seems to have served the purpose of taking her back to childhood. But pinned around her head so no one could grab and catch her.

The third notebook ends, the fourth one begins, in which she talks about the library book she is reading (*Katherine* by Anya Seton – 'very interesting and educational'). A gap of several more pages and the writing changes. A teenaged hand:

> *George is growing up so quickly. What a little tearaway he has become, he'll be the death of all of us when he's a big boy. I've had to buy him new trousers, he grows out of them so fast. His knees are losing their dimples. Still, you can't help wanting to eat him all up.*

I recognised this from earlier in the narrative. The words had been copied out, presumably by Evie, who was rewriting her mother's diary. She didn't change anything, she just relived it on her own account.

Several more sentences followed about George. Then an empty page and it started. I found the entries ... surprising, and unpleasant.

She wrote in the final notebook her sexual fantasies about her brother. Her dreams of incest with him, her aching and moaning for his body, for his cock, about what she wanted to do with her breasts, where she wanted him to put a finger. He was the love of her life. *Stevie isn't my type*, she wrote;

> *he's so thin and wan and unsatisfactory. I thought sex would be different, more tumultuous. We both try, we try to make it work in bed. He thought I was a virgin and he thought he should be gentle, but I didn't want gentleness. I wanted passion, I wanted George. I want George.*
>
> *I want a person who is more robust, more vital. I wish Stevie was like Adele. She reminds me so much of George, not to look at, but in her self. They are both winners.*

After I read this, I went back to bed. I lay beneath the covers in the mid-afternoon while Eddie toiled across the floor below and turned the radio on for a moment, punched the dials of the stations and then turned it off again, unable to find what he liked. The notched sounds of Professor Green. Bach. A play.

Then he walked up the stairs, paused outside my room.

'Mum?'

'Yes.'

'Are you OK?'

'I'm OK.'

He pushed open the door.

'What are you doing in bed? Are you not well? Do you want a cup of tea?'

'Yes, please.'

He went downstairs to the kitchen and came back a few minutes later.

'Here you are.'

He sat on the edge of the bed.

'Is there something you want to tell me? Come on, little mother.' He lifted his hand and gently stroked my hair. He picked up my hand and kissed it. 'I'm going to be fine, you know. I'm just in a stage, I'll grow out of it, you'll have your Eddie back. I love you. You've been a great mum. And you and the *padrone* make a good couple. I count myself lucky, honestly. I do.'

'Do you remember when Grandma looked after you when you were little?'

'Of course. She made me chicken soup and sang songs to me. I miss her. She was very fine, wasn't she? What was Grandpa like?'

'He was a wolf.'

'Not like me then.'

'You have his look, but inside, no.'

'I think I'm ... ' But he trailed off.

'You're what? Tell me! Are you ill, are you in trouble of some kind?'

He started laughing.

'No need. You already know.'

48

During our visit to Yorkshire, there had been an awkward incident on the last night when Rose had once again played the hostess at a dinner. She had attempted to present Gillian with a viola. Once we had been welcomed with glasses of champagne, she had made a signal to the maître d', who, smiling slightly, rather perfect in his oiled black hair and smooth-shaved face and measured sideburns, went through a door hidden by an oyster satin curtain and returned carrying a large package, wrapped in scarlet paper and bound in scarlet ribbons.

'This isn't for me, is it?' Gillian said.

'Yes, it's for you,' said Rose.

'But it's not my birthday or anything. What have I done to deserve this? I bet it's something really lovely, smellies for the bath, I expect. Though rather a lot of them! I still don't know why, though.' She undid the ribbons and attempted to remove the wrapping paper in one piece, as if she expected to fold it up and use it on a later occasion, and it was very beautiful paper, embossed with the outline of swans, and the ribbons seemed to be real satin. I, who had received many corporate gifts, had never seen such decadent wrapping.

'Oh. A viola.'

'It's a Mirecourt,' Rose said, 'like your original one. Look at the label.'

'Yes, I see the label.'

We all waited, while Gillian's hands lay inert on the table next to the rows of glittering silverware, the left one clenched slightly by her side plate near a silver dish with curls of butter and a basket of Melba toast.

'Well, pick it up and play us something,' said Rose encouragingly, with the expectation that a performance was about to break out.

'Oh, no, I haven't played for so long. I wouldn't be able to.'

'But isn't it like riding a bike or swimming? You'd wobble a bit at first and flounder, but then you'd take off.'

'Yes, I'd be terribly rusty, but it's not that. I don't know how to explain. I might be able to play it, but it's not really so straight-forward. I don't know if we would fit each other, to start with, I mean … the tone, and there's no chin rest. I would have needed … Anyway, it's very kind of you, Rose, I do appreciate it, and I know why you bought it, because I sold my old viola for the Party and you feel guilty, but you mustn't.'

'I used to love listening to you play,' Dora said. 'You played so beautifully in our room.'

'I know, I wasn't bad, was I? But that was such a long time ago and my life has been completely different. You can't go back. I've been without a viola for so long, you can't really pick that kind of thing up again. Music, I mean. When it hasn't been part of your life. I exchanged my viola for things I believed in. I couldn't have both. It just doesn't work that way.'

Rose was not used to being thwarted. She tried for a few more minutes to persuade her to play even a few notes, but Gillian had not yet even touched the instrument which lay in its coffin box.

'If you really don't want it then I suppose I can return it to the shop. How disappointing.'

'Or I could keep it and sell it and give the money to our Esperanto association.'

'Yes, do that then. Well, let's talk about something else.' Our starters arrived. 'I think I'll get us a bottle of Muscadet even though I'm the only one being fishy.'

For a few minutes we argued about Iraq. Brian had already returned home, so we did not have to endure his cynical indifference. Rose speaking quickly, with eloquent emphasis. Wearing a black Donna Karan suit, her once-chestnut hair now a complicated set of blond and beige highlights cut into a shoulder-length bob with side-swept fringe, straightened and glossy. Black Tahitian pearls at her ears, a matching necklace with the suggestion of a slipped diamond clasp approaching past her hairline towards her white throat. She was divorced. Her daughter was working at Barclays Capital in Moscow, a swan who turned into an ugly duckling, Rose said.

'I agree that with hindsight Blair turned out to have been wrong about WMD, but don't you think he was quite right to want to get rid of a tyrant? Hasn't the Arab Spring actually proved him right, in a way?'

'No. I'm a pacifist and war is always wrong,' said Dora. 'What is it good for? Dreamed up by old men for boys to fight in.'

'I have to agree with Dora,' Gillian said. 'I still think the war was completely wicked. And maybe the Arab Spring would have happened anyway.'

'Oh, well, I always lose that particular argument. I don't know why I bother any more. I know what you all think of me, I know you think I'm vain and shallow and have betrayed everything I believed in. How funny that seems. The experiment worked so well. I turned into exactly the person the founders wanted us to be. And I know because *I* was the original experimental subject.'

'What are you talking about?' Dora said.

'Do you know those psychological tests designed to understand how the mind deals with conformity? A group of people are given a series of questions, say, simple arithmetic, getting a little harder with each one. You shout out the answer, and soon the group is concurring on the wrong result. You think (or don't, depending on the strength of your sense of individuality) that you must be in error. Only when the test is finished are you told that everyone was in on it apart from you.'

Rose was who the university had been designed for. To decide a bet laid down over a couple of whiskies in a pub in Leeds in 1954, that a baby girl born that year could be moulded into a model social democratic citizen. Her father had been in Catalonia together with one of our founders in '36. They had returned together, wounded, on the same ship. Years after the war they had met and dreamed up the campus, this egalitarian plan for the production of children who would spurn totalitarianism, where the arts and the sciences would rebuild the world. She had been prepared for that place, or it had been prepared for her.

When the architect drew up his first plans for the plastic-bottomed lake, the covered walkways, the beige concrete CLASP buildings, he had drawn matchstick figures for scale, the future students. Her father had laid them out on the table in the public library, pointed to a matchstick with a skirt and a ribbon in its hair on the steps of the library and said, 'See this one? It's you.'

'Apart from that little rebellion, when I was so ridiculous, my life has never departed from the plan. It all worked, didn't it?, it worked terribly, terribly well. It's depressing to have been pressed out, like a coin. Oh, Gillian, please, won't you just play?'

But Gillian shook her head even more emphatically and lowered her eyes to her pâté and toast. It was her first refusal.

Since that evening, I have met up with the other three for coffee. 'Adele, did you ever track down that boy?' Rose asked.

'Yes, I heard from him, he lives in Sweden. It turns out you weren't the last person to see Evie alive, Gillian.'

'Oh, that's a *lovely* present. Thank you for telling me. I've always felt so guilty. But then who was?'

I explained as much as I could, from the emails and conversations, what had happened the night Evie died and still it all seemed to me unsatisfactory, as if you pulled a thread in a fabric and it unravelled until there was nothing left.

'So he was just a vagabond who was knocking at our door,' Dora said.

'How do we get people so wrong,' I asked, 'when we are so intensely curious about them?'

I have tried to recreate the little plot of time we once lived in, the Homeric legend of our youth. I have gone through in my mind all the possible explanations for the significance of Evie in our lives.

There were the metaphorical and metaphysical. Was Denise an *ibbur*, the receptacle for a spirit who wishes to do a good deed, to make amends? Maybe old Figgy Lassiter himself. The *ibbur* kept the notebooks, Evie's erotic fantasies about her brother, from the family. It would have finished them.

Another idea, which often comes to me when I am in the twilight state just before sleep, the dozing which if you relax sufficiently will take you down into the night's long adventure, is that we are not real, but Evie's dream of us. I do wonder if the dead dream. If amputees feel pain in limbs that have been cremated, could the dead have disembodied reminiscences, memories, scenarios, adventures?

On a more practical level, I understand now that the founders had missed something in their grand plan: the irrational. Evie – or, as I am reluctantly starting to call her, Lorraine – needed counselling from the start. She needed help and got none; it was against the founding principles to interfere. Instead she got us, who colluded with her. Do I hold us responsible? We were only teenagers, we hardly knew if the egg we had been cracked out of still held parts of its shell in our eyes and hair. But there were so many warning signs. Alison had seen them, we hadn't.

When, last week, I told my son about the sequence of events that had led to his birth, I could not help but feel that I had delivered him to the world as Rose's father had delivered her to the university. The chain of circumstances that began with me winning the poetry competition – *Elsie's room is clean* – my letter to Allen Ginsberg in New York, the reply on the back of the monochrome Jackson Pollock I first saw in 1995 in its true place at MoMA and in colour, my father's suicide, my letter to the university, the interview with Professor Fine and the random placement of me in a room of my own, opposite Gillian Braithwaite and Dora Dickie.

Nor was there any means of avoiding Evie and Stevie, both of them walking towards me, him wearing my Fair Isle gloves. Or George. I hate the feeling of determinism. I like the illusion of free agency that the university gave us. But there is no avoiding what might have happened had I not run into Stevie that day outside the library, not gone against my will to the flat and met George.

Still I remember it, the blond nape of her neck.

Eddie sees it as just a story, another of *my* stories, which he has grown out of. Having come out, he has brought home his boyfriend. 'They make a cute couple,' Juan said. I agree. Very cute. His bedroom is now piled high with material about Aids which I have placed by his bed.

'What's this?' he said.

'You never knew my friend Bobby, he died before you were born.'

'That's an old guys' illness, we're fine.'

'Don't do this to me!'

I took the exercise books and buried them in the garden. There they lie, with the dead of a thousand years ago, rotting down to their constituent molecules, charged with becoming something else.

I have made a big rush through life. Yes, I suppose I have run through it without too much introspection. Dora was right: some people are natural depressives. I'm not one of them. I cannot understand what we are here to do, if not to live. I share with Juan a dislike of damaged people and I do not care for the current fad for misery memoirs. I don't want to hear about your hard times. Both of us, Juan and I, are drawn to survivors not victims.

When Yankel died, of old age, a great and fine age, he was the last link with the world of my childhood, a world which comes back to me, stronger than ever, more real, and those now-legendary figures, the women in their gashes of lipstick and frosted eyeshadow, parade past me and turn and look and smile the bitter triumphant smiles of women who have not surrendered to or been defeated by death.

I wonder if we have done half as well, and how much longer it will take us to learn all their lessons.

They would have looked after Evie. In their hands, I believe, she would have survived. But they would have needed to understand sex, the great confuser. I don't have any idea if they did or not.

November 2013

Overnight the rippled surface of the water had hardened. A few ducks emerging from cold sleep in the crevices of the bank slid across it, the snow rising up past their webbed feet to the feathered underbelly, and they performed their comic turns.

On the island the rotting remains of Evie in her torn white dress had half fallen on to whitened ferns, reclining on one broken arm, propped up by a rock and the decaying stump of an amputated tree. Canada geese hopped over her, the moorhens built nests in her chest cavity, the swans pecked at her metal eyes.

From the middle distance a monochrome speck took shape on the prevailing whiteness. Only the concrete boxy buildings, faint and biscuit-coloured, gave a pale tint to the scene. An ashy light flecked with dark spots shone through the thin cloud. Now the moving figure became the lumpy black butterfly of a Rorschach test, an inkblot with two heads on a single winged body. I sat down on a bench and waited for them.

I never saw the place so deserted by human life, the windows with all their curtains drawn, as if everyone else had passed through already and we were late, hurrying to catch up with the crowd gone by.

The Rorschach shape reassembled itself and I saw that it was two people, their arms tightly around each other, thinly clad not for the frozen morning but for an afternoon in early summer, in ragged jeans, T-shirts, light black cotton jackets.

He looked round at me as they passed. '*Let all sweet ladies break their flattering glasses,*' he said, '*and dress themselves in her.*'

I turned my head and watched them walk on, into the garden where the yew-tree topiary was still in its infancy and the russet brick of the manor house glowed across the frozen grass. They had moved on out of sight now and there was no getting them back. They had taken the path into the remains of the medieval woods and soon they disappeared from view.

Acknowledgements

This novel is based on a particular time in my own life, but the characters are the product of my imagination. I would like to thank in particular Peter Hitchens for our three-and-a-half-hour conversation sitting by another man-made lake talking about an obscure and forgotten time. Many thanks too to Judith Mackrell and Matthew Marsh for their insights and to Robert Weston for his clear and fresh memories of Cornwall in the sixties and seventies.

My editor, Lennie Goodings, is as ever the closest reader, and my new agent Jonny Geller has offered sharp and very welcome insights into my work.

I dedicate this novel to my agent Derek Johns, retiring from agenting but not the literary world after twenty-one years together. A steady, calm, wise voice for two decades. A gentleman from a time in publishing that is passing away. I shall miss his counsel. And the lunches. Amazon don't buy you lunch.

Linda Grant was born in Liverpool and now lives in London. *The Cast Iron Shore* won the David Higham First Novel Prize. *When I Lived in Modern Times* won the Orange Prize for Fiction. *Still Here* was longlisted for the Man Booker Prize. *The Clothes on Their Backs* won the *South Bank Show* Literature Award and was shortlisted for the Man Booker Prize. Linda Grant is also the author of *Sexing the Millennium*; *Remind Me Who I am Again*; *The People on the Street*, which won the Lettre Ulysses Prize for Literary Reportage; and *The Thoughtful Dresser*.